MAYA OF THE NEW WORLD

MAYA RISING BOOK #2

SITA BENNETT

MYSTIC ADVENTURE PRESS

Contents

Dedication	VI
Part One	1
1. Chapter 1	3
2. Chapter 2	11
3. Chapter 3	27
4. Chapter 4	43
5. Chapter 5	51
6. Chapter 6	57
7. Chapter 7	65
8. Chapter 8	73
9. Chapter 9	78
10. Chapter 10	85
11. Chapter 11	97
12. Chapter 12	103
13. Chapter 13	107
14. Chapter 14	121
15. Chapter 15	127

16. Chapter 16   133

17. Chapter 17   137

18. Chapter 18   147

19. Chapter 19   161

20. Chapter 20   167

Part Two   173

21. Chapter 21   175

22. Chapter 22   183

23. Chapter 23   189

24. Chapter 24   195

25. Chapter 25   203

26. Chapter 26   207

27. Chapter 27   215

28. Chapter 28   223

29. Chapter 29   229

30. Chapter 30   237

31. Chapter 31   247

32. Chapter 32   255

33. Chapter 33   265

34. Chapter 34   271

35. Chapter 35   279

36. Chapter 36   285

37. Chapter 37   289

38. Chapter 38   301

39. Chapter 39   307

40. Chapter 40	317
41. Chapter 41	329
Afterword	331
About Author	332
She Who Rose From Ashes	333
I Don't have an Introduction	334
Acknowledgments	345

Made with Love in South-West Australia by
Sita, for the seers, the sensitives, the introverts, &
the innately curious.

For all who sense a richer existence available
beneath the surface of what we see & accept as
reality.

And lastly, for the love and preservation of our
planet, earth.

PART ONE

This chapter of our story began with death.

The end.

The end of the life we came to love so dearly, yet one that was never meant to last.

I'd grown to accept endings in a way that made this one carry less weight, less pain than it may have to a past version of myself. I *had* to. I'd been forced by life itself to develop a way of adapting to change so that when death inevitably came around, death of any kind, I was ready.

Centred.

Death had become a comrade, a teacher, even a friend. It's sublime ever-presence hung patiently behind me, a potent but welcomed Shadow, reminding me to *live*.

I'd both seen and experienced death enough times to comprehend how quickly life was born, only to grow and to end. The life of a being, an experience, a feeling, a moment—reborn with every inhale. Dying on the exhale.

Even now, before our adventure officially began, a sense of preciousness was present in every moment, under the awareness that this chapter too would someday, in some way, end. This chapter, in which we were returning to a place we once knew, certain that earth would be entirely new.

Like a wisp of dust floating in the breeze.

A leaf gliding down a flowing river.

Everything passes.

And only in death, life begins.

Begins again.

With the acceptance of death so near, upon the tail of each moment, we are forced to wake up from the dream that we might be invincible, eternal.

Wake up to the truth that we *are*, just not in body.

CHAPTER ONE

B RIGHT RAYS OF GOLDEN light. Light from a sun that shone down upon us through a wide-open window in the cloud-covered sky. My wet skin, deprived after days of trekking through harsh rain and snow, welcomed its warmth.

I gazed up through the glare at the two parallel skies, a rare sight. Two realms co-existing in unison, visible to eyes that were only meant to see one.

One was the sky of Santōṣha, a parallel dimension that was located in the centre of the earth. The other, only visible through this small, singular keyhole, was the sky of the Upper Earth: our homeland.

Illusion temporarily exposed, here we saw a glimpse into a truer, more mosaiced labyrinth of reality where two dimensions of our multiverse co-existed simultaneously. Yet still, they were only two dimensions of many.

Past the sun of Earth lay the stagnant sun of the Sky realm, and beyond that was an unknown myriad of realms stacked on top of each other, unexplored by humankind, or at least unrecorded by human history.

And that was how it was supposed to be. By will of natural law.

I reached out to hold Björn's warm, comforting hand, grateful for his stabilizing presence beside me on this journey. A journey that wouldn't have begun if he hadn't found me in the City of the

Old World, and forced me to escape with him. Escape here. To this more balanced world that had only existed on paper, on an ancient map, until Björn navigated our way to it, through a singular fracture, a glitch, a lapse in the solidity of Earth's architecture, where interdimensional travel became momentarily possible.

And there we were, willingly returning, but this time our old, desolate world would be brand new.

From the Village of Spring we travelled, through the white blizzarding mountains of an eternal Winter and over the auburn leaves of Autumn, to reach the wet season at the edge of the island, the edge of the world, *this* world. It was not vast like Earth. It contained only one length of land, surrounded by water that stretched an unseeable distance before reaching the invisible dome-like sky that held this dimension at the centre of the Hollow Planet Earth.

Here, rain was constant, dribbling endlessly from a weeping grey sky. Pools and puddles soaked the earth, gradually blending into the ocean that enveloped the island. In the opposite direction, a crevasse in the land captured the fresh rainwater, carrying it in an ever-flowing river along the length of the island that eventually opened into the sea of Summer at the far end.

Huddled under the only circle of sky where the untiring rain ceased, we stood waiting, shivering as the cold air whipped against our wet skin. We were all that was left of humankind. A new tribe for a new earth.

I looked around at the faces surrounding me: Phóenix, Bŏdhi, Chaṅtara, and their kids. Adam, Farrah, Cole, and Björn. They were wild now, as wild as the Samãdhi people, but still human in their subtleties.

Not human as humans were *before*, before the end—heart's diluted, polluted, the walking dead. Human as humans *are* in our pure and natural embodiment, with active hearts and clean minds, and light at the centre of our being.

The FξŸa people hovered in the air around us, dancing, always dancing, to no particular song, just floating, swaying to the song of all of nature combined. They had foreseen this day long ago and sent their strongest and healthiest to grace our expedition. ʒchŏ stayed especially close over our travels, perched on my shoulder or crown, leaving a trail of dust-like L·ight Måttęr in our wake.

Adam dumped a large, waterproofed travel pack on the platform of dry earth upon which we all now stood and began handing out snow coats, vests, boots, mittens, and head warmers weaved from the thickest furs and skins, in preparation for the wicked arctic.

Well, *if* the arctic still existed…or more accurately *re-existed.*

The portal was located on the edge of the Arctic circle, in a country that was once called Russia. But like every other country on Earth, all of the human infrastructure that made Russia what it was had been wiped out by natural disasters. So as far as we could tell, all countries were one and the same now, and we couldn't be sure whether the same climates existed in the same regions that they had in the Old World.

Still, we dressed clumsily beneath the portal's protection into our dry layers and handed our wet rags to the Samādhi who hung on the outskirts, still kissed by the drizzling rain. In their visions, the Nŏahls had foreseen the return of snow to the land, and even though both Arctics had melted in the Old World, their premonitions were rarely inaccurate.

As I laced up my boot, I knew it was only a matter of farewells before travelling back up to the Upper Earth, and nerves turned my stomach in nauseating waves. When embarking on anything new, unease around the unknown always had a way of creeping over me, but the stakes were especially high today. Both the weight of our responsibility and the uncertainty of Earth's condition were daunting.

With a full inhale, I pressed my hands gently against my heart.

Trust. Trust.

I wrapped my arms around Adam, not ready to say goodbye again. This goodbye was one I couldn't ever possibly ready myself for.

⟫⟫⟫ ⟪⟪⟪

"If the number of beating hearts we travel with is the source of our power, wouldn't it be stupid for them not to come?" Björn asked, speaking the same question on my mind.

We stood in the enchanting underground hollow where voices echoed, echoed like the pain of my heart that would not accept Chief Ħan's decision. All humans were gathering with the Samãhdi leaders to finalise plans for our return to Earth.

"Their heartbeats aren't strong enough yet to be of service. They're still susceptible to being influenced by the Sky Consciousness. They must stay until their minds are clean and clear enough to witness any thoughts that might be implanted by Sky Consciousness. If they attach and believe any foreign thoughts as their own, the risk of following them down a path of destruction once more is too high.

At this point, I'm afraid they don't have the clarity to make these discernments." Chief Ħan's words were stern and articulate. Non-negotiable. He turned to Adam.

"You can't underestimate the subtlety of their manipulation. You won't know you're under their influence until it's too late. And even then, you will be too deep in a fog of ignorance to see."

"I won't let her leave without me again. I'm going," Adam said, the stamina of his brotherly protectiveness hindering his ability to listen rather than just hear.

"I made it through the portal, didn't I?" He turned to Nirmala, for her Shamanic opinion.

"You must trust us," she said. "The portal allows for a certain amount of density to slip through, because the purity of our dimension will, over time, help you dissolve whatever Shadows

still linger in your system. For you, Farrah, and Cole, that process has really only just begun.

"It can take years to retrain your system into new ways of being. Your body grips onto its patterns more tightly than the mind can understand.

"You will be more valuable to the Upper Earth after spending more time here. Here, no Shadow can survive the expanse of light. If you return too soon, your presence might have the opposite effect."

Adam was quiet but not relenting.

"What about the kids?" Chantara asked, not hiding her concern about leading them into the unknown.

"They should go. They are very light. They haven't had the time or the exposure to accumulate Shadows."

Adams fists clenched—tighter, tighter—until his frustration could no longer be contained. His fists smashed down on the moss-coated rock in front of him.

➵➵➵ ‹‹‹‹

"As soon as we're ready, we'll join you. I'll find you," Adam promised as I squeezed him tighter for one more moment before finally letting go. "You are wise and strong. I know that whatever happens up there, you'll survive."

I nodded and a soft stream of tears dripped down my cheeks, blending into the rain all around us. In that moment, I did not feel strong. While his conviction was encouraging, I couldn't ignore the reality that the future might not be so kind as to bring us together again.

Adam stepped out of the circle and back into the rain to join Cole, Farrah, and the Samãdhi, taking Farrah's hand in his. I was glad he had her; she made staying behind bearable to him.

"This is as far as we can accompany you." Chief Ḧan's voice rumbled over the sound of the trickling rain.

In many ways he was like a watchful father and the tribe were all his children. His capacity to take care was far-reaching, and his presence alone was grounding, stabilizing. I would miss it. As I would miss them all for different reasons.

My attention fell on the three Samãdhi beings who stood in the rain. They had each had a significant impact on my life over my years in the valley. I was even more uncertain of how long it may be until I saw them again, and again, accepted the most likely reality that after that day, I wouldn't at all.

There was only one entry to their dimension, and it was through the Bermuda Triangle. Björn's inner compass and sense of direction was sharp and generally accurate, but there were so many factors that would interfere with our ability to relocate the triangle in the New World, one being whether it even still existed. Another being that planes certainly didn't. All human civilisations had been wiped out when they were. The earth was bare now.

A sinking feeling of finality settled in the pit of my belly with each passing minute. The sense that our purpose in the valley had been completed. And while the portal we stared up through was a rare and enchanted opening, it was also a closure.

Chief Ḧan stood back, a smile animating his kind eyes, as Ŋala stepped forward into the clearing. A glowing air of light beings swarmed towards her, landing over her body.

Ŋala had a special affinity with the FξŸa tribe. They were both fundamentally light and intimately close to the purest forms of magic in the world. Light magic. It's presence glistened in Ŋala's eyes, the same glisten that emanated from their bodies.

"Ahh, I'll miss you two." Ṭarō stepped boldly forward, wrapping his giant brown arms around both Björn and I.

Our feet lifted momentarily from the muddy earth, and Ṭarō flashed us a charismatic grin as he set us down.

"I'll miss you too, man." Björn and Ṭarō had developed a sense of brotherhood over our time in the Valley, and at times were inseparable.

"Make sure you laugh at his jokes." Ṭarō leant down to me, speaking in a fake whisper. "We can't have him getting all serious up there."

I didn't always understand their humour. Sometimes it seemed like *no one* did.

"I'll do my best," I promised.

After the boys said their final goodbyes, accompanied by banter that made their separation easier for each of them to accept, I wrapped my arms around Ṭarō's torso, the tips of my fingers only just touching behind his back, and squeezed my eyes shut.

"Goodbye."

He pat my hair gently, which flowed in waves that now reached my tailbone, and kissed my forehead. Then he turned to Phőenix, eyes sad. Feelings unexpressed and unexplored burned between them, feelings that now mightn't ever get the chance to be.

"Well, see ya, Phőe." He bent down awkwardly to hug her.

I looked back to Ṇala, who watched me with a knowing smile.

"Maya." Her voice was soothing.

She bent to embrace me.

"Ṇala," I started, my last image of her blurred by a sheet of stagnant tears. I wanted to thank her again for everything, even though no words could ever encapsulate my gratitude, but she shook her head, already aware. Words mean little when you can feel the true expanse of meaning beneath them.

"Here, I almost forgot." She reached into a pouch strapped across her chest and drew out a handmade journal filled with blank pages. Her smile was radiant. "You can record everything in this."

She handed down the carefully crafted book that already felt precious in my hands. The cover was made by robust animal skin, and engraved with five symbols. Nature's elements.

"I look forward to reading it one day."

"Thank you. It's beautiful." I wrapped my arms as tightly around her as her waist would allow.

I gazed over the circle of humans once more, meeting each set of eyes with a look of affirmation.

Björn squeezed my hand. Above us, golden rays of afternoon sun beamed down from the Sky of the Upper Earth.

Electric sparks of light shot through my body as the Fξ began landing on my clothes, encapsulating me as they did each human set to return.

"The world's on your shoulders, Maya! Don't forget it!" Ṭarō called loudly—not that it was *true*. I just felt that way sometimes, the pressure of it all. And this was his last chance to mock me for it.

"Your son's the devil in disguise!" I called back to Ḧan.

"It's a worry." Ḧan shook his head at his son, who was the tribe's heir chief. But even from my now light-drenched distance, I could see the loving humour in his eyes. In truth, he wasn't worried at all. Sometimes, rascals made the best leaders.

CHAPTER TWO

S EVEN GLOWING HUMAN BODIES rose from the swamplands, ascending gracefully in jackets of silverish blue light beings.

It should have been impossible. The FξŸa were so tiny, but the abundance of energy and vigor they had access to, by nature of the pure Light that they were, weighed more than a human body in that realm. United, they embodied the stamina to lift us skyward.

The channel we were being lifted through did not abide by the same laws of gravity that normally bound us to the ground either. The atmosphere was neutral, not drawing downwards nor upwards. The higher we rose, the less solid our bodies became, our physical form transitioning into its lighter, ethereal expression, tailoring itself to align with the agility required to pass between dimensions.

My vision was painted by an aura of light: a transparent veil over my eyes that left a luminous glow over all I gazed upon. From our height, the grand scope of fresh water that coated the Wet Season shimmered. The giants, who now looked like dwarves in perspective, were lit by luminous rings around their bodies, and the trees of Autumn in the distance also displayed an exuberant glow around their forms.

Infused with the essence of the FξŸa, everything was illuminated by white magic—including my body, which felt as light in weight as it felt bright. My mind became peaceful, free from distracting thoughts or intrusive stimuli.

I was floating.

Weightless.

I closed my eyes after taking in one last sweep of the enchanted Valley that my heart would always understand as home, and surrendered to the exquisite simplicity of what it felt like to float or fly. But even behind closed lids, the richness of the magic I was enveloped by was still luminous, drenching my vision in a pristine sheath of white.

Other senses heightened as my eyes rested, and the subtlest sound of ringing bells and acute chimes twinkled in my ears, the sound of magic itself in motion, washing my mind clean.

"Woweee!" Ṫasmai's squeal echoed through the silence, and the sounds of voices gradually drew my senses back to my body from the meditative state into which I'd fallen. Fallen deeply.

The bed I lay on was powdery and malleable, as if we'd stopped to rest upon a cloud.

My eyes blinked gently open to the bright, striking, clear blue sky. After they adjusted to the glare, I lifted my torso to discover that the powdery white substance beneath me did, in fact, look like a cloud.

But upon speculation I realised it was a condensed bed of fresh snow!

This meant the Nŏahls' visions were accurate. Nature had been repairing and renewing itself more rapidly than we believed possible. Snow had returned to the Arctic. Earth's climate was restoring balance.

My eyes explored the smooth, white sheets that rolled over uneven hills, uninterrupted but for the markings of our arrival. Patches of dirt were visible, but the amount of snow was still impressive.

Moānā and Ṫassie had already travelled a distance from where I lay, their thick fur coats dirtied by patches of white powder and steps leaving a trail of footprints over the otherwise untouched surface. Their joy was carried on the uncluttered airways in squeals and laughter as they chased each other, falling almost every second step as the weight of their bounding movements forged holes where their little legs fell.

"Don't go too far!" Chaṅtara called after them. "Come back this way, we don't know how deep the snow will get!"

Bõdhi placed his mitted hand over her shoulder, appeasing. The Fξ˙ were swarming around the kids in play; they were in safe company.

Chaṅtara had been the most hesitant of us to commit to the journey, mostly out of concern for their kids. Unlike Bõdhi, who was the first human child born in Santōṣha and had an unwavering trust in nature embedded into his being as a result, Chaṅtara was raised on Earth's surface at a time when nature's erratic and unforgiving destruction was at its peak.

Although she'd adapted to the ways of the tribe since jumping dimensions at the age of seventeen and *grown* to trust in nature, she still carried the trauma of Earth's history in her system.

I understood her turmoil over the decision. By joining us in the establishment of the New World, Moānā and Ṫasmai were sacrificing the opportunity to grow and evolve in a community with other kids their age, where they would learn, live, and breathe the way of the Samãdhi people.

But while Santōṣha felt like home to us all, our race was created to thrive *on* Earth, but closer to the natural, harmonious way we discovered was possible true during our time *in* it, not the destructive way we human's lived *before*.

Before she retaliated.

Before she reclaimed power.

And now she was steadily healing and regenerating, which made me wonder if our presence was even necessary in the way the Nõahls and Samãdhi convinced us it was...

Humankind was the reason for the Old World's demise. Would it not be a simpler, cleaner, quieter world without us?

A shiver ran up my spine as an image flashed across my mind's eye and swept me momentarily into a haunting scene. One that visited me many times before I had the courage to truly acknowledge it. One that returned every time I had a moment of doubt in our expedition. One that reminded me of the importance of it.

The vision was of the Sky People who had threatened to dominate the planet for decades; their iron ships descending, their metal structures and technologies colonising the land.

It may have been a simpler world without us, but it was also a vulnerable world, and we, apparently, had the potential to play the role of its caretakers—as opposed to the rulers we deluded ourselves into believing we were in the past.

It reminded me that it was not, in fact, humankind that caused the Old World's destruction. Not entirely. Not alone, in our natural state. We had been puppets, prisoners, under the influence of a plague. The plague of Sky People.

The dysfunctionality of the human mind *began* under the influence of their formless consciousness, implanted into ours.

And they were persistent, patient, tenacious. An ancient race, who had existed long before humankind, and were determined to live long after we returned to dust.

They had a plan and were unlikely to surrender in response to the defeat of their previous efforts. In fact, the planet was *more* appealing now that she was raw and exposed. Their potential survival here relied on nature's desolation, and for their metals and technology to dominate, nature would have to remain desolate.

Without plants, wildlife, *and* living heartbeats, Earth was scarce of protection. I was by no means deluded into believing that our heartbeats alone would protect her. For the vision to be still returning meant the possibility of it happening was still high. Not *definite*, but high enough to beg for our caution.

I understood the way my visions functioned better now and had learned the danger in ignoring them. It would have been foolish to deny their accuracy, no matter how inconvenient the truth.

Through vision, my mind's eψe presented to me possible futures: potential outcomes aligned with the course that was presently in motion—*potential*, only because change was always possible.

But usually, in all my past experience, not much ever changed. By the time we realised which change in direction on the path we followed would have made the most significant difference, it was too late. And so the future happens because of the past, and the present is both a product and a catalyst of the two, existing at once.

Now, here we were, the threat of Sky People still lingering, the future of the planet still uncertain, *our* future as a tribe even more so. If my flashing foresights were on point, nothing had miraculously shifted course because we had arrived.

Apart from that, it was all more real now than when we were tucked away in the comfort and safety of a co-existing dimension. It proved that as much as the Samadhi people stressed that our presence here was critical, we were not the sole saviors of the world, just moving instruments of a much larger mechanism.

While the wide-open sky was clear and the sun's reflection off the white snow created an inescapable glare, the temperature was freezing. Invigorating, but so freezing it burned the exposed skin of my face.

I rolled slowly to stand from where I still sat in the snow, and a hand spread over my shoulder. I turned to find Björn's chiselled face beside mine. His white blonde hair shimmered under the bright sun, cropped short, not hiding his sculpted features. Square jaw, smooth skin, defined cheekbones.

Everything disappeared for the time I swam in his electric blue eyes. It was like staring into a deep ocean.

They were the first thing that struck out at me when I saw him for the first time—although I'd seen them before, in visions before we met in reality. Dark, they carried the weight of his past; vivid, they reflected the clarity of his mind and awakeness of his spirit; and kind, they expressed the expanse of his wide-open heart.

I closed my eyes and breathed him in, his addictive scent, the warmth of his ambience, despite the numbing air. He pulled me into his chest and held my head against him gently, shoulders broad enough to envelop me entirely. The tenderness of his hand against my cheek while his arms wrapped around me felt more secure than anything.

He pressed his face into my hair.

"I love you," he whispered into my ear, warm breath rippling down the supple skin of my neck.

I lifted my head and smiled up at him. A breath of frost drifted like white smoke on his exhale before dissolving into the air it was born of.

"I already miss the warmth." He pulled me back into his body again, although our winter layers didn't allow for much heat transmission.

I was still wordless; gaze shifting back out over land that I once believed would be barren forevermore.

It felt surreal to be there, feet deep in snow, body called to life by the arctic air. I was different to Björn in this way; I enjoyed the sense of aliveness that colder temperatures ignited. The weather was always warm, still, and unchanging in the Village of Spring we had travelled from. Comfortable. Like everything else in that realm.

The settled snow appeared to me like an unfinished canvas would: a pristine white page awaiting the first footprints of its expected explorers to paint it with life.

But then again, the snow itself only existed as a result of life in its extreme expressions; the product of freezing temperatures, and howling winds and blizzards that shifted and shaped the falling flakes. Even as calm as it presently felt, there was an epic and unfathomable power in the atmosphere that demanded respect. Nature: a force to revere, not underestimate.

"I love you too." I turned, lips softly pressing Björn's cheek that was painted pink by the numbing air.

I could see Chaṅtara, Phőenix, and Bŏdhi approaching from over his shoulder. Behind them, squeals of joy spread through the air. I watched the kids as they played, warmed by their innocence and freedom. They were unaware of our true purpose for resurfacing.

All they knew was that nature had been ill and we were helping to increase the presence of light.

They didn't know of the pending danger of the Sky race, who threatened to take advantage of nature's illness. They didn't know that while we were hunting fertile land, we were also hunting Shadows.

Well, *I* was hunting Shadows. The others weren't so acquainted with the etheric layers of our world.

"Should we start hiking then?" Chaṅtara said as they reached us, not wasting a moment. "There's obviously nothing here to stick around here for."

The Fξϓa reassembled around us and Björn stepped back, unfolding the map from inside his jacket. We all huddled around him in a circle. Ȝchŏ lowered to rest on my shoulder.

At the centre of his map was the North Pole, and a bright red spot of tree sap marked our location on the edge of Russia. He'd drawn a number of maps in preparation for the trip, detailing as much of the earth as he could remember, although we were all aware there was a high chance that the earth's geology might be vastly different now. Still, out of all of us, he had the most extensive knowledge of what Earth looked like before.

Björn had been Governor Koen's highest-ranking officer for years in the City, and studied all the intricacies of the world map both for work schemes and out of his own private interest to escape the System.

His parents were also scientists that studied the minerals in the land. They had been aware of a rich network of fungi that existed beneath the earth's surface even though it appeared dead. They called it environmental Internet because it was the interconnecting substance that nourished all seeds of life underground, and the singular source of life that allowed nature itself to survive Earth's end.

Mycelium, it was more formally called. A substance that was easy to underestimate for its delicate appearance; Flossy and white like matted spiderwebs or woven threads of cotton. But like many things on Earth, appearance did not reflect its resilience. When natural disasters shook the lands, rocks fell and crumbled but Mycelium survived, unscathed *because* of its agility, not despite of it.

Björn was the only human with whom his parents shared their discoveries about Mycelium. They knew that if nature's secret underground source of eternal life was exposed to Governor Koen and the other authorities of the System (the Control), they would find a way to mine it as they had all other visible sources of nature for fuel.

The pressure of keeping the last surviving City on earth afloat made them blind to the long-term effects of short-term solutions. But Björn's parents were wise enough to see that the long-term affects of disrupting the Mycelium network would mean certain planetary destruction that would have been final.

And now, Earth survived because they had protected it. They protected it to the extent they sacrificed their own lives in order to keep nature's secret, and were murdered by the Control for their rebellion. Traitors of the Old System, Heroes of the New World.

Björn held a compass over the map's centre and adjusted it until the coordinates matched.

"Ok," he began. "If we split like we agreed to, our path will be in that direction." Björn pointed in the direction of inland Russia, although from where we stood all directions appeared the same, vast sheets of white nothingness.

The FξŸa slowly split into four groups and hovered patiently.

Björn looked up to one group. "Autumn FξŸa, you'll be travelling that direction." He gestured again in accordance to his map.

"Winter, that direction. Summer, there. And Spring, that direction."

We all nodded, knowing well the plan, but some time passed before the FξŸa finished their farewells and we watched as each group drifted away in opposite directions to explore different climates and areas of the land.

Three FξŸa stayed behind to travel with us in the direction that Björn believed had the highest probability to bare the kind of plant life we'd need to survive after our supplies ran out. But no one could be sure of the landscape's new blueprint.

Ȝchŏ, Théodren, and Lupïta were to act as the communication channels between the Fξ and human tribes. No matter their distance apart, the Fξ had telecommunication connections that meant they could always reach one another to share information on what areas of Earth were fertile, and which were still dead.

After watching the last group of light beings disappear into the distance, we tightened our shoulder straps and began our own journey.

I could feel Ȝchŏ's quiet sense of loss from where she sat on my shoulder, her vibrant spirit a little dimmer than usual. Théodren and Lupïta were less chirpy too. This was the first time the FξŸa had been separated from their tribe in all of their lifetimes, and their light was brighter, magic more potent as a unit.

By the time we'd stopped to set up camp, nightfall loomed upon us. The temperature dropped and an air of frost settled over the land as the sky dimmed.

We found a decent-sized patch of dry dirt, still kissed by snow but not drowned by it, and began unrolling our tents, pitching them in a triangle around a central opening where Bŏdhi carved out a fire pit.

The Fξ` were unphased by the weather—their light kept them warm. It was their own internal heating system—but we set out a fur for them to lie on near the fire. In their Kingdŏm, they slept in hammocks and homes in trunk indents, but since travelling, they preferred to sleep together, their magic regenerating as one imperial force, although that force was significantly condensed now.

They lay down to rest immediately, particularly exhausted after lifting us through the portal and separating with the rest of their tribe. Time and space were different in this realm; everything carried more weight and solidity, including the downward draw of gravity.

I began sifting through our food packs in preparation for dinner. We hadn't stopped to eat all afternoon and were weakened and ready for a decent meal, but at the same time cautious about sparing our supplies.

It was uncertain whether nature had begun the process of baring edible plants yet. We carried seedlings from Santōṣha, but to plant them we had to first find fertile soil and an adequate location to settle while they sprouted.

Bŏdhi ignited a spark of fire using flint stones from the village and blew purposefully, covering the mound with his hands until a few fine, wispy twigs caught alight. We waited quietly as the fire began to emit warmth.

I built a simple but sturdy stand over the fire and hung a pot of grains over its flames to boil in freshly melted snow.

Bŏdhi stood to join Chaṅtara and the kids where they sat on a smooth grey boulder, watching the last rich orange rays of daylight disappear behind white-tipped mountains in the far distance.

It was the most vivid sunset I'd seen above ground. In the past, any colour had always been lost behind heavy grey smog.

I was alone for some time while Björn and Phŏenix continued securing tents around me. I felt a sense of peace. Stillness. My mind's eψe drifted back to one of my last conversations with Nirmala.

We sat, sipping tea, on the grassy edge of the high hilltop where she alone resided in small wooden hut. An unceasing fog drifted through the sky between surrounding peaks in the lush green land, which made it look like the hills were floating.

It was one of her more informal lessons. Any time spent with her seemed to evolve into a lesson in one way or another. I was always listening for the pearls of wisdom she shared, usually without even realising the imprint her words left on me...

⇢⟫⟩ ⟨⟪⟵

"The Sky race are formless beings, desperate to find a dimension that will allow them to manifest in form again. Planet Earth in its natural state is not ideal, but they were given access into your realm by Revăthi centuries ago and seem determined to transform it into a place that is.

"You cannot be ignorant of their lingering presence. You cannot lean on the hope that they might leave when nature regains dominance and vitality. You have to hunt them."

"How can we hunt something that's formless?" I asked.

Her porcelain white skin almost glittered as the clouds momentarily parted, sun rays beaming through. The silk fur of her white shawl swayed under a light breeze.

"*You don't hunt with your eyes,*" she replied, which meant little more to me than her previous statement. She explained, "*It's a feeling, like a dark cloud looming in the ether. You're very sensitive. You'll be able to sense the presence immediately if you stay vigilant. It's foreign. It's not of Earth dimension, so your body wisdom will react. Listen closely, your body will show you what doesn't belong.*

"*The formless are the most dangerous kind of Shadow because they can get a grip on you in the subtlest of ways. They can pass by as thoughtforms, feelings, and emotions, and the moment you attach, the moment you believe the drifting thought, feeling, or emotion is you, they gain access into your mind. You can lose the clarity of wider awareness and that's when they can start running you.*

"*Nothing can attach to you if you remain fully centred in your personal power.*" She paused, then continued.

"*You must understand that they are highly sophisticated in their manipulation. Humans are not a dumb species. The fact that they slipped past your awareness originally proves their cunningness. They attack you from inside your own mind. They imitate your voice. You believe entirely that you are in control, but you are a puppet.*"

A quiet sizzling at the pot's base snapped me back into presence, and I quickly removed it from the heat before it burned. The last of the day's light was just a glimmer on the horizon now, and the family's silhouettes moved from where they'd perched on the rock back towards camp.

As I stirred the inflated lentils, Nirmala's voice continued to play in the back of my mind.

"*You have a responsibility that the other humans cannot undertake. They don't reside in the same level of clarity or sensitivity to their surroundings. They are not Seers or feelers of the unseen.*

"They will be ok if they remain in a witness state over their own mind. But your awareness spans wider than your mind alone. Once again, your sensitivity will be your greatest power and protection mechanism up there. Today, I will begin teaching you how to use it to protect them also.

"You've experienced yourself as everything in a way that rarely gets exposed to your kind. You can use that to intentionally spread your attention wider than the lines of your body, and tune into each member of your tribe to make sure they also remain clear and free."

Her voice faded out and I looked over our tribe, intimidated by this responsibility I'd been given over their freedom—of which they were unaware. The Shaman often assumed my mystical abilities were more advanced than they presently were. But I trusted her insight and hoped they would develop.

Everyone gathered around the fire as I passed around the food. We all carried a thinly carved bowl, plate, cup, and spoon clipped to our personal packs, but I was the carrier of extra cooking equipment.

"Thank you." Björn kissed my cheek gently.

We ate in silence. Each face mirrored a collective combination of hope, faith, and uncertainty.

"I miss the giants, Mumma," Ṫasmai said after some time. He'd curled into Chaṅtara's lap after we finished eating.

"I know." Chaṅtara patted his hair gently, kissing his forehead, and he yawned, closing his eyes.

"I'm going to tuck the kids into bed, they're exhausted."

"I'm not," Ṫasmai said, but he didn't resist when she stood with him in her arms and swept open the entrance of their tent to set him down on the furs.

Moānā was laying beside the Fξ`, quietly admiring their ever-glowing bodies while they slept. She also didn't need much convincing when Chaṅtara suggested sleep of her own.

Bŏdhi collected our bowls and washed them in melted snow.

I lifted my head from Björn's chest as he slipped a detailed map of Russia out from his pocket.

"Hmmm," Björn exhaled as he lifted the map to the sky, examining it against the constellations.

I looked upwards too. The stars were vibrant, glittering against the sweeping black sky.

I'd grown used to bare night skies in Santōṣha, where only the moon offered light in the sun's absence. When I lived here, in the Old World, the dense grey smog combined with the drowning city lights dulled the star's magnificence.

I lay back on the dirt, enchanted.

The open map dropped out of view and Björn's rough hand wrapped around mine as he lay on his back beside me.

In our time together, I'd opened and shared more with him than anyone over the length of my life, and spent those moments equally appreciating *him* as I did the clear air and sky.

While our lives before meeting shaped us in significantly different ways, I'd always known him. Somehow, he'd always been with me—in visions and essence before reality.

He felt like *home*.

Here, on foreign land, in the northernmost part of the earth, I was still home, because he was with me.

Chaṅtara emerged through the tent opening beside us and Björn released my hand, sitting up. The map lay flat on the ground, the fading, flickering flames and moonlight illuminating it just enough to see.

"I'd say we would have covered around this much ground today," he said.

He held his finger at the edge of the continent and trailed it inland.

"Tomorrow, we'll keep following the same direction, I suppose, and keep heading towards dryer land."

We all nodded again in agreement, and I caught myself yawning.

"I guess we should get a good sleep then," I said, only now realising how taxing it was to think so much about the future on top of the physical demands of travel. Travel that would only become more demanding.

"Yeah, I'm wrecked as well. See you guys in the morning." Björn stood beside me, wrapping me inside his broad shoulders, and held me there for a moment, swaying slightly to the song carried by the stars, moon, and light, frosty breeze.

My body swayed in rhythm with his.

I laughed as he spun me away then drew me back into him, sweeping me up from my waist for a moment's flight, then placing my feet lightly back down.

Bŏdhi and Chaṅtara retreated to their tent, while Phŏenix stared at the remaining coals, their fluorescent orange glow fading to ash.

She'd barely spoken the entire day, nor met anyone's gaze for any other reason than practical communication, and seemed relieved to be left alone to process.

CHAPTER THREE

I STOOD AT THE base of a large iron ship that towered high above my head, although it barely looked like a ship and more like a smooth, silver dome-shaped shell, glistening.

The sky was bright. The sun was hot.

I was alone.

Behind the shell was miles of barren dirt, blackened by the coals of scattered spot fires that burned bright red over the dry, cracked earth.

The chilling sense of a dark presence drew closer behind me, seeping into my back. Shivers raced up my neck, but no matter how much I willed my body to turn and meet it, face it, fight it, my body wouldn't cooperate. I was paralysed by fear.

Something touched the bare skin of my neck.

A hand.

Dead cold.

My eyes flashed open.

The first glow of dawn shone dimly through the brown tent canvas and Björn rolled unconsciously beside me, hand slipping from where it rested on my waist.

Sweat dripped down my hot forehead although the degree of ice in the air made my fast breath visible in puffs of white mist. My heart raced, chest thudding.

Why can't I turn and face it?!

It was the same dream that recurred every night over the week leading up to our journey, but no matter how many times I mentally prepared myself to face the darkness as a warrior, when the moment came, I was paralysed. Fear dominated every other sense in both body and mind. Pathetic.

So much for protecting the tribe. I thought back to my promise to Nirmala. *I can't even protect myself in a dream…*

I exhaled a full breath and sunk back into the furs, eyes wide open. The atmosphere was still dark and hazy, but I could feel in it the first hints of morning, and I didn't care to return to the realm of sleep. My subconsciousness tormented me there.

Soft sounds of chiming bells drew gradually closer until a silver spark of light drifted in through the tent flaps. She felt my fear. We were bound now; she felt all I experienced as if it were her own.

Ƶchŏ soon fluttered above my face, her tiny brows creased with concern. She knew the metaphysical world well enough to understand it wasn't just a dream that I dreamt. My heart dropped in my chest. I felt like a coward, and worse because she knew it too.

I'd been hanging onto the idea that if I changed the course of the dream, it might change the course of reality, but it seemed the stronger my will developed to fight the darkness, the stronger the darkness became.

Ƶchŏ's pristine white teeth glittered through a tiny but wide smile. I shook my head.

"I know," I told her. Self-defeat did nothing but feed the negative frequencies I was afraid of.

I'd assumed too quickly that the force tormenting me through my dreams had won. But it hadn't won. Not yet. Not even close.

I squeezed Björn tighter, lingering in the pleasant comfort of his warmth and the sense of protection I felt there, then rolled over, reaching my arm out and exposing my bare skin to the freezing morning air. I slid my clothes back under the fur rug and began awkwardly dressing before assembling the courage to rise and brave the weather.

When I peeled open the flaps of our tent flaps, there was just enough dawn light to see. I slid my snow boots over my already numb feet and stepped out onto the slush.

The three light beings were sprightly, skipping over the chalky black coals of last night's fire. In a way they were like children, in a state of constant play. But they were not at all immature. In fact, play was a bi-product of their maturity. They were wise enough to understand that at the core of our existence, the world was a stage, and we were all actors.

Overnight, the coals had accumulated tiny, Fξ-sized hills of polar-white powder, a sharp contrast for the freshly woken eye. Their blue auras were like floating candles, shining brighter than the sun that was still hidden behind the horizon.

When they saw me, chiming sounds rang through the air, but words were unintelligible.

"Morning," I nodded, curious.

While high in pitch, their voices were usually clear...

Lupïta flew towards me in an air of silver mist, reaching out to touch her electric hand to my cheek. An immense rush of energy swept through my body.

She was trying to speak, but I couldn't hear the words. Ȝchŏ flew over, followed by Théodren who also spoke something that didn't manifest in English.

Phŏenix emerged from her tent, stretching up her arms, and watched speculatively before moving towards us.

"Morning." She rubbed her hands together and pulled her beanie down over her ears. "What's going on? Why can't we hear them?"

I didn't have an answer.

Ȝchŏ perched on my shoulder, slumping her shoulders and crossing her arms, befuddled. Théodren and Lupïta started speaking between themselves at a fast, unfollowable pace.

"This is what it was like when Fξ and humans coexisted on Earth before," ꙅchŏ said.

Before utter chaos ensued, and the entire FξŸa species were forced back to Santōṣha permanently.

I could understand her, but I guessed it was only because we were bound.

"Can you hear her?" I asked Phŏenix. She shook her head.

"Even when FξŸa travelled to Earth in the past, they could not communicate with humans. Not through words anyway," ꙅchŏ explained.

I was aware of our history, but I never thought it would repeat itself with us. We could see and communicate with the Fξ before we travelled there. We were not ignorant of their presence nor their power.

Why was this happening?

Hands spread around my waist and I spun to meet Björn's soft lips, momentarily forgetting this new and unsettling situation. My stomach emptied of breath, heart pouring open as I leant back into him.

Home.

From dawn to dusk we trekked, trudging ankle deep through the compacted snow. My hefty pack rubbed, shoulders throbbing, back aching, feet blistering.

Our surroundings became one everlasting wash of white. The snow thickened the further we travelled, and the ground flattened. Simultaneously, it was like my mind was being washed clean from distractions, and all I could do was surrender to the fundamental internal simplicity that lay beneath the noise of the mind. Stillness within the movement.

When my attention wasn't on the aches, pains, and fluctuating waves of physical fatigue, a sense of deeper peace made the barren trek more like a moving meditation.

It didn't take long for conversation to fade between us, and we travelled in the serenity of silence.

The Fξÿa moved faster than us, soaring forward, only to float gracefully back to meet us in our slower step. Our ability to communicate hadn't returned, but we hung onto the hope that it wasn't permanent.

Nights were freezing. Sometimes there was no kindling to make fire, but we all made an effort to collect anything that was burnable along our journey. After setting up tents and eating dinner, we'd retreat quickly to our furs, where I was grateful for the warmth of Björn's body to help deepen the night's rest.

Björn kept his map handy, but his sense of direction was sharp. He remained at the head of the group, closely watching our surroundings and steering us as best he could within the limits of our uncertainty.

"Well, I'm starting to get the feeling that the map might not be as accurate as we hoped," he admitted after days of travel over unchanging terrain. "There shouldn't be this much snow. But it also makes sense that things are different now. Or maybe this is how is used to be."

Chaṅtara hung her head in defeat. She'd been trudging along at the back of the group with Moānā and Tasmai, who demanded constant encouragement to keep moving. They dragged their feet and complained about the endless discomforts of snow travel—which were easy for us *all* to sympathise with, but it was even tougher on their small, less developed bodies.

"It doesn't mean there isn't dry land ahead, I just think...I'm just re-thinking my strategy," he said quickly, sensing our unease about travelling blind.

He didn't seem worried though; he still seemed confident he was leading us in a promising direction, as if he could hear something on the wind that was outside our range.

"I think it's a *good* thing, for a number of reasons, including that the earth is getting nourished by all this moisture. When the snow melts, nature will grow back richly here," he said with conviction.

"I still have a good feeling that the path we're following will lead us out of the snow. I can't explain why, it's just a feeling, and I can't sense how far away, but there's fertile land ahead." He drifted off, leaving us all hanging in the same hope and uncertainty we'd felt since arriving.

I thought of Adam.

He had also been an officer for the Control in the Old World, before following the map Björn left him to the Bermuda Triangle, and making the bold jump between dimensions to reach Santōṣha. He wasn't as high in ranking as Björn, but he knew a lot about the vast expanse of land surrounding our limited sphere of existence that was contained by the high, electric City walls. He was one of the few humans who had the freedom to travel outside the City border without his tracking chip sending alerts to the Control monitor board, and either exploding or leaking poison from its careful position in his wrist. He travelled for his job, but still, he travelled.

He would have been a valuable addition to our tribe now. Another dependable source of stability and geographical knowledge.

I didn't know if it was his nature, or if it was because he was my protective older brother, but he had always made me feel safe. Björn did too, but Adam was fierce, and we were bound by blood. While I couldn't imagine it happening, there was always a possibility that things might end between Björn and I. A possibility I might lose him and the sense of masculine protection he offered me.

Adam would never abandon me. He proved that when he left everything that was safe and certain behind, to follow me into the unknown, even though the idea of a parallel dimension existing inside earth's core was impossible to him. *I* had believed in it, and that alone was incentive enough for him to open his mind to the possibility.

Missing Adam was bitter-sweet. His memory bought so much love into my heart, even though it was seeped in sadness.

Days continued to drift by before our eyes and so did the endless white blanket. As we travelled, hope for contact from the other light beings lingered in the air around all of us, but we heard nothing. Even the Fξ͏Ÿa were unnerved by their lack of communication, although they hid it well.

It was unusual for them not to be in close communication with their tribe at all times—if not in presence, then in at least spirit— but it seemed even their channels of transmission had been disconnected.

"There mustn't be much to report yet," Ӡchŏ justified, floating beside me. I could sense she spoke for her own peace of mind as much as mine.

But that was more unsettling to me than the idea of them having found new life and fertile land without reporting back to us. It meant the snow might have spread a lot further than we expected...

I watched my feet as each step compressed holes in the fluffy snow, until they started sinking less, and began to hit a hard, glass-like surface. I looked up, about to enquire, but was stopped by the echo of a shrieking *crack!*

I froze.

We all froze, even the kids who may not have understood what the sound implied. But their bodies knew. Primal instinct.

Bjorn twisted his head slowly. I was directly behind him. His electric eyes were sharp as they scanned the white land.

"We're walking on ice," he said, his voice low and steady, as if any fluctuating resonance might unsettle the unpredictable ground we stood on further.

The coating of snow was thin, but it was unclear how solid the ice was beneath it.

"I think the *smartest* thing to do right now would be to get off it," Phỗenix said, matching his even tone.

Still, no one moved. Apart from Björn who twisted his torso back around more carefully than I'd ever seen him move.

"It's hard to say where it ends."

The snow that covered the land blended into one unbreaking sheet.

"If we step lightly, we might be ok." Björn reached back to take my hand, signalling me forward.

I hesitated, but either way, we had to move at some point. Preferably *before* the ice weakened any further under our weight. I stepped forward, as carefully as I could step, then again. Björn's grip was tight around my hand, guiding me around him. He remained still.

"Keep going," he said, leaving me to lead the way while he waited for Phỗenix to pass him, followed by the kids, then Chaṅtara.

"I'll stay at the tail," Bỗdhi told him, and soon, we were all moving forward with the lightest steps, wishing we could float.

"Start spreading out," Björn directed.

I maintained the line I walked, but Phỗenix started drifting to one side of me, and Chaṅtara and the kids the other, evening our weight over the ice.

But it wasn't enough. Another crack broke the silence.

I stiffened.

"Keep going," Björn called.

The sound had come from behind. I felt its echoing murmur beneath my feet.

"Now run!"

Every set of feet broke into a run, relying only on the *hope* that we were running towards solid land and not further onto the frozen lake.

As to be expected, our thumping feet disturbed its surface. It continued to fracture behind us, but we didn't stop. I was the first to hit the snow-covered soil. I felt the difference the moment I did.

"Here!" I called, not stopping until I got a safe distance away from the well-disguised lake.

Phŏenix, Chaṅtara, and the kids weren't far behind. Neither were Björn and Bŏdhi. But they were far enough.

"Agh!" A rough voice called out, followed by a sloshing sound.

I spun.

"Agh!" Bŏdhi called again, this time in the pain of the severe temperature of the water he was now enveloped by.

His had fallen through.

Björn spun to help him.

"Don't!" Bŏdhi demanded. "I'll be fine!" His voice was compressed. I was sure all his recourses were channelled into managing the cold.

A hand may have been helpful, but not if Björn sunk with him. Björn hesitated, but the broken ice around him made it clear that Bŏdhi's only option now was to swim himself to land. And Björn's only option was to continue running.

Björn hit solid ground and turned back to offer what little guidance he could.

"Keep moving! We're right here!"

Bŏdhi was still frozen, expression reflecting the shock that paralysed him. His legs beat beneath the water just enough to keep him afloat.

His breaths were deep and loud but not panicked. He was using his breath to calm his system. Eyes wide and focused, he stroked forwards. The ice had cracked all around him, leaving a pool between us.

Björn knelt at the very edge of the land, waiting to pull him out.

"We're right here," he repeated.

"Daddy!" Ṫasmai called and ran to the edge beside Björn. Moānā followed.

Whatever breathing technique Bohdi practised seemed to work. He no longer appeared overwhelmed by the freezing water. He adapted to it, so entirely that his strokes were smooth, as if gliding through a warm pool.

"I'm fine kids," he assured them, his voice as smooth as his movements now.

Something caught his eye in the deep, dark blue water below and he paused, treading water, head tilted down.

We all watched, anticipating.

His head snapped back up with an excited smile.

"There's fish in here!"

I leant forwards with disbelief. The cold could have made him delusional, but it wasn't long before I saw a silver shimmer move through the crystal clear liquid beside him—the first sign of animal life we'd seen since arriving!

He swam quickly to the edge and Björn pulled him up onto the snow, helping him shrug off his soaked, waterlogged pack that would have doubled in weight.

"I see it!" Moānā called excitedly.

"I see it!" Ṫasmai repeated with equal excitement.

"I'm starving," Ṫasmai complained, his hunger clearly stimulated by the sea creature.

Chaṅtara had already taken out a dry set of clothes and rushed to the ground, helping Bŏdhi undress. But he was not crippled. He was invigorated, and unaffected by the temperature. I exchanged a glance with Phŏenix, who, being his sister should have known if he had some kind of super-human relationship with the cold. But she shrugged, as mystified as the rest of us.

"Wait," he said to Chaṅtara as he unclipped a spear from his hefty pack. He looked up at me.

"Maya, can you break me off some of our saltiest dried meat?"

Bohdi was almost naked, kneeling in the snow, and acting as if it were a pleasant spring day. He did not shiver.

"You're not going back in," Chantara told him sternly.

He touched a hand lovingly to her cheek. She flinched away. It was frozen.

He didn't say anything, but looked back up at me, waiting.

"Uh, sure," I slid my pack off my shoulders and took out a small cut of dried meat.

"We're already low on rations and now you want to waste some on fish you'll never catch," Chantara argued.

He didn't argue back.

If it was anyone else, I might have argued too, but Bŏdhi had been one of the greatest fishermen in Santōṣha and was skilled with a spear. I didn't doubt his ability and I was sure Chantara didn't either. She was just worried.

We watched him slide back into the water, breathing deeply and loudly again in a rhythm that seemed to make his body less reactive. Björn remained at the edge, watching the clear water as Bŏdhi dived under, ready to dive in after him if his body suddenly decided to freeze. But his movements were agile.

Ṭasmai and Moānā sat beside Björn, and Ṭasmai dipped his fingers beneath the surface.

"It's freezing!" Ṭasmai squealed, whipping his hand away. "How is he doing that?" he asked with child-like wonder.

Björn shook his head, dipping his own arm in to test the water.

"I don't know," he replied.

"Maybe he's part man, part fish," Moānā said, seriously considering it. "Back home, he used to swim with dolphins too, and they never swam away from him," she told Björn.

"You know what, Mo, at this point, I wouldn't discount it."

"But why would he keep it a secret from us?" Ṫasmai asked sadly.

"He wouldn't," Björn assured him.

The meat on the spear attracted shimmering silver fish immediately. They were probably suffering from food scarcity too. But they weren't small. They were decent-sized fish—and an even more decent-sized food source to us.

"See, he's doing it again," Moānā said. "Same as with the dolphins. They're not scared of him. They like him."

"Yeah, too bad for them," Björn said, half-jokingly.

It wasn't surprising when he caught one. It swam straight up to his bait. And after throwing it onto the dry land, he went back under and caught another.

That was the surprising part. It was as if he had suddenly become immune to the cold. And thinking back over our trip, I realised I'd never seen him complain or show any signs of suffering from the temperatures the rest of us were challenged by. Maybe he had always been immune to the cold.

He was a mysterious man and only became more mysterious the more I learnt of him.

Phŏenix pressed her palm over each of the fish's hearts, closing her eyes in a prayer of gratitude before slicing their throats with a small but sharp pocketknife.

We set up camp close by that afternoon. It was already late, and the sight of fresh fish made us all suddenly ravenous, our hunger no longer suppressible.

Björn and Phŏenix scaled and de-boned the meat, while I prepared the cooking equipment. Moānā and Ṫasmai built and lit a fire, while Chaṅtara kept her eyes glued to Bŏdhi, constantly checking he remained ok.

Which he did.

Dry clothes covered him again and his body started shivering. The cold caught up to him, but he didn't reveal any sense of severe discomfort. He appeared the opposite: satisfied and pleased by his catch.

His biggest problem was trying to dry everything inside his pack before he'd have to strap it to his back again the following morning. He and Chantara took everything out and hung it on tent poles over the fire. There was a light breeze that helped air it all out.

The smell of fish frying through the crisp air was exciting. By the time dusk began to colour the clear blue sky, the kids were playing and dancing around the blazing fire, chanting:

"Fish man, fish man!"

Bŏdhi leapt up from where he knelt by the fire with a wild and playful look in his eyes. He swept Tasmai up into his arms and ran towards the ice lake.

"How about I throw you in and make *you* a fish man!?"

"No, no, no!" Tasmai squealed while laughing hysterically.

"You don't want to be fish man?"

"No, no, no!"

"Oh, so you *do* want to be fish man?"

"No!"

"What are you smiling for then?"

"No!" was all he could reply between laughter as Bohdi spun him around, tipped him upside down, and tickled his ribs.

That night, we all gathered around the fire and ate with light hearts. Faith had been restored. Not that we had *lost* faith. It had just weakened with our bodies. The fact that there was at least one food source available to us on Earth was reassuring.

But it wasn't just the promise of food. For fish to have returned meant that the entire underwater ecosystem was being restored. Just like the land, the sea was coming back to life.

"So, fish man," Björn said. "As grateful as I am for this food on my plate, I am curious how you did it?"

"Yeah, *dad*," Moānā chimed in with an edge of resentment in her voice. "What's the secret?"

"Any normal human body would have shut down," Phŏenix added, but without resentment.

"It's obvious," Ṫasmai said, his mood still silly. "The secret is that he's half-human and half fish, duh!"

Bŏdhi laughed at his son. But Moānā didn't find the joke humorous anymore.

"Honestly, if there is a secret, it is The Mother's, not mine. And she has kept it from me too," he said.

Moānā squinted her eyes with scepticism, looking freakishly like her mother.

"Come on, Mo, you know I'd never hide something like that from you."

"Do I?" she challenged.

"There's no reason for you not to," he said, not entertaining her pre-teen drama any further.

"If anything, I think the way I was breathing helped," he said in answer to Björn. "It was like I dropped into the centre of my being or something, and the water didn't feel cold. It was just water. Sensation around my skin. I've never really been bothered by the cold though," He shrugged, clearly not seeing it as anything extra-ordinary.

Björn and I were more awake than usual when we lay down in our tent. We had rested for a decent amount of time that afternoon and been replenished by the energizing oils contained in the fish.

I wrapped my body around Björn's, and closed my eyes, appreciating the warmth that radiated from his skin.

"Were you serious earlier? About being close to dry land? Or were you just trying to make everyone feel better?" I asked quietly. The sweeping silence of the night was loud, and I didn't want the others overhearing from their tents.

"Someone has to, right?" His chest rumbled beneath my cheek, voice deep and low.

I lifted my head to check his expression. His light-hearted smile reached his eyes.

"No, Maya, I was serious. I do believe that. I can't say why, but I feel it."

I lay my cheek back down on his warm chest, trusting him.

"But since you're asking for honesty, I use the word *close* loosely. I think it's further away than we all hope. But we will reach it. And we are all more capable than we believe to keep going until we do."

He kissed my forehead and wrapped me more tightly in his arms. His lack of concern allowed me to relax. He was an officer —a warrior. He had been trained to fight and persist, and that training clearly served him here, even though many aspects of it hadn't in the past.

He had a robust quality about him that made me feel more robust and capable too, both within myself and in his care.

CHAPTER FOUR

WE'D BEEN TRAVELLING FOR weeks now over unchanging land. Days rolled into each other as if on repeat.

Our food supplies ran low and we were on strict rations, which only made us weaker and more irritable. After a few days of severe discomfort, my body adapted to intermittent fasting, functioning the entire day on an empty stomach, green tea and water until one evening meal rich in fats and proteins. All of our food had been carefully prepared, dried, and preserved; we had packed only that with the highest calorie and nutrient content.

We stopped at every lake we passed and cut into the icy surface to check for fish. Sometimes we caught them on hook-tipped ropes or long spears; other times, the lakes proved barren. I never caught any. Bŏdhi, Björn, and Phŏenix were our best fishermen.

We were all aware we couldn't last much longer without additional food sources, but we did not speak of it, for our energy was precious now and worry was draining.

Before leaving, the Nŏahls of Santōṣha had seen visions of wild gardens where edible plants were abundant. They were *sure* that nature was preparing the land for our arrival, just as we were preparing to arrive. But they didn't have the foresight to direct us to it, nor say how far a distance it would be from where we entered.

So we walked forth, *trying* to trust that it was in the right direction.

Still, there'd been no contact from the other light beings and the luminosity of Ӡchŏ, Lupïta, and Théodren's auric fields was dimming. The collective power of their union was fading.

They'd always been interconnected, even when apart, one force of light weaving them together, one *mind* almost, but the connection had been cut. They couldn't reach each other. The rest of the human tribe weren't aware, but through my marriage with Ӡchŏ, I could sense it; I could *feel* the separation as she experienced it.

I awoke at dawn to a lake of dense fog over the land between our camp and a mountain range that had, only yesterday, become visible in the far distance. The first break in the white blanket was near, and hope that the mountains bore more life than the low lands fuelled us with extra enthusiasm to continue forwards.

The sun hadn't yet risen, but the moon was bright, as were the stars, which cast a silver-blue glow over everything. I stood at the tent opening as my eyes adjusted with a rising sense of unexplainable nausea. It grew more urgent. I ran just far enough outside the camp and vomited.

The dream was getting more intense. The Shadow that lingered over my shoulder, darker. Yet, I still could not turn to face it. My feet remained glued in place.

That night, there were scattered fires over the dry land where there were usually only coals. The flames rose higher, higher, smoke dense and black.

It felt like the end again.

But this time, not just the end of an old and dysfunctional world—the end of the natural world too, and with it, the end of humanity.

I wandered back to the camp and boiled the kettle, brewing medicinal herbs to soothe the strange sickness in my stomach, then added some extra for immunity in case I was catching the flu that had been circling around. But this felt different. It wasn't a head cold. And none of the others had been vomiting.

I heard a round of coughing from one of the tents and left a strong dose of herbs in the kettle that should have served the whole tribe as morning medicine. Then I wrapped myself in a long fur-lined coat. The dark earthy-red patterns embellished into the brown material reminded me of the Samadhi tribe.

I sat on a stone overlooking the miles of snow still to be traversed before reaching new territory. There was, of course, a chance that past the mountains would be another unceasing blanket of snow, but the promise of an alternative was enough to lighten our spirits.

After some time of sitting still, sipping tea, and watching the land gradually awaken under the rising sun that hadn't quite risen yet, the waves of nausea slowly calmed, and my awareness expanded wider than the discomfort within my physical body once more.

I began to feel something.

A presence—not dissimilar to that in my dream.

Haunting.

A Shadow.

It loomed behind me. *Am I being paranoid?*

Unlike my dream, I was not paralysed. I spun my head, but there was no Shadow. No being. No cold hand reaching for my shoulder. And the rest of the tribe was still asleep in their tents.

I'm paranoid.

Inhale. Exhale. Let go.

But in the silence I could hear wordless whispers carried on the breeze like gusts of wind whipping against my ears and I tensed. The air was still. But there was a vibration in the atmosphere that was not pure, was not air alone.

I couldn't help but wonder if it was the whispers of Sky People before they formed words. Was this how it all began?

I shook my head and body.

Inhale. Exhale. Let go.

I'm blending the dream into reality. The feeling has become too familiar. I'm carrying it around as if it's real. Stay real. Stay real.

I closed my eyes and took another breath, trying to expand again beyond the fear, aware that it was my shrinking that held what I feared in place.

I lifted my attention up and out.

Full, black storm clouds were visible in the distance now under the increasing daylight. They hovered over the mountains we travelled towards. But here, all was clear and calm.

Hazy breaths of white mist escaped my mouth, and I hugged my knees tighter, but more out of comfort than in response to the cold.

After some time, a moving white mass caught my attention in the distance through the lake of dancing fog, and I leant forwards, sharpening my gaze. A track trailed behind it, two parallel tracks, footprints!

As I honed my vision in on the fluffy white body, a fluffy white tail whipped up in the air: the form of a small snow fox.

My heart pounded, overwhelmed with joy, for this was the first sign of animal life on land that any of us had seen since arriving!

The lone fox continued to trudge its own trail through the fresh snow, scurrying low to the ground, and I wondered where it came from, where it was going. The snow was bare. There was nothing else in sight.

Are there others, waiting for him somewhere? Maybe they live in the mountains...

After some time, the fox disappeared again beneath the fog and blended back into the landscape, but my heart remained warm.

I sank into a deeper sense of trust in The Mother's capacity to create and cultivate life even after all life had been gone. While it sometimes felt like she'd gone silent, she was there, always, omniscient, ever-present, shepherding our path.

While in every other sense, we travelled blind, with no true map and no certain path, and our journey had not been manifesting as optimistically we envisioned, all was still unfolding perfectly, as intended, in accordance with her plan.

A vaster, wider space opened up within me as this deepening of trust grew, and a sense of inner peace blossomed like a waking flower, re-opening to meet the day.

As the silence amplified, the whisper of another presence emerged. A lighter, benevolent presence.

Be careful, a ringing voice warned, a familiar voice.

Alarmed, my eyes flashed open only to discover I was still alone on the stone.

Qiąõhui?

But her voice didn't return.

Some minutes later, Chantara emerged from her tent and pottered around the campsite for some time before spotting me and moving in my direction. I knew for sure the voice didn't belong to her though.

Her stride was direct as usual.

"Morning Maya."

She sat down beside me and was quiet for some time before speaking again. But internally she was loud, her energy a little neurotic.

"It doesn't feel like we're getting any closer to dry land," she finally expressed.

She was experiencing the opposite of the trust I'd re-discovered, un-enthused by the promise of the mountains. All she saw there was *more* snow and the *additional* challenge of steep gradients to traverse along with it.

"What if the whole Earth, or at least this part of it, is covered in snow? Like an ice age. It's possible, right? It would make sense. The land has been dry for so long. Maybe we came up too early."

I turned to look at her. Her face was tense with the worry she voiced.

"How do you grow food in snow? What do we do when we run out of supplies?" She didn't expect me to have answers. "Our clothes are starting to wear in. The kids are freezing. We need thicker furs, or at least more options when our layers get wet."

I scanned over her dry skin, red cheeks, her rosy nose and cracked lips. It was true the conditions were harsh, and our wearing clothes made it feel even more brutal. My back ached constantly from the weight of my pack, and we all experienced similar responses to the severe environment. The snow was unapologetic. Unrelenting. It had no compassion.

"What are you suggesting? To go back?" It wasn't something I'd considered, no matter how exhausting it was to hike through snow from dawn to dusk.

At least the intensive exercise cultivated enough body heat for us to stay mobile.

"No. Well, maybe?" Chaṅtara let out a breath.

"I don't know." She stared at the sunrise.

The truth was, we couldn't go back. Even if we wanted to. Even if our survival depended on it. The channel that allowed us to enter this dimension would not allow us to exit. The only entrance to Santōṣha was on the other side of the world, in the middle of the ocean: The Bermuda Triangle.

"I just worry about the kids. Ṫasmai barely stopped coughing last night. I worry his immune system isn't strong enough yet to fight a chest infection. And now Moānā's got it again, or some other strain of flu. She's barely had a few days' break. Mostly, I just think we should have…left them behind." A tear fell from her eye, and she didn't bother to hide it.

I'd never seen her vulnerability before.

I leant over, wrapping my arm around her.

"We're here now," I said softly. "They're here. We can't change that, and feeling guilty for choices we didn't make won't help the situation either. Trust, if nothing else, that we're being taken care of. The Mother hasn't abandoned us, that I know for sure. I really believe everything is happening as it should."

She sniffed into my chest.

"It doesn't feel like that. Why *should* a small kid have to endure a never-ending flu on top of never-ending travel through never-ending snow? How could the Mother possibly support such unfairness?"

"I don't know," I said honestly, adding, "I guess nature has never been fair."

She didn't like hearing that. She wanted me to support her *slightly* dramatized version of reality.

"It will end," I said. "All of those things will end. And as of this moment, we're all safe right? We're alive, breathing, fit enough to hike miles each day. Warm enough to keep moving. Right now, there're no *major* issues, apart from the kids being sick. That's not ideal. But still, they're healthy enough to eat and walk. It's only in future thinking that these worries become pressing."

I reminded her as gently as I could because sometimes people just wanted sympathy. But sometimes, sympathy wasn't what they needed. Sometimes reality was a more grounding force.

"So, let's just stay with each breath, each moment, and trust that the future will be ok just as *this* future would have been if we looked at it from a past moment."

Her racing mind began to calm, and I leant my cheek against her fiery hair, then lifted my head, remembering.

"I saw a white snow fox."

She lifted her head abruptly, eyes searching mine for whether I was lying.

"Really?"

I nodded.

"It scurried along just over there." I pointed. "Can you see the tracks?"

She leant forwards, then after scanning the ground, nodded quietly.

"I trust in nature," I told her. "Can you trust her with me?"

CHAPTER FIVE

W E WATCHED NERVOUSLY AS the storm brewed over the day's trek, and by late afternoon the pregnant black clouds unleashed upon us. The temperature was below freezing, transforming the heavy rain into blizzarding snow.

We'd been hoping to reach the mountains where we could make camp under some kind of shelter before the storm struck, but we were still on flat land. We could barely see our own feet, let alone a cave or hill to dig ourselves under. We kept our heads down.

"When we reach the mountains we'll have protection!" Björn shouted over the winds that snarled at the snow and uprooted furious waves of powder that flared up all around us.

He was trying to assure us that there was a way out. That if we kept moving, we'd find a safe place to rest.

The only problem was we couldn't *see* the mountains anymore. We could barely even see each other. For all we knew we could've been walking in the opposite direction.

We gripped each other's hands and pushed against the roaring weather.

Moānā started crying.

Ṫasmai started crying and coughing, and moaning all at once; the sound competed with that of the storm.

We stopped as Bŏdhi held Moānā against him, comforting her while Chaṅtara held Ṫasmai, but she was barely stable enough herself to comfort anyone.

Björn, Phŏenix, and I huddled together for a moment's rest, chests pressing, backs to the storm, faces momentarily protected from the cutting weather.

We walked on.

"You lead ahead again Björn! I'll walk behind and make sure everyone stays together!" I yelled, even though he was still beside me.

I didn't trust Chaṅtara's current state of clarity.

Björn was hesitant, his body drawing mine closer, face pressing into my neck, hand tightening around my waist before letting go.

"Ok!" He sped to the front of the pack.

In addition to the external chaos, there was a metaphysical element of chaos in the air that was more disturbing to me...

The dark Shadow I had felt that morning hadn't disappeared. I still felt the presence of something foreign looming around us, but I couldn't discern whether it was the Shadow of my own paranoia or the Shadow of Sky people. It didn't make sense that they could find us so quickly. In truth, nothing about them made sense to me at all.

But, in the name of vigilance, I kept one eye, one aspect of my attention, on the demanding terrain, and the other on the realm outside of form. I spread my awareness wider than my body, scanning the energy bodies of the tribe to ensure they remained clear, to ensure that if the presence I felt *was* a Shadow, it wouldn't attach to anyone.

I was still sceptical as to whether what I felt in others when I tuned into them was true or projected.

Nala had taught me with great specificity how to split my awareness in two and step one aspect of my being into another. She taught me how to merge until I felt their experience as my own. I practised on her, and she gave me what she promised was honest, unbiased feedback as to whether what I experienced was accurate.

When I had been clear in mind and body, what I felt was generally accurate. My mind would become so quiet, and my being so still, that I no longer felt separate from anything around me. I felt vast, experiencing the interconnectivity of all of nature as if it were within me, while at the same time disappearing entirely into it. Held by one source. And from that one source, feeling others was natural, effortless, their beings extensions of my being. And all beings, extensions of the One.

But under this pressure, I didn't feel clear or still enough within to get an accurate read. I focused instead on casting something of a protective field of light around us, in an attempt to fend off any Shadows that may be present.

It was taxing to maintain, but it was less complicated than the energetic work I'd have to attempt to undo their hooks later if they were in fact trying to attach to us. Žchŏ travelled inside my coat, and her magic on my chest fuelled me with increased stamina. She understood what I was doing. She could feel the field of light around us, which gave me confidence it was working.

I watched the group as closely as I could through the blizzard and trailed along at Chaṅtara's ankles. She was weak, weaker than the rest of us, and her frustration wasn't helping. Phŏenix had taken Ṫasmai's hand further ahead to give her a rest.

Of everyone that I tuned into, her energy body carried the most density, stirred up by the same metaphysical chaos I had been sensing in the air. I checked a few times, just to be sure that I wasn't projecting it, but I definitely felt something off lingering in the L·ight Màttẹr around her body.

I couldn't be sure whether it was the product of her own negative thinking, creating a cloud of black smoke around her, or the presence of a Shadow, gripping on, wrapping her up. It could have been both.

"Keep your attention on your breath, Chaṅtara!" I tried to offer guidance. Being trapped in loops of negative thinking would only deplete her vital energy.

"Fuck the breath!" Her head whipped around to glare at me, but her eyes weren't her own. They were foggy, like the fog that enveloped her being, pupils all but a slit down the centre.

My vision sharpened in response, and I swore for a moment that the skin of her face had developed a silver, metallic shimmer. I shook my head.

I'm hallucinating. Still paranoid.

That's what I *wanted* to believe. It would have been more convenient than the alternative.

But when her head whipped back around, her shoulders shrunk in a kind of shame. She'd exposed something she'd been adamant to hide.

"Chaṅtara, listen to me. You have to stop your mind from racing, ok!" I called, even though it was obvious that she didn't want to hear it. It was becoming clearer that her active mind was fuelling something that was desperate for its energy. An entity, a Shadow. I was almost sure of it now.

"I know it's hard right now, but your mind is weakening you!"

She didn't turn or respond, but I sensed her body tense. I know she heard me.

An extended roll of thunder shook the earth, and an electric blue crack of lightning lit the land for one sweet second.

"The mountains!" Phóenix called, and just that glimpse was enough for Björn to adjust our course to a more direct route.

We had, in fact, drifted off course.

A forceful gust of snow hit us. I stumbled back. Something sharp flicked into my eye and I stopped to rub it out.

I saw Chaṅtara turn, then turn back, as if she hadn't seen me stop. My eyes blurred, but I propelled myself forward, determined not to lose the trail of footprints that were being quickly covered by the wind and heavily falling snow.

"Wait!" I called, but I was sure the wind swept the sound back into the emptiness behind me.

I skipped forward, fastening my steps.

"Agh!"

My foot landed on a deceivingly thin patch of snow-coated land—perhaps it was ice. Whatever it was, under the momentum of my foot, combined with the impact of the feet that had already passed over it, it broke and I fell through.

My body dropped into a waist high crevasse, and a sharp pain struck one of my ankles as it twisted on the way down. The icy ground was slushy and wet.

Everything became less clear under my rising panic. I hurled my body onto the ledge at my waist to pull myself back out.

But that crumbled too.

"Hey! Wait!" I called out again.

I couldn't see the tribe at all anymore, and the howling storm was too loud to compete with, so I focussed instead on getting back up to ground level.

This time, I pushed my body *into* the thin ledge, snow crumbling all around me, until I hit sturdier ground.

I slid my stomach onto the snow and swung one leg up and around after the other.

Another sharp pain kinked my ankle as it hit the higher ground on an unnatural angle. My joints were already worn from the excessive walking. One tweak was all it needed to be injured; I hoped it was less severe than it felt.

"Agh!" I called out again, louder than necessary in the hope the others would catch the sound.

As soon as they realize we've been separated, they'll turn to find me.

I forced myself to calm, pushing the pain into the background of my awareness, and let my ankle rest for a moment, knowing the pressure of standing would only add strain.

But after some minutes passed and no one came rushing back to collect me, I realised that I might be thinking too optimistically. Chaṅtara was the only one who saw me fall behind, and she was in a dangerous state of mind.

But even so, would she purposefully hide my absence?

I stumbled forward a step. The pressure on my ankle was acute, but I forced myself to walk. If I lost the tribe, my life itself would most likely be next.

The blizzard blew more fiercely. Snow spat at my raw face with more intensity now the others weren't there to catch some of its force. I pushed myself against it, each step cutting through winds that would have otherwise pushed me in the opposite direction.

"Hey!" I yelled into the storm again, stumbling.

No response.

Ẕchó? It was only then that I realised I couldn't feel her presence on my chest.

CHAPTER SIX

T HE INTENSITY OF THE blizzard calmed.

Snow fell in light swirls, falling onto my fur jacket and settling between each wispy strand. It did not melt, and with the relative stillness in the air, it did not blow off either. I was a walking snowman.

My faltering walk was weak but not defeated. It was more of a hobble than a walk too. My injured leg dragged behind me, limp, and my swollen ankle throbbed, pulsing with pain under even the slightest pressure.

Lost.

Directionless.

I was blinded by dense fog, stumbling my way through an endless cloud.

But I didn't stop. I *couldn't*. If I did, I wouldn't have the strength nor discipline to get back up.

Ȝchŏ lay in the safety of my jacket, but she was in pain too. Her glow was fading, fading, flickering in and out of exuberance.

I'm getting you to shelter. Hold on. Determination was the force that fuelled me now. I could barely believe I had the stamina to get *myself* to shelter, but I had to. At least for her.

It's ok. I'm ok. Her voice was so faint, so fragile.

She wasn't ok.

Hold on. I repeated.

I didn't know what caused her sudden weakness, but I knew that being severed from her tribe made it significantly worse.

My eyes stung, swelled, squinted open enough to see what was in front of me. My nose was so numb I wouldn't have been surprised to find I was noseless. My shoulders ached, burned beneath my straps. Each breath of air scratched my dry throat. Swallowing felt like sandpaper.

My exhaustion reached a level I hadn't been aware existed.

I was still in shock over the sudden turn of events that led to my estrangement. I couldn't be sure that Chantara had wittingly turned a blind eye to my falling behind, but she was the only one who saw me stop. If she told the others, if they had stopped to wait—which they would have if they knew—I couldn't have fallen so far behind as to lose them.

I shook with a tremor that ran deeper than the mere sensation of being cold. Freezing cold. Realising that if it *had* been Chantara's intention to lose me, it wasn't *her* intention.

Not really.

It confirmed my suspicion that the presence I felt had, in fact, been a Shadow. Looming. Waiting for an energetic opening to hook into. And Chantara was the most mentally unstable, the most susceptible to possession.

It made *sense* that if this was the case, my separation from the tribe was convenient to her. To the shadow entity.

I was its biggest threat.

Their survival relied on our ignorance. It must have been aware that I sensed it. Any thoughts that may have influenced Chantara's decision to ignore my fall must have been sent from the shadows. It was the only explanation.

Being two of the three only women on Earth, we knew how important our survival was to the future of our race.

I still couldn't comprehend how it was possible for her to have fallen prey to their radio waves so quickly. I always believed

Chaṅtara may have been the strongest of us all. She acted that way on the outside…

But it was not external strength that repelled such forces. Internal honesty and vigilance were the ultimate resistance. Remaining an unbiased witness of the mind.

I didn't have the capacity to ponder it any longer. While it was distracting me from my physical pain, any amount of mental energy was draining.

The atmosphere darkened. I couldn't discern through the cloud of fog that enveloped me if it was an issue of time or another wave of weather.

But as I kept my gaze up and outward, a momentary glimpse of the mountain range revealed itself, closer than I'd expected.

I almost fell to bow down on my knees in reverence, but instead accelerated my step, directing all the determination left in me towards reaching the promise of shelter. I had no other option.

Björn carried our tent in his pack to balance out the weight of all the food and cooking utensils stored in mine, and he was gone. I was well aware that there was no chance a tent would survive these winds even if I had one though.

By the time I reached the mountain's edge my feet were beyond ruined and my body beyond depleted, yet somehow, I continued. Mindlessly, blankly, walking, limping. The pain in my ankle was sharp. It begged me to stop but I wouldn't.

Ӡchŏ attempted to send me what was left of her light, her magic, to help propel me forward, but I couldn't accept it. Her once-blazing sun had reduced to the flame of a candle. Delicate, it flickered passively in the wind, susceptible to being blown out entirely.

Please, you're too weak. Hold onto it.

But so are you.

I'm not too weak, I told her. But our conversation was pointless. We both knew exactly how weak we each were.

I traversed closely around the mountainous walls, relieved by the way they served to barricade me from the aggravated weather. The elements were definitely rousing up another blizzard.

And then, as if the Mother herself decided that I'd endured enough, a cave-like overhang became visible up the face of an adjacent mountain.

Without even having to activate the mind, my body redirected course.

The snow was thinner on the ascending angle, making it easier to dig my feet and hands into coarser land as I climbed upwards. But invisible ice also hid beneath the powder dusting. I slipped and tumbled backwards time after time only to haul myself back up again.

"Argh!" I used the call of the warrior to keep going.

Keep climbing.

Get up.

Get up again.

The mountains were not disturbed by my roars, nor was the sky or the snow that fell heavily once more. No sound could compete with them that day. The wind howled louder, drowning out the scope of my meagre human lungs.

Where was Björn's comforting hand of encouragement? Or the kids' light laughter to lift me from the physical torment? Where were the glimmers of FξŸa dust to remind of the magic in the world?

Was there any magic in the world?

I was both the battler and the entire battle, all on the canvas of nature, who may well have been silently laughing in all her epic stillness and her chaos.

The cave was dark when I finally hauled my limp body over the edge. I slid on my stomach over the cold stone and crawled on my elbows to find it was deeper than I had let myself imagine, which meant more protection from the weather.

I collapsed against the back wall, curling into a tight ball in an attempt to conserve the body heat I'd accumulated through motion. The stillness within the cave walls felt so extreme, in contrast to the persistent severity of the elements against my body, that it was almost overwhelming. I felt as light as a feather but, at the same time, as heavy as a cold corpse.

The snow that clung to my furs gradually melted in the dry air and I wriggled out of my outer layers, spreading them flat over the floor in the hope they'd dry. My drenched hair, however, felt like it would *never* dry. Icicles formed where moisture was trapped between strands, freezing my brain.

When I summoned enough momentum to move my arm again, I drew a knife from my belt. I held my hair at the tips so it was taut, then hacked at it with the thin blade until it fell in damp bundles onto the stone, leaving just enough around my face for future insulation.

My upper body fell to the stone again, wasted.

But now I was cold, so I tended to that by sliding on dry clothes.

Then fell limp again.

But Ӡchŏ hung on my mind. I couldn't rest in the uncertainty of her livelihood, so I lifted my head once more and tended to her too.

She was tucked into a warm pocket of my pack, but I could barely see her in the darkness. Her auric field was barely aglow and her skin was grey.

I lifted and nurtured her limp body gently in the cup of my hands, but I felt tremendously lost for how to help her. It was only then that I realised I couldn't feel my fingers. They weren't even tingly, only numb. And they would barely bend at my will. Maybe they were dead.

Ӡchŏ's naked body shivered in the cold air, so I tucked her inside my coat where she could rest once more on my chest, my heart.

What happened? I finally asked, lying back against the rocky wall, closing my eyes, with no intention to move again now that we were both wrapped inside the warmest fur I owned.

I hadn't wanted to force her to speak, but I needed to know.

I don't know either, she whispered quietly, calmly. Tiredly, as if she'd been the one hiking through the blizzard.

It's ok, she whispered. *I'm ok.*

I didn't sleep yet. I forced myself awake for as long as I could, listening carefully to each breath Ӡchŏ drew, and tuned closely into the power that lay in my heart, visualising it seeping out through my chest and embodying her, holding her.

The sky continued to darken, but no stars or moonlight shone into the opening. They were non-existent that night. It was pitch black.

In my lack of sight, sounds became more concentrated. The dripping echo of melting snow, the wild wind and cracking thunder. But no amount of concentrated listening could keep me awake.

I fell.

Deep sleep.

Goodnight.

The storm continued for days, although the fluctuation of light between day and night was slim. I was too disorientated to notice. They blended into one.

For some time, violent shivers were my body's sole energy expense. Otherwise, I was dead weight. Dead weight desperately missing the warmth of Björn's alive skin against it.

I closed my eyes and gripped onto the memory of sleeping beside him, intertwined in our tent, as if my imagination could transport me there, or at least trick part of my body into thinking it was warm.

The first day, I barely opened my eyes, only waking to check on Ȝchŏ.

I built a fire with the twigs and sticks that hung in bunches from my pack, and with the dry kindling scattered around the cave, I was able to keep it alight until each layer of my skin eventually warmed. At some point, the warmth finally reached my frozen bones.

Once my body heat rose to a natural temperature, and the intensity of my physical discomfort lifted, I began slowly regaining strength. Or at least life.

I continued nursing Ȝchŏ close to my heart and she became like an extension of my chest. The luminosity of her being remained dim; she could barely move or laugh or speak, let alone fly. I guess she was dead weight too. But not weight. Just…

I tended to her closely, offering anything I possibly could to aid her healing.

But she wasn't healing.

And it was hard to help her when I still didn't know the cause of her deterioration.

I wouldn't acknowledge it at the time, I *couldn't*, because it was too heartbreaking. But her light had faded, and it wasn't coming back.

The severity of the storm passed again, but I remained in the cave. The dense, everlasting fog didn't, which made it hard to see past the entrance. It would have been unwise to travel blind of direction.

Presently, survival was my priority, and if survival limited me to this small, dark space, I was happy to do that in the name of simply being safe and dry. My body did not replenish itself quickly, and my ankle was sore and bruised and swollen.

I was quietly relieved that the fog excused me from travelling; I would have pushed myself through the pain in my ankle if it hadn't, even though I knew better than to push through pain.

Observing the rhythms of Ӟchŏ's breath as if I might my own was like an ongoing meditation. Her breath was my only gauge by which to monitor the quality of her livelihood.

When her last breath was exhaled, the lungs of her tiny body never to know a following inhale, I felt the central essence of the light that she was leaving her body. But it didn't leave the earth entirely.

It merged with mine.

A glistening silver river of L·ight Mátter lifted from the centre of her tiny chest and soaked into my heart where her grey body still lay, transferring all the magic and power that she was over into my being.

An electric rush of energy rippled through every cell of my body, so high in frequency I thought *I* was the one dissolving. It raced through my system like volts of lightning.

With it, I saw flashes of imagery. Memory. Ӟchŏ's life, as it flashed before her eyes in the final minutes of consciousness she experienced after her bodies death, flashed before mine. The beauty and love and divinity she experienced over her life was so rich it was not sad to see it end. It was full. And she was content. Free.

The rapid-speed film stopped rolling.

And the moment the transfer of her spirit into mine was complete, her physical body dissolved into dust, and dust into pure L·ight Mátter that trickled down my breast, spreading over my stomach and through my clothes.

CHAPTER SEVEN

ABSOLUTE DARKNESS RETURNED TO the cold cave. I was alone.

And the slow-seeping comprehension of what just unfolded landed.

Ӡchŏ was dead.

"No." I wrapped my arms around my chest, curling inwards, attempting to grasp onto any slither of Ӡchŏ that still remained with me in the physical realm, but she was gone.

Pure light flooded through my system, almost overwhelming in its exquisite effervescence, but still I ached with grief.

The noble, benevolent Light Being who had wholeheartedly bound her life to mine, in service of humankind and all of nature on Earth, had died before she even got to see the fruits of what she sacrificed herself for. For all I knew, her sacrifice may still be proven fruitless.

My heart burned with loss. Every trace of her existence had disintegrated before my eyes, as if she'd never existed at all.

But my emotions calmed, and I knew that nothing had been lost. Her presence lingered, undying. *Within* me now, no longer separate. We were still bound, more intimately than ever. The spark of light that she was had merged with the light inside me.

The pain I felt was not so much loss as it was the sudden realization that I was alone now.

But beneath the loneliness, my heart felt brighter.

My tears dried, and a river of peace and equanimity washed through me. I pressed both hands over my chest where Ȝchŏ had been and became increasingly aware of the flame that still burned in her absence.

Without Ȝchŏ's company, there was an eerie emptiness to my existence.

At first, it was unsettling. I craved company. But it wasn't long before a richer sense of trust began to permeate within, counteracting my despair.

While on the surface, it was frightening to be isolated from the tribe in unknown territory, I also felt an undeniable sense of being guided—the sense that this, too, was part of a preeminent plan that lay outside my comprehension but entirely within that of nature's.

It was a bittersweet reality. The pain of losing Ȝchŏ broke my heart, and my longing for Björn's presence was immense.

In daydreams, I'd imagine the tribe following the smell and smoke of my fire. I'd see their faces appearing over the ledge as they crawled inside. I heard Ṫassie's sweet young laughter and Moānā's sassy pre-teen comments. I imagined Bŏdhi's wild eyes and calm essence that was as still and rich and untamed as the deepest part of the ocean.

I welcomed Phŏenix's melancholy, and the quiet grief she had been walking with during our rough travels. I understood what she felt more than ever. I also understood *her* more now too, just by product of the time we spent together. She was a complex woman. Outgoing and talkative when she wanted to be, but sharp and mysterious at times too. For a long time, the distance between us seemed unbridgeable, but after letting go of the jealousy I felt towards her as a result of my conviction that Björn would inevitably fall in love with her, I realised she was just another young woman, with her own set of insecurities, interests, and ideas.

Even Chaṅtara's face was welcome, *more* than welcome. I was curious to know whether my assumptions about her purposely ignoring my fall were correct, both with anticipation and dread. If it *were* true, the whole tribe was in danger and there was nothing I could do about it.

I closed my eyes and tried to call them to me, hoping to spark some kind of telepathic connection like the one between me and Ӡchŏ. I prayed that even if they didn't find this cave, they'd at least found their own shelter from the storm. I prayed that even if I wasn't able to warn them, they'd be safe from the Shadow that had begun attaching itself to Chaṅtara's energy field.

I yearned to talk to Ŋala, but since I couldn't I took to journalling, as if the journal itself, made by her hands, might open up a channel of communication between us.

Dear Ŋala,

I failed.

I sensed the Shadow but didn't trust my intuition enough to take it seriously. I wasn't vigilant. I let my own thoughts, my own self-doubt, interfere with protecting the tribe. I think Chaṅtara's mind was influenced, and I don't know if it's permanent.

Now I'm alone. Ӡchŏ is dead. I'm weak and injured. I don't know if I'll be able to find the tribe again. I don't know if they'll all be infected by the time that I do.

If you were here this wouldn't have happened. I wish you were here.

But she wasn't. She and all her shamanic powers were not coming to the rescue.

Without you, what do I do?

Of course, there was no answer.

I sat at the edge of the cave opening, staring into the fog, and fell into silence when there was nothing else to do or think.

I was just there.

And as I surrendered to my new reality, I rediscovered a certain quietness and stillness within that was rarely available in the company of others. I remembered how *rich* it felt to be alone, how sweet and spacious.

A tingling sensation rippled up my spine, although I didn't feel cold. The air had actually warmed over the last day. The rain and snow stopped flowing and the cloud cover acted like an insulator, trapping any heat.

I began to feel a presence with me.

A breath.

An air of L·ight Mátter that wasn't mine.

A voice.

I didn't open my eyes for I was certain no human had entered the cave, just as I was certain the entity wasn't a Shadow. It was light, pure, benevolent.

"I'm with you." The voice was unfamiliar, the sound of a young boy. Innocent and innately loving in essence.

"Who are you?" I whispered. "Where are you?"

"With you," was all he answered. He had a very strange accent. Nordic, which I'd never heard before in its pure

expression. It was rich and undulating.

Well, that's helpful.

My attention stayed with the presence, so as not to let him slip away.

Then vivid images started flashing through my mind's eψe.

"In a day, the fog will pass," the voice told me, accompanied by the image of a clear blue sky and wide-open view.

Snow covered the ground, but it was thinner on this side of the mountain and the ground less flat. A patch of brown dirt sprinkled with grass was visible in the far distance: the first splash of green I'd seen on the New Earth.

"Follow the patch of green," the voice continued. *"That's the direction of dry land."*

His voice was followed by another sweeping image of clear land, clear skies, and an abundance of green. There were young fruit trees and berry bushes and edible plants. Compared to the rest of the land I'd seen, it was a utopia.

"You must move quickly." It was as if the boy was suddenly a man; his voice became rougher, deeper, masculine.

"Another storm is coming, more severe than the last. The temperature will drop, and ice will coat this cave. You'll be trapped." His colourful accent was harsher under the severity of his warning.

"In three minutes, you'll begin vomiting. Tomorrow you'll wake up so ill it will feel impossible to move. But you must move. Death is the only alternative if you stay."

I shivered away from the vision that followed.

It was my body, stiff and grey on the icy floor of the cave. Cracked purple lips and frozen white hair.

"Right now, both futures are equally possible, which is why I am here in warning. But you alone have the authority to choose life or death."

A thought of the others entered my mind, followed by the sickening fear of leaving and losing them for good. Of straying too far in another direction. By staying in the cave, I was gripping onto the chance of crossing paths again.

"Your survival is more important than your tribal concerns right now," the seemingly all-knowing man assured me.

"They are, and will be ok too," he added, as if he also had insight into their fate. *"But you will not be if you don't get to dry land. Tomorrow, when this mist dissolves, you must move."*

Then he vanished.

I choked on a gasp of air.

My eyes flashed open.

My body shook and my stomach began to twist and turn. Sharp cramps made it hard to breathe. I felt dizzy, and to my disbelief, after two minutes of lying flat on my back in an attempt to stabilize the feeling of spinning, I began hurling vomit over the edge of the cave.

I could barely believe the accuracy of the man's prediction, but also couldn't deny it, for there I was, overcome with an overwhelming wave of nausea that made it hard to think or function.

I lay on the stone's edge, head hanging over, spinning, aching. My vision blurred; my ears rang. I felt paralysed, glued to the ground, and surrendered, allowing whatever was happening to me to pass through. Even if I wanted to, no amount of force would have enabled me to move.

Time passed, but I wasn't tracking it. Gradually, the dizzy spell passed and I regained mobility. A diluted sense of nausea followed me into the night, but it was not severe, which I hoped meant the illness had passed and wouldn't return as the man predicted.

Who was he?

Benevolent entities had communicated through the In-Between to guide me in the past, entities that existed *in* the world but not *of* it, but none had been quite like him.

I shivered again at the image of my frozen body on the cave floor and began to gather my belongings and organise my pack in preparation to leave in the morning, just on the off chance the mist *did* in fact clear. If I woke up as sick as the man suggested, I didn't want to be stumbling around collecting everything. Not that there was much to collect.

I mixed a bitter tea of immune-enhancing herbs before sleeping that night, and a meal with detoxifying spices. As I lay on my back, staring up at the blank rock, I visualized myself waking up clear, healthy, and energized.

CHAPTER EIGHT

B UT THE NORDIC MAN'S premonition was inescapable.
The following morning, I was vomiting *before* even conscious of doing so, and immediately regretted the amount of spices I'd consumed. As I regurgitated the previous night's meal, the putrid smell and taste were so repulsive it only contributed to my nausea.

When my eyes opened to the light of day, I rolled to face the cave entrance but could barely appreciate or even *acknowledge* the crisp blue sky and the single patch of vivid green grass in the distance.

It was like all the fog that had filled the air now filled my head. And it *hurt*. Everything hurt. My whole body ached and throbbed and burned. For the first time since arriving, my skin shone with sweat.

Dizziness made thinking impossible. Feverish chills rippled through my body. I groaned and moaned, writhed around on the stone, and vomited some more. Then the image of my dead body flashed across my vision.

"Maya. Move. Now." The man's aetheric voice returned, rough, raw, blunt, and it now scared me.

"Did you do this to me?!" I shouted through the pain, then gritted my teeth together, trying to hold down another wave of vomit.

"No," the voice answered candidly, then disappeared again.

I groaned once more, *knowing* he was trustworthy, even though I didn't know why, and rose.

I slowly rolled my sleeping furs, strapping them to my travel pack that I was so grateful my past self had prepared for departure.

Then I crawled to the edge of the cave and looked down towards the ground, only now able to see how high I'd climbed. I drew in a full breath and rolled my weight over the edge.

I slid down the powdery mountain face on my backside, using my legs and feet to steer—it seemed like an easier option than walking.

A bubbling laugh escaped me as my turbulent descent down the slope ended with a thud, my body safely reaching flat ground with only a few bruises. But I quickly suppressed it when I felt something else wanting to escape with it.

I swallowed and stood, brushing snow off my backside. It was hard to focus on direction when everything was blurred and unsteady, even though I knew it was me that was off-balance, not the earth. But the vivid green burst of colour in the distance was hard to miss.

The weaving trek through the mountains was not *fun*, but in the back of my mind, the aetheric voice that warned me of the incoming storm urged me forward. I was on a mission. To survive. And somehow, I did.

I remember falling on my hands and knees to vomit a bit, but I got back up. I also remember the earth tipping upside down at one point, but still, I continued walking, even when the sky was beneath me rather than above.

I knew for sure I was tripping when the clouds began illuminating fluorescent sheaths of colour and morphed into perfect geometric shapes that swirled in unison. But the cause of these delusions remained a mystery.

I *clearly* remember reaching the patch of grass.

It was a holy moment, like arriving in heaven. My knees weakened, and I fell onto the waxy green blades and kissed the ground. I even chewed on a few sour strands before getting back on my feet and continuing forwards over more snow.

In time, more breaks in the snow started to appear and the white layer that coated the ground became thinner the further I travelled from the mountains.

Walking. Walking. Stumbling. Walking.

The yellow sun drifted across the clear blue sky.

Walking.

Time passing.

Ankle hurting.

Still walking.

More patches of dirt. Small plants poked their thin, premature necks up from the exposed soil that I'm sure had been nourished by the melting snow and I smiled the weakest smile of joy at the sight of these new wisps of life on Earth.

"Pick a handful of leaves from this plant," the Nordic man's esoteric voice arose from the prevailing silence as I passed an unfamiliar shrub.

I felt a shard of resistance. The shrub was not even a shrub yet; it was tiny. I didn't want to minimise its chance of survival by stealing its first few expressions of life.

"Raspberry leaf is more robust than it looks," he assured me. *"It will survive. And it will help you survive."*

I followed his guidance and picked a few leaves—the ones closer to the bottom, so the higher leaves could continue to catch and drink the sun.

"Chew one every half hour as you walk," the voice directed.

"Spit the fibre back onto the earth when the taste diminishes."

The leaf was sour and bitter, which almost immediately soothed my lingering sickness. My brain started to clear and re-centralize. Both the dizziness and the delirium gradually faded.

Raspberry leaf. I committed it to memory, studying the leaf in case I ever needed to find it again in the future.

The voice disappeared again, but his essence lingered with me and remained close.

Walking became easier after I'd chewed on a few of the miracle leaves, and by evening, I was no longer stumbling along in a hallucinogenic dream. My wintry skin felt rejuvenated by the beaming sun that had felt, over the day, like the embrace of a close friend or lover.

Lover…Björn…

I paused nostalgically in my tracks, turning in the direction of the distant mountains as if I might spot him now the air was clear enough to see.

But the mountains didn't look so clear anymore. Another congregation of dark grey clouds loomed, preparing to disrupt the land once more.

I looked up at the sky.

"Are you guiding Björn too?" I asked the man, assuming his presence existed somewhere in the aether of divine possibility above. My question was met by silence.

By the time the sun began descending behind me for night to proceed its duties, the landscape had significantly changed. Snow only appeared in small, passing islands now, exposing larger patches of dirt and rock.

I collected as much snow as I could melt in my water container, aware that the supply mightn't be consistent for much longer.

While relatively sure I'd be safe from the storm's growing threat, I continued walking long into the night. I'd spent so many days deprived of movement and the more the illness subsided, the more my inner vitality returned. I felt lighter, freer, and even more grateful for my general good health.

The clouds above continued to clear, and the first stars I'd seen in days became visible. As I stared up at the sparkling sky, an extraordinary phenomenon began to occur. A phenomenon that was once labelled the Northern Lights.

At first, I thought I was tripping again as I had when the clouds began to swirl earlier, but the sight was too vivid and filled the air with a rich effervescence that was impossible to deny.

It began as a dusty curtain of bright green light that floated across the shimmering blackness, striking and almost fluorescent in contrast. Another curtain of an equally brilliant shade of purple painted the night beside it, merging, dancing, swaying, its movement so subtle it could have easily been missed.

But as I stopped still to watch the light dance, it continued gracefully, spreading across all that was visible of the wide, open sky.

My feet began moving again beneath its everglow, the land tinted green, and I felt invigorated, sleepless. I walked until the moon was directly above me, and I presumed it was around midnight, then waited further into the morning.

Finally, I lay my furs down for a few hours' sleep under the majestic sky before sunrise.

CHAPTER NINE

I WOKE BEFORE MY eyes opened to something small and wet on my cheek.

A kiss.

A serene smile melted my freshly woken features, imagining Björn's soft lips against my skin, his face above mine.

He'd found me.

I nuzzled into it, then froze suddenly, realizing the high improbability of Björn finding me during the short hours I'd slept.

I squinted one eye after another open, afraid of what I'd see. The sky was clear above.

When I lifted my head, a smooth, scaly face appeared an inch away from mine. It was small and peculiar. Alien, in that I'd never seen any animal like it, and I had immediate doubts as to whether it was even an animal at all.

Its wide golden eyes stared curiously over my figure, and there was an unusual humanness about the way it examined me that made me equally curious in return.

It looked like a mystic creature from ancient mythology that I'd seen sketched in books I read when I was young. If I remembered correctly, they were called dragons, but I was sure they only existed in mythology.

My eyes searched the environment for its family, but the land surrounding us was bare apart from oddly sprouting plant life.

"Do you have a mother somewhere?" I asked, intimidated by the idea of meeting a full-grown dragon.

"Are you alone?"

The baby dragon lent his nose in to sniff me again, nuzzling into my side. It tickled and I couldn't help but laugh. He jumped back, startled, but his wide eyes remained in contact with mine.

"It's ok, you just tickled me." I doubted he'd understand the human language but didn't rule out the possibility.

He lowered his body to the ground and crept forward as if hunting, then sprung at me, only to nuzzle his head into my side again. I laughed, this time more in surprise over his sense of play, and my laughter seemed to encourage him. He hopped buoyantly over to the other side, his nose inadvertently flicking up my shirt.

"Agh!" Something sharp, one of his scales or spikes, sliced my skin.

The dragon froze, and I pulled up my shirt to examine the cut. It wasn't severe, but it was deep, and blood dripped down my waist.

I heard a whimper and looked back down at the dragon. His head tilted down too, as if he were guilty to have hurt me. I touched my hand to his long nose.

"It's ok," I reassured him, touched by his human-like compassion.

"It's not bad, just a small cut. It doesn't hurt," I added, still aware the words meant nothing to him.

He backed away a few steps, head still bowed.

After a few moments, his golden scales started to shimmer, and his body quivered. Violent shivers rippled up and down his spine. Then to my bewilderment, his entire form started to morph into something else entirely.

He slipped in and out of transparency as every part of his body transformed, shapeshifting, until a fluffy bundle of brown fur with four stubby legs stood in his place.

I stared in disbelief, sure I was tripping again. But as the dragon settled into his new embodiment, I was forced to accept that he was no longer a dragon but a brown bear cub.

I tilted my head, wondering whether he was a convenient illusion, a mirage to ease my loneliness. But he was solid as anything else around me. His size was about the only element that remained the same.

Instead of being armed by a skin of shimmering golden scales, he now wore a thick coat of chocolate fur. His ears were small and rounded, less erect, and twitched infrequently, catching sounds outside of my hearing range. But the same wide, curious eyes stared back at me.

He sat back on his fluffy round tail, his stubby hind legs stretched out in both directions, and leaned on his front paws.

He tilted his head, mirroring me, and watched me as inquisitively as I did him. I laughed again, shaking my head. He sprung to his feet and bounded boisterously towards me, leaping into my lap. This time when he rubbed against me, he seemed proud of his new, harmless woolly coat.

My arms relaxed around his warm body. In that moment, the company of another living being felt sweeter than he could have understood. Then again, it appeared that he'd been alone too, so perhaps the appreciation was mutual.

I turned, only then realising the black storm clouds that swallowed the mountains behind me were spreading, following me. They cast a dark shade over the land which motivated me to move.

"I have to keep traveling now." I rubbed the bear's neck. "You must have family around here somewhere," I said responsibly, while secretly wishing I could take the mystical creature with me.

He just stared at me, wide-eyed, not cognizing that this was goodbye.

I sighed and stood, meeting his innocent gaze once more.

"Stay." I held out my hand before turning my back on him.

A river of whimpers followed me, and each step away from him felt heavier.

This doesn't feel right.

What if he doesn't have a family? I can't leave a baby alone.

Just as I was about to turn back to re-evaluate the situation, a panting puff of breaths snuck up behind me and paws hit my ankles.

"You're *sure* you have nowhere else to be?" My eyes scanned the area again for any other signs of animal life.

He didn't answer, simply staring up at me with loyal eyes.

When I turned to walk, he continued to bounce along beside me.

Over the days following, Bear remained by my side like a shadow.

We'd travelled far enough from the storm to be safe. Now, I was lost for direction, but I continued to walk, my feet simply taking the reins. The air was frosty, but clear skies prevailed.

Pink flowers were the first splashes of colour to accompany the small spouts of green. As more days passed, Bear sniffed out odd bushes where berries grew and directed me to a kind of edible nut. They had hard shells around them that Bear cracked between his teeth, then spat out into my hand. His intelligence would have been unbelievably strange if I hadn't seen him transform from a dragon.

The landscape became less barren and more radiant, and I was filled with awe over the flourishing new life. It was unnatural for nature to grow so fast, but it seemed there were numerous mysteries to this new earth that were indescribable.

There was a new stamina within me too, which ran deeper than the relief and excitement of seeing nature's regrowth.

The divinity of Ӡchŏ's spirit had soaked through me, and I felt brighter inside. Brighter than ever before. It was a quiet kind of brightness. From the outside it would have been unrecognisable, but a sense of heightened clarity and simple joy brimmed within.

Magic.

An indefinable peacefulness and that wasn't reliant on external events. The kind that could remain ever-present throughout any amount of external chaos. It felt like the most natural part of my being.

When everything else dropped away, there it was. In the cup of my heart.

So simple, yet often just out of plain sight.

Days and nights bled together. I had no tent, so no option but to endure the elements in all their expressions beneath the full exposure of both the sun and moon.

After a significant amount of time spent walking, we reached a wide, open lake. It disappeared out of sight in both directions, flowing. Bear detected its scent in the air long before I registered where he was leading me.

Behind the lake was a high cliff where a number of overhangs offered shelter, and that combined with the fresh water was enough for me to drop my pack without hesitation.

But that was not all that was promising.

The lake was surrounded by vivid plant life, and already, I could see some that were edible. It was like stepping into an abundant garden of all we could desire after a long journey— well, abundant compared to the rest of the land we'd seen!

I fell to the ground beside Bear, wrapping my arms around his burly body, and showered his fur with kisses. I bowed over the dirt in reverence that such a place already existed. I pressed my chest and face into the holy soil. Then I pressed my palms together and sent a silent prayer to The Mother.

Something strange was occurring in my body. Even with all the walking and food rationing, it seemed to have been growing.

It felt swollen, and an indescribable discomfort made me particularly grateful to have found a place to rest.

Fatigue had begun slowing our journey, and while the strange illness in the cave dissipated, my stomach remained sensitive since with ongoing nausea.

I didn't know what we were travelling towards anymore either. We had no clear destination. The man's voice had disappeared, and I felt void of guidance, only my own intuition and the brilliant nose of a bear cub to follow.

There was no reason for us not to stop and set up camp.

At least for a little while.

The shrubbery was low to the ground, but numerous trees already met my height, and after exploring the area, we discovered that many carried fruit and other edibles.

Bear tore leaves off plants and chewed them with a nodding type action to show me which were safe; he growled when he caught me interested in anything poisonous.

I was still bewildered beyond comprehension over how an animal could be so intelligent, but I didn't over-analyse it. If I were to analyze anything, I would have begun with how it was possible for a dragon to morph into a bear, or for a dragon to exist in this realm in the first place…

Instead, I was simply grateful to be graced by such a caring companion.

When I explored further along the riverside garden, I found the offshoots of root vegetables like carrot and beetroot, and even stumbled across a patch of vines that bore small pumpkins!

The detailed knowledge of plants, herbs, and natural medicines that Ginger and Petāl had shared back in the village was becoming possibly the most valuable survival aid I'd been given. Most of the plants I found sprouting in this realm were the same as those in Santōṣha.

Over our two years in the Village, while waiting for the Noahl's insights into when it was safe to return to Earth, all seven of us humans became students of plants, both edible and medicinal. We were taught to hunt, and how to shape spears, bows, and knives out of nature's bare resources, and how to use the skins and furs of animals to make clothes, blankets, and a number of other necessities.

The Samãdhi were thorough to teach us everything they'd learned over all their time living in harmony with nature, to give us our best chance of survival.

And in that moment, it finally felt like it was all panning out. I finally felt a sense of security and stability, that maybe it truly was possible to survive.

While bathing on a still afternoon, I caught my reflection in the lake's glassy surface. My unevenly hacked hair dangled messily around the sides of my raw face. I hardly recognised myself.

My breasts had grown rounder and fuller than ever before. Apparently, according to my reflection, I was a *woman* now, or so I appeared. My hips were wider, and my stomach was somehow fuller too. I rested my hand gently at the base of my lower belly where a small bump of weight was accumulating.

It took me a moment to realise the cause of such an overgrowth for I hardly considered it possible, but it became undeniably clear that something occupied the space beneath my palm. Something other than my organs.

A being.

A human.

A baby.

I was pregnant.

CHAPTER TEN

A HOT, SHARP SENSATION struck my chest like a knife. My heart thumped and I choked on my own breath.

I tore my gaze from the fluid mirror, and looked down and my own body to check the bump I saw wasn't a mirage.

But the glassy surface of the water didn't lie.

How…

We were never taught much about babies and pregnancy at school. It was a taboo subject in the City. To uphold the single child rule, all women were forced to have monthly injections of a serum that stunted menstruation until they were DNA-matched and married and ready to birth their one perfect, genetically optimal child.

My menstrual cycle had only recently become regular after a painful, erratic period of hormonal rebalancing. Ginger and Petãl —the Samãdhi tribe's medicine women—said that my womb was full of toxins, and they gave me herbs that cleansed my reproductive system and supported hormonal balance, like ground maca root.

But still, I often missed my bleeds for months, then experienced an extended heavy one that would be debilitatingly painful for a few days. It was almost easier to take the serum and not have to deal with all the complications that came with menstruation.

But there was also a sense of a sacredness about the cycle that felt powerful, no matter how inconvenient. It was the sacred power of creation. The power that was the very essence of womanhood. Feminine. Yin.

I also understood the critical importance that rested on my being able to bare children. The children of the New Earth. But I didn't believe my body was ready for pregnancy yet, when it still struggled to simply maintain a regulated cycle.

My mind raced to understand it, but I quickly realised that no matter *how* it occurred, there was a baby growing inside me. And there was nothing I could do to change that fact now it was in motion.

"Bear!" I fell to my knees, nurturing the genesis of my pregnant belly in both hands.

I felt Bear's weight thumping the ground before he appeared beside me. He nuzzled his wet nose into my side to comfort me, but his heavy head almost knocked me over. It'd almost doubled in size since we met. Just like the rest of nature, he grew abnormally fast.

I lifted my head and smiled meekly when I met his concerned eyes.

"Sorry, I didn't mean to startle you." I patted his nose and looked down again.

He followed my gaze with a grunt that made me wonder if he already *knew*.

"You're going to have a brother or sister," I said, still in shock. "Actually, maybe you'd be more like an uncle…"

Then it struck me that the child might grow up without a father.

A tidal wave of emotion washed through me, spilling out in a burst of tears that I cried into Bear's neck. I dug my face into his mane while he sat patiently beside me, occasionally adding a howl of his own.

"I miss Björn."

It was the first time I'd expressed it out loud.

"I miss Björn."

I had acquiesced to my circumstances and found contentment in exploring these new lands, both alone and in the loving company of Bear. I adapted to the lack of human interaction. But a subtle undercurrent was ever-present, no matter how rationally I tried to stitch up the tear in my heart, that something, *someone*, was missing.

His absence followed me.

Inescapable.

An empty void in the centre of my chest.

Haunting.

Because I had travelled so far since losing him, them. And it was likely they travelled in the opposite direction, or *any* other direction. There was even a chance they were no longer alive.

The brutal truth was, considering the vast expanse of land and sea that was planet Earth, that it was highly unlikely our paths would ever cross again.

We were specks of sand at the bottom of an unmeasurable ocean now, dust drifting through the ether. Even Bear, who was double my size was an ant—no, the *antenna* of an ant— when held up against the scope of this planet.

And now I carried Björn's child.

And now I didn't want to. Not alone.

I was afraid.

A sense of bittersweetness washed through me as I realised that through our merging, a part of Björn would always remain with me now, even if we'd lost each other forever. His essence lived inside me and would live on inside our child.

I wiped the tears from my cheeks with tufts of bear fur and drew in a deep, composing breath. Bear wriggled beneath me to stand and nudged me with his nose to make sure I was ok before plodding off, satisfied that his emotional support was accomplished.

The next human I thought of was Adam. His support, in that moment, would have also been valuable beyond compare. He would have been the baby's real uncle. And he would have made the best uncle I could imagine for a child of the New World. But I did not crave his presence like I craved Björn's. Firstly, because it was impossible. And secondly, because the larger part of my heart to the part that wanted him there by my side, was glad he was still in Santōṣha. He was safe there, and I hoped he, Cole and Farrah did not travel back up to earth as he promised he would. He would never find us.

And if he had joined us originally, we would still have been split apart anyway... Or maybe we wouldn't have. Maybe things would have gone differently. He was my protective older brother. *Maybe,* I would have never fallen behind and been separated at all...

I twisted to face the glassy lake again, sliding down the muddy bank to dangle my legs in the crisp and cleansing water. I stared at my naked reflection.

I had thought about the baby's father and uncles.

 Mother. I trialled the label against my face.

I'd only recently embraced womanhood. Was I ready to embrace motherhood so soon?

The mature woman within me become more visible the longer I stared into my reflection. Barely a trace of the fearful girl I was when I first arrived in Santōṣha still existed in my eyes. My womanly physique was only a reflection of the inner transformation that had unfolded over the past few years.

But how can I be responsible for a child when I barely have the resources to care for myself? The voice of fear tempted me.

Without the etheric voice who guided me away from the storm, I'd be a corpse in a cave right now. Even since, Bear has been the reason for my ongoing survival, guiding me to berries, fruits, and edible plants, keeping me warm when the frosts of night set in...

Plus, if it's true that I'll never reunite with the tribe, this would be a terrible life for a child. There is nothing for it here. I can't bring a baby into a world in which it would inevitably end up alone.

A popping pressure throbbed in the front of my forehead as my thoughts continued down a darkening spiral. My head felt heavy and my mind felt cloudy.

That woman in the City I'd heard of a long time ago...She got pregnant after already having birthed a child. I heard she forced the second baby to miscarry before it was born by intentionally damaging her womb...

A roll of images flashed through my mind, possibilities for how I might achieve that same goal.

Then a moment of deeper awareness dropped in.

Or I dropped back into *it*.

I was suddenly horrified by my own thoughts.

Where are these thoughts coming from?

As I stared into the invisible space that drifted between all earthly formations with this curiosity in mind, I began to see a strange phenomenon that I'd sensed, but never seen in physical manifestation before.

Once again, I was drifting between worlds.

Between the physical world and the one of formless phenomena.

From the In-between, I could see a semi-transparent black fog drifting through the otherwise clean air in front of my forehead. A singular stream of dark mist reached outward, wrapping around the back of my head. A tingling sensation tickled the base of my skull where the black mist seeped into my brain. I shivered.

This was how Sky Consciousness entered our minds. They sent thoughts through to a space within the brain we associated with our voice, and from there the thoughts became our own. It was a very mechanical procedure that linked so seamlessly to the mechanics of our natural brain circuit, it was too easy not to catch the point of separation.

I understood quickly that what I was seeing in front of me, by the grace of the L·ight Måttęr that united both the manifest and un-manifest worlds, was an attractor field.

One thought had become a fear, and that fear attracted a field of fear. And that field of fear polluted my mind with a cloud of fearful thoughts that were so convincing; I could hardly discern my voice from the voice of the Shadow.

But it was, indeed, a Shadow.

It was so freakishly clear.

Frightening.

Empowering.

I stared directly at the interconnecting stream of dark mist—Black Magic—and touched my hand to the back of my head, brushing it gently, like a broom sweeping dirt. I closed my eyes and pressed my palm flat over the point on my skin where the channel had been flowing, and visualized replacing it with a bright channel of White Qi that flowed from my heart, down my arm, and out through my palm. I felt it wash through my mind, clearing, cleansing. White Magic.

Just as quickly as it appeared, the black mist dissolved and the Shadow of fear vanished.

I stared into nothingness for some time.

It seemed too simple, too easy to detach from something as sticky as thoughts. But after my usual, recurring scepticism in my own mystic ability to free myself from the hooks of Sky Consciousness, I realised I'd already detached.

The moment that the voice of deeper awareness entered and posed the question, *"Where are these thoughts coming from?"* the Shadow had already been seen.

I *could* have continued down that negative spiral, and the black thought cloud may well have fully enveloped me. But the question alone shone a light of higher consciousness onto the lower-conscious thought forms, and in that moment, the detachment had already begun.

I continued to sit, still, fascinated by the workings of the energy world.

I began to feel a great sense of power, understanding on some level the truth that the only reason the Sky Consciousness chose humans to feed from all those millennia ago, when they were invited to Earth, was because of the unfathomable magnitude of power within us. Power that was monumental enough to cut through the Sky Consciousness' tentacles just as it was to source their formless survival.

Humans had become targets, not because we were weak, but because by nature, we were vessels of immense energy, plugged into a source far vaster than the containers of our own bodies. One source. Infinite and divine.

Ignorance was humanity's weakness. Everyone fell into a state of collective amnesia, drifting through the world, not acknowledging their own innate divinity, and following the prompts of a mind that had been hacked. The operation station split in two. One voice true, one voice foreign, speaking through the same monitor.

I was beginning to understand in a more direct, experiential way what Nala had told me numerous times. With absolute vigilance and awareness of what thoughts filtered through the mind, moment to moment, the Shadows had no power over us.

> *"The formless are the most dangerous kind of Shadow. They can get a grip on you in the subtlest of ways."* Nala's warning returned to my mind.

> *"They can pass by as thoughtforms, feelings, and emotions, and the moment you attach, you're gone and it's running you. One thought can lead you*

*down a dark alley, and before you know it you're
locked in a cage, enveloped by a fog through which
you can't see clearly..."*

The Shadow had caught me for a moment. But the moment I
detached was the moment it fell away again.

My mind quietened as I fell deeper into the power I'd
discovered—or *rediscovered,* for it had been within me all along.
Thoughts thinned, and the tension that built up in my forehead
dissipated.

I closed my eyes.

The muscles of my face softened, shoulders dropping back,
chest stretching open, heart pouring open. I drifted back into
another memory of one of Nala's lessons.

᠁᠁ ᠁᠁

*"Because the time you must wait until re-entering the Earth
realm leaves you at a disadvantage, it's important to understand
all we can about how the Sky People accessed your minds in the
past, so you have the best chance of avoiding it happening
again.*

*"I don't know much about the workings of Sky Consciousness
apart from what I've gathered from studying common threads in
the humans who have travelled here," she said.*

*"When I was healing you, there was a tight knot at base of
your skull that stored dense negative energy. It was black. But it
wasn't unique. I've found it in all humans from the Earth realm.*

*"I realised it's not innately human either. It does not exist, nor
did it ever begin to develop in Bŏdhi, Moānā, Ṭasmai—humans
born here. In some humans, it's been so dense it's almost solid,
and has a metallic essence, like a foreign installation—some
kind of iron substance that links your minds to something else."*

"The Sky Race," I gathered.

"Exactly."

What she said sparked a memory. "In the City, some people's skin had a weird, metallic shimmer to it, like they were morphing into something else. I thought I was delusional, but now, looking back..." I drifted off.

"I don't think you were delusional," Nala confirmed.

"The iron entanglements at the base of your skulls spread through your energy systems like tree roots, with different degrees of severity depending on the human. I can't be sure, but if it leaked into your veins, if your blood turned metallic, I imagine your entire human form would be modified. It seems that was the next phase of their plan. They'd already transformed your natural world into iron. It would make sense for your bodies to be their next target."

I opened my eyes and took my journal from my pouch, recording my experience in writing.

Dear Nala,

I knew there was a thin chance she'd ever read it, but it made me feel closer to her. It made these intangible experiences seem more tangible, for she co-existed entirely within the world of the intangible. I knew if I could talk to her in real time, she'd get it.

You were right about the central entrance of Sky Consciousness. I just experienced, clearer than ever, something foreign accessing my mind through the base of my skull. It manifested as a black fog. The thoughts it sent were destructive. I felt immediately weak and drained.

If I continued to follow them, I might have believed it's a good idea to kill the child growing inside me. It also made me realise that to them, it is. They don't want the human population to grow.

Oh yeah, um.

Surprise?

I'm pregnant.

I shut the journal and peered back down into my reflection in the water.

The eyes staring back were warrior-like, of a woman finally starting to grasp the surreal reality of Earth's multi-dimensional and mystic nature. They were almost intimidating, but I held contact.

The only sound was that of my heart thudding. I could *hear* the blood pumping through my veins, and I *knew* that within my being lay a power beyond my own comprehension, the power that was naturally unveiled when fear was no longer present. Trust swept through my body.

Ok. I nodded silently to the Mother.

Ok.

If I've been blessed in your image to carry a child into the New World, I surrender. I surrender myself to the role of motherhood.

And thank you.

I sat silently for a time that became timeless and allowed my trust in this *slight* change of circumstances to settle in and become permanent.

I drew my attention to my womb, the very centre of where I could now feel the energy of creation dancing within. The previously pervasive cramping felt sweet now I understood its purpose. I released my resistance to the discomfort. My body was growing a human from the tiniest seed; discomfort was non-negotiable.

Love swept through my being. Unconditional.

The more present I felt with each breath, the more I sensed the additional presence that was being nourished by my body, moment to moment. No thought required. Like every other aspect of nature, it was all simply and exquisitely happening, beyond my control.

"Now I know you're in here," I whispered, "I'll take care of everything you need."

As my eyes gently reopened, all the colour and vibrancy of the environment around me poured back in. It took time to find the motivation to move, but my rumbling stomach encouraged me to gather ingredients for a nutritious meal, not just for me, but also a baby.

CHAPTER ELEVEN

N OW I KNEW A baby was due, I couldn't risk leaving the sanctuary. While the temptation to continue exploring was promising, there was no guarantee we wouldn't reach barren land again after leaving the rich and generous riverside soil.

Travelling was harsh on my body too. This baby may have been the only baby I'd ever have the opportunity to birth, so every move I made from the moment I registered its existence was to support its best chance of survival.

As I settled in over the following days, I revisited the moment of clarity I had with the Shadow by the river, and wondered if the tribe had any experiences with the Shadows in which they could *see*.

"You have the capacity to spread your awareness wide enough to protect them also. Spread your attention wider than the lines of your body. Watch everyone closely. Tune into them regularly to make sure they remain clear." Nala's words returned once again.

After receiving confirmation of the presence of Sky Consciousness in the very air we breathed, it was torture knowing the tribe might be in danger and there was nothing I could do.

Was it really possible to feel across incalculable distances just by connecting with someone's heart?

Nala had suggested it was, but doubt still rang in my mind. Still, it was the only possible means I could think of to check if they'd been influenced. Now I had a more direct understanding of the workings of the Shadows, I would be able to detect if they were. I could check the base of their skull for any sense of pressure, and their forehead for fog.

In body, it appeared all beings existed as one singular organism, but in multidimensional reality, we had five bodies stacked on top of each other that together, formed our holistic experience of consciousness. The physical body, energy body, etheric, mental, and light body.

Nala had shown me how to shift my attention into each of the different bodies, and separate my experience to focus on certain aspects of my own consciousness.

To feel another's experience required me to shift solely into my etheric body and travel from my physical body to momentarily reside in theirs. It may have proved impossible from my distance, but I could try.

Inhale. Exhale. Begin.

When my mind quietened, my awareness dropped three layers deep, merging with something vaster than the confines of my skin. The One awareness. And from that space of stillness and silent interconnectedness, I held the tribe dearly in my attention with unbending focus.

It began like a radio signal.

Immense light waves of a frequency that I hoped would pick up their heartbeats extended outwards from where I sat. The centre of the signal was my heart.

When my signal met no match, I tried a more refined approach by focusing on Björn's heart alone, for our hearts were the most intimately intertwined. I felt a heightened sense of love and magnetism as my heart called out in light waves to his, but still, there was no spark of connection.

I returned to my initial approach of calling to the tribe as a whole.

But after some time of sending out energetic detector fields as far a distance as I felt capable, I accepted the fact that my metaphysical radio wasn't working as it had when I trialled it in the Valley with Nala's guidance. That made it all the more disappointing, because I couldn't fully blame its failure on my mere lack of skill. I knew that it *could* work because it *had*, just not at so far a distance.

When I tested my skill in the valley, the tribe were in sight, or at least at a close radius. We had not prepared for a situation in which they might be lost to me all together.

I kept the detector field running lightly, but I let it drop out of focus and expanded my awareness even wider.

The border of the field, where my skin closed around my body, felt like it evaporated as a vast, boundless sense of presence enveloped me. Time stopped. The only sound: a high-pitched, static ringing. I began to lose my sense of grounding and gravity.

No visions accompanied the experience. I was beyond the realm of imagery. But I could feel vast expanses of land sweeping by, as if I were travelling at impossibly high speeds across the earth's surface, even though I knew that my physical body remained still. I could almost hear the wind whooshing by, the planet spinning, spinning.

I felt dizzy, as if my awareness was being sucked down a vortex where time, space, ground, were all irrelevant.

With a gasping breath, I drew myself back into my body entirely.

The dizziness remained. I felt disoriented. My body felt less solid, but an immense sense of power and awareness dwelled inside. I don't know what would have happened if I'd allowed myself to keep falling, but I doubt it would have helped me find the tribe.

My awareness had dropped a layer deeper, into the fifth layer —the light body—where the experience of bliss prevailed and all was both perfectly simple and incomprehensible. Pure consciousness. The foundation upon which all the other bodies were stacked. The realm of nothingness, that simultaneously gave birth to everything.

I'd entered such places before: the realm between life and death, where nothing and everything co-existed at once. But I wouldn't find the tribe there, for they still existed very much in the realm of form on Earth.

Well, I hoped...

A hard kick to my lungs from inside my pregnant belly winded me of breath and I rested my hand over the bump. It made me reconsider whether it was safe to play and extend my energy so far outside the realm of my physical form when a fragile being was trying to use my resources to grow.

I felt torn. I wanted to try again, but I decided to wait until I restabilized.

Dear Nala,

I can't find them.

More failure.

But I'll try again.

Maya.

After considering what a baby might need once it was born, I realised that a safe, stable environment was important. A home.

So, I began nesting.

I built a cooking burrow near the edge of the cave and collected the biggest stones I could find, tessellating them into a wall all the way along its edge to create a wind barrier that sent the fire's warmth inwards rather than out.

I collected and spread the seedlings of germinating edible plants far and wide so there'd be no shortage. After exhausting what was available in the vicinity of our camp, I began exploring the surrounding country for other food sources.

My belly continued to inflate until hobbling and shuffling replaced my usual swift stride. I became unbalanced and clumsier than usual. If I spent too long on my feet, my lower back would ache under the pressure of the extra weight, so I gradually transitioned into gentler activities.

I weaved baskets with flexible twigs to make food gathering more efficient, but I never picked too much at a time. The sun wasn't hot enough in this season for drying and preserving, nor was there presently snow or ice to build a cooling container; everything had to be eaten fresh. I also weaved a long, sturdy oval-shaped basket with a flat base that I lined with furs and soft cushioning for the baby's cot.

Over the heavier months of pregnancy, I started painting again. I collected fallen bark, smooth rocks, and other flat materials and experimented with finger-painting using berries, tree sap, beetroot juice, and pollen from bright flowers.

I also practised cultivating my more masculine side by crafting a few long and sturdy arrows that I used to attempt spear fishing in the river. The longer I spent there, the more fish and water creatures moved through, populating the lake just as other nature did the land.

As a result of both the shimmering surface and the fish's slimy, scaled bodies, fishing was a lot more challenging than Björn and Bðdhi ever made it look. But when I did catch something, it was the kind of victory that left me satisfied until nightfall.

One afternoon when I was especially fatigued, I took out a small leather pouch of wooden beads Björn had carved for me when we were in the Valley. I was glad I hadn't decided on what to do with them before.

I admired the fine detail in each individual bead as I threaded them onto a leather rope. I was making a bracelet or necklace for our baby.

Tears slowly blurred my vision, the floodgates of my hormone-infused emotions bursting open, which I had managed to remain in the eye of the storm of until this reminder of Björn's love, and Björn's absence. They streamed down my face as I thread the last bead onto the rope. I held it to my chest.

"How am I supposed to do this without you?" I whispered, my throat thick. "The baby needs you. *I* need you."

I felt exhausted and defeated for no particular reason. I walked my hands forwards until my forehead touched the ground. Curled over in a child's pose. I became the riverbed through which my emotions poured. The grassy ground was fresh and somehow soothing beneath my squashed face. I didn't mind the smell and taste of dirt as I inhaled it.

I closed my swollen eyes and drifted to sleep, still grasping the painfully dear reminder of Björn.

CHAPTER TWELVE

T HE SUN BURNT DOWN on the bare skin of my back when I deliriously awoke. Time had escaped me.

I sat upright. The intensity of my sadness had alleviated, and I felt a peaceful sense of release. I folded up the blanket and placed it in the baby's cot inside the cool cave, then walked back out into the afternoon.

I began to wonder where Bear had disappeared to. Tracing back the day, I realized I hadn't seen him since sunrise.

I wandered down to the stream and washed my face, then went for a stroll, but there was no sign of Bear.

As daylight dimmed and brilliant streaks of colour began to splash across the sky, anxiety crept over me. He'd never disappeared for this long before.

I hope he's not hurt, was my first concern, but reason counteracted the likelihood of that.

He's big and strong now. No animal I can think of could compete...

As the night progressed, the more likely explanation hit me.

Bear has left.

Pain pressed down on my heart again like a hot iron.

Of course he'd leave. He's a wild animal. He's not made for domestication. He got bored and is out searching for his own kind now. Whatever 'his kind' may be...

Another wave of emotions swept through me as I tried to come to terms with another loss. I could barely breathe as I comprehended the fact that *everyone* I'd ever cared about was now either dead or gone in some way or another. My ultimate aloneness seemed inevitable, and I began to wonder what this might mean for the baby's future...

He's a bear and I'm a human. I returned to the catalyst of the emotion. *We were never going to be lifelong companions. I shouldn't have expected anything more than a fleeting friendship...or become attached to his presence at all.*

But my heart told a different story. It had developed a deep love for him and ached at the idea of never seeing him again. He was more than just a bear.

I didn't make dinner that night, even though hunger was present. I was numbed by grief.

Loneliness.

Loneliness usually rose and fell in waves, and that day, it rose. The swell was turbulent, too rough to control, so I surrendered to its tide.

I held my belly, knowing I wasn't truly alone so long as I carried this baby, but I felt even more so.

I *tried* to believe I was strong enough to give birth alone, that the body's natural instincts would take over. I knew it was possible, but it was intimidating. All I'd known of births were women in a room surrounded by other women, doctors, nurses, healers; people with knowledge and experience in labor.

I felt raw, fragile, and sensitive to *everything*.

In the Old World, in the City where I grew up, women were hard and men even harder. Their hearts were cold, dead. All humans were expected to be robust, hard working, and unemotional. There, I believed I was weak for having and acknowledging feelings.

But that was the Old World. And there was a *reason* that it was us more sensitive humans, and us alone, who survived to create the New World. In this New World, it became more and more apparent that sensitivity was power.

It was a power because it gave me the ability to sense the world beneath form, and gage what was of Earth and what was foreign in terms of energetic phenomena.

But it was also obvious through all I'd learnt and observed in Santōṣha that while the tenacity to comfortably stand alone was an asset in times like the one I found myself in, great strength and power also lay in the tribe—in the union of people coming together, meeting in the heart, and existing in support of the whole, instead of the separate self alone.

Through the experience of being pregnant, and reaching new levels of vulnerability and physical weakness, I saw the value in the support of a tribe more than ever. Until now, I had always felt capable and content with the idea of existing alone.

In the void Bear's disappearance had left, it became obvious that his company had been surrogating the role of the tribe in a strange way. Even just the simple warmth of his big, furry body under my cheek made me feel safe. Curling up against his soft tummy in the dark frosts of night was enough to ease the weight of Björn's absence, who I'd grown used to sleeping beside.

I fell asleep that night curled up on the flat stone of the cave, wrapped in fur, accepting the warmth of my own body as enough. And it was enough.

The waves of emotion drifted back out to sea as my mind calmed. I'd exhausted its capacity for thinking, hoping, considering a different now than the now that was. The emptiness of deep rest became me.

I was ok.

I was healthy.

I was alive.

I was breathing.

I was, simply, ok.

CHAPTER THIRTEEN

I T WAS DARK, THE moon not even a slither in the sky.

My eyes blinked open in alarm at the sound of an unusual shuffling, but I was only met by the same pitch black as behind closed eyes.

More movement.

My heart beat rapidly.

A giant Shadow loomed over me and just before a scream left my throat, a familiar, gentle roar rumbled off the rock walls. The most heavenly sound my ears had heard all day.

"Bear!" My heart still pounded but now in overjoyed relief.

I hopped to my feet, not thinking to care about the freezing night air on my skin, and threw my arms around his neck.

"I thought you left me!" I curled my fingers into his fur and he whined, rubbing his nose against me.

"I'd be ok if you leave me," I reasoned. "I understand if you need to find your own kind. But I'm happy you're back." My nose pressed into his neck, appreciating his Bear scent more than I ever had before.

A shiver rolled up my spine as the cold air caught up to me. Bear responded immediately, gently nudging me back to my sleeping furs where he collapsed.

He's exhausted. He must have travelled a long way.

He lifted his paw, tapping my leg insistently and I curled happily against him, wondering—now that I knew he hadn't left me for good—what it was that he'd been out doing so late.

When the sun rose, I woke to the sound of birds chirping.

The sounds of birds chirping. Numerous.

A dream?

Bear rolled and grumbled beneath me, clearly not ready to rise from his slumber.

After lying there, waiting for the dream of consciousness to take full shape, I realised nothing was happening. Nothing but the sounds of water rushing through the river over small rock falls, and *birds*, still singing somewhere outside the cave.

I sat up and looked out through the large opening, but there was no immediate sign of birdlife.

When I stood and stepped out from the cool shade, the sun was higher than where it usually greeted me from for the first time each day. I hobbled down the rocky track and over the bridge-like plank I'd secured over a slender bend in the river that flowed along the base of the cliff. When I reached the canopy of small trees on the other side, I scanned them closely.

And there they were.

Three small birds took to the sky, soaring in unison from one tree to another. Wings spread wide, they chirped merrily in their motion. I spun, not wanting to lose sight of them, but they were not alone. More birds danced from tree to tree, and in the distance ahead, another bird hopped along the bright moss that was gradually spreading over the rocks and bark and wildlife across the young forest floor.

It wasn't as if an *army* of birds had invaded the area overnight, but there were enough to ponder from where they suddenly appeared. I bent down next to a little wren who glided down to peck for small seeds in the dirt, careful not to startle it.

"You've come to the right place," I said in a hushed voice, glad to finally share the abundant sanctuary with other living beings. I couldn't possibly utilize it all myself.

I continued walking with a particularly light heart, still pondering their sudden arrival, then froze in my tracks.

"Bear...?" I turned back to face the cave.

He's way more exhausted than usual. I'm sure it's because he travelled a long way yesterday.

Was he on a bird hunt? Did he lead them here?

Now I felt selfish for getting upset in his absence.

But how...

I shook my head, unable to truly *know* but mystified by the potential explanation. It was completely unrealistic, but after witnessing all the other enchanting things that Bear was and did, it almost made sense.

He wasn't just a bear.

That was clear from the moment he shapeshifted into one.

I found a flat area of fresh grass as I neared the round, pool-like opening in the lake, and began stretching while appreciating the joyous sounds of birdsong that animated nature's otherwise serene silence.

Yoga had become more challenging with the addition of my balloon belly. Cramps were consistent and I was always hot, no matter how active or still I was. I moved instead through a simpler but more precise sequence of movements taught to me by Qiạỗhui. Tai Chi.

Gaze soft, I lifted one arm, then the other in an orbiting motion, hands gently brushing in the centre. My breath became like medicine, and my body lightened as it washed through every cell.

I moved my arms so meticulously that it hardly felt like movement at all. My chest began to glow. Or at least that's what it felt like. I felt emptier, but at the same time brimming with radiance.

As I completed each movement, flashes of gold L·ight Mȧttẹr started to flicker in luminous sparks before my eyes. A faint mist became visible in the air, which was evidently not just air alone;

it washed over everything. All the colour of my environment began to drop away, drop out of focus. All the shapes and edges that were usually sharp became more indefinite.

The sporadic sparks of L·ight Mȧttęr densified into one sweeping, golden fog, which compressed further into a mass, then an image. I continued the movements, attention single-pointed although the ethereal substance could have been distracting.

I'd been through this process before. I knew to remain still while the world shapeshifted around me.

The movements were transportational tools that Qiạȯhui had taught me when I was a teenager. She visited me in dreams, sharing the wisdom of this ancient set of movements that were purposefully designed to expand the human mind and access higher realms of consciousness.

I didn't know this at the time, but as I practiced and refined each movement, I discovered that the sequence allowed me to access a realm of consciousness through which interdimensional travel was possible. It allowed me to travel through the In-Between and meet her in her dimension: the realm of the Aẋscendants.

The vibrant land around me continued to blur into a wash of colourless mist, and the gold L·ight Mȧttęr continued to solidify until I stood in the centre of three royal walls crafted from the solid gold.

I recognised quickly that I was inside the Pyramid that I first entered in Santōṣha. There was nowhere else quite like it in any world. Grand. Magnificient. Light enough in substance to sustain the image of the Aẋscendants, who used this as an interdimensional meeting place.

I did not know that it was possible to enter it from the Earth realm, but here I was, bare feet on the pristinely polished lapis lazuli stone. Above me was the perfect intersection where the walls met and a thread of gold L·ight Mȧttęr seeped through.

The walls glowed brighter, brighter, becoming more and more real as the movements continued to flow through me, and my body through them. Soon, the river of gold mist that fell through the tip of the triangle compressed beside me into the form of Qiaǒhui herself.

She performed the same movements in perfect unison, and we both continued. As always, the grace of her presence was so divine it was hard to remain focused, the vibration of her being higher than anything else to hold form. Perhaps that's why she didn't.

I still didn't understand the nature of her dimension, of how she drifted in and out of form at will—nor did I ever expect to. But I was sure the frequency of light inside the Pyramid, and carried by each Axscendant, was about the brightest that the constitution of my being could cope with. Any lighter and I might explode into light itself.

Her porcelain beauty was breathtaking, skin so white and unblemished it was like whipped cream. Her movements were smooth and sweeping beneath her golden silk robes.

More bodies started to manifest around me.

No, not manifest: *appear*. They'd been there the whole time, waiting.

Waiting for me.

My hands rose above my head and in one sweeping spin the movements were complete. I stood still in the centre of a circle of beings. The three Nŏahls. Their guiding Axscendants, and—

"Nala!"

Tears filled my eyes and just as the emotion of seeing her struck my heart, the vision vanished in a blink and my legs buckled under me.

My body fell heavily onto the grassy ground. I was back in the realm of solidity, of earth.

And it was *solid*.

"Agh!" I gasped. A sharp pain shot through my pregnant belly, leaving me breathless.

I pressed my hand to my womb and closed my eyes, feeling movement almost immediately, and assumed that meant the baby was ok. I rolled onto my back and tried to calm my mind enough to return to the Pyramid.

But a blue sky replaced the gold walls that had dazzled my eyes, and there was no trace to which I might return.

I had not *intended* to travel there to begin with. I was performing the movements as a meditation as I often did. So why was it that, this time, I'd travelled through time and space?

All interdimensional travel required a balanced collision of metaphysical practices with clear intent, and at the same time, surrender of mind. If it wasn't my intent that drew me there, it must have been theirs.

But if that were the case, shouldn't it enable me to return?

Opening a channel demanded immense clarity, openness, and White Magic. To have arrived there only minutes ago was one miracle; to return so promptly was probably impossible...

I performed the movements again on repeat until my body weakened, and I was forced to let it go and accept the fleeting experience for what it was. But the nagging curiosity of what they drew me there to communicate pressed on.

A message. I knew they had a message.

I crawled to the water's edge to wash off my regret for my inability to stay internally still in a critical moment. I stripped off my wrap and dipped beneath the frosted surface without another thought.

My entire body was shocked to life the instant it made contact —every cell, every vessel awakened.

Clarity returned to my mind and I lay back, taking deeper, more concentrated breaths that expanded my capacity to stay in the icy water for longer than my body may have wanted.

My gaze softened as I watched light clouds drift calmly across the endless blue sky. Then, as if the clouds were a canvas, an image started painting itself upon the sky. A Symbol.

This time, I remained still, simply watching, absorbing, as the sky dissolved back into nothing, and in its place another celestial Symbol was drawn by some invisible hand, and then another. A whole series of Symbols began flickering past at rapid speeds. One sequence on repeat, too rapid to fully comprehend immediately.

It seemed that the moment my receptive channels cleared and opened, I was able to witness the message, which was transferred to my consciousness from that of the Axscendants. Or at least part of it.

I knew immediately that my moments in the Pyramid had not been wasted, nor completely ruined by my premature exit. Whatever their message was had been implanted in my mind. I just had to decipher it.

My head shot up with a gasp and I rushed to the cave.

I took out my basket of charcoal and began fiercely sketching the symbols that continued flashing over my mind's eψe on repeat, transferring them onto the rocky walls surrounding me.

A perfect circle. A six-pointed star. A flipped triangle inside a ring. A sun. A crescent. A maze. A bird. A spiral. A wave. A flame. A tree. Two trees.

They were all simple pictures, but interpreting their combined significance hurt my brain.

I immediately read the last four as representations of the earth elements.

A bird, a wave, a flame, a tree—two trees.

Air, water, fire, earth—two earth symbols.

Spirit—the spiral?

The elements were the foundation of all shamanism and white magic. Did all the symbols combine somehow into a spell of white magic? I didn't know what one might look like, or how I might use it. Nala never discussed the art of spellcasting.

Maybe whatever it was would lead me back to the others?

I hoped that was its purpose. If I had the ability to use White Magic, Nothing else seemed more important than first using it to reuniting with the tribe.

I sat back, legs crossed, and stared at the wall.

The symbols were familiar. Basic, primitive, obvious—so obvious that their meaning was lost. Their style was the same as the pictures engraved into the walls all around the Pyramid in Santōṣha. Although I had tried, I could never fully grasp the Axscendants written language that was primarily symbolic.

Lengths of time passed as I stared, hoping for the language to miraculously make sense just as it had miraculously appeared when painting itself upon the sky.

But no amount of waiting exposed any amount of sense.

I analyzed each picture, considering what they might represent independently of one another, but I didn't want to impose pontificated meanings that might have led me astray from their true symbology either. The sun and crescent moon were as obvious as the elements, but again posed the question of *for what purpose*?

I took an outbreath, stood, and shook my body to loosen up, then sat again. So much surrender and patience were required in this game of mysticism, and sometimes, I desperately wanted to *make* things happen or *make* things make sense.

I waited, this time more patiently, for the drawings to click together like a code.

My mind was now blank. Still, no amount of information entered, nor did Nirmala or Qiǎ̊hui's presence return to explain.

Morning became midday and nothing happened.

I finally let go of the need to know and decided that at least I had the symbols recorded. Perhaps just having them in my living space, day and night, would spark an understanding.

Patience and surrender.

I left the cave to clear my mind again in the icy lake.

Bear finally emerged from his slumber with a spring in his step, bouncing around with the birds as if they were old playmates. Watching their interplay made me almost *certain* he'd led them there, even if the question of 'how' remained a mystery.

After the bird incident, he spent more days exploring further than my eye could see, but my heart was able to rest for when the sun hit the horizon, he'd always return home.

I often wondered what he did out there—and more so, what was actually out there.

My adventurous spirit yearned to join his expeditions, to behold what was beyond the border of the little sanctuary we'd settled in. But my body yearned for other things, like simplicity and rest.

I spent time rearranging the sequence of symbols on different sections of the stone wall, experimenting with different patterns and combinations that may inspire it to click into sense. Soon the cave interior was covered in an array of possibilities, yet still not one *clicked*.

Cravings for certain foods became intense. The craving for broccoli became so loud I couldn't ignore it any longer, but the seeds I'd planted had only sprouted, so late one morning I took a walk with my harvesting basket in the direction I found the original plant.

From memory, it was a fair distance away, and the pace of my walk had significantly decreased, but the day was clear and bright. A stroll seemed like a nice way to spend it.

I also interpreted the cravings as my body calling for certain nutrients it needed for the baby's development. I had become very attuned to what foods were most attractive each time hunger struck, to ensure the baby was nourished enough with the limited variety of foods we had access to.

Broccoli felt rich in iron and protein, and I assumed that must've been what both our bodies needed at that stage of the process.

The more time I spent alone and the clearer my mind became, influxes of wisdom and knowledge of the land became accessible without the aid of books, or even thoughts. It was a deeper understanding that arose from a space *behind* the thoughts, the space of silence. Without the input or influence of others, an exceeding trust grew in my own intuition.

The walk was long but pleasant. But after collecting a few heads of bright green broccoli, I was squatting down to pick up my basket when a sharp cramp pierced my lower belly.

I'd been experiencing more cramps over the last few days, so I initially didn't think much of it, but this one didn't pass like the others. My womb tensed, and the wall of my cervix started thudding, compressing.

I gasped, suddenly breathless, and dropped the basket, pressing my hands into both knees and bending my torso over my legs.

"Uh!" Another kick.

The simple act of drawing air through my lungs required concentrated effort.

"Baby, are you ok?" I asked between breaths.

I held my belly, overwhelmed by another round of cramps, and lowered myself to sit with the soles of my feet together, knees falling out wide, which helped to open my hips.

I drew my focus inwards, following the steady rhythm of each inhale and exhale. The contractions intensified and then softened, intensified and then softened, until eventually fading completely.

I rolled to lay on my back, suddenly exhausted. I hardly felt the strength or stamina to walk back home, especially with the addition of a loaded basket to carry.

I closed my eyes. Eventually, the throbbing spasms alleviated, and I was able to appreciate the calm that fell over my body. After drifting in and out of sleep a few times, I felt a cold, wet cold nose on my cheek, startling my eyes open.

I was greeted by Bear's round face leaning over me.

"How did you find me?"

He just nodded his head, nudging me to get up off the ground.

"Ok, ok, I was just resting," I laughed, moving onto my knees and then my feet. I felt momentarily dizzy, ears ringing, before I adjusted to being upright again.

Another sharp shard of pain stung my lower abdominals in response to the movement. I leant my hand on Bear's shoulder, sucking in a loud breath of air. No matter how deep my breath, my lungs were never quite full.

Even when standing still, I could feel a permanent pressure pressing down. My back ached before I even started walking.

Bear flicked his head around, nudging me again.

"Sorry, Bear. I don't know if I can move too far right now." I stroked his shoulder, but he nudged me again with a persistent groan.

"Bear, please." I was feeling too sensitive to be nagged.

But Bear wasn't one to nag.

When I studied him more closely, I realised he was trying to communicate something. His chin was pointing upwards. I looked in the direction he was nodding, to his back.

"What is it?" I reached my hand up to feel through his fur, thinking he was hurt, and as I did, he nudged my backside forcefully.

"Bear! What do you want from me?!"

Again, hormones...

But he simply and plainly looked at me, then at his back, then to me, then his back, until finally, I caught on.

"Ohhhh...." He was offering to carry me.

"Really?" I tilted my head, doubtful. It wouldn't just be me he'd be carrying. It would be me, a baby, and a big balloon of water weight. And the basket.

He made another insistent whining noise, so I let out a breath and accepted; we could at least try it. I studied his back, considering the easiest way to climb up, but he leant his chest to the ground, making it easy.

I awkwardly positioned my legs to hang on either side of his back, and my fingers gripped the fur of his neck tightly as he slowly raised his chest back upright. His wool was thick and soft, making for a comfortable but unstable seat. I squeezed my knees into his sides and hung the basket over my arm.

"Woah." Each step forward interrupted my sense of balance, and riding became an exercise of engaging the muscles of my core and thighs to remain steady.

He walked slower than usual, only increasing his pace to a normal step once I was stable. The fresh breeze that brushed gently against my face and hair was invigorating, and I started to relax, grateful for the ride. I bent my chest lower to Bear's fur, my belly resting on his back, and patted his neck.

"Thank you," I whispered against the wind.

But after a while of walking, I realised we were not heading in the direction of home.

"Where are we...?" No landmark was familiar.

In the distance, movement caught my attention. A silhouette, a body. As we got closer, I saw it was a deer!

Bear slowed, stepping more carefully now, treading lightly under the shade of leafy treetops. The deer was grazing calmly, head to the ground, unaware of our presence.

We reached a cluster of shrubs and Bear lowered to his knees for me to slip off his back. He nudged me, cautioning me to stay hidden, then stepped away.

His whole body started to tremor. Shivers ran through him from tail to crown. His head dropped to the ground as he quivered, shoulders rolling back, then a shudder lifted his fur in shackles as his whole body began to transform, for the second time, before my eyes.

Standing before me was now a proud and mighty stag, the male equivalent of the deer that grazed a yard away. He stood tall, head high, giant antlers pointed to the sky, and round chest puffed.

He stared back at me with the same trusting eyes I knew, then blew air through his lips and rubbed his front hoof in the dirt as he looked back at the deer with longing.

When Bear galloped into the paddock to meet her, I watched her ears twitch as she sensed his approach, before she cautiously lifted her petite head.

Bear strolled across the paddock with an almost arrogant sense of pride, only meeting her watchful eye enough to encourage a developing interest.

As the space between them closed he stood still, and she moved closer to sniff him. They walked a few rounds of each other, just sniffing and watching, then as if a spark ignited, she lowered her front legs for him to mantle from behind, and they began mating.

I was shocked and accidentally let out a laugh, then quickly pressed my hand over my mouth, remembering Bear was serious about me staying hidden.

This is what you've been doing! I was bewildered once again by the mystery that was Bear. *Mating with any female you can hunt down to reproduce the species!*

After their time together was finished, he nudged her neck affectionately, planting a kind of kiss, then strolled back in my direction.

"What *are* you?" I was curious whether he was of a whole new species, or an anomaly of the Mother, created to assist with procreation.

He approached and nodded for me to mount his back again. I eyed him again, considering whether he could still carry my weight in his stag form.

He crouched his hind legs this time and I carefully climbed aboard. His muscular back felt steadier, and the ride was more graceful.

We arrived back home when the sun was beginning to set, and I steamed the broccoli with wild leek and dandelion flowers to finally satisfy my craving and enormous hunger.

The stag that kindly carried me home disappeared, then reappeared in his big, friendly bear form. He curled up next to me by the fire. He leant his chin on the ground, and I rested my arm over his shoulder, rubbing his fur.

"You're a wonder, Bear."

I pondered over how many animals he may have already mated with and felt a rush of excitement for all the babies that would be born soon if it was, as it appeared, a daily practice! I held my tummy, thinking of all the playmates this baby might have.

As dusk settled, I caught sight of a rabbit hopping from one bush to another, its cotton-bud tail and long ears flopping as it did.

I smiled warmly. The Earth really was blooming back to life.

CHAPTER FOURTEEN

I WOKE TO THE same sharp pains I'd felt during the day and cried out loud, for the intensity had vastly increased.

Acute contractions twisted through my womb. The little being that had been quite calmly living there for the past nine months had decided it might be a fun time to start kicking at the upper left side of my stomach.

Its head was turned down now, sitting against my cervix with such pressure it was hard to breathe.

Sweat dripped down my forehead and chest, and my skin was sticky. I couldn't tell whether it was an unusually muggy night or if I was burning up inside, but it was irritating.

All I could think of that would feel nice in that moment was to be submerged beneath the ice-cold water of the lake. But with my body in the state that it was, the idea of walking down to it seemed a lot less nice. So, I just imagined myself there.

There was a wet patch between my legs, but it wasn't sticky like blood, nor did it smell like urine. It was just spilled water...

I rolled around over the furs, wringing, curling, but nothing could soothe the severe discomfort, cramping, and pressure between my hips. The furs suddenly felt a lot less soft and snuggly, and they became plain itchy against my sensitive skin.

Finally, I gave up and stood, hobbling towards the cave opening with both hands supporting my lower back. The night air was refreshing and the sweeping purple green light of the

Aurora was painted across the sky. The land looked more majestic under its luminous, otherworldly glow.

Being out in the open helped me regulate my breathing, and somehow standing upright felt less tormenting. I paced like an ogre with bent knees and legs spread wide, no direction, just breathing heavily as I rode the waves of sensation.

Whenever the Aurora lit the sky, it carried an exquisite presence, an air of divinity that made me feel less alone. The entire sky emanated with the sense that an intelligence was watching over the land, protecting and guiding.

If the Earth was in essence like a mother, the sky was like a father. And in that moment, I couldn't have been more grateful for even just the illusion of fatherly guidance.

Deep, chesty moans escaped my lips and the expression relieved some of the discomfort. I found myself chanting, mostly impulsive, spontaneous sounds. The word "Ouuummmmm" repeatedly vibrated through my lips, the sound soothing, opening up a space within that dissolved my angst.

There was no time for angst. It was happening.

I wandered down to the riverside and dropped onto my hands and knees at the water's edge, rolling my hips gently to the rhythm of my breath. A huge amount of the pressure in my aching spine was relieved as the movement opened up my vertebrates, allowing my back to untie itself of tension.

The water's glassy surface glimmered and shimmered under starlight, reflecting the fluorescent purple and green light of the Aurora. But beneath, it was dark and enigmatic. Its mystery drew me in.

I cut my hands through the mystical reflection and splashed cups of water over my sweaty face. The contrasting temperature was thrilling, and I closed my eyes, massaging the icy water into my face, neck, and shoulders. I crawled forward, through the muddy bank, gradually immersing my naked body in the water.

It was perfectly shocking.

For some moments, all was still. I was simply floating. Frozen.

But I didn't want to freeze the fragile baby.

As I crawled back out, knees spread, I could feel a wide passageway opening between my hips. The pressure of the baby's head dropped lower.

This is it, I thought. *The baby wants to be born now.*

Fear struck. I felt sick, and wrapped my fur tightly around my body.

How am I supposed to do this alone? What am I even supposed to do?!

In the city, all I really knew of the childbirth process was that once the time between contractions got shorter, women were rushed to hospital, and nurses took care of the rest.

Even in the valley, when a woman went into labour she was always taken to the Shaman's hut. I'd never heard of a woman going through these final hours alone, nor had I ever been exposed to what happened behind closed doors.

Panicky and overwhelmed with emotion, I began to weep in fear it wasn't possible to birth a child naturally without help.

I moved to a squat, bouncing my knees slightly up and down as tears leaked from my eyes. Every movement now was intuitive, mindless. I could feel the penetrating weight of the baby's head pressing on my uterus and cried more in the worry that it could be stuck there forever.

Dwelling in the frequency of fear became too exhausting to sustain on top of the amount of strenuous activity that was occurring inside my body. At some point, I felt too drained to feed any more thoughts.

Tiredness drove me back to the cave where I lay, curving my back over Bear who still slept soundly. The vivid Northern Lights were fading in the sky.

The contractions were lasting longer now, sharper, and the sweet gaps between them were closing. Consistent pain throbbed both through my front body and back, demanding all my attention.

I closed my eyes, building a relationship with the contractions through which I could simply be with the waves of sensations moving through me, *feeling* but not *suffering*. Semi-detached.

It became a state of meditation, where I was so present in my body that nothing else existed, and the cramps didn't feel so painful. Beneath the dark Shadow of the cliff, it was just my body, and the baby gradually transitioning out of it.

Time passed and I remained lying over Bear, a slight arch in my back, breathing and groaning, bending my knees and pressing my feet into the ground, bouncing my hips gently up and down, then submitting all my weight back down onto the earth.

Humming and singing. Gritting my teeth, then surrendering all tension. Shedding tears of overwhelm, then of joy in the knowing that soon, this precious little human would be on my belly instead of in it.

Then, in the early hours of the morning, just after the sun began to rise and saintly golden rays of light began to shine gently through the cave opening, I felt the head so close to my outer opening that I began to push. I shrieked and moaned as the skin of my opening tore, pain ripping through my body.

Bear was awake now but didn't rise to move; he just lay there, eyes peeled open, holding my weight.

My knees fell out wide and my feet spread apart, and I felt the top of a head as it began to pop through the whole.

I moved to a squatting position, leaning my hands on Bear.

"Agh!" The pain was too much. I was too exhausted. Too weak to push.

I was sure I was going to die.

Blood was pouring out.

I was going to die.

And without a mother, so would the baby.

A moment of hopelessness. I wasn't strong enough.

I could just let go. Give up. Forever.

But instead, something inside me encouraged me to push. A quiet, loving whisper. Somehow, at the centre of all this pain was the subtlest warmth of something loving. And in it I felt held.

I found that I was, in fact, strong enough to push again. And while I knew there was a chance I might not survive, I had a slither of hope that the baby still could, even if I didn't. And I had to give it that chance.

It was the only thought that made the process of dying sweeter.

"You have to take care of it, Bear." My voice was haggard and raw. "When it's out, promise me you'll do your best to help it survive."

Bear moaned loudly, meeting the rawness of my ruined voice.

"Thank you—" I whispered.

I pushed with another breath.

Another shriek escaped my throat, this one deafening as the rest of the head slipped through. Then another as the shoulders followed.

I was still squatting, feet balanced firmly on the earth, as both hands cradled a very delicate, sticky head.

Finally, I felt the pressure release inside my outer tract when the rest of the body fell through. Everything was blurred behind my tears; this was the most precious thing I'd ever held, even through all the pain of getting it here.

I leant my weight back on Bear as I pulled the tiny body up to rest on my chest. It was wet and so delicate I had to be careful not to crush it with a simple squeeze.

The moment it was safe on the warmth of my chest, I passed out, falling, dropping back, back into a realm of dreamless nothing. Black.

The In-between.

I had been there before, as the channel between life and death that each human spirit passed through on their way back to nothingness.

This time it felt different.

And I was sure it was because I was the one who was dead.

Within the all-encompassing blackness, an exquisite spark of gold appeared.

A star.

It shone brighter, brighter, until all the black in the atmosphere was replaced by pure, luminous gold.

CHAPTER FIFTEEN

W HEN MY EYES OPENED, I lay in the same position over the cold stone. But this wasn't the rough stone of the cave floor. I was inside the Pyramid. The three pristine golden walls that met to form a central tip were not easily mistaken.

My body was heavy. Drained. I had no energy to lift my head, so I simply stared at the majestic ceiling. I was still hot, sticky with both sweat and blood. I was sure I would leave a puddle of crimson stains on the immaculately polished floor.

"Sorry," I mumbled to no one in particular, barely even moving my lips. This was a holy place. Sacred and divine. And I was a mess.

But still, I couldn't lift an inch of my body, which was curled up on the ground. The ground was blue, electric blue with threads of gold. My body hardly even felt like it was mine anymore. I felt disconnected.

A Shadow brushed past the gold wall somewhere in my periphery, then a figure. As I tried to sharpen my gaze, I realised tears still blurred my bloodshot vision.

The figure standing above me gradually became clearer. The beautiful soaring birds on her gold robes, her porcelain skin and sculpted features. An air of wisdom and love swept from her heart to mine.

Qia̯ǒhui.

"Have you—" I could hardly speak. "Come to take me to—" But I couldn't finish the question.

"This is not your time to die." Her voice was kind, always kind, but resonant.

I was surprised by her words.

"It's ok. I'm already dead." I thought she was trying to comfort me in what she assumed were my final hours.

I had read once that after the body had spent its last breath, our consciousness could live on for as long as ten minutes. That's all I was now, pure consciousness alone, detached from my body, ready to merge back into the one.

"This is not your time to die," she repeated firmly, towering above me, although in true relativity she was smaller than me. *Older*, but smaller, her frame delicate and petite.

"He needs you. You need to return. He needs to survive. The future of your kind depends on it." Her tone was serious, not to be ignored.

"We're alone. I lost them," I told her, regaining energy just from being in her loving presence.

Light of the purest kind radiated from her being, soaking into my skin, filling me with life. She crouched down and placed her warm hand on my crusty cheek, unbothered by the mess.

Her touch was electric, jolting my system back into full circulation. My heart felt as golden as she was. As bright as the sun and as luminous as the moon. The immense frequency of love that was stored there came pouring out, washing through my body, clearing, cleansing, purifying.

"They are not lost," she said. She didn't know what happened.

"It's been a long time. It's just us. I'll die one day. He's destined to die alone, whether it's now or in a hundred lonely years."

"You do not make that decision. Death is the decider. And right now, death does not choose you. It will not take you. And I will not take you to him." She spoke of death as if it were a being, as if they were comrades.

"But look at me," I whispered, still corpse-like on the floor. Even with this degree of separation, I knew my physical body was still too broken to comprehend returning to it.

"You are a warrior. Stronger than you may ever know. And you will survive this."

I finally stopped to allow the possibility of her words to penetrate me. Breath continued to revitalise my body on every inhale. The aliveness of my heart continued to expand and ripple through my being. My sense of eternal internal power was returning.

It seemed that what she said was true. I was not dying.

I began to process what she might have meant by her earlier words.

"You said the others aren't lost. So, they're alive?" I lifted my head. The sharp spasm of pain in my stomach wasn't too unbearable to prop myself up onto my elbows.

Her glimmering eyes were like golden diamonds staring down at me.

"They are not lost," she said.

"Why can't you just say things clearly? Can't you just tell me if they are alive, where they are, how I can find them?" I was irritated by the way she spoke in riddles. "Don't you think that would be helpful?"

The corners of her eyes wrinkled in amusement. I was too raw to be polite.

"No, I don't think it would be helpful," she said simply.

"Life moves as it does. It is not my role here to tell you what may come to be, for anything that you discover in advance could influence you to do something that may change the course of the future that has been perfectly set.

"I only encouraged you to stay on course. And right now, your course is to return to your body and your newborn baby. Your course is to survive. Just as it was that day in the cave when you could have chosen to let the weather take you, and fallen willingly into the arms of death, who still does not want you."

"That was you in the cave? It didn't sound like you…" I was confused, trying hard to remember again the tone of the voice.

"It wasn't me. Aáric is an Axscendant I have been closely intertwined with for a long time, but not one who is linked to Santōṣha. He has chosen Earth."

"But the voice disappeared."

"And it will not return in the way you expect, nor will he return as the man he was when he Ascended. But he is one of the reasons you must return."

Aáric…

I opened my mouth, but she interrupted before I could speak.

"Do not ask me questions I cannot answer," she said knowingly.

"Now go. Your baby is crying."

In a flash, the floor fell out from underneath me and my consciousness dropped at the speed of light back into my body.

The moment I fully embodied the experience of being back on Earth, I was overwhelmed by pain.

And I cried. I didn't mean to. I guess it was my body's only logical response to my harsh return to reality. But it wasn't the only cry that echoed through the cave.

The baby on my chest was shrieking loudly, shivering. I quickly put my own pain aside and rolled over to wrap the tiny body in a fur.

The tiny boy.

I wrapped us both in another larger fur and as I held the sweet light of his being to my chest, tears continued to flow down my cheeks.

This time, they weren't so much tears of pain, although the pain was still present in the background; they were tears of joy. Relief. Emotion. Release.

I was alive.

I survived.

He survived.

An outpour of love enveloped the fragile body I held in my arms. I could feel his tiny heaves of breath on my chest.

We survived.

It was a true miracle.

"Baby, baby, baby." I rocked gently, holding him closer until both our tears faded, and my eyes cleared enough to see for the first time his squashed face that was sculpted against my bare chest beneath the fur.

He was so small and barely looked human. Thin rolls wrinkled his fair, blotchy skin, and his limbs curled inwards like he hadn't quite comprehended that he was no longer confined to the tight space of my womb.

As I gazed over his pinkish face, his puffy eyes still sealed shut, I felt the first sense of his essence. It was familiar—maybe because he'd been growing inside me, so of course he felt tremendously close…but there was also something else about it that made me feel like I knew him in another way too.

He squirmed in my hands, so I lay him on my chest again, holding his delicate body against me, careful to be gentler than I'd ever been with anything. My heart was swelling with immeasurable love I barely knew how to contain. It beat so potently it was all I could hear.

It almost felt surreal to be holding this baby in my hands, that was, only hours ago still safe inside my stomach. I was silenced by the miracle of childbirth.

"We did it," I whispered, my voice so rough I didn't recognise it as my own. "You're here. I'm alive. How am I alive?"

My laugh was rough too, and my head fell back, looking skywards.

I felt a fountain of gratitude for my interaction with Qiaŏhui, who instead of guiding me to death sent me back to life.

"Thank you," I whispered up at the sky, my throat dry and scratched, but that didn't stop me from whispering again. "Thank you."

I'd barely acknowledged Bear's quiet presence still curled up behind us. His chin rested on the ground as if he was sleeping, but his eyes were wide open, watching us inquisitively.

I transferred the baby's weight into one arm and reached behind me to rub Bear behind his ears. He whined then laid his chin back down. He knew my appreciation for his support without words. A primarily sensory being, he felt it, flowing from my heart to his.

I felt elated, although I'd barely slept. The intense agony and physical demand of childbirth should have left me exhausted—which it did, in body. But internally, I was wide awake. A deeper, more eternal awakeness that didn't rely on physical energy.

While my body was heavy, an exuberant lightness radiated through my cells, as if an eternal sun was lit inside my chest. I couldn't fathom the thought of moving again. But I didn't need to.

All my attention fell on the precious human within my arms.

His tiny hands and fingers began to curl and grasp onto my skin as he discovered their mechanics for the very first time. His plump feet were like silk, rubbing against my skin as he adapted to the new amount of space and textures around him.

I pat my hand lightly over his velvet head, taking note of how fragile it was. His breath was uneven but gradually regulated as he adjusted to this new requirement of being alive. I paced my own breath to match his, chests rising and falling in rhythm.

His skin was sticky and blotchy but warm, and I held him close, ensuring he remained snug beneath the furs. In those first hours of his life, I simply lay there, watching him, and all was perfect. All the pain was forgotten, swept like dust beneath a blanket of all-encompassing love.

CHAPTER SIXTEEN

W HILE THE SUN WAS still soft but warm in the mid hours of the morning, I decided it was time to wash.

I sat in slow motion, keeping my baby pressed against my chest as I lifted myself up to stand. The feeling of being inside my own body was odd, uncomfortable. I felt off-balance, and the skin that had stretched tightly around my balloon belly was now wobbly and awkward to carry around.

Cramps twisted through my abdominals as I walked with my legs wide, careful not to agitate the torn skin that stung between my legs. But I was so mesmerised by the baby that I didn't care. It was a worthy sacrifice.

I carried him unhurriedly into the day, gradually introducing him to the outside world. He wriggled, unsettled by the crisp outside air.

"It's ok." I wrapped him tighter in the fur. "This is what fresh air feels like."

My gaze moved between the baby in my arms and the serene environment we walked through. The morning sun shot down in rays through branches, bouncing off leaves and leaving a luminous yellow glimmer over all they touched.

When we reached the water's edge, its still surface twinkled and glistened. My baby's eyes were still shut, but I knew he could sense the shift in atmosphere, the freshness and moisture in the air.

I sat on a flat stone, dipping my feet in the cooling water, and rocked him gently. My eyes shut as I inhaled his powdery scent.

"Do you want a name?" I asked, not expecting an answer. I hadn't really thought about names.

"I could call you Björn, in honour of your father," I suggested, feeling suddenly emotional over his memory.

"But you're not Björn." Even though he already somehow looked like him.

I couldn't help but drift there for a moment. His face was clear in my mind's eye, ocean eyes piercing into mine like they had that very first time I saw him across the street in his officer uniform. His smooth skin, square jawline, and chiselled cheekbones, cropped blonde hair that was lighter than the ray of sun that I imagined shining down on it.

But my baby's essence was fresh and new, light and pure and clean. There was barely any quality to grasp onto that might inspire a name. Like the bare expanse of sleek, endless snow that coated the land in all directions when we arrived back on Earth, awaiting the first footprints. Clean and crisp. His spirit was too, like a canvas.

"Snow," I said out loud, considering.

In essence, and the pale white complexion of his skin, it felt fitting. Even the premature wisps of hair on his head were so blonde they were white.

"Let's try that. For now."

I held him out in front of me and carefully unwrapped his furs. The muck on his skin from childbirth was dry and cracked. He whimpered as the crisp air struck his bare skin for the first time, but he needed a wash.

"Shhhhh," I cooed. "It's going to be cold, but I promise you'll feel even *more* alive afterwards."

I slid down the riverbank to sit in the muddy shallows, immersing my own body into the water before introducing his. I held him high on my shoulder as I rubbed myself clean, then began gently wiping my wet hand over his delicate skin.

I was so careful with Snow over the first few days, but I was surprised by how quickly he adapted to all of nature's elements.

We spent most of the first weeks just cuddling and feeding, and I was grateful I'd spent the time during pregnancy preparing a comfortable nest. Every few hours he'd show signs of hunger both day and night, so although I wasn't very physically active, breastfeeding was draining, and I woke frequently during the night to feed, which left me in a mildly delirious state of ongoing exhaustion.

All my attention was on caring for him. My body called for deep rest and healing too, and it felt special and sacred to spend the time simply being with Snow and getting to know him.

He was very quiet and still.

His eyes began to squint open after a day of being in the world. They were a strikingly pale but clear and vibrant shade of blue. Ice-like.

But after entering deep sleep, Snow often woke up crying severely, urgently, shrieking, as if traumatised. I wondered whether he was being haunted in his dreams.

I did everything I could to calm him and create an environment in which he could sleep peacefully. But I couldn't control what he saw in dreams.

It was my first experience of a mother's pain, when every cell in her body yearns for her child to be ok, and well and content. A fierce sense of protection that demanded from me an equally fierce amount of surrender when dealing with things that were outside of my control.

When he wasn't crying, he was very placid, simply watching everything with wide-eyed curiosity. Calm. Serene. I watched him as he watched the world, equally curious of who this silent being here with me really *was*.

Already, there was wisdom within his eyes and unfiltered expressions, and at the same time, more innocence than anything I'd ever seen. He had no knowledge of the world, yet perhaps in his purity *understood* more than anything knowledge could teach.

I felt full now he was here, my heart an uninterrupted outpour of love. The elated feeling carried with me over the days following his birth, and then weeks.

Every new day became more exciting than ever because I got to share it with him and watch him learn and grow. The days carried an additional air of mystery, events even more unexpected and spontaneous as I adapted to his moment-to-moment needs.

His survival was entirely dependent on me, but I didn't care that for that short while I was his slave because it felt more natural than anything. I discovered in a brand new way, the power and beauty of absolute service and devotion to another.

CHAPTER SEVENTEEN

A FTER LAYING SNOW DOWN in his sleeping basket one afternoon, I took a moment to meditate on the symbols, which had fallen into the background of my attention since he was born. I sat cross legged on the stone and simply stared at the pictures on the wall, not expecting anything miraculous.

But I was still open, listening, waiting.

In time, Qia̗ȏhui had told me.

All would be revealed *in time*.

I picked up a shard of hard coal from the fireplace to play around with different combinations. No language was interpretable if it wasn't written in the right order.

Instead of drawing them in linear sequence like English, I used each individual symbol to create a bigger, overlapping picture. I began with the maze at the centre, then aligned other symbols into a perfectly spaced circle around it. It looked correct in some way. It flowed.

A ripple ran up my spine. It was the first time I'd received any kind of intuitive confirmation like this, so I continued to piece the remaining symbols into the sequence.

Now it looked slightly out of balance, so I began again on another blank space of wall beside it with the same positioning, but I swapped a few pictures around. Still, a sense of imbalance evoked me to open my mind to a less obvious solution.

I drew the five elements inside each leg of the six-pointed star, but one leg was left bare. As I examined it, the earth element began to emanate a faint, greenish glow. It was only subtle, but I was highly aware it wasn't a delusion.

I remembered that when I was originally shown the symbols, the earth element was repeated, so I drew an identical earth symbol in the blank space directly across from where I'd placed the first.

With the maze picture inside the star's centre, I drew a ring around the image.

The moment the two lines met, the circle lit up.

A striking golden beam of L·ight Mȧttȩr shone where the lines merged into one, then ran seamlessly around the ring like a golden river, or a canal that held the image in place. Secure. Protected.

The symbols lit up too, in a very precise order.

In identical timing, the two earth symbols flashed to life, emanating the same deep green glow I'd seen earlier.

Then the spiral lit up in a pure, pristine shade of white.

The bird was sky blue. The wave also shone blue, but deep, dark, electric blue. The colour of the ocean.

Finally, the fire symbol lit up, flame red.

I leant back, watching in wonder.

The potency of L·ight Mȧttȩr that spurred each element to life was so tremendous that it began to burn crevasses into the stone they were painted upon, transforming each soft coal drawing into a permanent indent.

The central image was the only one that didn't light up, nor did it sink into the wall. Instead it darkened, the black of the coal I'd painted it with blackening until it finally began to dissolve then vanish completely.

I leant in. I hadn't touched it. The atmosphere was still, the stone dry. But there was a blank space where the maze had been.

It took some moments to process that the animated sequence that had occurred on the rocky screen before me may have been a direct insight into its real-life purpose, a representation of what would manifest if I could figure out how to gather and align the live versions of each symbol.

It seemed that the central image represented the force that the surrounding pictures were deliberately positioned to counterbalance. The force of the Sky Consciousness?

And what of the crescent, sun, and upside-down triangle? They all lay outside of the circle and had not lit up.

I caught myself leaning forward, both in mind and body, and sunk back again, reopening my mind to the greater intelligence that could not be accessed through the contracted aspect of it.

The cave echoed with the silence that fell upon it.

Silent apart from Snow's occasional sleeping sigh.

Bear was outside seizing the day. I almost wished another set of eyes could share the sight I witnessed.

The river of gold that ran around the circle didn't fade, even after both the central image and the rainbow of colour that had lit the surrounding symbols had.

It shone brighter, brighter, blinding, projecting a rich, ring-shaped ray of light outwards into the air in front of it.

But it wasn't entirely transparent like sunbeams were. Within the circular golden hue was an exhibition of glittering, star-like specks of L·ight Màtt̞er. They drifted unhurriedly upon the air towards each other, gathering to form a mass.

The veil between worlds had thinned again, and I knew better than to let thoughts interrupt what was unfolding this time. Any amount of mental activity or spike in emotion had the potential to break the channel.

The gold stars blended to become one beaming light from which a being was formed, then a woman.

It wasn't Qiạỗhui, although it was one of the Aẍscendants.

Ídã̃.

Her eyes were such a clear, deep, dark shade of blue, they carried the totality of the ocean. Wild and wise. Erratic and serene. The same colour that had animated the water symbol moments earlier.

I wasn't close to Íðã in any significant way, which heightened my curiosity in the purpose of her visit. She'd always been present in the Pyramid with the other Axscendants in important meetings. She'd spoken to me through the Noahl that sometimes carried her spirit as a vessel for her to interact through. But she'd never visited me alone.

I didn't speak.

I was silenced by the resilience of her being, which was so different in essence to that of the gentle, loving, yin nature of Qiąõhui. Not because Íðã's nature wasn't also loving, but it was an entirely different expression of it. Again, the kind of love you might feel at the foot of the vast ocean. Unfathomable. Untamed.

"We have been where you are." Her voice was resonant, accent rich and unusual—only because the undulating sound was still foreign to my ears. But as she spoke, it reminded me of the man whose voice visited me in the cave. It was the same accent. He, too, must have been Icelandic.

The fair skin of her aged but ageless face was exposed by cropped white hair that was tucked behind both ears, and the contrast made her eyes appear even darker and more brooding. Mysterious.

In a flash, her image dissolved, but the L·ight Mátter that it manifested within did not. It simply morphed into another being, and soon, in her place, stood Nala's Ascendent, Chaiţãnya.

Like Íðã, she did not appear solid. In no way was she mistakable for someone of this world. She was semi-transparent, an exquisite projection of light in Chaiţãnya's image.

When she spoke, she continued as if finishing the thought that Íðã began.

"We have been what you are, in human form. Thousands of years before you." Her vivid green jungle eyes were piercing, and her Nepalese accent rich.

She was tall and elegant, her dark skin smooth and long black hair like silk, not too dissimilar in texture to the golden robes it fell over. Gemstones glistened from rings of golden jewelry that were stacked along the line of her bare arms and neck.

"We once didn't know it. And it was only through exploring, experimenting, and embodying it, fully, in its entirety, that we were able to transcend the human forms we were originally born of, to become what we are now."

Axscendants.

"Guiding you on your journey of becoming.

"There were two in our cluster who ascended higher than we did, beyond *all* realms bound by space and time. But we chose to stay. As guardians of the Light that we fought to invite back to Earth."

Like with the image of Ídã, the L·ight Màtter that formed Chaiṭãnya dissolved in another flash, shattering, only to reconfigure itself in the projection of another Axscendant.

This time, it was the built and burly, warrior-like image of Âdja. His blue eyes were also bright and piercing in contrast to his skin, which was so dark he could have blended into the Shadows of the cave if it weren't for the aura of gold that lit his image.

Again, he continued the stream of information the others began.

"What you are becoming is what you already are." He had a Kenyan accent that matched his exotic appearance. The epic power of his being was so grounded and fully embodied he could have been solid, although I was aware he wasn't.

"There is nothing new to discover. Uncover what already lies within you. The symbol is simple if you understand your part in it. Just one role, within the whole. Put your attention there. On your role."

Âdja's image burst and shattered back into gold dust and the image of Ídã returned.

"We have been where you are," she repeated, just as she began. "We have done what you are being asked to do. This is a continuation of our work. Work that we thought was finished when we Ascended but cannot be truly finished until the Sky Consciousness find another Planet to make their own.

"Earth is not equipped for their frequency of being. It never has, nor ever will it be."

Ídã evaporated and in another flash the remaining gold mist washed back into the wall it was being projected from. The river of gold that filled the circle faded, faded, until all that was left was a simple carving in the stone.

Why was it that every time I was given any kind of celestial insight, I was left with more questions than answers?

Understand my part in the symbol...

This seemed like the most actionable insight I'd received. Thank you, Âdja. He always spoke in more direct ways than the other Axscendants, who perhaps found pleasure in mystifying me.

But still, this sparked the question of what my part in the symbol was?

Snow's cry startled me. I'd leant in so close to the stone my nose was almost touching it. His cry increased in urgency but not in demand for attention. It was an agonised cry, full of pain.

He usually calmed the moment he could see me standing over his cot, but it was like he couldn't see me, his mind still caught in another one of his sleep terrors. I held him against my chest, rocking.

"Shhhh."

He shook, the kind of convulsions that were usually the body's way of letting go of trauma. It pained my heart, but he slowly calmed as I pressed him more tightly to my chest, realising he was safe here.

I stepped outside into the sun and sat on the grass to feed him, wondering what kinds of images caused him such fright. It could have been past life trauma, still trapped with his spirit, resurfacing through his subconscious.

I also wondered if he was like me and saw visions of the future, of the Sky People. This was more concerning because they were clearly not positive visions.

I began to ponder over more of what the Axscendants had shared. They seemed to believe there was a way to influence a future in which the Sky People were eliminated for good. I focused instead on that.

I couldn't imagine them in human form. They were too holy. Too magnificent. I assumed that an Axscendant was all they were and all they had ever been. I didn't think it was something one could *become*, through benevolent work on Earth. They called it work. Working with the symbols. And each other. Their cluster. They all had a part. A role.

Understand my role...

I tried to retain every word they spoke, for in all my past experience, they were never flippant with words. They only ever shared precisely what I needed to hear to serve me on my path. Nothing more, nothing less.

"Ouch." A sudden, sharp pain in my breast brought my attention back to the baby that fed there. This happened sometimes. For something so natural, the constant strain of breastfeeding became quite painful and even left light bruises.

Snow's eyes were wide open now, wide awake, and there was no trace of the fear he awoke with. He stared up at the sky, almost drunk off breast milk, watching the clouds drift by. He was as calm and content as usual, so I lay him down on his back on the spongy grass beside me.

When he was younger, even just this simple action would have caused him to panic over our separation. His tears demanded we be physically attached in one way or another at all times, but I gradually showed him that he could be detached while still safe, still loved, still cared for. I felt a lot less pressure now, and he was happier too.

My gaze was soft over the land—land that continued to blossom and grow more vibrant and lush each day, just as Snow continued to grow bigger and pudgier.

A gust of wind blew, creating ripples over the lake, and the leafy branches of its surrounding trees swayed. In it, I saw the dance of nature's elements, living, breathing, and moving in unison.

The elements...

They were the only aspect of the symbol that was obvious, positioned inside each leg of the interconnecting star, working in harmony to counteract the maze in the centre.

Upon reflection, I could see the parallels in what the Axscendants mentioned of their 'work' when they too lived on Earth in human form, working in harmony to counteract the force of the Sky Consciousness.

Maybe the elements don't just symbolise nature. Maybe they symbolise people working with nature, united by the same purpose to heal and restore the natural world to its fullest, most thriving expression. Which meant erasing the Sky People, the maze.

My part.

Maybe 'my part' lies within understanding not all but one of nature's elements in its entirety.

But that would have meant that the rest of whatever the symbol was proposing relied on an unforeseeable future in which I found my tribe, who were perhaps my 'cluster', and also each represented one of the elements.

I knew, by that point, that that idealistic future was, in brute reality, far more unlikely than it was likely.

It had been so long.

Too long.

If we were to somehow find each other, it would be a true miracle.

My part.

I returned to contemplating my part alone. Âdja had stressed that it was all that was in my control.

My part in the balance of the elements.

Earth. Water. Fire. Air. Spirit.

Water. *Ídắ's eyes*...Perhaps she'd been water? Perhaps she still was.

Air.

Spirit.

I could quickly discount Fire and Earth as possible affinities. I was not fiery. Not in character or spirit. And I had to work hard to ground myself. I generally felt so malleable and easily influenced by my environment that I was like a feather in the breeze…

Air.

When Nala taught me the qualities that distinguished each element, she said Air was the element of the mind and metaphysical senses.

If I was capable of embodying any kind of extracelestial power, it would be within my ability to feel the dance of life that moved beneath the surface of form. To see and travel through realms that were usually inaccessible to humankind, and communicate with celestial beings who, by general rule, also remained strictly invisible to the human eye.

I would have the ability to travel through space and time, uninhibited by the physical vessel of my body or any solid substance.

Like Air.

When I lived in the Iron City, these 'abilities' felt more like a curse. I would have never imagined they might become my most valuable asset. Seeing and feeling the interplay of the energy world, of what lay in the Shadows of humanity, caused so much pain and confusion there was a time when I would have given it up to live a simple, single-layered existence.

But since I accepted the multiple dimensions that made up reality, and the complexity of the universe that could never be fully grasped by the mind, life had certainly become more interesting. Richer. Fuller.

Letting go of the pressure I felt to live a refined existence, limited to what the Control declared as the only version of reality, opened up space for true freedom of expression and perception that only continued to expand.

Just as it was in this moment of new self-discovery.

Was it my constitutional alignment with the force of Air that allowed for my experience of the veil between worlds to be thin?

Was it the force of Air that the Ascendents encouraged me to understand?

Was my part, my role, somehow affiliated with the Air symbol?

CHAPTER EIGHTEEN

BEAR REMAINED CLOSE AFTER Snow's birth and Snow immediately warmed to him. Bear was impressively patient and tolerant with the small, curious human.

Over the first few months of Snow's life, we lived a very simple, basic existence. He was a late spring baby, which meant the un-dramatic weather treated us kindly during the first seasons of his life. And I had time to gather herbs and preservable foods to sustain us both when winter hit.

Presently, there wasn't much to maintain other than our health and wellbeing. And for this he quickly grew into a healthy, plump baby.

I couldn't tell if it was just the pale tone of his skin, but I swore it glowed, closer in quality to that of a Fξ than human. Sometimes I'd catch glimpses of his aura, which was pristine white. No colour expressed itself with his essence. There was more pure light carried within his being than any human I'd known.

Time had become less tangible.

Days and nights flowed like one seamless dance of light and dark.

Soon enough, Snow began reaching for the ground instead of my arms. He watched Bear's method of travel more closely than mine and mounted on his hands and knees. After some lopsided experimentation, he could crawl.

The land around us continued to flourish with a wild abundance of plants, flowers, fruits, vegetables, grass, and *life*. I could barely believe the speed in which the area became a sanctuary. The laws of nature that I'd known to be true in the past had certainly been twisted.

More animals congregated into the area. Rabbits, squirrels, deer, birds, and beavers all shared the land we called home and Snow adopted each one as his brothers and sisters.

The moment he was on the ground and my attention elsewhere, he'd crawl over to the closest creature in sight and because he was as small and plump, baring no claws or sharp teeth as possible alarms of danger, they weren't intimidated by his inquisitive presence, welcoming him as if one of their own.

The first time it happened, he set his eyes on a grazing rabbit and crawled towards it. I watched closely as he approached, assuming the rabbit would flick its ears and dart away, but to my surprise it barely flinched. Snow simply sat beside it. The rabbit was aware of his presence, watching him out of the corner of its eye as it grazed on bright blades of grass, and in time, it grew curious enough in return to hop across and sniff him.

Snow earned permission to bring his hand to its silky fur, and it didn't seem to mind as he stroked down the line of its back.

He was gentle and made high pitched noises like he was attempting to talk to the rabbit in the way he'd witnessed me talk to Bear.

The rabbit hopped around him playfully and rubbed its long, floppy ears against his leg, making him giggle. The sound of his pure joy rang through the space and seemed to attract more animals to the surrounding area.

Two more rabbits hopped over, and a squirrel crawled down the trunk of a tree to join them. Splashes of colour swooped down from the sky in the form of birds, dancing and chirping about the harmonious gathering.

I continued to watch from my distance as the group of playmates was forming. The oddest group I'd ever have expected to witness.

Seasons passed, but not in the timing of the cycle we had known before. Winter finally came after an extended amount of pleasant weather, and it was rough, but I was prepared. I had built a waist-high wall across the cave opening with all the stone and sticks I could collect, weaving them into something solid enough to withstand and protect us from the weather.

Snow got ill, his first illness since entering the world, and I got ill with worry until he was better. His immune system proved strong for a newborn.

Bear barely left the sanctuary to wander. He barely left our cave. His fur, and mass amount of body heat kept us warm, and that, combined with an ever burning fire that I was sure to keep stoked with the piles of kindling I collected and stored during the dry months, helped Snow's fever pass.

I killed an animal. Just one. A deer. Our furs wore down and it became challenging to keep them dry. We needed more warmth, and I used every part of the animal, including its flesh for food, and bones, which I cleaned and tied together to create an art hanging.

It blew and tinkled in the wind and reminded me of the circle of life. The preciousness of life. The brutality of nature, and the inevitability of the fact that one-day, near or far into the future, I too, would be refined down to bones.

The dear was an easier catch than it should have been. The animals of the New World didn't know humans as hunters yet. Up until that moment, we had co-existed non-violently. But still, the hunt wasn't *easy*.

As soon as the dear sensed the intention behind my creeping step, and glanced the sharp, hefty spear in my hand, it dashed sideways in the snow. I chased and lost a number of them before finally catching one, which felt both rewarding and disheartening.

Days grew shorter and shorter, until, during the peak of winter, only a few hours of sunlight graced us each day. I used every second of those hours to work and be and bathe outside, even on the most freezing days accompanied by heavy snowfall and cutting winds. It felt invigorating to experience the elements as they were.

The long nights were not bland. All throughout winter, the vivid, mystical Northern Lights danced across the sky as if visiting from another world. All three of us would stare for hours from our comfort in the cave, our glassy eyes reflecting our enchantment. They reminded me of the exquisite and incomprehensible vastness of the multiverse we existed in.

The only haunting thing about living in extended darkness was the night terrors that Snow woke with more and more regularly, screaming. Crying. He did not have words to share with me what he saw. I could only share his terror.

I realised after some time, however, that although I couldn't ask him to explain the dreams to me in words, but he had learned to communicate in other ways.

He had watched me draw on the cave wall with chalk since he was born, and began to copy me as soon as his hands were developed enough to hold and control a piece. Pictures and drawings seemed like a natural expression to him, just like they had been for me for as long as I could remember.

I gave him a stick of charcoal and asked him to draw what he saw. His hand wasn't elaborate at transferring the images from his mind, but he went into a kind of trance, his little eyebrows creasing as he focused all his attention on the images in his mind's eye, and when he lifted the chalk from the stone, the markings he left were simple enough to interpret.

It was a human. But not a human. Taller. Sharp-edged. Shaded grey. I knew immediately it was a Sky Person. Surrounding it were many wisps of chalk. Fire. And behind it, a dome shape.

He was being haunted by the same vision that haunted me—which haunted me more. Because I could not dismiss what it meant. The future had not changed course. Not yet. If we continued upon the course we currently cut, this image would inevitably manifest.

Would this be the end of our world? Me and Snow alone in the face of the indefeatable Sky People? Would they win?

But they couldn't.

It was wrong.

It went against every force of light in the world. Everything that was most natural.

How could foreign entities win over the natural forces of our own planet?

The reason we received these visions was to ensure they wouldn't. They were warnings. Gifts of awareness. And I realised that the fact we were *still* receiving them was not necessarily a bad thing. It meant we still had a chance to influence some kind of change. We still had a chance to win. If that weren't true, whatever forces of light sent the premonitions would have given up, surrendered to the inevitable.

It wasn't inevitable.

Still, I didn't see why Snow had to suffer night after night because of it. He had seen the vision now. We *both* had. We carried the awareness with us. And so, I sought a remedy that would help him sleep more peacefully.

Spring came.

One evening I walked to a garden by the lake with Snow on my hip where a magnolia tree grew. I'd learnt from the Medicine sisters in Santōṣha that Magnolia bark was a powerful relaxant and sleep inducer.

The previous night, Snow had woken again in intense agony from another night terror. I had tried many of the limited herbs I found growing during winter but nothing had been strong enough. I only now recognised the magnolia tree for what it was.

As we walked, tiny sparks of light flashed in and out of sight around us. They'd been appearing often, usually at dawn or dusk, but I couldn't discern whether they were physically occurring, or glitches in my eyesight or the atmosphere.

Bear followed and stopped to roll and scratch on a patch of grass just out of view.

I let Snow down, who crawled around my legs as I used a sharp blade to shave off bark from the tree trunk. I watched him with peripheral vision as he wandered over to a nearby bush where a red bushy-tailed fox lazed.

He crawled straight up to it and reached his arm out to stroke it the way he did rabbits.

"Let the animals warm to you, my love," I called. "Wild animals can be dangerous and prey on smaller beings. It's just one of the laws of nature."

He hadn't started talking yet but watched me closely as I spoke and appeared to understand in some way. He reached his hand up more cautiously to the fox's nose, who was sleepy and passive and sniffed it with apparent indifference.

I turned back to pick some chamomile flowers from a nearby plant before heading home in the dusk air. And while my back was turned, the pleasant scene unravelled quicker than I could process.

Snow's high-pitched yelp pierced the serene silence, followed by an aggressive snarl that was quickly broken by the wild growl of an almost full-grown bear.

Fear struck me like an arrow and something burst to life inside my chest; a sense of immense power rippled down my arms and into my palms. When I looked down at my hands, a bright sphere of sky blue L·ight Mätter formed between them.

I knew immediately what it was. Intuitively. Without the interference of words or thoughts to affirm or deny.

It was White Magic.

Air Magic.

Manifested as a beaming blue ball between my pulsing palms.

I whipped around to intercept the fox in whatever it cunningly attempted behind my back; her nonchalant behaviour had been a deception, in hindsight.

But to her disillusionment, Bear was more aware of her maliciousness than I. From where he'd been hidden just out of sight, Bear leaped into the scene. He towered over the fox on all fours, his razor-sharp teeth exposed through growling lips. The fur along his spine shackled.

Snow was safe beneath him.

My heart seared with relief.

The sphere of Air Magic in my palms dissipated as fast as it had manifested.

Snow burst into tears, shocked and confused by the charged giant above him who he'd only known as gentle and placid until that moment.

The fox slit her eyes at Bear before slinking backwards and disappearing into the bush.

I dropped my basket and threw myself beneath Bear's legs, retrieving Snow and wrapped him tightly in my arms. I felt a wave of maternal guilt for turning my back on him as I examined the mild but bleeding claw marks on his body, followed by a more immense wave of gratitude for Bear's unusual, human-like protectiveness over us.

"Shhh," I rocked, pressing his precious body against my chest and rubbing my cheek against his silky hair.

I looked up at Bear. "Thank you."

But he didn't need my words.

He nodded his head and let out a low growl, then rubbed his wet nose against Snow, turning his tear-stricken expression into a beaming one. Bear nudged the boy, shifting into a more playful manner, and it didn't take me long to recognize his signals.

He looked to Snow, then to me, then to his back in sequence until I finally surrendered.

"Ok." I stood with Snow still in my arms, and hooked my basket back over my elbow. "But only if I walk beside you," I added, not that he could understand me.

I lifted Snow onto Bear's back, his little legs falling around Bear's neck, and helped him stabilize before beginning the walk back to camp. His hand gripped mine tightly while the other hooked itself into Bear's fur.

As with me, it took a few steps for him to stabilize, and I remained by his side, ready to catch him if he fell. But he didn't fall. And the more balance he maintained, the more his joy grew, taking in the world around him from his heightened view.

Once home I boiled the magnolia bark, then added a palm full of chamomile and lavender flowers, brewing a strong tea.

We huddled by the fire. Snow sat between my legs and hummed with me as I stirred. The sound attracted a pair of white/grey rabbits who had become regular visitors to our cave. They hopped straight up to us, sniffing and rubbing their heads against our legs, then spread their long torsos over the warm stone beside us to soak in the flame's heat.

Snow crawled over to sit between the rabbits, resting a hand on each of their fleecy coats, giving them a gentle stroke. The incident with the fox clearly hadn't broken his trust for animals, although he now wore wounds to remind him of the more dangerous kinds.

But it did more than just offer Snow an insight into nature's ruthlessness.

It offered me a gift. An insight into something that lay dormant within me. Something impossible, yet proven now. Something I could no longer deny.

Not only was Air Magic real, it was available within me, in expressions I would never have guessed to attempt to harness it by. Nor was I certain how to access it again.

It was sparked to life in a moment of thoughtless urgency, fear. Dictated by emotion. *Could I summon it to return in a controlled way, or was it only a spontaneous arising?*

My gaze was soft, but something caught my eye in the atmosphere above Snow's head. Glittering sparks of flashy silver light. This was the second time they had appeared that day. I couldn't dismiss them any longer as mere glitches in my vision. They weren't flickering in and out of sight this time; rather, they remained present in a calm drift.

This time, a high-pitched twinkling sound also rang through the air that I was sure was associated with their presence.

Snow's gaze turned upwards, eyes darting between them, sparkling with their reflection. One landed on his arm, and he watched it closely as it rose again just as gracefully. His hands lifted from the rabbits, reaching up in an attempt to catch what looked like a tiny fallen star.

I leant in, reminded of a strikingly similar experience I'd had when I was in the Valley of Santōṣha, then jerked back as a tingling sensation rippled up my arm from where one of the stars landed on me.

They're not glitches in my eyesight, or the atmosphere...

The FξŸa have returned!

It was obvious now that I could feel the presence of a being inside its glow.

I stared at the light on my arm, but I still couldn't see a body. It was hidden by its bright aura, which was smaller than I remembered.

"What happened to you?" I asked faintly, so as not to blow the wispy being from its resting place.

A high-pitched sound twinkled through the air, but no words were carried with it. Our ability to communicate was still lost.

I looked to Snow, who also seemed blind to their true form, then to Bear. He was watching the Light Beings too, but he seemed less curious. I got the feeling he'd been aware of what they were for some time before I finally got out of my own way and *saw*.

To my surprise, the sound of a voice made me scan the Fξ` more closely, searching for whom spoke it. But the soundwaves it travelled upon were more refined than usual, and I realised that the sounds were transferred from mind to mind instead of ear to ear. I knew it well because this was how I used to communicate with Ẓchǒ.

Snow appeared deaf to the voice, and Bear's ears didn't twitch like they usually would when he was listening. I wondered if my ability to hear was part of my affinity with Air—the element of the mind—or a product of my old affinity with Ẓchǒ. Or both.

"We never left as you were led to believe," a male voice rang in my mind like a gong, both high and low at once. *"This Earth's atmosphere doesn't support our physical form. It can only comprehend us as sparks of light, for at our core that's what we are. We embody very little density and the Earth realm relies on a certain amount of density for something to be visible."*

Another Fξ landed on my arm. While small, her presence was familiar. Lupïta and Théodren were never far apart.

"Why can I only see you now?" I asked.

"Historically, humans have rarely been aware of our existence. In some ways, to see is to believe, and to believe is to see. It happens only when the rational mind does not interfere with your sense or sight, which by its nature, limits your perception.

"You've been seeing us in glimpses but dismissing it as something else, so we disappear to you."

Théodren paused for Lupïta to continue.

"We thought the New Earth would be different, at least for your tribe, because you were already aware of our existence, but

we've been proved mistaken. It appears the Mother created the human/Fξ relationship this way with reason."

Her voice was sweetly feminine and girlish just as his was boyish, but neither lacked wisdom.

"*You, however, are eternally bound to the FξŸa world because of Ʒchǒ's pledge of benevolence to you. The connection has rippled on to live within the blood of your son too.*"

I glanced back at Snow, who was still mesmerized by the playful, magic light beings, and I felt a wave of sorrow at the mention of Ʒchǒ. Lupïta felt what I felt and explained what I hadn't understood about her passing.

"*A human can live on if the FξŸa bound to her passes, but if the human dies, the FξŸa, by law of the pledge, passes too. Your body was under extreme pressure that night, and Ʒchǒ was physically weaker than you. We are not built to endure the kind of weather that you endured.*"

Memories flooded back, memories I had buried.

During that storm, my body suffered more pain than anything I'd experienced before in the physical realm. But I was so determined to survive that I ignored the call of death that loomed over my shoulder, whispering in my ear, encouraging me to surrender.

To give up.

To give *in* to the boundless peace that would have welcomed me if I just stopped and let the blizzard bury me.

"*You were close enough to death for her to simultaneously hear its call, and she couldn't hold on to life the way you did. Perhaps she didn't want to. But the bondage that intertwined you remains unbreakable. It is a commitment for life, and therefore, although Ʒchǒ has left this world in body, her essence is still with you, within you.*"

A memory I *hadn't* forgotten was when the epic glow of her being merged with mine while her delicate body dissolved and disappeared into my chest. It was true; I still felt her essence with me, but it had become a *part* of me now, always.

Théodren rose from my shoulder, leaving a stream of L·ight Màttęr beneath him that softly fell and faded.

"How did you find us here? When did you leave the others? Where are they? Are they alive?" I suddenly realised they might have answers to a plethora of more critical questions.

Lupïta and Théodren looked between each other. My anticipation rose. Then Lupïta began. *"Their ability to see us faded. They thought we'd left them long before we had. But our light was fading faster than we knew was possible. Like Ẓchó, we became weak, our light dim. Even our ability to fly was fading. But we are more ancient than she was. We had more life force stored within us to survive.*

"It didn't take us long to understand that it was the separation from our tribe that was causing our loss of stamina. We have always been more powerful as one."

Théodren carried on from Lupïta.

"We were able to live separately in the past, in the early days of the Old World when the frequency of light here was still more supreme than the forces of Shadow. But we realised that until nature is thriving and light on Earth prevails again, we are not strong enough to be separate.

"We left your tribe after the great snowstorm to find our own, and it was through finding them that we found you. But in leaving the other humans, we lost connection to their whereabouts, and we have not gone searching for them again.

"It was difficult enough to find our kind after separating from them the first time. Even once we had, it took a long time to regain our full exuberance. We could not risk separating again for a human cause." Théodren said both simply and sternly.

Lupïta continued again.

"Both the Spring and Autumn Fξÿa were already here. They were here before you, helping nature grow, preparing for your

arrival. We have been in communication with Záphire, and she advised us to remain here, with you, emphasising the importance of you and your child's survival.

"The other humans have a destiny that has fallen outside of ours. There are other divine beings guiding them. But you are one of us. And so your destiny lies in alignment with ours."

The Fξ had been present since I arrived? *They*'d been the celestial force assisting the rapid growth of flora here?

"We have been communicating with the mycelia webs of life beneath the ground and sending our light, showing them that it's safe to re-emerge."

I suddenly felt blind to not have acknowledged them earlier. Lupïta could read either my mind or my energy, for she spoke kindly.

"All is perfect as it is and has been Maya. We can never assume The Mother's intent, but it would seem that it was within your story to face true and deep aloneness over the past year, as it was within ours to be invisible to you.

"Until now. And so, our paths intertwine again. And for this we are happy."

I couldn't argue with her words.

Upon reflection, the resilience within me that only developed as comprehensively as it had through believing and accepting that I was utterly alone, shaped the woman I had become in so many ways.

I truly knew what it meant to stand alone and survive, in my power, against whatever hardships life thrust upon me, at a level that could only be found through experience. Since being separated from the tribe, I realised that I had the capacity within me to withstand and behold so much more than I would have otherwise believed was possible.

In this way, life had been so kind.

Under the disguise of cruelty, life gifted me with the kind of strength that cannot be feigned or bought. The kind of strength that can only be built, experience upon experience.

Through being ground down to the core, I was able to find the true expanse of power that lies there. Patiently waiting to be rediscovered and embodied.

No more words were spoken, but a chime rang from Lupïta's bright body as she rose from my arm, joining Théodren in the air, leaving me to process what had been shared.

My heart felt lighter, an immense wave of gratitude sweeping through me as I realised the extent to which even in my darkest hour, there had been support, and an exquisite expanse of light, all around me, aiding my survival.

I felt a deeper sense of the perfect harmony that governed the mysterious and unpredictable flow of life, moment to moment, as I comprehended how all of nature had been cooperating seamlessly with the same divine intention, to see Earth prosper once more.

From the plants that burst through the dirt, determined to be born, to the seasons working in sublime balance to provide the ample climate for each area of land to thrive. The animal's dominating drive to procreate, and my own body's intuitive ability to give birth alone.

I thought of Bear, the extraordinary shapeshifter who'd contributed to the evolution of *multiple* species, and the FξŸa magic that had the power to accelerate the growth of nature...

The New World was going to survive.

Of all the forces working in its favour, there was just one working against it. And we could overcome it this time.

I felt trust, as bright as the sun in my heart, that the New Earth would survive.

I still didn't have any clear insight into whether my tribe had survived, but Théodren assured me that they too were being guided. For now, that was enough.

CHAPTER NINETEEN

S NOW AND BEAR BECAME close playmates as Snow grew. After the incident with the fox, Snow was adamant to ride him again and again. We began riding on his back together, Snow between my legs, and Bear's initial slow pace became a free-spirited run. It was the closest thing to flying I'd experienced.

With the new awareness of the FξŸ̈a 's effervescence in the air all around our sanctuary, I felt more at peace than ever to simply live and be and let life unfold as it did.

With peace in my heart, I developed more confidence to explore my apparent affinity with the Air element. The more deeply I tuned into the inconspicuous but exquisite essence of it all around me, the more it revealed itself as a force that was also present and accessible within.

I knew it so intimately already; I just hadn't been conscious that that's what it was.

I came to understand through experimentation, that it wasn't so much practice as skilful mastery that Air Magic demanded of me. The element, as might be obvious in its invisible nature, revealed itself more through *not* doing. Through meditation. When my mind became silent, Air Magic became more freely available to play with.

Inter-dimensional communication was the most obvious ability associated with the affinity. It also felt the most natural to me because it had been occurring long before I ever considered it a product of Air.

But experiencing a sphere of it manifest between my palms opened my curiosity to what else might lay within the realm of Air Magic. I could not cultivate the same phenomena again, and began to doubt my own memory of it, sceptical of whether I had glamorised it in some way.

Still, I discovered I had the capacity to do more than what lay in the limits of my imagination. When my mind was crisp and clear, and my intent singular, I found I had the ability to move and manipulate things with my mind.

Impossible things.

Things I would not have even attempted to move and manipulate if it wasn't for my allies in magical phenomena, who encouraged me to breach the boundaries of my own self-limitation.

I was no longer alone in my experimentation.

The magic of the FξŸa beings wasn't so different to the magic of Air. They, too, were closely intertwined with the element. They danced with Air and Spirit in a harmonious equilibrium, fuelled by and functioning in alignment with the grace of these agile substances.

They taught me how to tune more totally into the epic force that lay within me, to merge and become an open channel for the magic to move through, rather than trying to force it to work for me.

"We are of the same L·ight Mátter. Your essence may be even more aligned with that of the Fξ than that of humankind. It is evident in the aura that surrounds you, silver blue, like us." Lupïta and Théodren became my primary teachers. They spoke and moved in a synchronized manner, like extensions of one another.

"The blue of your L·ight Mátter is the shade of the Air element. Silver means White Magic is with you, which is highly uncommon in humans," Lupïta explained.

"White Magic is not a force available to those with even the slightest potential to use it with ill intent. Humans are known to be easily tempted and swayed by forces of both light and dark, and driven by egocentric desires. White Magic can only be used selflessly. Whatever it is called upon to assist must be prosperous for all, not for singular gain."

The day was still and serene. I sat at the edge of the cave looking out over the vibrant land, the glimmering lake, the bright green grass. Snow was asleep behind me.

In that moment, the entire image before me appeared as if it could have been sprinkled with a little magic.

Théodren continued.

"For as long as we've known you, and I would assume, long before our paths met, the central attention of your being has not been self-serving. Your expanse of consciousness is unusually wide and all-inclusive. You think and act and behave in ways that support all sentient beings, not you alone.

"It has been this way for a long time. You are a giver. It is within your nature—simply the way The Mother made you."

I had no words to add. I only listened, opening my ears to hear and receive their insights into things I didn't understand.

"White Magic may sound fantastical, intangible, but it is only a term, a label we use to describe the more sophisticated ethereal forces of the universe that work in alliance with light to lift and enrich its expanse here.

"In contrast, we could call what the Sky Consciousness has done to your minds Black Magic, for they too are sophisticated, ethereal forces that work instead with Shadows, to breed Shadows and enrich the negative frequencies here.

"The point is that, conscious or not, you have had valuable experiences with both White *and* Black Magic, and both will serve you moving forward.

"White Magic has always been the substance present with you during interdimensional communication and seeing. It was the force of light governing your safety when you became the channel between life and death for humanity to pass through all that time ago in the Valley.

"It trusts you, and that in itself should encourage you to trust yourself with it. Self-doubt stunts the flow of life in its most divine expression. And it *wants* to express itself through you, as divinely as you will allow it.

"You are *partners*."

Partners. It was all great knowledge and all, but I was still unclear on what exactly it wanted to partner with me for. What purpose?

Snow let out a high-pitched sound and I turned to check on him, but he remained in deep sleep. My eyes fell onto the Symbol engraved in the stone.

"The Axscendants said the symbol represents a continuation of their work from when they were humans on Earth. Do you know what their work was?"

"The Fξ have never been closely involved with the Axscendants. They live in the frequency of L·ight Mȧttẹr that is golden. They are aligned with any expressions of gold Light, gold Magic. We live in the realm of silver.

"Our work on and inside Earth is different," Théodren explained. "But I am aware of the Legend of the Θ.R.A, which is what I assume they were referencing." He paused, hesitant, and Lupïta spoke.

"It is not our place to share their story or why it might be relevant to you. Our knowledge of the legend is that it involved a cluster of five sorcerers, each diverse in skill—but interwoven as one by White Magic, and complementary of each other in that they each embodied one of nature's elements. United, they were a force of absolute balance.

"It was them who lifted the veil of ignorance that was cast upon Earth in the dawn of the dark ages. You may have heard the story of Revǎthi?"

I remembered back to one of my earliest memories in the Village, when Chief Ħan shared the story of Earth's history. He told of the Black Witch Revǎthi, mother of all Shadows, who opened the original portal that invited Sky Consciousness to Earth, to share and exchange resources for knowledge.

I nodded. Théodren continued.

"The Aᵡsᴄendants, then in human form, undid Revǎthi's curse over Earth that suppressed the forces of benevolent light here, which allowed for people like you and Björn and others aligned with higher frequencies to populate the earth again.

"But they could not reverse the presence of the Shadows once they had infiltrated the land. They were already attached to the human mind and being carried through human DNA.

"It became within the power of each individual to detach from their hooks. But the workings of the Sky Consciousness is complex, and their intelligence cunning. Most of humanity was already too heavily trapped within their loops of suffering to desire freedom or to even suspect another way of being existed. And so the patterns continued.

"When they ascended from Earth, their work was done."

"But the Sky Consciousness had not left," I concluded. "That's why there's room for continuation."

"I don't know what the Aᵡsᴄendants know, nor where your paths collide. I only know where the Fξ's purpose lies within it all. Our work is with nature and the land. Our most efficient use of energy is in creating and cultivating abundance and beauty, not destroying.

"Humankind is both creative *and* destructive. I would think it is the destructive aspect of your nature that is being called upon to destroy the grip that Sky Consciousness has over this planet," Théodren said.

"The consciousness of Sky People is not fundamentally bad or evil," Lupïta added. "Their intent just clashes with what is life-giving and life-supporting for Earth. They are simply ignorant of the truth that Earth can never sustain an iron species, or an iron civilization. They're too desperate to see reality as it is. The reality is that nature is earth, and earth is nature. All will burn out if nature cannot grow freely again."

I nodded again, still unsure of what exactly I was supposed to do with all this information. If it was true that the power to eliminate Sky Consciousness from Earth for good lay in the formation of a human cluster of element benders, there was nothing I *could* do alone.

Understand your part entirely. Âdja's voice rumbled through my mind again, reminding me not to get overwhelmed by the scope of the task, and to instead refine my role within it to the finest degree.

At least until the opportunity to form a cluster arose.

Air.

Air and White Magic.

Air-infused White Magic.

A high-pitch chuckle rang in the air beside me where Théodren floated. They did not say anymore, taking that as their cue to leave.

CHAPTER TWENTY

I T WAS AUTUMN NOW. The leaves I watched bloom in Spring and brighten in Summer were now fading and falling, dry and bronze, onto the ground. The temperature was cooling down again.

Snow and Bear roamed free that afternoon while I bathed in the gently flowing lake. I closed my eyes as rays of sun soaked into my exposed face, while my body sunk beneath the fresh water, awake, alive.

Another entire cycle of seasons had passed, which in old time would have meant a year. Snow had learnt to walk, but I had been slack with teaching him to talk.

Our lifestyle didn't require many words. We had the ability to sense one another in a way that allowed us to communicate in subtler, direct non-verbal forms, so his use of the spoken language did not develop as it might have if he were a normal child raised in a normal community. Although there was no such thing as normal anymore.

He *had*, however, developed a kind of silent, intuitive language with Bear. I now trusted them to ride out on short adventures alone, knowing Snow would be safe, or at least as safe as he might be under my supervision.

Part of that trust rested upon the field of light I'd cast around the vicinity of land we called our home, that worked to repel all forces that could not meet it. And Bear knew to remain within it when he was with Snow.

It began as a protective sphere around my heart that, under the force of my intent, expanded and encompassed my body. It wasn't just the *sense* of a sphere either; it was visible, a semi-transparent sheath of bluish silver L·ight Mȧttȩr, Air Magic, just like the magic that manifested between my palms that time by the river. But bigger and controlled.

With unbending focus, I expanded it wider, just to test its potential magnitude, until our entire area was protected beneath a dome of Light. It was so potent, so bright. I was confident that no Shadow could enter.

Within it, we were safe from Sky Consciousness. Of that, I was sure. Shadows could not survive the frequency of Light held there. They would dissolve into it. It was a matter of White Magic vs Black, and White, at least in this case, was superior.

After establishing the sphere, I continued to experiment more boldly with Air Magic, attempting to understand both its scope and limitations. It came through me. Through my body and out the channels of my palms.

My hands became my tools, and my body a vessel through which the magic flowed—freely, but *only* when I was light and clear within. It demanded detachment from emotion, need, force, and thought to run through me without getting blocked. My mind, when still and attuned with my vibrant heart, became the instrument from which all my inner power was unlocked.

With practice, I discovered I could align my intent with the motion of the wind, and manipulate its direction and momentum, from harsh gales to a gentle breeze. And through working in synergy with a force as wild and seemingly untameable as the wind alone, so much became possible. It became an unprecedented ally.

I could enhance the flames and heat of a weak fire by fuelling it with the right amount of Air.

I could send messages along a breath of wind to both Bear and Snow, from far distances away, who would hear my voice as if it was carried directly from mouth to ear. At first, I dismissed their responses to my calls as coincidence, but after repetitive evidence, I surrendered my scepticism and accepted that magic-infused wind could truly carry my words across unnatural distances.

I experimented sending messages along the wind with Björn in mind, stretching the limits of how far I believed they could possibly travel. I didn't expect anything of my trials, and there was no way of knowing whether they reached him unless he followed them back here, to me.

Which he didn't—or hadn't yet. He was either very far away, or not receiving the messages.

After bathing in the lake, I began performing the movements of Tai Chi, feeling the force of Air rising through my system the more I surrendered.

The air was still and the atmosphere calm around me, until a whirl of wind swept violently up off the ground, moving in an upward motion with the momentum of my body. It rose and fell with my hands, sweeping forward as I pushed and back again as I pulled.

My concentration was singular and acute, watching and feeling the exquisitely nuanced flood of Air Magic moving fluidly both within and outside of my body.

There was no baby to distract me.

I was alone, but not alone.

Air was a profound presence in itself. Infinite and eternal. There was no beginning nor end to its existence. It was everywhere, ancient and sublime, moving through and around everything.

Omniscient, it was the life source that maintained all living form. And because of this, it was also the force that determined death. The moment that Air chose to leave the lungs of a being and not return was the moment it ceased to be.

I tried my best to honour the almighty force by remaining as clear a channel as I could. The preeminent nature of its intelligence was still beyond my comprehension. It was intelligence that lived outside of the realm of mind, but I was fully open now to listen, receive, merge, learn.

Each movement of Tai Chi that my body performed that day, after so many years of repetitive practice, was brand new. It was accompanied by something that may have always been there, but now I could see it.

Air Magic.

Qi.

In those moments, it manifested in a bluish silver stream of L·ight Màttęr that poured out from my chest, my heart.

I could feel it more vividly than ever too, glowing, vibrating on a frequency that barely felt containable by my body that was suddenly so minute in comparison. But I remained calm and centred, and dropped my awareness deeper, witnessing, feeling, but not letting the sensations overwhelm me.

The L·ight Màttęr trickled from my heart like two forking streams down each arm, forming bright wells of pristine light in each palm.

I didn't know what to do with the Magic now that I held it. There was no demand for its purpose. But I was learning how to cultivate it, which was probably a purpose in and of itself. When the situation arose, I would be able to repeat the process.

I stood still with my palms open, chest open, heart open, simply allowing myself to hold this amount of power in my body, and then I slowly raised my arms and pressed my palms onto my chest, where the Magic was transferred back into the well of my heart.

No loss of energy.

I closed my eyes, breathing. Everything was so still, so quiet, yet so alive.

In the silence, I heard a whistle of wind.

My eyes flashed open just in time to catch sight of a fast-flying arrow, shooting through the air towards me, but not *at* me.

It shot into the dirt at my feet, so close it could have clipped my toe, but I remained unscathed.

I examined the arrow swiftly, its wooden tail thin and smoothly sanded. The blade had disappeared into the ground.

My heart beat fast.

I didn't have to look up to know a human was present.

The first human I would have been in contact with for years.

I was initially confused because my tribe were the only humans left on Earth, yet I couldn't imagine why any of them would greet me with such a warning.

And it *was* a warning.

Whoever shot the arrow clearly had impeccable skill and precision. They *could* have aimed for my body. They *could* have struck me down in an instant. But they didn't.

They established their presence by alerting me of the threat of danger they posed if I were to be in any way uncooperative when they revealed themselves in body.

The sound of my thudding heartbeat made my ears ring.

I finally dared to look up, and the archer stood in plain sight on the top of the cliff ledge.

The archer*ess*.

There was no way she could have been mistaken as one of my tribe. She was brand new to my eyes: tall, dark-skinned, with long dreadlocked hair and a fit, toned body. Her shoulders were rolled back, chest lifted in full ownership of her space, and her expression, even from this distance, was cautious, unwelcoming.

Was she a Sky person? I was *sure* that my shield protected us there. Maybe I was naively confident in my own skill...

But she was not made of iron. Her skin was *brown*, not silver, and her clothing was earthy, sourced from natural materials.

I sent a gust of Air Magic up to wrap around her, using it to scan her energy body like a laser beam from head to toe.

She was clean of Shadows.

I closed my eyes for just a moment to intensify my concentration. Still clear.

An outbreath of relief.

Then a wave of confusion.

If she wasn't one of my tribe, or a Sky person, who was she? How was she here? How had she survived the end of the Old World?

She continued to stare down at me for some time, establishing with her body and eyes the same sense of warning she had with her arrow. While I understood to an extent the wisdom in caution when meeting strangers, hers seemed to verge on the edge of paranoia, and I wondered why.

I stared back up at her openly, defenceless, more curious than anything.

We may have been strangers, but we were also two humans on a planet where humans were supposed to be extinct!

PART TWO

THE UNEXPECTED TWIST

CHAPTER TWENTY-ONE

T HE WOMAN FINALLY BROKE her stare, turning abruptly and disappearing behind the high cliff edge.

I didn't move to chase her, almost certain she was making her way down to me. No matter her cold exterior, I knew she was curious too. Any human stranger was cause for both great surprise *and* celebration in this time of human scarcity.

My mind fell onto Snow's whereabouts, not necessarily concerned for his safety as he was with Bear—he was *riding* Bear—but cautious all the same. I wanted to inspect this woman more closely before they returned. And I was in no hurry to give her more reason to mistrust me, which I was sure might happen if she saw a full-grown bear carrying my baby.

I called upon a body of wind, whispering into it a message with Bear in mind and heart.

"Don't come home. Not yet. Keep Snow safe, away, for now."

I closed my eyes and with a sweep of my hands and breath sent the message on the wind to find him.

Sounds of movement approached behind me—the crack of twigs under carefully treading feet, the crunching of dry autumn leaves. I turned and bright white eyes cut into me from behind dark skin.

The woman stepped out from behind the trees, bow drawn, its sharp, hand-carved arrow directed at my chest. I didn't flinch, doubting she would let it fly. *What human would kill another without solid reason in a time like this?*

Not this woman.

The closer she came, the more I could feel the softness of her spirit and the kindness of her intent. Her heart was open. She was human, *true* human.

A human of the New World.

She stepped with caution, but I could tell she hoped with all her heart that I was not dangerous. I could feel her so clearly, within the One, interconnected to a finer degree than I'd felt before. It proved that my merging with the element of Air was refining my ability to see and feel.

All beings on Earth lived and breathed and walked and thought and felt within the omniscient arms of the air. On this level, it made sense that the more I dissolved my sense of singular solidity into the expanse of its vast embrace, the more receptive I became to the energetic interplay that was but another aspect of each being, dancing beneath the surface but carried through the air just as legitimately as form.

"Who are you, Witch?" Her voice was as cutting as her eyes, but it was only an act. Her heart was warm, speaking to mine with joy she was barely able to suppress.

"I don't know," I answered honestly, although I knew 'Witch' didn't encompass all that I was and all that I was capable of doing within the realm of magic. "I am Maya. Born to humans of the Old World, but in heart, of the New World."

I saw a flicker of a smile over the woman's features.

"Also a Witch?"

"Not Witch. But I practise White Magic for the purpose of staying vigilant against the Sky People."

She tensed—at the mention of both White Magic and Sky People. Her bow was still drawn but not tight. Maybe I was being too transparent. Up until recently, I too would have been skeptical of anyone claiming the existence, let alone *use* of magic, white or otherwise.

"Sorry, I've been alone for a long time," I said, apologizing for my lack of social skills.

A smile flickered over her features again. She must have sensed the aliveness of my heart as I sensed hers, or at least saw the authenticity in my eyes, for she lowered the arrow.

"I am Anya. Also born of the Old World, but in a place that has become the New World."

"How did you survive?" we asked in unison, then laughed.

The tension eased between us.

"To be honest, I…it will sound crazy," I said.

"To be honest, I have heard the story of how you survived the end, but I am curious about how you have survived since, alone."

My heart beat fast and my mind raced with excitement over all that her words implied.

"And yes," she added. "It does sound crazy, but I can't discount the existence of this 'other realm' because it is true you are all here and you are different to other humans. Your tribe has learned things beyond what our kind had ever known." She watched me closely as she spoke, reading every flicker of movement across my face.

"My tribe?" My chest was on fire. I could barely hear my own thoughts.

"Yes, they live with us now."

Us?

Tears struck my eyes, suddenly overwhelmed with emotion.

"I'm sorry, it's just been a long time since…I didn't know if they were even still alive. This is…this is…" But I couldn't find a single word to express it.

She smiled freely for the first time. "I can imagine. Although I don't understand."

"So...?" Again, I didn't know where to start.

"Björn sent me here. He said he heard your voice on the wind with directions of where to find you," she shared.

I was surprised that my message had actually reached him, that the magic I sent it on actually *worked* and survived the distance.

"We initially thought what he told us confirmed his insanity. But we also couldn't ignore the possibility that it might be true. Of everything else your tribe shared with us of your past years since the Old World's end, this was one of the less obscure concepts to grasp."

"Why didn't he come here himself? Why did he send you?" I felt suddenly afraid of who these people she spoke of were, these survivors. If they were anything like the people of the Old World I had known, Björn may well have been trapped within a new system of control.

"And what do you mean by we? How many of you are there?" I added before she could reply.

She became less transparent, and I became less trusting.

She took some moments to decide on what to reveal and what to withhold. I didn't want to hear her calculated lies. I wanted to know if Björn was ok, if Björn was *free*.

"Björn is injured. He couldn't have travelled this far. He sent me because…he trusts me, I suppose," she began, somewhat easing my concern. "But he is ok and will be very happy to see you. As for the history of my people, I'm not sure where to start…"

"Let's sit down."

We both lowered onto the grass.

"We are a small clan of humans from different parts of the Old World, although the majority are from this country, which was once called Russia. We survived because we live underground. We were sure we were the last of humankind until your tribe found us."

Underground. Of course! Nature was never depleted underground, only above. But how did they escape the City?

I didn't have to ask.

"When the Institute of Technology was gaining more momentum and control over each country it governed, a group of Russian rebels formed, who foresaw the inevitability of the total lack of freedom that was falling over humanity.

"Long before the System locked everyone into the Iron City, they began building our underground city as a safe haven for people who were reluctant to serve the Control but still wanted to live in relative safety from the constant threat of natural disasters.

"At the beginning it was just a handful of them, acting under both their own ability to see the madness of what the Control was doing to our planet, and the guidance of an old, otherworldly Shaman, who shared insights into the true driving force behind the Institute of Technology.

"He was aware that an aspect of the human mind had been bought by foreign entities and shared what he could *see* only with those who had the clarity to *hear*. Still, very few believed him. But to some, it was the only explanation that made sense, and those who did believe were determined not to let their hearts die."

When I lived amongst them in the City, amongst the walking dead, I believed there was something wrong with *me* for having a heart that was warm and awake, not dormant like those around me. Until I met Björn. I would never forget the moment our hands touched for the first time. It was like a spark of fire. His skin was warm, hot, like mine. Up until that moment, I'd only ever been in contact with skin that was dead cold.

I had also believed that I was the only one who saw the world through a lens in which there was something not quite placeable in the picture, that it looked fundamentally *wrong*.

To hear now, after all this time, that there were others who saw, who survived in secret, and who still lived on, even after the rest of humanity was wiped from the planet, was the most impossible and relieving news I could have heard.

But their existence was not a complete secret.

The Mother had known. The Mother protected them. She had the power to wipe them out with the rest, but she *let* them live. And she was now, somehow, guiding us all together.

My heart was full of wonder.

"Both the Shaman and the rebels foresaw that as long as the Sky People had dictatorship over the Control, humanity, in their ignorance, would continue to deplete Earth until there was nothing of it left. They saw the inevitable end," Anya continued.

"So, they sought out environmental activists and scientists from across the globe and invited anyone who aligned with their mission to join them in creating a self-sustainable, biodynamic, underground community that could sustain a population of people, even if the earth's surface continued to self-destruct."

Anya spoke with the kind of clarity and presence that I'd grown used to seeing in the Samãdhi people. Her senses were sharp. She was not trapped in ignorance, or a self-indulgent, ego-centric existence. It gave me hope that this underground clan she spoke of was also free from Shadows, as her story led me to assume.

It took some time to process this new reality—the reality in which the humans in my tribe were not, as I had previously believed, the only humans left on Earth.

She was still watching me closely, and now I knew she was watching for any hint of my being infected by Shadows.

"Why here?" I asked. It all seemed too convenient. "Why did they choose to build it in Russia?"

She was patient with my questions.

"Dmitri, the man who had the initial idea to create an underground city, was from a family of cave tour guides. They owned one of the biggest natural caves in Russia. By the time the plans had been developed and finalised, his parents had retired and passed the cave into his ownership. He closed it to tourists and began building it into what it is today.

"It was a risk—on a number of levels. The Arctics were melting fast and the waters were rising, but the cave was located inland enough not to drown. The planet was overheating and many areas of land were already unable to sustain human life.

"But the cold climate here was maintained enough for freshwater not to stagnate, and Dmitri believed it would freeze again if the conditions on Earth somehow improved, which it has. Faster than any of us imagined.

"When the earth is in a state of global warming, ice—or even just the potential of ice—is a treasure," she explained.

"You said it's inland. To be honest, I have no idea where I am geographically. Are we close here?" I asked.

"Russia is, or was, a large continent."

"And you travelled alone?"

"I prefer to travel alone. Being so closely contained with people underground can get…claustrophobic."

Every one of her answers only sparked more questions, but I realised that if she had travelled so far, she would appreciate a rest.

"Are you hungry? I can make you something. You've probably already noticed this area isn't scarce," I offered.

"Thank you. That's kind of you. It's…very impressive." Her eyes left me for the first time to take in the abundance of nature around us.

"I haven't seen anything like this outside of the farms of our community. But we planted our gardens and put a lot of work into maintaining them." She shook her head with a sense of disbelief, but the evidence was right there.

CHAPTER TWENTY-TWO

ONLY WITH THE ADDITION of company, I could see with fresh eyes how the once bare cave had been transformed into a cosy living space. It truly felt like home now —although I was acutely aware of Anya's speculation over my obsessive drawings over the wall, which were now also decorated with more abstract art by Snow.

Anya wasn't a passive guest. She helped me chop vegetables and answered patiently as I asked question after question about the underground city that had survived the Old World's end.

I was eager to see it, and even more eager to see Björn. My excitement made it hard to speak or think clearly. But it would have been unkind not to offer her at least a night's rest before asking her to begin back on the roadless road again.

When it was obvious she wasn't dangerous, I called Bear back.

Just be calm and extra friendly. We have a visitor, I warned him, still not entirely sure the messages were being received— and even if they were, how he understood the human language. But the fact that it was already so late in the day and he hadn't returned yet was evidence he understood; he'd never kept Snow out this long before.

The vegetables we prepared were boiling and the sound of the bubbling water elevated my anticipation.

Until now, we had lived in a bubble of our own, protected. Just us. I was nervous about introducing the rest of my unconventional family to this stranger. But I couldn't ask Bear to keep Snow away all night, and I knew that come tomorrow, we'd all be travelling together to a place full of strangers. It was inevitable.

The sky was pink when I heard the thumps of a four-legged animal moving closer to the cave. Anya caught the sound shortly after and studied me with suspicious eyes.

I didn't prepare her for the sight that would confront us only moments later. I didn't know how to explain it. So, I just let it happen.

Anya leapt swiftly up onto her feet and drew her bow.

"It's ok." I jumped up beside her and stood in front of her arrow.

"They're not dangerous."

"They?"

"Just trust me. Put the bow down. You'll see."

She lowered her aim but still held the arrow between her fingertips, ready to re-draw.

A low whining noise came from outside the cave and after a few more crunching sounds, Bear stepped around the rocky edge.

Anya stepped back, her eyes wide and sharp and not leaving the hefty animal as he continued slowly and harmlessly inside. He whined again, nodding his head at the unfamiliar woman, as if in greeting.

Her eyes flickered to me then back to Bear, before noticing the small child who was nestled behind the thick fur of his neck.

Snow's fair face broke into a sweet smile when his eyes landed on me. He bent down to kiss Bear on the top of his head before reaching out his arms as I walked to him.

"Hey Snowy," I lifted him from Bear's back and onto my hip, then turned back to Anya who waited impatiently for an explanation.

"Anya, this is Bear and Snow. They are my family here."

She nodded slowly, unsure of which of them to be more surprised by. Björn wasn't aware I'd been pregnant, so he couldn't have prepared her to find me with a baby. And nothing could have prepared her for the friendly bear he rode.

"The bear is your family," she repeated.

"He's been with me since he was a baby. He's the reason I found this place. He led me here not long after I'd been separated from my tribe." After a pause, I added, "I was pregnant when I lost them, but I didn't know it until it really started showing. Björn is Snow's father."

I let that information settle before going on.

"They kind of grew up together. Bear behaves more like a human than an animal. He's very intuitive and caring and..." I paused, watching as Bear stepped cautiously towards the woman.

"And Snow sometimes behaves more like an animal than a human," I laughed, eyes skimming the innocent boy in my arms.

But all of Anya's attention was on Bear. She lowered her arrow to the ground and held out her hand. Bear sniffed it, then leant his forehead down to rest on her palm. She closed her eyes, taking a full breath, allowing herself to connect into his essence, which was unmistakably kind and loving.

"Hello, Bear," she finally said, reopening her eyes. "He's beautiful."

I smiled. The water in the pot was loud, almost boiling over. Dusk was settling in the air.

Bear continued inside and slumped down in front of the fire. I placed Snow down beside him while I removed the pot and finished preparing the food.

Snow was wary of the new woman in our home. This was the first human he'd met aside from me.

"Hello, Snow. I'm Anya." She knelt down to his level.

After staring with eyes as cautious as they were curious, he crawled closer and reached out to touch her cheek like he did when greeting animals. He was intrigued by the dark shade of her skin and features, and her black hair, which was twirled and tied into long knots. I watched them in my peripherals but tried not to impose.

Anya camped with us for the night, although she slept just outside the cave, respectful of our private space. I slept lightly, waking at the slightest sounds. She seemed trustworthy and already felt like a friend, but I couldn't be *sure* she didn't have alternative motives. Snow slept curled up in my arms, and I in the arms of Bear, who acted like a shield.

I got the sense she was withholding information. She wouldn't speak in detail about my tribe, only saying they had been living with their underground community for about a year. It was still strange to me that she was the one who came to find me if they were all there. She explained that Björn was injured, but what about the rest of them?

After lying restlessly for some time, I heard the light twinkling sound of the Fξ drifting towards me and sat upright.

The exuberance of their beings shimmered like stars in the darkness, moving towards me. Just two of them: Théodren and Lupïta.

We can trust her, right? I asked when they stopped to hover in front of me, knowing I could trust their sensitivity to light and density more than my own.

Her energy field is not corrupted by Shadows, Théodren confirmed. *She is light and open in both heart and spirit. I sense no danger.*

Lupïta agreed. *You can sleep peacefully Maya. We will stay with you tonight in case anything changes.*

Thank you.

When I slid to lie back down, Snow's eyes fluttered open. He smiled lazily at the vibrant light beings floating above us before drifting back to sleep.

CHAPTER TWENTY-THREE

A S SOON AS THE slightest glow of dawn touched the dark sky the next morning, I was wide awake and rose from my furs to pack for a relatively long journey, uncertain of when and whether we'd return.

I packed essentials for both me and Snow, and anything of significant value, and stored everything else at the back of the cave. The FξŸa stayed in the sanctuary, and I left the protective light shield active around it—not that it demanded ongoing effort to maintain.

Bear made travelling easy by carrying Snow and a few of my bags strapped to his back with agility that made the extra weight seem like no burden at all.

I walked beside Anya, and we walked for days.

The landscape was relatively barren compared to the abundance of nature we left behind. Nature was regrowing but not as rapidly. We walked over miles of dry, undulating lands and rocky plains, through grassy valleys, and between mountains. There were odd trees and animals, but it was all spread out.

We followed a fresh, flowing river that led us to a mountainous area where nature was richer and fields of farmland were evenly sectioned out over the flat ground around. The river became a wide lake that snaked through a crevasse between two peaks and continued an unforeseeable way into the distance.

There were human silhouettes in the distance, and I heard the echo of voices calling to one another. I assumed they'd spotted us too. They may have been aware of Anya's hunt for the woman of Björn's heart, but like her, nothing could have prepared them for Bear or the boy.

Anya held up her hands in a peacekeeping gesture, along with a sound that was like a bird call. The high pitch would have been sure to carry the distance where a normal, human call could have easily been lost in the space between.

I couldn't see the cave entrance yet, and Anya stopped us before continuing any further.

"I'm sorry." Her expression was truly apologetic as she drew a long-torn material out of her waist belt.

I stepped back, alarmed.

"Is that necessary?" I asked, *sure* she was aware it was not.

What could I possibly do to harm them? Just one girl against an entire community?

The more logical question was what could *they* do to harm me? An entire community against one girl. The possibilities that followed seemed far more threatening.

"It's an over-precaution. But security is important to our leaders. It's not often we get outsiders," she justified, which was an obvious overstatement.

But I understood their vigilance and surrendered to their game. Even if they *were* dangerous, I wasn't going to do anything to jeopardize my chance to reunite with Björn and the rest of the tribe.

I let Anya tie the material around my eyes. Bear growled in warning and I'm sure she understood it would be foolish to put me in any kind of harm when I had an ally like him on my side.

I reached out and patted his nose gently.

"It's ok, I'm ok," I told him.

She didn't cover his eyes or Snow's. As long as Bear was with us, I felt secure enough to go in blind, trusting him to be my eyes.

I slid my hand along Bear's back and found Snow's small, silky hand, while Anya guided my step with the other. The lack of sight made my other senses naturally switch on, including the more celestial senses.

Before we reached the opening, I felt the weight in the air of numerous bodies ahead containing warm, beating hearts. Their auric fields radiated far wider than their bodies. The collective energy field wasn't negative or dark, just dense because they were all mixing and merging, making it harder for me to get a clear reading.

I couldn't sense the eerie, black presence that was distinctive of Sky Consciousness, which was an immense relief. Even if there were a few amongst them gripped by Shadows, they weren't a dominant force within the community.

The atmosphere began to cool as we stepped beneath a canopy of shade-bearing trees. The breeze was refreshing against my sweaty skin.

The air grew cooler still when we reached the mountain base where I heard swift footsteps approaching.

"What is this?" The man's harsh accent exaggerated the sense of urgency in his words. I assumed it was Russian, but I'd never met a Russian, so I couldn't be sure.

There was fear in the Air.

Bear growled.

My hot heart skipped, and I was milliseconds away from tearing the pointless material from my eyes when Anya intervened. She dropped my hand, and I felt her warm Shadow as she stepped protectively in front of us.

"Stop." Her tone was authoritative.

The shuffling sounds ceased.

Her energy spoke for her intent, and I trusted her. I remained still, to prove that I was unthreatening and so as not to add to the tension.

"They are *all* safe.*"

Bear let out a low, surrendering whine. I assumed she'd touched his nose, which to him was a peaceful gesture.

Snow, on the other hand, let out a slight cry of distress and in it I could hear his uncertainty. He wasn't used to people, and these people sounded fierce, sharp-edged, much like Anya. I could only feel two unfamiliar human auras at that point, but I imagined they wore expressions that matched the severity in their voices.

"This is Bear." I was still blind but spoke in their direction. "He is my companion. And Snow is my son."

The people shifted slightly in energy, opening. While still guarded, curiosity replaced their initial fear.

"We will come through and introduce them to the community at once," Anya told them.

They wanted to hear the full story immediately but didn't argue. I wondered what her role was there.

"Are you suggesting we lead the bear inside?" one of them asked.

"It could feed us all for days. And the fur..." the other said more quietly.

Bear growled again.

"He's not a bear," I said before they could entertain this idea any further.

"Do you not understand the word *companion*?" Anya followed with disdain, as if disappointed in his response.

But I realised he might not be the only one to see Bear as food.

My blindness became more burdensome. I wanted to monitor the community's reaction when we entered and be one step ahead, not behind. But I laid my trust in Anya. Off what I'd heard just now, she would protect us.

I squeezed Snow's hand and he squeezed mine back.

"Denis, make sure no one does anything stupid when they see him ok? And Maks, call everyone to meet in the community centre."

The sound of feet shuffling gradually faded as Maks disappeared into the mountain. Denis stayed with us, as an extra bodyguard.

Anya reached to take my hand again, leading us forward.

"Wait," I said. "I want to ride Bear too."

There was a pause.

"If I can't see them, I need to feel them."

I'd gone from years of living in uninterrupted freedom to being forced to walk into a new environment completely blind. It was unsettling and gave me chilling reminders of the Control. I caught myself hoping again that this community wasn't anything like the Old Society was…

Anya had assured me that they lived freely under the *guidance* of a leadership, but 'freedom' could have immensely different implications to different people according to circumstance.

"Ride the Bear," Anya said, and helped me step my leg up and over behind Snow.

His little body fell back into my embrace. He was unsettled too but less so now that I was up there with him. At least he could see. He was far more intelligent and alert than anyone would assume for his age; he would warn me if anything was alarming about where we headed.

I reached my hand down to rub Bear's back.

"Follow Anya inside," I told him, and when the woman stepped forward, so did he.

CHAPTER TWENTY-FOUR

T HE AIR WAS DAMP within the cold stone walls when we entered the mountain opening, and the tunnel into the ground was long and downward sloping. It wasn't very high. I could feel the presence of the roof close to the crown of my head from my raised position on Bear's back.

I didn't feel claustrophobic as we continued deeper underground. There was ventilation, a flow of fresh air moving through. It was quiet but for the shuffling and crunching of our feet over the sandy stone, and the echo of odd dripping sounds.

The echo of voices also began travelling down the tunnel, and the walls that enveloped us gradually moved further away. We were reaching another opening.

I anticipated the moment that Björn rushed towards us. Word would have spread about our arrival by now.

But he didn't. No one did.

When the voices became louder, Anya stopped us again.

"Ok Maya," she said quietly. "You can take off your blindfold."

It took a moment for my eyes to adjust after being squashed behind the tough material. The blurred light pouring in from the opening was bright and yellow, but the light that lit the tunnel was unlike any I'd ever seen. The stone was lined with vivid, electric-blue, bead-shaped lights.

At first, they could have been mistaken as FξŸa, but they weren't FξŸa. They were glow worms. Their delicate strings of sticky silk hung elegantly down like chandeliers, glowing the same fluorescent glow as their bodies.

I momentarily forgot where we were and why we were there.

"This is the communal meeting place up ahead. Everyone will be waiting here to meet you. Are you ready?"

I nodded in a state of mindless wonder, still staring at the natural, living lights.

Anya walked on with Denis by her side, who I saw now for the first time. His build was tall but slim, and he had short black hair and white skin. They both held their bows at the ready, although I doubted they expected to use them. It allowed me to relax, knowing that we—and most importantly Bear—were under their protection.

Bear walked on behind them, each step rocking me gently from side to side. I bent down to kiss Snow's crown.

He'd been very quiet, his eyes wide as he too took in the new surroundings. He reached out his hand, as if expecting one of the glow worms to drift over and rest on his palm.

"They're not FξŸa, Snowy," I told him.

My heart beat faster as a mob of people came into view through the high rock opening at the end of the tunnel. This room was lit by artificial lights, and I was surprised. I didn't think electricity still existed—though, later I learnt that the whole underground city functioned on solar power. Power from the sun and wind and running water.

The founders were explorers, environmentalists, and environmental scientists, after all. This was a manifestation of their creative, unconventional thinking combined with their passion for the preservation of the natural world, and nature-based sustainability.

I couldn't help but wonder though, why they still chose to live underground when the land was safe and nature was steadily growing again above.

All casual conversations ceased the moment our shadows imprinted themselves upon the stone floor in front of us.

I took a breath, rolled my shoulders back, and looked out over the crowd as Bear stepped through the archway, into the light. There was a giant, round Persian rug in the centre where the community gathered, woven into geometric patterns from earthy shades of deep red, orange, yellow, and brown.

Sounds of surprise and disbelief rippled through the crowd, and when I scanned each face, they wore expressions that matched. They were, in body, generally fit, strong, healthy-looking humans, of all different colours and racial blends, but there was a dominating race among them that appeared pure, which I assumed was Russian.

Pure races were rare in the Iron City of the Old World, where mating was based on DNA matching. Race wasn't a considered factor so over time, they all blended. All that mattered was that each offspring was the most optimized possible version of each genetic pair.

My heartbeat accelerated, pounded, stimulated by the amount of human energy in the room. Again, not because it was inherently negative or dark; it was just a lot to take in at once.

Then something strange started happening.

Thoughts.

Thoughts began racing through my mind. Before that moment, my mind had been relatively clear—or at least organised. Now, it rushed with a river of thoughts, too many at once to make sense of them.

As I listened more carefully, it became obvious they weren't *mine*, nor were they sent by the Shadows. They were thoughts that gave words to the surprise and curiosity of the humans in the room.

I was hearing other people's thoughts.

She's riding a bear!

What is she?
Is she a witch?
Food?
Animal whisperer.
My head swirled.

I felt hot and took deeper breaths, attempting to block the sounds that drifted upon the airwaves from entering my mind.

"This is Maya," Anya introduced me loudly, her voice echoing off the rounded rock walls. "This is her companion, Bear, and her son, Snow."

Companion? A bear? Not possible.

She must be a witch.

Anya should not be so quick to trust strangers. She already bought in a contaminated one.

This thought captured my attention and I tried to stay focus more directly on the mind that thought it but I lost the stream. If this was part of my Air abilities, I had no control over it. What did they mean by 'contaminated'?

I tried to be polite by smiling but it was weak. I sat once again on the edge of two worlds, not entirely present in either. In-between.

One was the simple world of the physical. Simple only in that it existed in plain sight. Anyone with eyes could read and interpret its interplays relatively accurately if they chose to watch closely.

The other world, the energy world, was ever more complex because it was subtle, invisible. Well, invisible to others, but less so to me.

"The bear is under my protection until they are all settled here. No one may touch him without my permission, which will, of course, come through Maya. She is the one who can communicate with the animal."

Communicate? She is an animal whisperer!

Anya looked up to where I sat, braced on Bear's back, then continued introducing us, recognising that I was a little too overwhelmed to speak to the eager audience directly.

"The three of them have lived alone for the past years since being separated from their tribe, the tribe that also belongs to Björn…"

I couldn't focus on her words any longer, but they were accurate, so I trusted her to continue. She was an engaging storyteller. The audience was captivated.

Upon hearing Björn's name I felt his presence like a wave breaking over me, swallowing me.

Our connection, now that we were in close proximity was intense, like two sparks meeting, merging. He felt so close he could have been right beside me, but my eyes scanned the room, searching. He wasn't there.

His presence, however, became so intense I could barely discern what was my experience and what was his. My awareness and point of centre were no longer locked into my body; they became loose, malleable. And my etheric body, the one that was a less dense formation of L·ight Màttẹr than my physical body, began moving, skipping between locations through the portal of an In-Between dimension.

It was a dimension of the Earth realm—not separate like Santōṣha, but a less defined dimension, where the laws of density were not fixed. It was the dimension where the etheric elements of our existence co-existed with the manifest, inconspicuously dictating what occurred in solid form.

It was a silent dimension.

White. But not white.

Transparent, but not entirely.

It was like soaring through a vast unending fog, so fast it felt slow, timeless. Everything was hazy but at the same time, crisp, pristine. Sounds didn't register in the same way they normally would. Everything sounded foreign, muffled, as if occurring beneath a blanket.

It wasn't frightening.

Fear didn't exist there.

The frequency was so light that I barely felt any emotion at all that wasn't sweet and loving and calm.

Still.

So still.

It was just I alone there, but at the same time, the me that I was wasn't me in the same way that I usually experienced myself to be in form. I was not separate from the essence of life through which I drifted. A mass of L·ight Màttẹr within the one mass—that's truly what it felt like.

At first, from within the fog, a sense of being in two places at once developed, or at least jumping between the two at impossible speeds. Then my vision began travelling with it.

I began to see stone walls around me that were different to the ones in the room I arrived in. It was a smaller cavern within the same cave. And there was no one else in this one but the human whose eyes I was looking through.

Björn.

And when my awareness was seeing through his eyes, I felt what he felt, and he felt…off.

He felt…not afraid…but agitated. Angry. A little desperate. He'd been trapped within the confines of that small, dark, cold space for some time. Some time that was beginning to feel like too long.

Isolation was wearing on him. But something else was too. Something even more prominent...

My vision flickered again. Back into the timeless mist, back into my body in the cave. Back into the mist. Back into Björn. Back into the mist. Back into my body.

Disorientated, my weight swayed on Bear's back.

Björn wasn't in the crowd, and I finally knew why. He couldn't have been even if he wanted to. And he was calling to me, just as I was to him. He knew I'd arrived.

"Björn," I muttered mindlessly.

I'm sure I looked drunk, but I had no control over my body. No centre.

"Mumma," Snow's quiet voice echoed.

He turned to touch his hand to my cheek. He knew I wasn't *there*. But I didn't know how to fully return.

My weight swayed again, and I slid sideways from Bear's back. By this point Anya had noticed, and both Denis and Maks raced to catch me.

My eyes rolled back.

CHAPTER TWENTY-FIVE

S ILENCE.
  Nothing.

White. But not white.

I had no sense of place. The totality of my awareness was inside the In-between now, away from the safety of my unconscious body.

Beauty.

It felt so beautiful, so exquisite.

Free and uninhibited.

Life.

In the appearance of nothingness.

It was the fabric that all of life was weaved upon. The vast sea that each wave fell back into once its dance was done. It was not an unfamiliar place.

Why is it that I often end up here?

The agreement of human form generally bound our experience to the one dimension of which we were born. What lay beyond, before, and after life was a mystery. It was *supposed* to be a mystery. But apparently, not to me.

Apparently, I was not supposed to be confined to the earthbound body I wore, although I kept returning to it. There was still a pull, a purpose to complete in the physical realm.

But here, I was nothing and everything all at once. And through the interconnectivity of everything, I was being drawn towards Björn.

My drifting awareness travelled once again from the mist and back into his body, joining him there.

This time, as I experienced what he experienced, I knew for certain that something was very wrong.

He was heavy.

Weighed down by a density that I could only conclude were Shadows. I could not feel his heart. It was blocked.

He'd been infected—to a degree that I hadn't seen before.

Well, at least not quite so clearly, and not quite like this. This was how the humans of the Old World lived. Worse, actually. But they had for years, from the very moment of birth, accumulated the negative patterning that dimmed their hearts and attracted Shadows.

The Old World was a maze of thoughts and belief systems and social conditions that all supported the survival of Shadows.

Björn had developed his new armour too quickly, in a place that was relatively clean of outside influence. But something was missing. *Where is Björn's light?*

When I felt the Shadow wrapped around Chaṅtara, it was thin. Her light beneath was still present, just dim.

With Björn, all I felt was pain. Immense pain.

Too much. I could not stay there.

He'd been writing and drawing things on the walls, scratching them into the stone with a sharp blade. Things that were not human. Things that were channelled through him from Sky Consciousness.

Harsh lines. Structures. Numbers. Codes. Machines. As if he alone planned to rebuild the Old World.

Maybe he's not alone.

Maybe this is what the cave people want. They fed him to the Shadows and now the Shadows are feeding him their knowledge.

Did they plan to do it to me? And Snow? Snow was pure. Where was he? Where was Snow?!

My eyes opened abruptly.

All the colour of the world rushed back in, although the dominating colour was grey.

Everything was crisp. Every curve and indent in the rough stone appeared to me in high definition.

I was on a cushioned bed, comfortable, but the synthetic kind. It had been a long time since I'd felt anything so…machine-made.

"Where's Snow?" I demanded before moving to look at the person shuffling in the room beside me.

I knew it wasn't Snow.

"It's ok, he's safe. He's with—"

"Don't touch him." I sat up.

The woman's eyes were kind. Genuinely so, but I couldn't trust her. I couldn't trust any of them until I knew exactly what was going on.

"And Bear?" I was suddenly afraid I'd been tricked and they might have already captured him, or worse.

"They're together. They're ok. Really."

"And what about Björn then? Is he ok? Because he definitely doesn't feel ok." I was attacking the woman with my words, perhaps a little indecently, but I didn't care for decency when everyone I loved may well be in danger.

Her expression shifted from hospitable to uncertain. She was dressed in what looked like nurse attire.

Maks entered the room, the one who had suggested Bear be food.

"If you touch Bear—"

But he cut me off.

"The bear will come to no harm here. He is our guest. We can see he is not just a bear, like you said." He was speaking gently now too, as gently as his harsh accent would allow.

My eyes darted around the basic medical room. "And our stuff, where's our stuff?"

"Me and Denis took it to your room."

"What if I don't want a room? What if I want to leave?" I suddenly felt trapped. A wave of fear rushed over me. Control. This was my biggest fear. It pressed down my chest.

"Maya, you are a guest, that is all. You are free," the woman said softly.

"And Björn? Is Björn free?"

Why were they being so *nice*?! I knew they were hiding something. But I had to find Bear and Snow before interrogating them.

I stood up a little too hastily and staggered to the door.

"Woah, careful." Maks put a hand on my back for support. I barely let him make contact before flicking it off.

"Don't touch me."

I swung open the door, stepping out into the communal space where we'd entered. There was a gathering of kids in the middle.

CHAPTER TWENTY-SIX

B EAR MADE A WHINING noise as soon as he sensed my presence. He lifted his head, drawing my attention to where he rested tamely on one of the old, oriental rugs, in the centre of the swarming kids. The adults in the room stood back respectfully, but their attention was on the big, brown animal.

He was highly alert in the company of so many strangers, and while he acted placid on the surface, I sensed his underlying agitation and unease.

Snow was uneasy too, but he did not hide it. He'd never seen other human kids before, and in that moment they were buoyant, lively, and excitable, not quiet and cautious like the animals he was used to interacting with upon first meeting. He sank back into Bear's fur, watching the kids with wide eyes as they watched his bear friend.

Anya was beside Snow, holding his hand, and I was grateful that he trusted her—we'd only known her a short time. She was also monitoring the kids who tried to pet and poke at Bear, knowing well he was no toy.

Some of the adults turned their curiosity towards me as I walked towards them, and Snow looked as relieved to see me as I felt to see him safe.

He twisted, using Bear to push himself up to stand, and walked to meet me. The kids around him moved aside to create a passageway between us. The rugs were warm beneath my bare feet, counteracting the chill of the cool air.

I rushed forwards and wrapped him tighter than ever in my arms. It had been a long time since I'd felt such a rush of emotion. Motherly protection was a force not to be messed with.

I sat down beside Bear with Snow in my arms, comforted by their warmth, and looked beside me to Anya with appreciative eyes. She nodded, understanding.

But my relief didn't last.

"What happened to Björn?" If anyone was going to tell me the truth it was her.

Her expression tensed. She looked down at the small group of kids in front of us, then to their parents, who caught on promptly and began chaperoning their kids away.

Her piercing eyes seemed to put both adults and children on edge, intimidating them—but not purposefully. They were just honest and alert. Hyper-alert?

Her wooden bow was still strapped around her chest and a handwoven pocket of arrows fastened to her back. Maybe she just forgot to take them off...

"I'll take you to see him. He's been quarantined," Anya said plainly.

Quarantined? Is that what they call imprisonment here?

"What have you done to him?" The fire in my heart had not been ceased by her apparent cooperation.

She squatted down beside me so we could speak more intimately, although the room was swiftly clearing.

"Tried to save him. That is all. We found him this way. Both him and Chantara. They were inside one of the iron ships. That's how they were surviving. And it affected their minds. Severely. We knew the ships were dangerous, but…" She trailed off.

The room was quiet now. I struggled to accept her words.

"You've seen the ships of the Sky People? They're here?"

"You haven't?" She sounded as surprised as I was.

"No."

"Sorry, I assumed you'd have seen at least one. There are a number around. We've mapped all the locations we're aware of so we can avoid them. They're the reason we still live underground. They send out frequencies that are...painful. It's hard to explain.

"But nature has power over them. They can't penetrate deep earth. I'd say that's probably why they didn't land anywhere where you've been living either. Nature is too dominant there."

"If there are so many, why didn't we pass any on our way here?" I asked, sure I would have noticed if we had.

"You think I would lie about this?"

It was a fair point. But Anya explained herself anyway, aware my interrogative tone was only a product of my fear and lack of knowledge.

"I passed one on my journey to you but made sure to steer a clear path on our way back. Even from a distance, our bodies react against them, sometimes so violently we can't think straight. And loss of mental clarity is something we all know we cannot risk."

So, she knew more about the Sky People than she originally let on.

"Why didn't you tell me any of this before?"

"I didn't know I needed to."

"About Björn, I mean. Don't you think that's important information to share?" My mind was skipping between subjects, trying to piece it all together at once.

"I didn't know how you'd respond or if you'd believe me. I couldn't be sure you weren't infected too." Anya paused.

"I didn't want to say anything that might interfere with your decision to come," she said more directly. "If it's true that you have insights into the Shadow world that we don't have, and potential powers over them. You might be able to heal him in a way that no one here can. You are our last chance." Her tone was serious now.

The words 'last chance' sent another spike of fear through my chest. What would happen if I failed?

"He may be new here, but we understand that the life of every human on Earth is valuable to its survival. We don't want to give up on him, or anyone else who might get infected in the future, but no one here has the skills to help him."

I suddenly felt crippled by the weight of responsibility. Pressure had never been a motivating force for me. It only made me want to shrink and hide. But beneath my lack of confidence in the rumoured 'healing powers' I might have, I knew that if anyone could draw Björn out of the Shadows' grip, it was me.

Love is a force that can achieve impossible things.

But does he even still love me? After all this time?

"What about the blindfold and all the secrecy?" I was still confused by what Anya's actions spoke of her intentions. "Can you be straight with me now? I'm here. And I won't leave until Björn is free." Both internally *and* externally.

"I can," she said. "And it is true, I have been withholding things from you. In honesty, it's kind of a test we do. To see how people behave under pressure, and lack of understanding creates pressure. Anyone can be nice on the surface, and it can take a long time before their true inners are exposed.

"We can't afford to have dangerous people here. It's too precious. Putting people under some kind of pressure from the beginning has, historically, been our way of weeding out anyone who might otherwise be a burden to our community later," she explained.

"I trusted you very soon after meeting you, but one person's judgement is not enough to put the whole community at ease."

I let out a breath and surrendered. I couldn't argue with their logic. In fact, it was comforting to know that they had filters for the people they chose to build their community with.

For all they knew, I could have been like Björn, or Chaṅtara—who hid her infection well. It was only in the storm, when she was under extreme pressure, that the Shadows stirred fully to the surface.

"Where are Bǒdhi and Phǒenix, and Moānā and Ṫassie?" I hadn't seen them in the crowd either, but Anya had mentioned they were there.

"They don't know you're here," she said. "I was lying when I told you that they were out hunting when Björn shared with us the message. But that is where they are now. They left a day ago and should be back soon."

At least she was being transparent now.

"I suppose there's a good reason why you kept Björn's message from them too?"

"We didn't want to raise their hopes in case it was a delusion, which we considered a higher possibility than it being true. We haven't had anyone with those kinds of...celestial abilities here, not since the Shaman who helped establish the city, and he died a long time ago. It all sounds very otherworldly to us. We live a very raw existence here. Survival is our priority, and maintaining this system of living without it getting polluted like so many systems have in the past..."

There was a sense of curiosity and mystery in her eyes around the idea of 'celestial abilities,' but she didn't probe.

"We also could not risk your tribe's attachment to you clouding their judgement if you were found in a bad state. It was a problem when Björn arrived."

"So, who is 'we'?" I asked. "How many of you are there in this inner circle of decision making?"

Based on what Anya painted with her words, the leaders of the underground city were wiser and more reasonable than those in Control of the Old System. But I was still skeptical.

She glanced up over my shoulder, expression hardening as she watched someone approach behind me.

"Maya." Another harsh Russian accent. A woman.

I turned.

She had white skin, brown eyes, and long, silk blond hair. She was dressed in a floor length, scarlet-red velvet dress, and antique golden jewellery featuring a rainbow of diamonds, which made her stand out from the rest of the people who were casually dressed in old, worn-down clothes. The manner in which she carried herself spoke of her authority.

"Welcome to our home," she said with a courtsea. "I am Katya."

A dark-skinned man came up behind her, placing a hand on her shoulder. I'd met enough leaders now to recognise them as the headman and woman of the community.

"This is Yegor," Katya introduced her partner.

A welcoming smile reached his brown eyes. He wore a matching scarlet-red velvet suit that made them, together, appear like ancient royalty.

"I hope my sister has been welcoming," Yegor said with a hint of humour in his eyes as he glanced at Anya.

When Anya had spoken briefly of the leaders, she never mentioned her brother was one of them. It made sense of the heightened respect people treated her with.

But she did not dress like them to earn it.

She didn't seem to take any pride in her appearance at all. She wore practical brown leather, animal hide, and hemp.

"She's been very kind," I said honestly.

Katya readjusted the spotted fur shawl around her shoulders that looked like it came from a snow leopard.

She must have caught my look and detected my distrust. "We may live underground, but that does not mean we must be primates," she said.

"Our ancestors prepared this place for decades before The End finally hit us. They collected many of Russia's fine treasures while more and more people evacuated the crumbling country. It was hurricanes that hit us the hardest. They tore up our towns, and the rebels went around scavenging anything they could use to develop city. They also stole treasures from ruined museums and sacred sites," she explained.

"Not that they have any value in the New World,' she added. "They are just pretty to the eye. The true treasures in present times are nature and harmonious existence."

As she spoke I realised her costume was less self-important and more playful. When I tuned into her heart it was light, as was her partner's, and they seemed to function with high clarity that was not clouded by self-obsession.

But there was tension between them and Anya—or more accurately, tension in Anya. She had turned cold again in their presence.

I watched the behaviour of the few people still scattered around us. They behaved freely. They didn't close or shrink in fear in their leaders' presence, which would have been an immediate sign of a toxic dictatorship.

"Come, let us show you around," Yegor offered.

"Thank you, but I want to see Björn first," I told him.

"I was about to take her down," Anya told them.

They were hesitant, which made me more determined to see him immediately.

"Actually, would you mind showing me? Snow trusts Anya. If she could stay and look after him that would be better than having to take him with me." I trailed off, hiding the wave of sadness I felt.

This was not the reunion I'd imagined in *any* of my countless fantasies over our time apart. While part of me was impatient to introduce them, Snow's first meeting with his father couldn't happen while Björn was in the state that he was. Above all, he was dangerous—apparently so dangerous he had to be quarantined in the farthest cavern of the deepest tunnel in the largest cave in Russia.

I took a breath.

I let it go.

At least he was alive.

"Of course," Katya finally said. "Maybe we can give you a tour on the way back."

I bent back down to kiss Snow's forehead.

"I'm going to leave you with Anya ok?" His ice-like eyes stared back at me. "You like Anya right?"

"Anya…" He looked up at the dark women, then nodded. Anya bent down and sat beside him, her cold exterior melting again to meet him in his openness.

I stood. "I won't be gone for long, ok?"

It wasn't like he wasn't used to being apart. He just wasn't used to being around so many people.

"If he gets overwhelmed just take him and Bear somewhere quiet, or back outside," I told Anya, hoping we weren't trapped now that we were inside. Just the thought made my heart compress.

She nodded.

"Ok, let's go," I said to the leaders, back up on their level.

CHAPTER TWENTY-SEVEN

T HE CAVE WAS DEEP and spacious, with many tunnels leading to different sections, some man-dug, some natural, most altered in some way. I began to understand why they called it a city. Its structure was clearly thoroughly considered and mapped before its construction.

There were sections that resembled urban streets, with sleeping hollows built into the walls. We passed through a tunnel lined with 'shops' organised into different food groups—dry, meat, vegetables, fruits, and so on—while the following tunnel was dedicated to clothes and other material goods.

There were only two women running each tunnel. There weren't enough people in the city to create high demand. A few children ran around playing, and I assumed the shop holders were their mothers.

"How do people buy things?" I'd been set on going directly to Björn without interruption but became curious about their system.

I'd never seen or imagined anything like it, and still wasn't sure how I felt about it all. There was something eerie there, even with all the smiling, apparently peaceful faces I saw. Humans were a cunning species. I couldn't believe that this entire clan survived, free of Shadows. It didn't make sense when the rest of humanity had been swallowed by them.

"There's an exchange of tokens," Yegor began.

"Money," I interrupted.

"In some ways it's like money," he agreed. "But it's simpler. No one is any richer than anyone else unless they choose to work more hours. There is no need to be rich here though. There is a certain standard of living that is not really possible to climb above," Yegor explained with a slight laugh.

"What about you two? You dress like you're richer. Are you a special exception because you're the leaders?"

His heart remained light, unbothered by my scepticism, and he exchanged a look with Katya.

"It's just a game, Maya. Anyone is welcome to play. Including you, if you'd like?" She rubbed her hand along her extravagant scarf in gesture.

"No thanks."

Yegor returned to the previous topic.

"We all work around the same hours each day, doing what is necessary to keep the city running, but no more. And we encourage our people to take on jobs they are somewhat passionate or naturally skilled at. We have our growers, harvesters, water collectors, cooks, storefront servers, hunters, medicine people, solar energy converters, public cleaners, and so on.

"It all seems to work quite well, although there are always adjustments being made. No system is perfect, but we all understand how lucky we are just to be alive and safe in a place not dictated by the Institute of Technology."

"It must get intense sometimes though, everyone being so close," I probed.

"It is true. The conditions are not always ideal or easy, especially for introverts. But there is also a mutual understanding among us that every human life is both a miracle and of the highest value to the earth as a whole. We don't harm one another.

"Again, it is not perfect, there are arguments and fights, but nothing brutal. If certain people clash and people cannot get along, we'll switch and change jobs and living spaces around to keep the peace. And we have leaders in each field who monitor such things."

I appreciated his transparency and began to relax, accepting that they might have less to hide than I assumed. But I didn't drop my guard.

"We don't take advantage of the fact that we are safe from the iron ships here. And no one would do anything to sacrifice their own safety, so there's an element of fear involved that keeps people in line. We have had to force people to leave in the past. Not many, but it has happened."

We turned a corner into a tighter tunnel. We hadn't passed any other humans for a while.

The air was growing colder, and the echo of Yegor's voice between the walls louder, although it had not raised in volume. The skin along the back of my neck prickled, my body suddenly hyper-aware of being an unnatural depth below ground. The expanse of solid earth behind the stone walls felt compressing. My instincts urged me to turn back.

Katya had been relatively quiet while Yegor explained to me their ways, but they both tiered off talking, allowing me to prepare myself for what was to come.

Again, I could feel his disturbed presence in the Air before we turned another bend that revealed the bars that held him.

Björn.

I tried to remain separate from the density he dwelled in. It would be of no service to join him in the fog when I was in a position to remain clear. But staying unattached demanded immense vigilance, for when my heart was this intertwined with a person, it naturally wanted to merge.

I understood the logic of his isolation—he'd been infected by the Sky People's intentions. Intentions of destruction and reconstruction. Intentions that could creep seamlessly into others' minds if they weren't sensitive enough to feel the shift. I couldn't be naive to the cunning subtlety of their infection after witnessing Chaṅtara hide my fall that day in the snowstorm, consciously leaving me to face potential death alone.

But seeing Björn behind bars still looked wrong to me.

He must have heard us approaching, for he was at the bars within moments of us entering the tunnel.

"Maya. Maya is that you?" His German accent was subtler now than when we first met, but the distinct rhythm and deep resonance made my body respond in a way that felt so sweetly familiar.

All the emotions I'd felt for him over the past years flooded to the surface.

"We'll hang back here," Katya said, stopping.

I barely heard her. All of my attention was on Björn. Not on the Shadows that enveloped him but the warmth of his heart that was still alive beneath.

I stepped closer, closer, and finally, under a beam of artificial light I saw him.

His eyes at first were wide and desperate. Desperate to know it was true, it was me, that my message had been real. And as soon as he saw that it was, his energy shifted. He went cold.

"Don't come close."

He retreated abruptly back into the Shadows.

His turmoil was transparent in both his body and his words. I felt it as if it were my own, removed just enough to understand that it wasn't.

When his words didn't stop me from moving forwards until I was at the bars, he continued backwards until he hit the stone at the far end of the cavern.

But his eyes didn't move from mine, begging. Sincere.

"Please."

A wave of déjà vu hit me.

We'd been here before. Not *here*, but here in this same drama loop.

Of course. This was his pattern. Guilt and shame were his nemesis.

"Björn, let's not repeat the past," I said simply, trying to appear robust, invincible, impenetrable by the Shadows, so that he would allow me into his space.

The pain on his face was almost too much to witness.

His face, like his body, had transformed over our time apart, much like I'm sure mine had. His jaw was more square, and cheekbones more defined. The Shadows under his dark eyes were even darker against his fair, sun-deprived skin.

He'd always had a fit, muscular build, but now he wore the body of a fully matured man. His shoulders were broader, his chest and arms built like a soldier trained for battle. He was the perfect recruitment for the Sky Consciousness, just like he'd been the perfect recruitment for Governor Koen when he was seeking a ruthless general—and that was when he was still a boy.

He was not a boy anymore.

He was dangerous. And he didn't appear to be weakened by the Sky Consciousness's that inhabited him, at least not externally. He appeared more invincible than ever.

"This is nothing like the past, Maya. I am nothing like I was in the past. We are strangers now."

I watched him, trying to read how much he believed his own words, or whether they were just a defence mechanism he was using to protect me.

"We could never be strangers. Even if it's true that you've changed." I said, reminding him of the closeness between us. The way we came to understand and know each other better than anyone.

"You are still you. I can feel you, you are—"

"You're deluded. You *want* to feel me. You want things to be the same."

"Not the same. Neither of us could possibly be the same. But the love I feel for you is the same. Eternal. It cannot be dimmed by time or change. And you cannot persuade me into believing it isn't real, because it's something I feel, not think. Right now. Here."

He shuffled, irritated by my sincere declaration of undying love that at any other time may have sounded romantic, beautiful. But his present ears could not hear beauty.

"Well, I don't feel it," he said coldly. "I stopped loving you a long time ago." There was an edge of apology in his words, but not enough for him to retract them.

"No, you didn't." I could barely believe the confidence in my quick reply. In the past, his words would have made me shrink.

But with the support of Air Magic, I could read energy unbiasedly now. And the love in his heart, like mine, was immense, as vast as the ocean that was reflected in his eyes, no matter how many Shadows were dulling its expression.

"I thought you were dead, and I fell in love with Chaṅtara," he told me. "Sorry."

I inhaled deeply. If he was truly going to repel me, he was going to need a new approach.

"Björn, that won't work this time." For a number of reasons that I didn't presently care to list, for it was clear he wasn't actually *listening* anyway.

One was that jealousy wasn't a frequency that existed in my system anymore. I'd worked on it when it proved itself as the destructive force it was the last time it came up. In the Valley. Towards Phỗenix.

I was so sure that Björn would fall in love with her over me. I was so certain that I was nothing compared to her. Plain. Boring. Strange.

But he proved me wrong, and through accepting his unconditional love, and more significantly accepting *myself* in all my quirks, the sensation of jealousy had dissolved, healed. I no longer felt the burn of its presence, even in that moment, when Björn outwardly confessed his love for another.

The fact that his tone was completely unconvincing probably had an influence too. He was lying, and not a cell in my body believed him.

Even in his blurry state of mind, he was smart enough not to waste his breath trying to convince me.

"Well, I still don't want you near me."

I scanned him closely. The pain my mere presence caused him made my heart throb with sadness. He was trying to protect me, and I knew at that moment that the kindest thing I could do for him was to let him. For now. Until the intensity of this guilt he felt softened.

"I will leave now," I told him.

The tension in his body loosened, just slightly.

"I've missed you," I couldn't suppress the tears in my eyes, nor did I attempt to hide my emotions. He *had* to realize that the love I felt for him was a flame that couldn't be extinguished, no matter how determined he was to try.

He looked away.

Before moving, I said, "Well, thank you for hearing my message, and sending Anya to find me. It would have been easy to dismiss it."

The fact that he had heard my etheric words, words sent by the Magic of Air, was evidence that he maintained a pocket of receptivity and openness within him somewhere.

He nodded once but didn't look back up to meet my eyes.

I stood there frozen for a moment, my body dreading any amount of distance between us again. Even when he was closed to me, there was something so sweet and comforting about being close to him. His presence, his essence. It still felt like home.

But I forced myself to move and felt more of his tension relax when I was out of sight.

I found Katya and Yegor waiting patiently around the corner of the tunnel.

They didn't speak but led me unhurriedly back through the tunnels, allowing me time to process the well of feelings that swirled through me before returning to Bear and Snow. I noticed more of the details that were crafted into the otherwise plain pathways too.

There were hangings all along the walls of old, symbolic art and shelves carved into the stone, displaying some of the ancient treasures Katya spoke of. Elegant golden ornaments, giant gemstones and jewels, vivid glass-stained lamps. Some hung from the roof, weaving splashes of colour into the sweeping warm light.

After some time passed in silence, I realised I had only seen one prisoner down there when I had expected to see two.

"Where's Chaṅtara?" I asked.

They looked between each other.

"Anya didn't tell you?" Katya finally asked, a little too gently.

I didn't have to answer.

"She's dead. She never made it here."

I suddenly wished I'd never asked. On top of the feelings I was already processing, the sensation that overwhelmed my body was too much.

My feet stopped moving and my body went weak. I leant against the wall for support.

"The Sky People?" I didn't know how to phrase my question.

But they nodded.

I took a moment to process yet another unexpected turn, then walked on without another word. I didn't want to know the details. Not yet.

CHAPTER TWENTY-EIGHT

T HAT NIGHT, WE ATE at a communal dining space, within one of two community kitchens at opposite ends of the underground city. Not everyone ate together but many did. It was a large, dome-carved room; littered with vivid, multi-coloured stained-glass lamps that hung down from across the entire ceiling. They were round in shape and emitted a warm glow with rays of colour beaming through.

While the cave structure itself was primitive in the sense that it was all carved out of cream stone rock, each room was decorated with the reminiscence of antique Russian, Siberian, and Persian décor.

Each table was old, long, and carved from dark wood, and placed over rectangular Persian rugs woven from warm, deep red wool. The chairs were unmatching, with vibrantly embellished cushions that added to the rainbow of colour in the room.

I ate with Anya. She kept to herself, hanging on the outskirts of their small society, which I understood. And for that reason, it was easy to be around her. To speak or not to speak. The feeling seemed mutual.

I didn't trust the community enough to leave Bear out of my sight for long. It would have only taken a few rebellious or desperate people to strike him down in a moment of unawareness—although as placid as Bear acted, he was rarely unaware.

In fact, his underplayed hyper-awareness of his environment was what allowed him to remain calm and at ease in any situation, undefended. But the moment any danger arose, he was quick to respond, and when threatened, he could be as ruthless as any ordinary brown bear. I'd seen it. Just not regularly.

So, Bear joined us for dinner and lay against the rounded rocky wall beside us. We took the farthest table, and the other diners left a decent gap of empty tables between us. It seemed the suspicion was mutual. We hadn't earned their trust yet either. Some were just being polite, giving us space to settle in.

Bear's eyes were watchful, and his body agitated. I knew him too well to miss it. The overlapping noise of human interaction was over-stimulating; up until then, he had only been familiar with the peaceful serenity of wide, open spaces, and the sounds of uninterrupted nature.

I sat close to him with Snow on my lap, occasionally reaching down to pat his fur. I understood the way excessive talking could sound like an interruption to the already rich and prevailing sound of silence. I also acknowledged that words were a valuable form of communication. Just not so much for bears.

Imprinted in my mind was the image of Björn's face.

I couldn't let it go. I probably didn't truly want to. It felt wrong to be sitting there, simply enjoying a meal while he was condemned behind the bars of a cold cavern far, but not too far, away.

"He locked himself down there. As soon as he arrived. Well, he basically forced Yegor to. He was paranoid about infecting people," Anya was speaking about Björn. She didn't have to say his name.

I didn't have to ask her to go on.

"He knew more about the 'Sky People' than we did—he'd been living inside their ship. He was aware that his chances of freedom increased the deeper he could be inside the earth.

"He's aware of what has happened to him, and I'm guessing he was aware while it was happening, yet still, it happened. I don't understand." There was a question at the end of her sentence, although she did not voice it.

I ate a spoonful of soup then fed a spoon to Snow in my lap.

"The Shadows seem more powerful now than they were in the Old World," I said.

"Maybe it's because humans are aware of their existence now, so they've lifted their game to meet our resistance...I don't understand it either to be honest.

"In the past, the Shadows only had power over us when we were ignorant of their existence. Those who hunted out the beliefs and thoughts and feelings that were stirred by the Shadows they carried, freed themselves from their grasp."

I paused, remembering my own experience of a Shadow weaving itself into my thoughts in a moment of fear. The time by the lake, when I realised I was pregnant. It was the clearest reference I had.

"We all have personal areas of weakness which they can use to access our mind. They seem to be able to sense any negative thought or feeling in the air, and can tune into its frequency waves and start sending more. Negative thinking cultivates negative energy in our bodies, and it's this energy they feed on," I explained, unsure of how much she already knew, but aware she wanted to understand as much as possible.

"Once attached to our mind, they produce more negative thoughts, and our bodies produce more negative energy." I returned to its relevance to Björn.

"I think part of him believes he deserves to suffer. He still believes he deserves to be punished for...things he did in his past. Guilt is his area of weakness, which is one of the lowest, heaviest frequencies of consciousness we can dwell in, because it feels so valid when we're in it.

"He believes his suffering compensates for what he's done in some way. There is no justice system anymore, so he's taking it upon himself to be both the punisher and the punished. And through doing so he believes he's protecting and serving us. He still has the soldier mentality that was programmed into him in the Old World," I was piecing things together as I spoke.

"That's what I've gathered anyway, off what I know of his history and the darker pockets of his mind. In the Valley, he let it go. He was free. But it appears that all this baggage was still hidden in his subconscious."

Anya listened intently. It was clear she'd never heard these concepts expressed in such a way. The psyche, especially when entangled with the Shadows, was an intricately designed web of a thing to try to explain.

A couple approached our table hesitantly. I watched them from the corner of my eye. They were careful not to step too close to the wild, but not so wild, animal beside me.

"Can we sit with you?" the woman asked respectfully. "We won't be offended if you say no."

I looked at Anya who did not oppose, though nor did she appear welcoming.

"Sure," I did my best to smile, but seeing the couple's hands casually intertwined struck a chord of sadness.

It reminded me that my love was there, in the vicinity of the underground city, but at the same time not there, not accessible. Holding his hand would have been more painful than pleasurable as long as his energy body remained full. Almost black.

Charcoal. I called it charcoal in my mind just to make it seem less intense. Easier to work with. Charcoal was still a pretty dark shade of L·ight Màtter compared to what I was used to interacting with.

The woman registered the emotion in my eyes that still lingered on their interlaced hands. She let go.

I smiled more genuinely. "It's ok."

They sat beside Anya, leaving a decent gap between.

"I just want to you to know how impressive we think it is that you survived alone all these years and birthed a child alone. I know what childbirth is like." She looked to her partner who shared a knowing expression. "Mine was hell anyway. I couldn't imagine doing it alone."

"Trust me, I prayed to The Mother for help, but at some point I had to embrace reality and just let my body do what the female body has done since the beginning of time," I said, brushing off her sense of awe.

I hadn't done anything special. All I'd done was survive, in the very way we were built to survive by the hand of nature itself.

But her eyes remained awestruck, so I continued thoughtfully.

"It was interesting to realise just how much the body knows and does and can do without our interference. In the Old Society, we were so domesticated. There were so many structures set up that took the pressure off us, both as individuals and as a community, to take care of our own survival. It was all taken care of for us. All we had to do was follow the System and we were fed and housed and supported by many comforts that don't exist in nature's raw expression.

"But when it comes down to us in our bare form, us and nature, instinct takes over. We are genetically built to survive all sorts of hostile conditions and weathers. Survival is our primal instinct."

I don't know what made me say so much. But the couple were interested, so I didn't cut off the flow of words. In the past, in the Old World, the main reason I didn't bother speaking much was because people—humans distracted by their dysfunctional human minds—were generally not actually *listening*. Not really.

Two young girls walked up shyly to their parents. Their eyes were wide, skipping between me, Snow, and Bear. The youngest girl waddled up to her mother's arm, who lifted and wrapped it around her shoulders. The eldest was more confident, his posture tall.

"Hello." He greeted me with a mature nod.

"Hello."

Some moments passed. He stared at Bear.

"Can we…pat him?" he asked.

I felt conflicted by the question.

"I'm going to say no," I answered. "Only because he's not a pet. He's been a great friend to me over my time alone. And he's not used to being touched by many human hands. When he settles in, he might show that he likes it, but right now, while he's still adjusting, I think we need to respect his space."

The boy nodded, disappointed. He sat down on the opposite end of the bench to me and continued to watch Bear with even more intrigue, now that he couldn't be refined down to being some kind of mascot or toy.

A wave of murmurs rippled through the room, capturing my attention. Eyes were darting my direction even more than they had been before. It put me on edge.

I heard sounds in the hall, feet, bodies moving swiftly towards us. I stood for no reason but an impulse, shifting Snow to sit on my hip.

My heart began to race, as if it knew before my eyes or mind what was coming.

Who was coming.

CHAPTER TWENTY-NINE

E MOTIONS SWEPT HOTLY THROUGH my system, which only made sense when the first body stepped into the doorway.

His eyes fell straight onto me, and I was frozen. Tears struck my eyes as a jolt of uncontainable joy beamed through my heart. Another body became visible. It was Phőenix, stepping through the doorway beside her brother, Bŏdhi.

They froze too, expressions of disbelief painting their faces. It could have been disbelief over seeing me alive, or the sight of the baby on my hip and the great bear behind me, who also stood, sensing these humans were important to me. Perhaps it was all those things at once.

I turned to Bear.

"Stay here, ok?" I could barely speak. My vision was blurred by a thin sheath of tears.

I didn't notice Anya standing, but she was beside me, offering her hands, and I mindlessly passed Snow into her welcoming arms.

I stepped towards the siblings. They stepped towards me. Then I ran.

I hit Bŏdhi first, who wrapped me so tightly in his arms I couldn't help but let my welling tears fall. He kissed my cheek and forehead. I'd never seen or experienced his affection before in the way I did at that moment. There had always been a sense of distance between us, but presently, I felt so close to him he could have been my brother, lover, or at least a dear, dear friend.

My heart was lit, so bright it could have burst. Burst because his was too. Two hearts colliding in light was an immense force.

I let my body fall into his body. Every guard I'd upheld since arriving there dropped away. I felt safe. Held. And he let me express all the tears I hadn't let myself cry since being separated from them.

Phoenix hung back behind him, allowing whatever this expression was to unfold without interference. I barely noticed her. I barely noticed anyone. I forgot I was in a room full of strangers. Strangers who were watching my outpour. I didn't care.

It wasn't like Bodhi was the one I'd missed most, because we'd never had the deepest connection. Not on the surface anyway. We were both quiet and never knew quite what to say to each other. But there was always a gentle undercurrent of connectivity running beneath the words—or more accurately, wordlessness.

He leant back when my tears calmed, but only slightly, tucking a curling lock of dark brown hair from his face to better examine me. His jungle green eyes were striking, vivid, as clear and wild as ever. And somehow, more loving than ever too. Even though his partner, wife, and the mother of his children was… dead.

Still a word hadn't been spoken between us, but it felt as if so much was said.

I looked away, cognition of our environment rushing back, remembering the number of eyes that silently watched our reunion. Remembering that he wasn't Björn, so perhaps I shouldn't be so expressive, so in Love…but in that moment, love was the only force present in the world. Love with a capital L. The Love that existed beyond all labels.

I let out a light, nervous laugh, wiping my eyes, then looked over his shoulder to Phőenix for the first time.

While her hair was light blonde, she had the same vibrant green eyes and smooth brown skin as her brother. Their exotic appearance reflected the untameable wildness in their blood, and of the interdimensional Valley they were raised in.

I stepped around Bŏdhi to embrace her. She had a sterner sense about her, but she hugged me warmly.

"Katya told us you were here. I didn't believe her." Phőenix stepped back, holding my shoulders as she scanned my face, then body.

"You look different." She shook her head, unable to place why. There were probably a few reasons. I'm sure motherhood had something to do with it.

"And you have a baby." She shook her head again, releasing my shoulders and lifting her gaze to the small boy who sat on Anya's lap.

Is that...dreaminess I can see in her unusually sparkly eyes?

I was not the only one who had changed. The facial tension she usually wore had eased and her features were warm in a way that was new to me.

"I guess he's not really a baby anymore," I said.

Snow was watching our interaction with unease. I had left the table abruptly, and he wasn't used to seeing me cry. Phőenix was already moving towards him, infatuated. I followed.

"His skin glows," she said, more so to herself, then she looked back at me. "Is it always like this?"

His skin wasn't really *glowing*. It wasn't strikingly luminous like the Fξ. But it had a glowing quality about it that was more radiant than regular human skin.

I didn't really have an answer to her question. She wasn't really asking for one.

"Is it ok if I say hello?"

"Of course," I said. "Snow. I call him Snow."

Snow watched as she approached him, and she bent down beside the bench.

"Hello Snow."

He held up one of his small, silky white hands and touched her bronze cheek. She closed her eyes.

"I knew your mum when you were in her tummy. But I didn't know you were in there. You were very quiet about it, weren't you?" She poked his belly playfully and he giggled.

I looked back at Bõdhi questioningly and was surprised to find his eyes already fixed on me, not the interaction in front of us.

He shrugged, then leant over my shoulder, his voice somewhat husky as he lowered it "She's been getting pretty...hormonal about babies since meeting Ivar."

"Ohhh." It suddenly made perfect sense. She was in love.

Bõdhi's presence so close to me was electric, his breath on my neck sending a light wave of shivers through my body that I attempted to hide. It was probably just because I hadn't been that close to a man in a long time. Pure biology.

Well, that's what I told myself.

"Where are Moānā and Ṭassie?"

"They were exhausted after the trip. I put them straight to bed. We wanted to see you before telling them. To make sure..." He didn't finish the sentence, but I knew what he meant.

"Are you hungry? You must be hungry. I'll get you both some food." I turned, but Bõdhi's arm at my chest stopped me.

Another jolt of energy pulsed through my body.

"Maya, sit down. I can get it."

For a moment, neither of us moved. His touch was calming after the initial spark, touching something that felt closer to my heart than the outer shell of my chest.

"I just thought, you must be tired from your trip and..." I shifted my gaze down, away from his clear eyes.

"I can get it," he repeated, then disappeared into my periphery where I watched him more discreetly.

My cheeks were hot, and I hoped they were not red. That would have been even more embarrassing than my unanticipated and irrepressible feelings. I could hide feelings, but I couldn't control the colour of my skin.

I sat back at the table beside Phœ́enix, who, to my relief, was too distracted by Snow to notice.

Bear, however, watched me closely. I gave him a look, then pretended all was normal, even though I knew that hiding was not an option between us. We were too interconnected to miss the subtleties in each other's behaviour.

I hadn't seen them move, but the small family who had joined us were now eating at a different table. The young woman lifted her head when my eyes fell on her, and gave a me a nod. It was small, considerate actions like this that allowed me to build trust for the community.

Phœ́enix's attention drifted from Snow when a tall, dark-haired man walked into the room, and she leapt up, throwing her arms up around his shoulders.

I took Snow back into my arms and held him close, kissing his forehead. He was wide awake and content. I'd never seen Phœ́enix happily in love before, and smiled as I watched her.

"Maya, this is my partner, Ivar." She wrapped her arm comfortably around the back of his waist. Everything she felt for him was announced in the revering way she pronounced his name.

"Hello Maya." He said, not overly kind nor cold. He was another Russian, with pale skin and black features, tall and handsome in his own unique way but not the kind that I would have expected for Phœ́enix. Maybe because I only pictured her with the giant Tarō.

"Have you met them already?" She tilted her head up at him. "This is her son, Snow."

"Not met. But I saw you arrive. Interesting family you have," he noted, his alert brown eyes calculating me as I calculated him.

I got the sense he was intellectually smarter than the average human and aware of it. It was visible to me through a faint blue auric field around his head that was crisp. Functional—not the fog of sky consciousness.

As the couple sat down, Anya stood.

"Goodnight," she said simply, and took her bowl to the wash sink before retreating. We were in good company now.

"Oh, Ivar." Bõdhi returned, holding two bowls. "Are you hungry?" he asked, offering him one of them.

"No, I ate, thanks."

He passed it instead to Phõenix, his arm accidentally brushing mine.

I shrugged away impulsively. He didn't seem to notice.

"So, this is the Bear that replaced Björn," Phõenix mused lightheartedly.

"He didn't replace Björn," I defended a little too quickly, taking her words *less* lightly.

"We all know nothing could replace *Björn*," Bõdhi said before anyone could analyze my response—including me.

I laughed, a little forcefully.

"Of course not." She looked lovingly at her partner. "They were perfect. When they finally acknowledged it." She turned back to me with a humoured expression.

"Speaking of, you couldn't make him miraculously emerge from his dungeon?"

I looked down, shaking my head. "Not yet."

"You will," Phõenix leant over the table to touch my hand gently. She spoke with conviction that almost made me believe her.

But I wasn't The Mother. There was no guarantee I could do anything.

"I found Bear not long after we got separated," I said, returning to a simpler topic. "Well, he found me actually."

Bŏdhi slid calmly down the stone wall to sit beside Bear. He didn't make any move to touch or pet him, and for this, Bear seemed equally at ease beside the stranger.

Neither Bŏdhi, nor Phŏenix showed any sense of alarm in his presence. In the realm they were raised in, animals and humans weren't regarded with the level of separateness that they were on earth. Even when hunted, their life was honoured and their sacrifice never went unacknowledged; their spirit always thanked.

We all went quiet. There was so much to catch up that none of us knew quite where to start.

"So, how *did* you get separated?" Phŏenix finally asked. "It's always been a mystery to us how you fell behind without anyone noticing." She looked to Bŏdhi whose expression was in agreement, then back to me.

My body tensed, conflicted, because what she said wasn't quite true; Someone *did* notice. It was Chaṅtara. And she intentionally ignored it.

But she was dead now.

Could I really taint their memory of her with another shade of darkness?

Not until I knew more about her death, and what stage of the grieving process they were all in.

I let out a breath, and told them the story, leaving out the part that involved Chaṅtara.

More people in the community gathered quietly around us to listen. The attention made me uncomfortable, so many eyes and ears on me at once, but I understood why what I shared was interesting to them, so explained it in detail, from the moment I lost them, to how I managed to survive since.

Well, the important details. It would otherwise have been a very long story.

CHAPTER THIRTY

AFTER EATING, WE ALL showered. I hadn't bathed properly since leaving the lake, and the hunters were still dirty from their travels.

I was shown to a room that was large enough to comfortably fit Bear, where I changed into new clothes. They were simple, earthy.

I should have been tired, but I was wide awake.

Apparently, Bǒdhi was too.

There was a light knock on my door. I was drying my hair with a towel when I opened it.

"Oh, sorry, I don't want to intr—"

"No, it's fine. I'm dressed. I just," I looked at the soft towel in my hands. "I forgot how good towels are..." I said with a laugh.

"I know, right! I'd never used this kind of material before. They're very good." His hair was wet too, and he smelt as fresh and clean as I felt.

Uncertainty drifted between us.

"Do you mind if I come in for a bit? I just...I can't stop thinking about the things you went through alone and," his eyes drifted to Bear who lay in the room behind me. "Well, you know what I mean."

"It's ok. Yes, come in, I feel the same. I mean...you know what I mean," I spoke in a hushed voice, so as not to wake Snow, who was curled up on the floor next to Bear.

He stepped inside, closer, and took in the room as I secretly took in more of his scent, before turning my attention back outwards, examining the room in a timelier manner than I had before.

The cream-coloured limestone walls were raw, and the room was simply furnished.

A bed. A small wooden table. A chair with a velvet purple-lined seat. A shelf. A cupboard with elegant floral patterns carved into the dark wood. A sink, tap, and round face mirror. And a dark purple stained-glass lamp.

None of the furniture matched, all antique and scavenged from the Old World, but it had been assembled in a way that was coordinated into a theme. There was a large round rug in the centre, woven into patterns with bright purple and electric blue wool, and the bed was styled with an array of blue and purple embroidered pillows.

There was a communal bathroom in each section. My room was in the family corridor, to allow space for Bear. There were also sections for singles and couples. Considering it was all built before the world's end, and everything inside salvaged in the same timeframe, was impressive. There were pockets of beauty crafted into every section, making the entire cave feel like a work of art.

"Weird, huh," he commented.

"If you think this is weird, you should have seen our rooms in the Old World. They were basically plain white boxes. And all identical. Well, until I started painting mine. Which was actually illegal." I shook my head, remembering back to when I was *imprisoned* for painting. Well, that and a few other 'rebellious' things.

"You were painting the valley, right?" We'd never talked about this part of my past before, which wasn't surprising. The majority of our communication in the past had been practical, survival-based.

"Yeah, when I still believed the visions were coming from my dangerous imagination."

Bõdhi's eyes lingered on Snow who shifted in his sleep.

"Should we walk? I don't want to wake him." His voice lowered to a whisper.

"I'm already talking too much. I haven't talked in a long time," I said apologetically as we moved to the door.

But he smiled. "It's ok, I like it."

The corridor was dark, lights dim to match the night. We stepped lightly, although our bare feet barely made more than a shuffling sound.

So many questions, but neither of us spoke for some time. His company was enough.

"He's a special kid," Bõdhi said. "I mean, all kids are in their own way, but he's very pure. Abnormally calm."

"I guess he hasn't had anything to disturb his innocence yet. No other kids to create conflict. No siblings to fight with. No technology to distract him from reality. No schooling structure. It's just been us, nature, and animals. He loves animals." I smiled at memories from our camp.

Our conversation tailed off again, but he was thoughtful.

"So." He tried to envision the sequence of events that was our story more clearly. "You fell behind in the storm, you got to the mountains. You found a cave. Ӡchŏ…died."

"But the FξŸa returned!" I said excitedly. "They were the reason nature grew so fast where we've been living. They never actually left; they just became invisible to humans again. But I've talked so much, I want to know more about your time." I laughed, a little too loudly.

"Shhhhh." He reached around my shoulders, momentarily pressing a palm over my mouth.

His skin was cool, but not dead like the people of the Old World. His touch shocked me like an icy sea. It was unlike any other energy exchange I'd felt before, as if something deeper than anything we were conscious of was speaking between us, speaking in a language I didn't yet understand.

Did he notice? Did he feel it too?

If he did, he acted casual, dropping his hand as we walked on.

"Hm, I know where we can go," he said, steering me around a bend, then another.

The artificial lighting faded, and the tunnel darkened until a luminous bluish glow became visible from inside one of the upcoming openings.

Inside, glow worms littered the domed roof like stars across a black sky.

The sound of trickling water drew my eyes to a thin, gently flowing stream that ran through the centre of the cavern; it glistened under the silver lights. On the other side were garden beds of dainty white flowers and other wild plants.

It was like we'd stepped into another realm—a mystical realm, dreamlike in its otherworldly beauty—but the air was crisp, fresh, and breathing it in, I was unmistakably awake.

We sat on a patch of surprisingly spongy bright green moss for a place where there was no sunlight. He sat close beside me.

"No one really ever comes here. Probably because it's pretty far out of the way. That's why I like it though." Bŏdhi spoke with consideration, his voice low. In the time I'd known him, he'd never spoken for the mere sake of filling the space with noise.

"I found it early on, when I was still adjusting to everything. I planted the gardens and use caretaking as an excuse to come back regularly. Mostly I just come here for solitude."

"It seems harder here for introverts," I said, thinking of Anya. "I don't know how long I'll last." I laughed.

"People like Phŏenix thrive here though. She's so happy to be part of a community again. I am too, and I'm grateful we were welcomed into it. I don't know if we would have survived out there alone. We never found a place where nature and edible plants were abundant like you did. I just also appreciate having a space like this to retreat sometimes."

The sound of trickling water was soothing. Meditative.

"When did you realise Björn and—" I caught myself too late. "Were infected."

"It's ok, I'm not grieving her anymore. It was weird, she drifted away from us in spirit so gradually. It felt like we'd already lost her before we truly had," Bǒdhi said of Chaṅtara's death.

"Björn was similar, actually, but we thought he was just grieving your absence. After losing you, he became distant. He stopped speaking. I think the Sky Consciousness found access into him through his grief, but it wasn't obvious at the time, and we couldn't discern what was natural pain and what was Shadow.

"He just became more reclusive and inward until one night when we were all asleep, he left. We woke up and he was gone. He did well to cover his tracks too. But Chaṅtara found him a few days later. It was the first of the iron ships we came across." He looked over his shoulder to check I was ok to hear the rest of the story.

I was.

"She was drawn to it. At first, we all were. We thought it was a structure left behind from the Old World. It was the perfect shelter. But I remembered the visions you had before arriving and realized it matched your description of the Sky People's ships too well to be an old relic. It was shiny and new, and conveniently placed in the middle of dry, open land. Nature hadn't started growing in that area yet." His eyes glazed as he stared back over the shimmering stream.

I seemed to be the only one who hadn't been aware of the ship's descent, even though I was the one who'd seen it long before it manifested. I'd been living in a fantasy, a tiny pocket of reality that was beautiful but sheltered from the bigger picture.

"We tried to persuade her not to go near it, but she was in a kind of trance. The look in her eyes when I tried to pull her back was so fierce I knew I couldn't force her," Bõdhi continued.

"I followed her, to protect her, but the ships emit frequency waves that are so piercing I couldn't continue. My vision blurred and my ears rang so loud I couldn't hear anything but a low, mechanical hum." He closed his eyes, sinking back into the memory, knowing without me having to say a word that I wanted to hear every detail.

Any insight into the Sky People was valuable to me.

"I could feel the weight of a force darker than anything I'd felt before, black, pressing down on me. I felt paralysed, but Phõenix pulled me out. The touch of her hand on my arm was like being splashed with a wave of light that gave me the clarity and energy to run back the opposite direction until the Shadow had no power over me."

"Chaṅtara wasn't affected the way I was. She functioned perfectly, which was when I realised that she was already in tune with its frequency. It wasn't painful to her because she was already infected. The same energy that repelled us was calling to her with a kind of magnetism I couldn't break." He paused.

"We hung back, way back, watching her disappear into the ship, waiting for her to come back out. I felt cowardly for not going in after her, but I also knew that staying clear of their field was the only wise option. Our tribe had been cut down enough. The kids had already lost their mother. I couldn't afford to get infected too.

"Time passed. Wind picked up and the sky grew dark with heavy clouds. We pulled the material of one of our tents over our heads to stay dry as rain began to fall. But we didn't risk setting up camp. We knew sleeping near them would make us too vulnerable.

"A being did eventually come out of the ship. But it wasn't Chaṅtara. It was Björn. He called out, gesturing we join them inside to shelter from the rain. We had to make the decision to wait there and hope they'd come to their senses, or leave without them. When night fell, we left."

He looked at me, his eyes exposing a glimpse of guilt even though he knew there was nothing he could have done. They made their choice. He may not have taken action to rescue them, but refraining from the temptation of shelter, Shadows, and the hope of saving Chantara and Björn demanded a more significant amount of internal strength.

He didn't wait for me to respond before continuing.

"We remembered their location though. And it wasn't long after we left them that we found this tribe. When they grew to trust us, we asked if they would return there with us, hoping we might be more powerful and persuasive with more beating hearts on our side.

"But they wouldn't risk it, and we understood why. To be honest, we already believed that if they were still living inside one of the ships, they'd be beyond saving anyway." Bõdhi paused and turned to face me again.

"It was Anya who went out to find him. She didn't tell anyone, she just disappeared for a few days alone, which wasn't unusual for her. The ship wasn't too far from here.

"No one knows how she persuaded Björn to follow her back, or how she even got close enough to communicate with him without being impacted herself. All she said was that he was ready. And Chantara was dead."

He went quiet.

Anya was the one who saved Björn.

Well, he was not saved yet, but she was the only one who had enough optimism to try. Just like she was the only one with enough optimism to follow Björn's 'message from the wind' to me.

But it wasn't optimism alone. What she did demanded bravery. *Courage*. She walked voluntarily into a danger worse than death for the unlikely possibility of saving two lost humans—and returned unscathed.

Only the truest of warrior hearts contained such courage.

"How have the kids been since losing her?" I asked gently.

"At first, when we thought we were the only four humans left alive, it was a little depressing. Our future, and the future of humanity on Earth, was starting to look pretty bleak. But their innocence and lack of understanding of the scope of it all helped them process their sadness.

"Phỗenix has loved and cared for them like a mother. And since arriving here, being around other kids has lifted them. Especially Moānā. She's very much like her mother was, very social."

"And what about you? I mean, how are you *really*?"

"You must be getting tired of listening to me talk," he said, deflecting my attempt to access the part of him that I hadn't seen anyone access before. His heart, his emotions.

It was so clear in his eyes, and the way he moved through the world, that there was more going on within him than he revealed. He was a deeply feeling and perceptive being, and in that moment, I wanted him to let me into his world.

I shook my head. "I want to know."

It was true I'd never heard him talk so much, but I wasn't tired of it.

He contemplated his answer, eyes momentarily suggestive of inviting me in, but then a sense of distance reaffirmed itself. Now that I considered it, I realised I'd never even see him open fully to Chaṅtara, and she was supposed to be closest to him…

Without thinking, I blurted out, "Did you love Chaṅtara. I mean, truly?" Then quickly wished I hadn't. "Wow. Sorry. That was inconsiderate. You don't have to answer that."

But he didn't react as if offended. He turned to look at me, a half smile lifting one side of his lips. "It's ok."

He was quiet for another amount of time. As he stared simply into my eyes, I felt the distance between us dissolving.

I assumed he wouldn't elaborate but did not shift my eyes from his. They said so much, while at the same time only mysteries. And I was too curious as to why they suddenly made me feel all things I couldn't explain.

"Over my life," he finally began. "I've loved many people. But that certain kind of love you speak of for one special person alone, the kind that's so obvious between you and Björn...I've never experienced that." He paused, opening a doorway into his past.

"When Chaṅtara arrived in Santōṣha, I guess I felt like we *had* to be partners. She fell in love with me immediately, and the Samādhi believed it was written by The Mother's hand that we would be together.

"But you're right in your assumption. My heart never opened fully to her. I felt a kind of...duty to humankind to have children. We were all aware of the prophecy that predicted this Earth's end. It would have felt selfish not to get together, even if it was just to keep our species alive."

He paused, justifying;

"I love Moānā and Tasmai. Because of them, I do know what selfless, unconditional love feels like, and that's something I would never wish to reverse. So, I see the perfection in the way it all unfolded.

"But I have also always felt partly guilty for committing myself to a partner I knew I didn't love in the way I'm sure I have the capacity to." He drifted off.

I continued to watch him.

"She was an admirable woman. Resilient. Strong. Maybe too strong. I cared about her deeply," he assured me. "But she experienced a lot of trauma during her time in the City, and I guess our upbringings shaped us very differently. She was hardened by hers and it's something she was never able to let go of.

"I always sensed a shield that made it difficult to love her. She didn't let me take care of her, and that's really all I wanted. Anyway, it's all in the past. And now you know more than anyone how I feel about it."

"I feel honoured," I said. "Sorry. I didn't mean to impose myself into your love life though," I added.

"No, don't be. It feels good to admit. Are you tired of listening to me yet?!" He laughed.

I shook my head. "The opposite, actually."

There was a sense of softening occurring between us.

Now that we were up to date on each other's pasts, our present was beginning to feel richer, all-encompassing. The sense of being right there. Only there. Just us. Alone in the majestic cavern, faces faintly lit by a luminous blue glow.

"You know, I don't know why we never talked properly before," Bõdhi commented, then after a pause added, "I guess maybe this is why." His untamed eyes met mine, unafraid of what his words implied. For a moment, I was unafraid too.

But then a thought came rushing in, or more accurately an image. A man's face. Björn. Followed by the image of our son, Snow. The son he had not yet met but would. Soon. When he was well enough.

"I should go back and check on Snow. He doesn't really cry much, but he's never slept without me close by," I justified. "I wouldn't want him waking up the whole hall."

Bõdhi stood and pulled me up to stand.

We walked back without any further exchange of words. It was late now. Or more accurately, early. Everyone was asleep but us. And within the stillness and silence of the night, a resounding sense of aliveness danced between us.

CHAPTER THIRTY-ONE

I ONLY SLEPT A few hours, but I didn't wake up tired. I felt so awake inside that it discounted my body's need for sleep.

Bear was in the opposite condition, sleeping deeply, so when Snow woke, I perched him on my hip and left the room so as not to disturb him.

I pushed the door closed behind me, careful only to make the lightest sound—although it's not like Bear couldn't sleep through noise.

When I turned, Anya was standing close beside me, leaning on the wall. I jumped, almost dropping Snow, which amused him.

"Shhhh," I told him.

"Sorry," Anya whispered, "for startling you."

I stepped away from the door. "Is everything ok?"

"Yes." She began down the tunnel, expecting me to walk beside her.

"I just wanted to make sure you're still ok," she said.

"Oh, thank you. I am. I'm good, actually."

"Good."

Without the reference of the sun's position in the sky, I had no way of calculating time, but I assumed it was early. None of the shops we passed were open and the tunnels were not busy.

We stopped at a wide opening. The rocky roof was impressively high and there were man-made cracks through which direct sunlight poured down. Elegant white marble benches were placed all around and there were garden beds positioned where rays of sun could reach them.

Anya sat down on one of the benches. I sat beside her. There was a small stream running through the room and I wondered if it was connected to the one I was at with Bỏ̃dhi the previous night.

"This place is…" But there wasn't a word that quite captured it.

"The environmental engineers who collaborated on the building plans were some of the smartest in the world. They *had* to be to pull it off."

I sat Snow down on the ground under a ray of sun. He crawled straight over to the nearest garden bed, reaching for the leaves of a plant.

"Just don't tear them, ok?" I told him.

But he didn't have a habit of picking leaves or flowers. He had an intuitive respect for all living things, and even though plants didn't have faces, he treated them in a way that honoured their livelihood.

"Everyone has a job that contributes to keeping everything running," Anya said. "But we don't want to assign one to you."

"I'm happy to help, really. As long as it's something I can do with Snow, I'd rather be of service in some way than just be here as a taker."

She shook her head. "Firstly, mothers don't usually work until their child becomes more independent. And when they do, it's just simple jobs. Childcare is recognised here as possibly the most important job of all. The Mother's natural ability to nurture children into capable, secure individuals is valued, because it means the following generation of adults will be capable of maintaining what we've built," she explained.

"Our people choose jobs that best suit their natural skills. But it's clear your skills don't fall into the general categories," she continued. "We want you to focus on helping Björn. If you can find a way to help separate people from Shadows, that would be the most valuable work you could offer our community."

When her eyes met mine, they were both sincere and sorrowful.

"Björn isn't the first human we've seen fall victim to the Shadows," she said. "Even here, where we have taken all the precautions to shut them out."

She didn't say what happened to these 'victims' but spoke of them in past tense, which stirred my nerves.

"Your tribe told us that you worked closely with a Shaman in this...other land. I think I already mentioned the Shaman who was part of our original settlement, but we haven't had one here since he passed. He lived the length of two human lifetimes in full health.

"He was waiting for another Mystic to be born, to whom he could transfer his shamanic knowledge. He believed it was only valuable to those with the right energetic constitution to use it, and in the wrong hands, could be dangerous.

"But even over the span of his double lifetime, no one met his requirements. So, instead of taking on an apprentice as tradition would have it, he recorded his knowledge in journals that are still waiting, in the same chest he originally locked them in, for a new Shaman to arrive."

She paused, her eyes drifting across the people in the room who were quietly going about their business, watering plants, socialising in respectful volumes, enjoying the rays of sunlight.

There was even a young girl leaning against one of the far walls, drawing. She reminded me of when I used to draw to escape the dull reality of the Old City. Escape into my dream world that ended up revealing itself to be less of a dream and far closer to reality than I could have ever imagined...

Anya continued directly, making sure to meet my eyes.

"If it is true that you have shamanic skills, you are more rare than you know."

Her gaze drifted again up to the cracks in the high roof where the golden sun shone through, then down to land on Snow, who was now sitting in the garden bed, rubbing soil into his skin. He clearly felt more at home there, with nature. Nature was all he'd known up until now.

"This city is an incredible achievement, but humans weren't created to live underground. We need sun and air and open space. We can't stay here forever. We've adapted, and most are content here, but I envision a future where humans can walk freely upon our own land. Every time our hunters go out, they're voluntarily risking their sanity, and we're all aware they may not return the same.

"We've had to make difficult decisions, and we've lost perfectly good people. We can't afford to lose people. Humans are scarce as it is."

As I listened, it was becoming clear—as it gradually had been over time—that I could no longer allow self-doubt to cripple the power within me. I could no longer deny or downplay the extracelestial abilities that were apparently available to me alone.

Anya wasn't finished. She turned to me sincerely once more.

"I want to ask you formally to take on the role he left us void of. And if you agree," she said, slipping her hand into her loose brown button shirt pocket and pulling out an aged leather journal, clearly prepared for this conversation, "I will share with you his chest of knowledge, although it isn't mine, or anyone else's to share. It is his. And something in this book will help you unlock it if you prove yourself to be what I really hope you are."

She handed it to me, and I felt the magnitude of its power in my hands. Ancient knowledge that had not been accessed by any human on Earth for decades.

But I wasn't intimidated. It felt at home in my hands because I knew that these hands were capable of ancient Magic that also had not been accessed by humans for a long time. By the laws of physics that defined our world, the magic shouldn't have been possible at all. Its manifest expression was, in itself, otherworldly, its colour not natural to Earth. But I couldn't deny what I had seen and experienced, what had been conjured by my own palms. And I knew I had only just scratched the surface of the true power that lay dormant within them.

The book felt alive in my palms. It was speaking to me, although I hadn't read a word, through the same channels of intelligence that magic flowed outwards. Light Magic, White Magic, whispering from the soft leather case. Encouraging me to step even more boldly forth into everything I had the capacity to do and be.

In that moment, it became clear that it was time to embrace and embody what I already *was*.

No more hiding.

The situation on Earth was too critical. The situation with *Björn* was too critical.

"I can help you," I said. "And I'll start by helping Björn."

Now that I had committed myself in words, I felt the responsibility to live up to them with even more urgency than before.

When I arrived, my intention was to *try*, try my best to help him. But now, I couldn't allow myself to fail, because it had finally dawned on me that there was no one else around that would, or more accurately *could*, take over. Nala would not miraculously appear and finish what I started.

At that moment in history, I was the closest thing to a Shaman that existed on Earth.

"Thank you." The relief of Anya's heart was evident as it washed through her body, softening the tension of anticipation she'd been carrying.

The sound of feet running stole my attention. I turned to watch as two kids entered.

"She's here! We found her!" a girl called.

It was Moānā, followed by Ťasmai. I tucked the thin book into the rim of my pants.

Bõdhi came running out a few moments after them and stopped to catch his breath. But the kids ran straight ahead, and I stood just in time for them to slam into me, squashing me between them.

I stepped back to take them in.

"Hey, you guys! You grew so quickly!"

"Not that quick," Ťassie said. "It's been aaaaages."

"You're right, it has been a while," I laughed.

He carried himself a little less shyly than he had before, his posture a little taller, and his words a little more fully committed.

Moānā was tall and lean and beautiful. Her silky, light orange hair almost reached her hips. She must have been an early teen now. They both had matching eyes—Bõdhi's eyes—but in every other way she looked like a younger version of Chaṅtara.

Bõdhi reached us with a smile on his face.

"Morning." He carried zero awkwardness about the previous night. Not that anything awkward happened. I was just still confused by the intense feelings that sparked between us. Feelings that returned the moment he was near.

I told myself they were simply a product of my elation over seeing a familiar face after so long. But I knew that if that were true, I would have felt the same amount of elation with Phõenix, or right now, with the kids.

I couldn't ignore that it was his presence alone that made my heart beat faster again, and his smile that made me smile. There was a sense of urgency about it that I didn't understand.

"Wow, this is your baby?" Moānā asked. "He's very pretty."

Snow's ice blue eyes looked up at her from the garden bed, wide and inquisitive. She sat on the ground next to him.

"Hi, I'm Moānā."

Instead of using words, Snow reached out to touch her cheek like he had done when greeting others.

Ṫasmai sat down with them. He waved. Snow mimicked him, waving back.

"Can I be his sister?" Moānā asked, playing with his tiny white fingers. "I'm basically his sister, right?"

"Um," I laughed a little nervously.

"You're not related," Bðdhi told her.

"But if you want to be a sister to him, he would probably like that," I justified, watching him crawl closer to her.

"He looks like Björn," she said, touching his white-blonde hair. "But an ice-prince version."

"Where's the bear?" Ṫasmai asked. "Dad said you came here riding on a bear!"

"He's sleeping," I said. "Bears like to sleep a lot. Or at least this one does."

"Well," Anya said, standing. "That is all I wanted to talk to you about. I will come check on you again later."

"Thank you, Anya," I said, and she nodded, knowing what for.

She left, and I stood in silence with Bðdhi, watching the kids as they showed Snow how to play.

"Do you ever go see him?" I asked. "Björn."

"You probably noticed he's not very welcoming at the moment...but I do go down to see him sometimes." He paused thoughtfully.

"You know, I never would have expected he'd be one to get infected. I mean, Chaṅtara always had an aspect of darkness within her, waiting for an opportunity to express itself. I could see that when I met her. I thought it would fade away the longer she stayed in the Valley, but it seemed only to fade into her subconscious.

"Björn seemed to have genuinely worked through all his Shadows. When we arrived here, he was so buoyant and optimistic and clear. But maybe the Shadows never fully left him either," he drifted off, then caught my expression.

"Sorry, does it upset you? If there's any chance of him coming back, I'm sure it'll be through you. They won't…" He didn't finish the sentence.

"What? What do these people do to people they think are too far gone?"

Bỗdhi stared at the kids as if he hadn't heard me, but I knew he heard me. He lowered his voice. Instead of answering directly he told me a story.

"You get the sense that Anya is kind of…not paranoid, but…" he searched for the right word.

I nodded. He continued.

"Well," he hesitated. "I don't think she was always this way. Her trust was broken. A few months before she found us, her partner, Devon, went out on a hunting trip and got infected by a Shadow. He was less aware than Björn, and it completely dominated his mind.

"I don't know if you noticed the drawings on the cave wall down there, but they're not from Björn alone. Devon was determined to reintroduce technology from the Old World, and it looks like Björn is adding to the plans he left.

"They did everything they could to help Devon, but just his being here became dangerous for the whole community. The Shadow spread and started to affect other people, who started to think like him about our future. To those who stayed clear, it was obvious that these advanced ideas would only serve the Sky Consciousness in the end. Anya was able to stay clear. She was desperate to heal him.

"One night, without her knowing, they took him outside and…" Again, he didn't finish his sentence, but answered my question directly.

"What happens to people they think are beyond saving is…"

"They kill them."

CHAPTER THIRTY-TWO

B EAR'S BROWN EYES GLISTENED up at me when I re-
entered the dark cavern that was my room. I turned on the
soft purple shaded lamp and slumped on the floor beside him,
holding Snow against my chest.

"Bear," I said thoughtfully, and he lifted his head.

"What do you think about going out for some fresh air?"

I rode through the cave on Bear's back with Snow between
my legs. My eyes remained set ahead, ignoring the attention we
attracted.

No one stopped us on our path, which confirmed that we were
not trapped there. We were aware of the dangers that lay outside
in open air, but it was ultimately our choice to risk leaving the
safety of being underground.

Bear sniffed his way back to the entrance tunnel that was dim
but for the glow worm's star-like glimmer, following it up to the
exit.

A line of animals from the tribe's recent hunt lay on the ledge
of the cave opening where a handful of men prepared their
blades and buckets for skinning. One of them paused mid-
movement after throwing one of the carcasses over his shoulder
—to move it from the entrance, I assumed—at the sight of Bear's
burly body stepping out of the Shadows.

More heads turned our direction.

Bear let out a growl and broke into a run.

I let the worries of my mind be swept away by the wind, which was like ice against my forehead, striking me back into clarity. It blew my hair back, exposing my face to the elements.

Snow laughed in elation of our speed and I held him tight, secure.

In contrast, I felt like I could scream, but I tried to release it without the sound only to protect his sensitive young ears.

Pressure. Too much pressure.

I understood what Anya was implying between the obvious lines of her words now.

If I couldn't find a way to heal him, Björn was dead.

Bear kept running, and running. Refuelled by his long sleep.

Running and running.

Running and running.

We jolted up and down on his back, but I didn't mind the erratic nature of the rhythm. It helped shake out the erratic energy I felt inside.

Running and running.

Running and running.

We slowed as we reached the top of a wide, scoping cliff and came to a stop at its edge. A wall of rocky earth dropped down below us and a far-reaching view of open land spread for miles ahead, disappearing into the flat horizon.

Bear whined. He didn't know the cause of my emotions, but he felt it.

The land was relatively empty and dry, but something out of place caught my eye in the far distance.

Something shiny.

Metallic.

Silver—iron silver.

It stole my attention from the imploding pressure I felt inside, as I recognised it immediately as one of the ships of Sky Consciousness. I leant forwards, sharpening my gaze, but I was sure that's what it was. I'd seen them before in dreams and visions.

When I rode Bear, it was like the undercurrent of our beings were not separate. He sensed my impulses and intentions, and adjusted course according to the direction I held in mind. But in that moment, I was unsure, hesitant in my intention for our next move, and so Bear was too.

My impulse was to ride down to the ship and examine it more closely. But that was in conflict with my recently learned knowledge of how easily people were being infected in their vicinity.

The ship was so close. So tempting. If I was alone, I may not have been so cautious. But I wasn't alone. I couldn't risk Snow's safety.

And while I was contemplating all of this, he was having a response of his own to the sight of the metal ship. He had seen it before too, in visions just like me. Possibly the same vision.

His body began to quiver in my lap, and when I looked down, his expression was frozen in fear. It had been a long time since he'd woken from one of his night terrors, but his body remembered.

"Mumma." He pointed.

"I know, I see it too," I said in a soft voice. "It's ok, it can't hurt us here."

Bear lowered himself to the ground and I slid from his back, holding Snow against my chest. It was surreal to see the ship in real time and while part of me wanted to get closer, I was grateful for the distance between us, to be able to examine it from afar.

Snow was equally curious when his body stopped trembling and we sat on the rocky ground at the edge of the cliff, all three of us staring out over the land. It unnerved me to wonder what his connection to it was, why he received the same visions I received. He was too young to play any significant role in their expulsion.

Maybe it was just a gift of divine intelligence warning him of their danger, warning him to steer clear, to not be deceived if they ever tempted his thoughts. And if this was its purpose, I was grateful. It had already worked. Even from this distance he recognised their danger.

And as wrong as it sounded to hear the humans of our new tribe were ruthless enough to kill their own, I knew it was *only* to protect those uninfected. There was no black or white in a situation like this. Only grey. Black with white intentions. And their white intentions made their black actions forgivable.

Each breath of fresh air continued to clear my mind, and I stared at the silver ship as if I might miraculously gain the ability to see through it, into it. But nothing changed.

Nothing changed apart from the state of my being, which became lighter, less weighed down by the pressing intimidation of being Björn's last hope of redemption and survival, now that I had more space to process and accept reality as it was.

The reality was that I could not force Björn into freedom by demand of my own will, just like I couldn't force the metal ship in front of me to lift back up off Earth, or unite all the elements of that damned symbol at once so that we could put it into practice.

All I could influence, as emphasised by Adja, was my own role in each situation. Björn's fate, if I was unsuccessful at helping him detach from the Shadows that were presently bound to him, was outside of my control.

What I *could* control were the actions I took in alignment with my own determination to succeed. I could control the expanse and quality of light energy I poured into helping him, as opposed to wasting resources and draining energy on worrying about the alternative.

I could control the extent of my own detachment from self-doubt, and instead cultivate a kind of self-belief that would allow me to access a vaster, more infinite expanse of light and healing energy.

I remembered the book that pressed into my side and pulled it out. I slid my hand along the soft, worn leather cover then peeled it open, anticipating what kind of knowledge was inside.

The first page was blank.

So was the following.

And the following.

I flicked through the entire book at a faster speed, but there was not a drop of ink on any one of the aged, cream pages.

"It's a joke." I laughed pessimistically and shut the book, trying to remember if there was any hidden hint of humour beneath Anya's expression when she handed it over, surely knowing it was empty. At the time it had appeared only serious and urgent.

"Or a test…" I realised.

Anya had said that the Shaman believed knowledge in the wrong hands was dangerous, so to leave this lying around for anyone to open and read would have been against his wishes. And Anya did not seem disrespectful of his wishes. If anything, the opposite.

I remembered back to when I escaped the City with Björn. He showed me an ancient map of Santōṣha, but upon first glance it was like this book, one big blank page.

"The ink only reveals itself to those who are ready, who can see beyond the one-dimensional world we are taught to believe as the only reality." Björn had told me. And when I opened my mind, it did.

The ink only reveals itself to those who can see…

I reopened the cover and looked more curiously at the paper, then closed my eyes and ran my hand lightly over it. I felt both the power of the journal and the White Magic present in my palm, amplifying it as I held it there.

When I reopened my eyes, ink began writing itself on the title page as if by an invisible hand, sharing the message word by word.

This is a book of Shadows and freedom.

I turned the page, and the ink continued revealing words written long ago by the old Shaman, words that had been hidden from the ordinary eye by some kind of alchemical enchantment.

Over my years of lifting Shadows, and keeping my community clear, I learnt many effective tactics. Every human is a combination of varying belief patterns, physiological pathways, and energetic composition. They all require customised attention and tailored strategies to help them unfold.

In this journal, I have recorded the fundamental rules that seem to apply to all humans on their journey to freedom.

If you reach the end, you will gain access to my full chest of knowledge. But it is not my knowledge that will be valuable to you. It is your own integration of it. To avoid the study of magic becoming a distraction to your practice of it, I have charmed this journal so that each page will only become visible to you when the frequency of your being aligns with the frequency of the information.

What you see is what you need, and that is all.

Over-complication is a curse of the mind. It is a trap that will not serve you where magic is concerned.

I turned the page.

Rule One.

The lifting of a Shadow is only possible if it is in accordance with the intent of the one who is intertwined with it.

I had heard this before. As I read the words, it was Nala's voice who spoke them, even though I was aware they were written by a different Shaman. While it wasn't new, it was the most important teaching for me to remember in that moment of despair.

As much as I felt impassioned by my own will to see Björn free, it was not possible for my intent alone to save him.

Ink continued to fill the page.

If one can't see the value of freedom, or if their mind is too polluted by thoughts that defend the Shadows they dance with, it is impossible to set

*them free. And a waste of your precious resources
to try.*

*As Shamans, we have no business in playing god or
choosing for another their path. We are only guides.
Guides of the spiritual. We have extraordinary
powers to work with others to help them heal. But
the choice to heal must always be born by their own
intent.*

*Disturbing the will of the Shadows is a dangerous
game. And disturbing another's path by forcing
upon them your own desires is just as so—no matter
how pure your heart is in its wanting.*

Nala had been persistent in making this truth very clear to my
optimistic, hope-polluted mind when I arrived in the Valley. And
it seemed I hadn't quite learnt the lesson yet, for here it was
again, appearing through another hand of Shamanic wisdom.

I was stubborn back then, because I was so desperate to save
the rest of humanity before The Mother wiped them from the
earth completely. I was so *sure* that every human had something
pure within them that would see the value of freedom if they
could just be shown it was a possibility.

But they were too heavily influenced by the Sky People's
desires, and their beings so intricately interwoven. There was no
separation left between their true and pure spirit, and the spirit of
Sky Consciousness. Their desire to be free was non-existent
because they were unaware they were even trapped.

And nothing I could have done or said would have had any
persuasive power over their recognition that who they thought

they were was only a fraction of what they had the potential to be outside of the Shadow's reign.

As I absorbed the Shaman's words, I knew I had begun to repeat the same stubborn pattern.

But as I considered Björn more deeply, under a lens that was as far removed from my own prejudice that I could see, I had no doubt that there was at least a fraction of his being that *wanted* to be free. His will was just buried beneath the belief that he didn't deserve to be, buried in equal parts by the Shadows, and his own shame for falling victim to them.

I was aware this was still an assumption, but it was one rooted in hard evidence—evidence I'd gathered from all I had observed over time, of the workings of his mind.

Somewhere within him, he still carried the guilt of his murderous past, and in turn, believed he deserved to suffer. He may have even believed, in response to the amount of death inflicted by his own hand, that he deserved to die.

A shiver rippled up my spine.

I shut out the image.

And I shut the book.

The ink had stopped writing. That was Rule One.

I understood my next step.

Before attempting any kind of metaphysical work, I had to somehow uncover and draw Björn's organic will to be free to the surface of his attention. The work I performed would be smoother and less taxing if he was not actively resisting it.

I wasn't like Nala, and perhaps this Old Shaman, who had been long attuned with an infinite connection to source through which she was tireless. I wasn't practiced enough to know the limitations of my own energy, nor the expanse of my potential powers. And I knew it would be counterproductive to delude myself into thinking I was capable of more than I actually was.

So, to begin by establishing some kind of mutual meeting of will was the wisest move forwards.

I felt calmer and more focussed, and took one last look out over the land and the silver dome before leaving.

"Bear, can you remember this location?" I asked of him as I stood, picking up Snow and sitting him on my hip. I knew I needed to return to properly examine the ship—but next time, without Snow.

Whether Bear understood, I could never tell.

CHAPTER THIRTY-THREE

T HE HOLLOW TUNNEL ECHOED in its silence.

I sat against the stone wall opposite Björn, who initially ignored my presence, shrinking into the shadows of his prison. His guilt and shame, while appearing valiant, served only to feed the Consciousness of the Shadows that inhabited him.

Energy. All they needed was his energy. And with it, they grew more dominant, settling comfortably into their new home.

His skin shimmered with a silverish metallic shimmer that hadn't been present previously. He was morphing, shapeshifting into one of them—into what they were in their original form.

I could only afford to witness him objectively. I *had* to remain detached. I tried to drop any sense of clinging on to who he was inside and what he meant to me. I couldn't allow myself to be weakened by emotions.

Time was more critical than I had realized. He was transforming faster than I had believed was possible.

I had left Snow in the care of Bear and Bõdhi. Bõdhi had a natural way with children, gaining Snow's trust almost immediately. He was a father. He had experience, but he also had a deeply feeling, intuitive sensibility, able to detect Snow's silent needs in a way that many might otherwise miss. They shared a similar sense of internal calmness that created space for a special kind of meeting between them, beneath the surface of both their beings.

And knowing Snow was safe and comfortable in the care of a capable man also created space for me to relax, and focus on my work with Björn.

I had not spoken yet. I'd been simply watching.

He was stubborn.

But so was I.

My eyes scanned over the pictures drawn across the stone walls around him. City plans, apartment buildings, mining sites, machinery, technology. Structures that would make life more convenient and comfortable—but at the cost of nature, which was a sacrifice we'd all learnt was not one this planet would ever endure. Not if we were moving towards a future in which humanity would survive.

But the Shadows communicating through Björn were not concerned with the survival of humankind or nature.

"It happens when I sleep. I wake up in trance with all these images in my mind." He broke the eerie silence. "They feel urgent. I have to get them out somehow."

He spoke with detachment, understanding at least, that the images he drew weren't his own brilliant ideas for material advancement. In fact, they were Old. The Sky Consciousness didn't seem to have adapted to the changing times. They wanted us to repeat the past, to rebuild what nature destroyed.

They didn't seem to realise that humanity had evolved. We may have returned to primitive ways in terms of survival, but our consciousness had risen. We were wiser. No longer so naive and manipulable. We had *learned* from our mistakes.

And even Björn, whose hand they used to record their undying plans, was aware that while he felt the urgency to get them out of his head, the walls of his prison were as far as he would take them.

He edged out of the darkness, exposing himself under a faint streak of light, and stared back at me with dead eyes. He wore the same mask he had worn in the Old World—the mask of a murderer—in his best attempt to scare me. But it didn't scare me.

"You're wasting your time trying to save me. You should leave." His voice was as cold and spiritless as his expression.

I didn't move.

"Why are you here?" I didn't let any emotion slip through my voice.

The question, as simple as it was, disturbed him. But he didn't answer.

"If you really want to be left alone, why did you come here? Why did you agree to this arrangement? Why didn't you just stay in the ship, where you could freely—"

He cut me off.

"Freedom," he said. "Is not what I want. I, *Björn*." He emphasised to make it clear that it was *him* speaking, not the Shadows.

I wasn't so convinced.

"Why would I want to be free if I'm infected by this darkness? The world is safe from me here. I can't infect people or nature. And I'm hidden from Sky Consciousness."

"But you're not hidden," I argued. "You're carrying it."

"You don't understand," he snapped, without stopping to consider his words. "When I was out there, they were everywhere, it wasn't just one Shadow. There were too many to keep track of, desperate for energy. The longer I lived with them, the more visible they became to me and—"

He cut himself off, shying away as if he'd revealed too much, and it was then that I saw what was really trapping him.

He was afraid.

The frequency of fear was a magnet that both invited Shadows towards him and held the Shadows that had already attached to him in place. His fear fed their fear. And fear was one of the most destructive frequencies in the universe. The destroyer of life, of love.

Love and fear were two extreme in their differences to coexist at once. As long as fear was at the foreground of his experience, the eternal love beneath was inaccessible.

But even inside the magnitude of his infection, he was still conscious that that's what it was. His clarity had not been blurred by the fog that permeated through the rest of his system. He was intelligent enough to register that his current state was in no way positive to humanity, the earth, or its future.

Intelligence was a highly regarded quality in the Society of the Old World. Intellectual knowledge was valued above all else, because it was the intellects who transformed the world.

But sometimes, intelligence—the ability to analyse and understand complexities—could tie people up in knots of confusion, knots of the mind.

And knots of the mind were always a catalyst of suffering.

There was a tight rope to walk in life, so as not to tip off balance, a razor's edge to remain central of, whether it be physical or emotional. His efforts to *protect* us had tipped off balance and become more destructive than positive. But he was too deep inside it to see clearly, objectively, that the most efficient way to protect us was to *heal* and free himself from the Shadows, not isolate himself in spite of them.

"So that's all you're going to do about it?" I challenged him. "Just rot away here."

Discomfort stirred through his body, so pronounced I could feel it as if it were my own, the dominating Shadows in conflict with the buried desires of his heart.

"It's kind of a pathetic solution, don't you think?" I spoke harshly, but it served its purpose. It was affecting him, although his attempt to suppress, to not react, to lead me into thinking he didn't *care* was thorough.

But beneath the Shadows, he cared.

"Wow. I really thought you were a warrior." I turned up the heat by challenging his masculinity.

"A *true* warrior would stand up against the Shadows. Maybe you only know how to go to war with people who are weaker than you, who can't defend themselves."

I was referring to his time in the Old World when he was Governor Koen's highest ranking General. When he was forced to punish and murder people for acting rebelliously against the System. Sometimes they weren't even rebelling. Sometimes Koen simply saw them as 'weak links' in the System, and therefore undeserving to live and waste the City's limited resources.

Instead of shielding up with defenses, my words made Björn's body weaken, which indicated a shameful response.

From what I had observed and studied over time both within my own body and those around me, every emotion had a distinctive and distinguishable impact. Shame, guilt, and apathy were perhaps the most debilitating emotions.

Emotions of fear or anger were debilitating too, but they were slightly more energised versions. They occurred in sharper, hotter spikes that rushed through the body, stimulating the system into action before depleting it.

But Björn's shame didn't simmer for too long.

A flame ignited in his chest. The smallest spark of light.

It was the flame of determination.

Determination to reclaim his power over the Shadows.

There it was.

And within it was a spark of power itself, of light, returning to his weakened being.

"You know, it's never too late," I said a little more kindly, standing.

"It's never too late to just let go. I know it might sound inconvenient to you right now to hear this, but the truth is the light of your heart is still alive. It still glows, no matter how much you believe you're too far gone. It's not true. There's no such truth unless you choose it."

My voice remained detached, less harsh, but still cutting.

"If you *really* don't want to be a burden to humanity and the planet, turn the attention of your warrior spirit onto the Shadows, and fight."

I took one last look at him. I felt my own internal power burning. Power he couldn't ignore. The power of Light. Truth. Freedom.

And with it, I walked away.

Only when I turned the bend of the tunnel, out of his sight, I stopped to process what just happened between us.

These games we played with each other were twisted. Because beneath our masks, both of our hearts only wanted to love.

I leant against the stone for a moment, appreciating its solidity against my back. Grounding. Breathing.

CHAPTER THIRTY-FOUR

O VER THE FOLLOWING DAYS, I moved through each moment with singular vision. Nothing was more important than freeing Björn.

Snow's trust for Bŏdhi continued to grow, allowing me to leave them together whenever I needed to. A sense of attachment was growing between them too, and I wasn't sure if I felt quite as positively about it as I did the fact that it gave me independence I hadn't had since Snow was born.

Bŏdhi was the first man Snow had spent time with, and while he never grew up seeing the traditional mother/father parenting situation around him, his biological nature seemed to know it. The presence of a man spoke to something within him that I couldn't, and Bŏdhi became the significant face of masculinity to him very quickly. Too quickly.

It seemed wrong that his true father was in close enough proximity to be what Bŏdhi was becoming to Snow, but in essence I knew he was too far away.

And the fact that Snow was happy to be left with Bŏdhi for long extents of time meant that I could work more thoroughly with Björn on healing, not that we were quite at the healing stage yet, and nor could I quite claim to be working *with* him.

But he was slowly reopening to me the more he reopened to himself. And I had little doubt he would soon surrender his resistance entirely.

He was painfully stubborn. That was something I'd learnt very quickly after meeting him in the City, when he was too stubborn to leave me behind, even though I was a stark stranger to him at that point, and he was well aware that it would have been a far simpler, easier, and less dangerous journey to travel alone.

As long as his stubborn resistance was directed at me, any significant progress in helping him was challenging. But I knew that it could work in his favour when his attention shifted from shutting me out to shutting out the Shadows.

His will, when set on something, was as solid and unshakable as the earth itself, and it was this very quality that would give him the tenacity to transcend the pit of darkness he had fallen victim to.

I was merely a guiding presence to remind him of the light. And so, I sat with him, as often as he would allow, with my attention on the aliveness of both my heart and his.

This was *Rule Two* from the Shaman's journal: *Merge.*

> *Once a willingness to step out of the darkness has been established, one must refamiliarize themselves with Light through spending time with those who live in higher frequencies.*

> *When an energy body is full, it takes time to empty. A reawakening of consciousness can only ever be gradual. The expanse of consciousness that is available to us is so exquisitely vast, a sudden shift from darkness into pure Light would be too radical on the system. Like an electric shock, it would stop the heart.*

Your subject must rewire their entire system to realign with Light, swapping toxic habits, beliefs, actions, environments, and people, for positive ones.

At this stage, spending time with someone who is already empty and embodies a high amount of Light and power is critical.

We are all products of our thoughts, actions, environment, and the people we spend the most time around.

The expanse of Light a Shaman carries, in combination with their Mystic constitution and capacity for healing, can discount the negativity carried by thousands. That is how potent you are when you return to your full power.

But in the current state of the world, this is rare. And that is why darkness prevails.

Even in the spheres of those who claim to want to help, there are many people who think they are further ahead than they are in reality to be of any significant impact. Many egocentric frauds wearing benevolent masks.

It is critical that the Shaman in training rids himself of all egocentricity. A true Shaman is a non-identified being whose intent has shifted from inward facing to outward serving. A true Shaman must be empty of all baggage, for his heart to be full enough to truly heal others.

If the ink of this rule has appeared for you, you are this.

And the kind of merging I speak of is within your ability.

Now practice.

Björn's heart was reawakening. Gradually, but truly. And it was usually in the moments that it was beaming back to vitality that he would demand I leave. But it was not his voice I heard. It was the voice of the Shadows, sensing what I sensed: his shift back towards freedom, which would mean their loss of an immense energy source.

My presence irritated them, which irritated *him*. His entire body was in conflict. Light reverberating against Shadow.

His eyes would sharpen and his skin would glimmer with a metallic effervescence that was not pretty to my eyes; my eyes could only see within it the Iron beings from which the substance originated.

I experimented with the force of air, calling it in to work with me as I worked with Björn.

It would announce its presence through a rush of wind that could not be mistaken as natural in a location so deep below the earth's surface.

Even Björn could not ignore the paranormal waves of fresher, cleaner air that began to wash through the tunnel. And it restored his being as it swept into his lungs and into his system on each inward breath, the way a tree might be restored after only knowing the air of an enclosed greenhouse.

I could *see* it, as clearly as I sensed its effect on his state of being.

Luminous, sky blue L·ight Máttẹr. Light Magic, through the expression of the Air element.

He couldn't see it, but I'd be shocked if he hadn't felt it, moving through his airways, clearing and cleansing the tension he had been accumulating. Everything within him that had begun to harden like iron was beginning to soften, dissolve into the expanse of healing light that was more supreme than any amount of density.

Moānā, Ṫasmai and a couple of other kids were playing with Snow by the stream in the open, park-like area, where the sun shone down through hand-carved cracks in the high roof.

Moānā was quite territorial over Snow, which was amusing, but also consoling, for it meant he was always fiercely protected from any kid who might have otherwise chosen to be unkind.

He was smaller, purer, and more innocent and naive than the rest of the children there. He still didn't often use words to communicate, and he had a calm, placid way about him that could have easily become the target of childish games. To see him lose any amount of his clean, untainted perception of the world would have been devastating to me.

Bỡdhi and Phỡenix were keeping an eye on them nearby, while Phỡenix worked on sanding a wooden handle with concentrated precision. She had taken on a job as a toolmaker there, which was what she used to do in the Valley, and still appeared as passionate.

She looked up as I approached.

"You look…tired. I was going to use a stronger word, but that captures it." She never concealed her honest thoughts for the sake of niceness, which I appreciated about her, although when we first met I found it confronting. Where I came from, in the City of the Old World, people only interacted through masks of politeness and communicated through veils of lies.

"How's it going?" Bŏdhi asked.

I took a breath in, unsure how to answer the question, then a breath out.

"Yeah…" I drifted off.

Phŏenix's observation was accurate; I felt more drained than I had in a long time.

Calling on Air and trying to work with the unseen forces of this realm was still a new practice that required a high amount of concentration. I was exhausting more energy than I might have if my skills were more refined and I knew precisely where to direct it.

Magic had always been something that happened spontaneously, so spontaneously that I didn't know to call it magic. Learning to summon it and use it in alignment with my will was the challenge. I had to be in both a state of absolute let go, and absolute precision at once.

Bŏdhi and Phŏenix looked between each other.

Bŏdhi jumped to his feet. "You know what, Snow's really happy just playing with the kids. Phŏenix, can you keep an eye on them? I want to get cleaned up and she could probably use a shower too."

His clothes and skin were still stained with brown smudges of dirt and soil from his morning shift of farm work.

"Of course," she said.

"Where's Bear?" I asked.

"Outside."

I nodded. He'd been spending more and more time outside, roaming and exploring the area. If I had the option, I would be out there with him. I wondered if he was finding more animals to mate with, and smiled inwardly at the fact that no one there knew what he truly was. Nor was I planning to tell them. It was easier if they believed he was simply an abnormally noble bear.

Everyone in the community had grown used to his unthreatening presence now. There had been no drama around anyone assuming his rightful place was on the table. There was no food shortage, so as long as there continued to be an abundance of animals around to hunt and plant-life to eat, Bear was safe.

"Thanks," I said to Bŏdhi as we walked back into the tunnels, towards the showers.

"You need to look after yourself too," he said.

"I mean for everything. Snow likes you a lot."

"I thought that might bother you actually."

"Oh, I..." But since he was being honest, I decided not to fabricate my answer. "Well, it does a bit. But it's stupid. Björn will understand. And the truth is I feel grateful that he has a solid, male presence, and you're so good with him. I think I'm probably more bothered by the fact that..." I trailed off, realising my ability to self-edit was declining at the same rate as my energy, and I was moments away from expressing too much.

I could suddenly feel the electricity of Bŏdhi's presence beside me in the way I had been so determined to ignore.

"The fact that...?"

"Nothing. I'm just gonna stop talking."

I felt him watching me, but he didn't press it.

"I want to show you something. If you're up for it," he said after walking a distance in silence.

"Something started...happening recently. You're the only person I can think of who might understand it in some way." He looked over to see my reaction.

I was curious.

"Sure, now?"

"I understand if you're not up for it," he said.

"No, I want to know what it is."

He led me past the shower block but picked up two towels on our way. It was only when we followed a dimly lit, vacant tunnel towards a familiar, luminous blue glow that beamed out from an opening up ahead that I recognised where he was taking me.

It was the glow worm cave he'd shown me the night I arrived, and while I'd been there once before, it felt equally as enchanting when we stepped inside.

And equally as isolated.

CHAPTER THIRTY-FIVE

I T WAS ONLY WHEN we stopped moving that I realised no echo of human sound or activity carried the distance, and the echo of silence replaced all other noise.

We paused beneath the arch-shaped entrance.

"I hope you don't feel uncomfortable bathing here. The water's fresh, I promise, and deeper than it looks."

I walked over to the shimmering pool in the centre of the cave and touched my hand through its surface.

It was shockingly cold, and relatively deep, as promised.

He lifted his shirt and lowered into the water in his shorts. I felt unsure of his intentions, but he acted casual. He said he wanted to show me something, and I was sure it wasn't his fit body.

I slipped out of my outer layers, leaving only my underwear. In the Valley, the tribe had no shame around bathing naked in public, but in this circumstance, it didn't feel appropriate.

I lowered into the water, which immediately shocked my system. Thoughts vanished. I let out a shrill sound in expression of the shrill feeling.

Bŏdhi hadn't spoken.

It was dark, but the bluish glow from above illuminated his face where he floated. He was watching me again with a certain look. But one I couldn't read. Once again, I felt drawn to him in a way that was both electric and calm, like the water we bathed in.

"So, what did you want to show me?" I asked, with the water up to my chin.

He didn't answer, but held my gaze and stood slowly, chest lifting up from where it too had been hidden beneath the silver surface. I shifted back discreetly, my mind hoping he wasn't about to move towards me in the way my body hoped he might.

The water was only waist deep, and he lifted both hands up from beneath the surface with a sense of meticulousness that drew my attention to them alone.

His palms faced the water, and as he lifted them higher, two channels of water lifted up with them from the centre of both palms.

He flicked his hands, letting the twirling streams drop and splash lightly back down to the water that was otherwise dead still. So still it reflected the starlike shimmers of light that coated the roof above, as if we were bathing, floating through the galaxy.

His expression was calm and focussed, barely cognizant of my presence. His eyes watched the flow of his hands while they seamlessly lifted two more channels of water, closer together this time. He made a quick spinning movement with his fingers and the channels twisted around each other as if they had an intelligence of their own.

But the intelligence they moved to was not their own—it was Bõdhi's, and perhaps that of the water itself.

He moved his palms in different directions. The water moved with him.

I knew immediately what it meant.

But I didn't say it yet.

I didn't say anything.

I simply watched as he showed me, without explanation, other subtleties of the unbelievable yet very real affinity he had discovered with the element.

Finally, he stopped.

"You're shivering," he said, and it was only then that I realised I was cold to the bone.

"Oh," I looked down at my body, which generated slight ripples in the water that enveloped me.

When I lifted my gaze, Bŏdhi was by my side. His hand sent a shock wave through my body as it touched the base of my spine to guide me out of the water. Not because his skin was any colder than my skin. His hand was still warm, hot, and I realised that while I was shivering, he was insensitive to the freezing water, just like he had been in the snow. It made sense now. It was part of something bigger.

The sensation of his hand on my bare skin spread up my spine and over my back, his touch even more electric than before. I realised it might have been the electricity of the water element in his blood, reacting to the magic of air in mine.

It was then that I also realised this immense draw I felt to him ran so much deeper than the attraction of my mind or body. Beyond chemistry, even.

It was the draw of the magic we both carried, speaking to each other, wanting to be acknowledged. Explored. Explored *together*.

He wrapped a towel around me. My body was numb. He wrapped his arms around the towel, around my shoulders. His chest against my back was as warm as his hand had been.

There was no tension in his body. He was not waiting or anticipating my response to what I'd witnessed.

When I felt mobility beginning to return, I turned in his arms and looked up into his eyes. His breath was hot, and his scent was as fresh as the water we'd emerged from.

I didn't quite know where to begin in words.

So instead, I stepped back, to show him in return just how deeply I understood what he'd shown me.

But first, I hugged myself tightly inside the towel once more, and shrugged on my clothes to calm the shivering, though they didn't do much to provide warmth and were no match to the heat I received from Bõdhi's body.

I stood still, closing my eyes for just a moment, letting my awareness drop more deeply into the stillness at the centre of my being, from which I could access the infinite source power of the Air element.

He waited as patiently as I had, watching every manoeuvre I made, excitement rising. Something deep within him knew what I was about to reveal.

A howling sound swept through the tunnel outside the cavern as I drew a force of wind towards me. I didn't know yet what to do with it. It rushed into the tunnel and blew my hair back, then wrapped around me in a tornado.

I drew the power of the wind that spun around me into my chest, then focalised it into my palms, still deciding on what to use it for. I wondered what would happen if I released it onto Bõdhi, if it had the power to propel him backwards, but I didn't want o hurt him.

Instead, I closed my eyes and connected the Air magic in my palms to my mind then let it out in a gentle, glistening sky blue stream that drifted towards Bõdhi and wrapped around his head.

I have been waiting for a long time to meet you, I whispered silently into the wind that travelled through his mind.

He jumped back, knowing my lips had not moved. I let the Air drop out of my body. As alive as I felt in spirit, my body was suddenly exhausted.

I stepped forwards and fell into Bõdhi. He held me tight, uncensored, and I felt all his relief and wonder as potently as I felt his arms around me.

He let out a laugh and kissed my hair, the crown of my head, and then my lips. I kissed him back, energy rushing back through my body, but a different kind of energy now. Passionate and free. Then sense kicked back in.

"Woah." I stepped back.

"Woah," I repeated as I processed the full spectrum of everything that just happened.

He was unapologetic and laughed again, acting as if the kiss didn't have the implications that it did.

Maybe he wasn't acting.

Maybe it didn't have implications at all.

Maybe it was innocent and non-romantic. A fleeting moment of elation between two people who had just realised they were of the same cluster. An *enchanted* cluster with access to celestial powers that no ordinary human could possibly understand.

The feeling of joy and consolation when it washed through my system, the immense power, was beyond description, beyond words. But with Bǒdhi, I didn't need them.

"What does it mean?" he finally asked, expecting I knew.

But the meaning I had begun to understand was still fractured. I was still piecing it together, and that moment was another piece. But I knew more than he did, so I began by laying what I held in my mind of the unfinished puzzle out for him to see too.

"There's this symbol I was shown by the Axsⅽendants in a… vision. It took me a long time to understand it. But it is basically a formula for defeating the Sky People, and sending them from the earth for good," I began.

"It involves a cluster of five people who are all embodiments of the five fundamental elements of nature. It didn't take me long to realise that all the mystic abilities I have access to are, in essence, distinctive of the Air element. But I was alone. I wasn't sure if any of you were still alive, let alone know that there was this whole community of humans that had survived down here. Which kind of makes finding the other three elementals harder…" I realised.

I had assumed our original tribe would reveal themselves to be the cluster. The tribe had grown significantly. There were many humans here I hadn't even met yet.

"But I haven't really been looking yet. I've been so focused on Björn."

I looked to Bõdhi to read how he was interpreting the information. He didn't seem to be in any kind of disbelief.

I tried to think of whether anyone immediately came to mind when I thought of the other elements.

"Can you show me the symbol?" Bõdhi asked.

"Is there anything I can draw with down here?"

"I have chalk in my room. Well, the kids' room." He was already slipping on his shirt and threw both of our towels over his shoulder.

"Thanks," I said. "And thanks for…showing me."

He reached for my hand and led me back out into the tunnel.

The power pulsing between our palms was so immense I couldn't think about anything else over the entire walk to his room. My mind was blank, but my heart was full.

CHAPTER THIRTY-SIX

T HE CREAM WALL WAS covered in black chalk drawings, and I smiled as I saw one of Bear, with two people riding on his back. One tall, one tiny. I assumed it was me and Snow.

"They admire you a lot," Bõdhi said on behalf of Moānā and Ṫasmai, who had clearly drawn the picture.

"So do I," he added as he rustled through the kids' things until he found an old tin of charcoal.

I took a stick and sat in front of the wall. The symbol was imprinted in my mind, but I was mindful to sketch each curve and line accurately, and each picture in their precise positions.

Bõdhi sat beside me.

I explained to him my interpretation.

"Two earth symbols, but only one of the others," he commented. I shrugged.

"And the Axscendants didn't explain it in any way?"

"Apart from that, it's connected to the work they completed as humans. There're five of them. I think they also embody each of the five elements. I also think that's why my connection with Qiạ̃hui is stronger than the others. Because I *think* she's also air.

"They wouldn't share in detail what it meant to them because they don't want us to confuse their past with our future. They were clear that our work is an *extension* of theirs. Not a repetition."

"Mmmm." Bǒdhi returned his gaze to the image. "Simple. But not simple."

"Yep."

"So, the fact that there're two earth symbols means we need to find two Earth people?"

"I don't know. It could mean anything. Part of the magic of the earth element could even be the ability to split oneself in two," I suggested.

I stared at the central symbol, the one I was almost certain represented the Sky People. I wanted to know more about their physical manifestation. To be able to work against them, we needed to understand them.

I stood.

"I'm going to find Bear."

Bǒdhi looked up at me. "Ok."

I turned to leave.

"Wait." He stood.

I turned back.

"Ah, I just. I don't want things to get weird now—"

"No weirdness," I agreed.

"This is…obviously important." He looked back at the symbol. "I just don't want anything to get in the way of it."

"Agreed," I said.

I assumed by 'anything' he meant the kiss, or the inconvenient feelings that swirled through me in his presence, which would have made things a lot easier and less guilt ridden for me. So why did my heart drop a little?

"See you later," I turned.

Tension hung in the air. Unspoken words. Unexpressed feelings dragging behind me.

"You know I've been *trying* to act normal," he confessed.

I paused.

"As long as that's what you want, I'll keep trying."

I nodded but didn't turn. I was confused. *Conveniently* confused.

CHAPTER THIRTY-SEVEN

*B*EAR.

Dense clouds coated the sky and there was a light dusting of mist in the air. The moisture in the clouds made the air humid, rain waiting patiently for the right moment to fall.

Bear, I'm at the cave opening. Can you meet me? Can you hear me? I tuned in to the essence of his being, sending the message from my mind to his.

I waited, looking out at the farmlands. The sky was growing darker. Most of the farmers had retreated inside for the evening, and the few that were still in the fields were collecting their tools and wrapping up, which meant night would soon be falling.

Daylight would have been more appropriate for what I wanted to do. But there I was. I was too curious to wait.

Distant footsteps began to thump the earth, footsteps that were heavier than humans. Bear swung around the edge of the cliff ledge, his hefty body swaying as he came to a stop. He'd been running.

"You heard my call."

He rubbed his nose against my side enthusiastically, and I stumbled back.

"Woah," I laughed.

Instead of communicating through voice, I practiced sending my words to him through mind-to-mind transference.

I want to go to the cliff we came to the other day.

Bear hesitated, as if already aware my more direct intention was not quite so simple, but he lowered for me to climb onto his back.

He ran across the open land tirelessly, and when we reached the cliff's edge, he didn't slow. He continued forth at full speed.

I thought he was playing some kind of bearish game, but he leapt into the air, and I clung onto his fur more tightly in horror as I processed my absolute lack of control.

We were falling, falling…

Flying?

Violent shivers rippled erratically through Bear's body, and he began to morph and shapeshift mid-air, faster than I could comprehend, until instead of clinging to the neck of a burly bear, I was trying to find my grip on a soaring dragon.

His coat mutated from thick brown fur to smooth golden scales that shimmered brilliantly in what was left of the day's light. Impressive wings shot out from his sides and his head grew significantly larger, neck longer, ears sharper.

His wide-spread wings saved us from hitting the ground, and instead of falling, we were gliding. He flapped the air and we began to rise higher.

The thrill of fear and exhilaration rippled through me at once as I found my balance aboard his tremendous back. Fear for my life. But exhilaration for being, in that moment, so unmistakably alive.

Somehow, as I settled into place, the sensation of flying felt familiar, natural, as if it wasn't my first experience. I supposed it was similar to riding Bear when he was in bear form, in the sense that I could feel the air sweeping past me at speeds I normally wouldn't experience unless caught in a wild wind. But without the heavy thump of each rhythmic step, this experience was smoother, freer.

We were flying at cloud height now, and the air became denser, warmer as we sailed through a cloud. My vision was blurred by the grey fog.

Woah, Bear! I cautioned as he took an accelerated dip after a significantly high peak, simultaneously thrilled by the adrenaline rush. *I don't have much to hold onto!*

You won't fall. Trust me. His majestic voice replied. *And if you do, I'll catch you. I can fly faster than you can fall.*

As if a practice of trust, he took one big swoop of his colossal wings and soared low again, this time spinning a full rotation.

I shrieked, recognizing that in a split second I'd be upside down but had no time to argue. Then, by a miracle, I was sitting upright again, floating through the sky as if my head had never dipped towards the ground. My heart beat rapidly.

He took an abrupt turn one direction, then darted back the opposite way.

A rumble erupted through his chest and I realised he was laughing!

You are bound to me as my rider now, Maya. You have been for a long time. You just haven't had the opportunity to discover it yet.

I wondered just how long was 'long.'

You couldn't fall unless you desperately willed yourself to, and even then it would take a lot of effort. It's a part of an ancient bond between our species, so that a rider is always safe and protected with their dragon, he explained.

I took a moment to process his words, then with a spark of courage tested it for myself. I jumped my weight off his back, separating momentarily, but a magnetic field more pronounced than gravity immediately drew us back together.

"Hahaaaa!" I felt liberated by a new sense of freedom now I knew there was no chance of falling.

I turned my attention inward to the intimate kinship that interlocked us, realising that our connection ran so much deeper than I could have ever imagined.

With eyes momentarily closed, I felt my heart pouring open more completely with every inhale, and in direct correspondence, his heart merged more completely with mine.

We had already developed a way of sensing the subtleties of each other's intentions and emotions, but it was reaching a new level now.

The sense of separation between us continued to dissolve until his body was an extension of mine, and mine his. We were flying as one being, hearts beating in synchronised rhythm.

The air flicked back my hair as we soared against it, threatening to throw my body back with it, but I knew it was not possible, so I held out my arms, opening my chest to the endless expanse of incoming sky.

I was not only one with Bear now but in complete unification with the air itself, light as a feather while its invisible, intangible but unmistakably divine force pinned me upright.

"Weeheeeee!" I called ecstatically to the wind, then felt the beast beneath me slow, my hair dropping with our loss of momentum.

What is it?!

The ship is not far ahead, he replied tentatively. *That's where we are going, right?*

In my elation, I'd forgotten my own intention for being there.

Bear lowered cautiously towards the earth and in a swift scan of the land below, I saw it too. The singular silver dome, in the middle of miles of otherwise untouched land, was unmissable.

We landed a distance away and approached slowly. Bear's pointy ears were spiked upwards in high alert, and I suddenly felt lost for what I actually wanted to do now we were in the ship's vicinity.

I felt Bear's reluctance to continue any closer, but he did not voice it. Perhaps part of the dragon/rider relationship meant that he was bound to serve, not to interfere.

I was reluctant now too. Part of me would have gladly received Bear's interference. But I could not yet feel the disorienting pain that others described when they got too close, so I assumed we were relatively safe.

I circled the perimeter a few times, examining the shiny, smooth silver structure. While a high amount of my awareness was on the ship, I split myself in two, and an aspect of my attention remained inwards. The moment my state of internal clarity was disturbed, I would leave.

I stopped circling and became still, which allowed me to feel more directly the frequencies that lingered in the air.

There was a sense of something dark and haunting. As my gaze softened, I began to see a black mist seeping out from the ship and spreading gradually around it.

As if mirroring the impregnated storm clouds that coated the sky above, etheric clouds of dense black L·ight Måttęr consumed the space around the ship. It spread through the air, drifting discretely over the land, creeping our direction, edging closer, closer.

But the consciousness that was present within the black fog was ignorant to the fact that I could see it.

Instead of retreating, I drew the power of Air into my heart and then into my hands. I felt the rush of its magic flowing from my chest and down both arms to create wells in the centre of my palms, where it pulsated, ready, waiting. When I looked down, the scars were glowing.

I raised my palms and gently pressed the magic outwards where it began to flow in airborne rivers of silver blue mist that was a stark contrast against the black.

The black fog reacted as if in fear, retreating backwards from the glistening L·ight Måttęr, as if aware that if they met, it may well dissolve and disappear.

Both masses of mist moved with agility. It was like watching a graceful dance, although nothing about what was happening was, in essence, graceful. It was war. Dark vs Light.

"You're not welcome here," I spoke firmly, unsure of what I was actually speaking to, or if the dark matter had the kind of consciousness that would understand.

The assertive force of my words seemed to reach it though. The brooding Shadow swept back as if propelled by a violent wave of wind.

"If you are not in service of love and light, you're not welcome in this body. There's no room for you here," I stated.

The ship creaked, an eerie echo ringing through the air that was followed by a shrill, shrieking sound, like sharp nails scratching its shiny exterior.

A shiver rippled down my shoulders and spine.

"That's right." I collected all the courage left within me and held it in the centre of my being. "And if you're not here in service and support of nature, you're not welcome on this land."

The Air Magic pouring from my palms reached the ship, enveloping it in glistening silver blue mist.

Another loud creak echoed from the ship. It began to vibrate, emitting a low, mechanical hum that gradually became more piercing. My ears rung, the pitch rising so high it stung, reverberating through my brain.

I lost my capacity to focus. I couldn't maintain the sphere of Air Magic that was working as a protective shield around me, and the mist that enveloped the ship swept back into my palms.

I was bare. Naked. Exposed.

I clasped my hands over my ears to escape the shrieking, but it penetrated straight through the weak armour of my human limbs. My mind began to blur. I knew what this meant—I'd been warned—but I was determined not to become a victim.

The air was dark now, with night approaching; the looming black fog progressed towards me once more.

"Bear! We have to leave. Now!" I called, the intensity of my objective cutting through some of the fog that had already

seeped into my mind.

My forehead thumped. I could feel the pressure of Sky Consciousness wanting to implant itself into my mind. I could not hear their thoughts yet, but I could barely hear my own either. My mind was weak and, in response, so was my body.

I felt heavy, weighed down by bricks I could not see and could not shake.

I ran to Bear's side to find him shuddering and breathing heavily, drawing back his neck as if choking.

They've reached him too! How could I have been so ignorant to bring him here!

I had believed he was the most robust creature on Earth, utterly invincible, and impenetrable by such forces of lower consciousness.

Stay back. He stepped forward, guarding me behind the armour of his impressively muscular body, and thrust his long neck back on a mighty inhale.

I froze as he exhaled a trajectory of dark smoke, followed by a funnel of vivid orange flames that devoured the metal exterior of the ship. The cloud of dense black L·ight Måttęr retreated inside, hiding where the brilliant, almost blinding vigour of fire couldn't reach.

The violent reverberating sensation in my brain ceased immediately, but the Shadow's determination to return in full force only escalated under its attack. A shrill screeching sound that was alien to my ears resounded from the ship, even more piercing than the previous sounds, deafening.

Get on my back. Now. Bear directed me and I followed his demand without hesitation, leaping briskly aboard as he lowered his broad chest to the ground.

As soon as I was locked in place on his back, my vision blurred, the lens of my eyes flickering in and out of focus. The world was painted by flashes of fluorescent colours that were not of this Earth or this realm, and I began to see a more intricate mosaic of reality that was not usually available to my human eyes.

But it wasn't a side effect of my state of delirium. It didn't take long to realise that my eyes were no longer mine alone. I was seeing through Bear's vision. Through the eyes of a dragon, a multiplex of dimensions that existed outside of limited human perception were visible.

He watched the ship, which was now stained bronze, with sharp eyes as he spread his wings wide, and did not shift his attention until we were high in the air.

I felt drained as we glided back the direction we came, even though I'd barely exhausted much physical energy. The energy it took to remain free from the tenacious clutch of Sky Consciousness was greater than I had prepared for.

My brain was foggier than usual, but I maintained enough clarity to understand it hadn't been permanently violated. I tried to let go of the tension pulsating through my forehead, tension that would have generated a matrix of looping thoughts if I let it, if I listened.

But instead, I surrendered, not to the tempting hum of mental noise, but to the space that lay beneath it, to my heart, the air, and all I knew to be pure and true.

I leant my stomach over Bear's warm scales and watched the earth sweep by below.

The land, while under the shade of falling darkness, still appeared crisp and vibrant through Bear's night vision, and a wider expanse of everything around was perceivable. His eyes, which viewed the world not single-pointedly but in full peripheral vision, had the enhanced capacity to catch the slightest movements miles away, and zoom in and out like a camera lens as desired.

It was dizzying to adjust to his magnified vision and made me recognize just how little of the vast scope of reality I had been cognizing just as a by-product of being human.

Finally, rain fell from the pregnant storm clouds, and vivid flashes of lightning lit the sky in fleeting moments.

The icy droplets cleansed my mind as if a gift from the sky. As the rainfall became heavier, and the accompanying wind whipped against my exposed forehead, my brain fog began to dissipate.

I'm sorry for insisting we go. Let's not do that again.

Bear didn't reply, but I sensed the firmness of his agreement.

While our adventure shook me more than I had prepared myself to be shaken, a valuable sense of understanding was brewing. My intention to gain insight into the workings of Sky Consciousness was successful, and I had direct experience in how to cut through the blur of their infection now.

Only on the surface did the Shadows appear powerful. In reality, they were weaker than I had imagined. Fear was their one and only power, and without it, they were but black clouds of empty mist, drifting through space and time as they had been for centuries.

If they carried any true amount of power, they would have already successfully dominated our species. They would have stolen our bodies and established permanent residency on our dying planet long ago.

I suppose they almost did. But the true, patient, and eternal power that lay in the heart of humankind and in the core of Earth itself shone through, brighter and more robust than any amount of force could rival.

It was obvious now that the Sky Consciousness only had one weapon. Fear was the sole frequency of their being. They cultivated fear, fed on fear, and stimulated fear in other beings with the singular desire to absorb it.

They were not innately evil, just desperate to survive on a planet where energy sources that supported their livelihood were scarce. But once a source was found, it provided an abundance of fuel that had the potential to feed them for the length of their life.

Every living entity relied on energy to survive. The dance of energy through each expression of nature was the foundation of all life. It was nature's way, natural law.

We could not *hate* or despise the Sky People for their primal determination to live. In comparison, we humans were not innocent.

We also fed on the energy of other living entities to survive, just in different forms—forms that existed within the circle of life. Animals, plants, water, air. All born of earth, and to earth they would inevitably return, just like our bodies.

The energy that sourced our livelihood was only borrowed. It cycled through many different forms. From the beginning of time, forever in transit. Eternal.

No amount of compassionate understanding could discount the fact that the energy the Sky People cultivated to survive was not in alignment with the cycles of our natural world. It was, in fact, destructive. Foreign.

It was of another planet, another realm. A denser realm born of black matter and an infrastructure of negative-drawing energy. It would destroy humankind and Earth alike if it won dominance here.

Earth's energetic constitution was of a fundamentally positive nature. Pure Light was the fabric upon which all that existed here rested upon. The contrast between the two coexisting frequencies was too great to be upheld.

One force would survive this metaphysical war, but if it was the Sky People, nothing would survive for long.

So, the only solution was their extinction. At least from this planet.

And I was beginning to see that their fear of being dissolved by light when we stood unbending, and in full embodiment of its omniscient power, might be the key to driving them away.

That, and the united force of all of nature's elements, working through five humans, in harmonized balance.

The combination of heavy rain, dense cloud cover, and nightfall made it hard to see ahead, but when the mountain that announced the underground city appeared through the storm-induced fog, Bear, in his brilliant and almighty dragon form, swooped low to land.

I slipped from his back as he shook and shapeshifted back into his familiar bear form, then reboarded, wrapping my fingers through his warm and welcoming fur.

We rode on, both in silent agreement that to the rest of the community, he should remain a bear, and bear only. At least for now.

It took them long enough to adjust to co-inhabiting with a bear. Neither of us were prepared or interested in engaging with the attention we would undoubtedly receive from anyone who caught a glimpse of the great golden dragon.

CHAPTER THIRTY-EIGHT

T HE NIGHT WAS BLACK when I returned, and Snow was upset. I'd left him for too long. My clothes were soaked, skin dripping, body shivering, but not to a bothersome degree.

The arctic air had reinvigorated me. Winter would be upon the land soon enough and I was grateful. The cold temperatures and wild weathers of the new season would help us maintain clarity as we progressed in our work with the Sky People, as it kindly had that night.

Anya was waiting with Snow beneath the shelter of the cave opening, their faces hidden in shadow. The glittering blue glow worms that lit the tunnel behind them were more star-like than the brooding sky that night.

Rain still fell, although a little more lightly now, and the repetitive sound as it patterned down onto the stone was soothing.

While I felt centred again within, my body was still rattled by what happened, a little on edge, and the surprise of their presence startled me more than it usually might. But I hid it. I thought I'd have at least a moment of stillness to breathe before having to see anyone, but here I was, and so were they.

I slid from Bear's back and knelt down to where Snow sat in Anya's lap.

A curtain of rain dribbled down from the overhang above, leaving puddles along the ledge, but they remained dry. In the glimmer of light, I could see Snow's eyes were red and his cheeks were lined with dry tears, but he was no longer crying. Perhaps the serene sound was soothing him too.

"I'm sorry, baby," I told him as I held him against my chest, then looked across to Anya.

"I'm sorry for leaving him with you for so long," I repeated to her. "And thank you."

"It was fine until an hour or so ago. I think he just panicked that you weren't coming back. He's pretty worn out too. I fed him, but he wouldn't sleep without you."

"I appreciate it," I said as I breathed in his mild baby scent. I wasn't used to spending so much time away from him either.

In my arms, he immediately relaxed.

Anya didn't ask what I'd been out doing. She simply stood and patted Bear's head gently as she waited for me before beginning back down the tunnel. I had noticed that she often disappeared from the cave for extended amounts of time too, and never shared what she went out to do. She treated me with the sense of nonchalance that she preferred to be treated with in return.

"How was your day?" I asked Snow as I stood, sitting him on my hip. "Did you have fun with Anya?"

He nodded and tucked his head into my chest with an affectionate smile.

Bear was breathing heavily and after we'd walked a distance into the tunnel, he shook. Drops of captured rain splashed off his fur in all directions.

"Bear," Snow called over my shoulder.

Bear jogged up and touched his wet nose to Snow's cheek. Snow wriggled and laughed and reached out to pat his damp forehead.

I lifted him up to sit on Bear's back and held his hand as we walked.

"How are things going with Björn?" Anya asked.

"He's changing." I was tactful with my choice of words.

I knew she'd most likely pass on whatever I shared to Katya and Yegor, and was careful not to convey any possible cause for concern that might lead them to consider extermination as a plausible option.

"I can see his will to be free now. His intent is becoming more dominant than the Shadows' intent, which is the beginning of the end, I think."

We walked quietly. I could sense her lingering curiosity, but she didn't impose it onto me by asking more questions. I continued anyway, both for her enlightenment and to explore out loud new understandings of my own.

"Our problem, when this happened to us in the past, was that we didn't realise the human mind is more powerful than the Sky Consciousness. The levels of consciousness we have access to as human beings are so much higher and vaster, but we dimmed ourselves to meet and merge with theirs, which is of an innately low frequency."

The more people that understood this, the better the chance we had of remaining free in this New World we were co-creating.

"When humans live in direct alignment with their heart and call their personal power back from all the areas in their lives where it has leaked, internal freedom is almost inevitable.

"It's a choice to serve the Shadows. A habit. Hard to break once we start believing that the thoughts they send are our own, and even harder when we can't discern between what is the voice of the Shadows and the voice of truth within our own mind. But not impossible.

"The extent of our freedom rides upon the tail of our internal choices alone. No one else is responsible."

Anya listened intently. I knew the workings of the etheric world were hard to grasp when one had only existed and thought within the one-dimensional laws of physical form. But she was open. And she didn't seem to doubt or resist my words, even though I'm sure they sounded foreign.

"And the book?" she asked.

"I thought it was a joke."

She bowed her head, disappointed.

"But I've seen something like it before. It can only be read by those who are aligned with the information."

Anya looked up, hope in her eyes.

"It reveals itself to me page by page, only when I'm ready to use it."

"You are the one he was waiting for."

I let out an exhale.

"I guess I am."

Shaman. Air-Bender. In-Between. Eliminator of Shadows. From humans, and from Earth. The Mother was not frugal with the important roles she bestowed upon me to fulfil, and I wondered why she didn't split the load. I felt like I was juggling, unsure of where to direct my attention. Save Björn. Find the rest of the cluster. Master Air-Bending. Eliminate Sky People. I supposed they went hand in hand.

The Mother never overwhelms or overburdens us.
She knows our limits.

Qiaŏhui had said this to me after I was used as the In-Between. All the deaths I experienced felt like too much. I carried them with me, haunted.

A mind untrained in equanimity may choose
overwhelm. But when you live pristinely now by
now by now, it is not a valid response, for time is

not stacked on top of itself to create that pressure. It is only now. Birth and death, rising and falling with every breath.

Experience, let go.

It is not natural to hold onto the past, just as it is not natural to hold onto the breath.

Let go, let go, let go.

And be with what is now.

So, what is now?

I thought of Adam for the first time in a long time, realising that we had found a safe, stable place where he could join us. Now that my mental abilities were being confirmed as one of the key mystic elements of Air Magic, maybe there was a way to call him there the way I had sent a message on the wind to Björn, detailing my location. But was it possible for wind to cross dimensional barriers?

If he came up to earth from Santōṣha with Farrah and Cole, there was a chance I could guide them to the underground city, to safety. My connection with him was strong. I didn't doubt my ability to tune into his essence and direct the Airwaves carrying my messages his way...

But first, I would have to breach the Veil between our dimensions. It would be more complicated than making contact with someone in the same realm. I was almost certain it was outside of my current limits. But I could try. I would. After completing my work with Björn. And Bŏdhi...

CHAPTER THIRTY-NINE

S LEEP SEEMED IMPOSSIBLE THAT night. Every cell in my body raced while I lay on my back, still, staring up into the blackness.

There were two critical scenes approaching climax at once, and the magnitude of energy available within my body rose to meet the momentum of life that was suddenly urging me forth after some time of contemplative stagnation.

Sharing the mystery of the symbol with Bõdhi enforced a more complete sense of trust in what was unfolding, for it confirmed that its message was real and actionable.

I felt more determined to find those linked with the rest of the elements, who, I was sure, were within the same cave I presently lay. Whether they were aware of their own mystic abilities was another mystery. But at that late hour, there was nothing I could do to hunt them down, so I switched scenes.

Björn.

I rose slowly to sit upright, careful not to wake Snow, and crossed my legs on the hard mattress.

Accepting my inescapable awakeness, I lit a candle and opened the old Shaman's Book of Shadows. I had reached Rule Five. I ran my hand along the blank page, feeling a river of White Magic flowing through me.

I sought more direct sorcery that I could use to manipulate Björn's energy field now that he was more open to receiving my help—which was a victory in itself.

And it seemed I was ready to receive it. But the ink that began to reveal itself on the page was not another rule; it was more of an aside.

> *A note to consider on the heightened power and danger of working with people when they are unconscious.*

Perfect. It was night.

> *This may or may not be relevant, depending on your ability to remain clear when the force of Shadows entering you is intensified. You must be wise and honour your own limitations.*

> *The sleeping state opens the energy body in a way that makes it both more vulnerable and malleable. The grip of the Shadows loosens, and people became easier to work on because their mind's defences cannot hold the Shadow patterns in place.*

> *Sleeping beside someone who is full of Shadows makes you more susceptible to being infected by what they carry. A clear human is a fountain of exceptional power, uninhibited by anything impure. And Shadows are attracted to power.*

If two energy bodies open subconsciously beside one another in sleep, Shadows can jump and merge more cunningly than when one maintains the waking awareness to deflect their intrusion.

Any Shaman knows the danger of sleeping near any infected human. It should be avoided. Even if you believe you are robust, you cannot control your energy field while in deep sleep.

But I wasn't planning on sleeping, and I was sure merely visiting a sleeping body wouldn't initiate the same dynamic.

I stood and slipped on a jacket.

Bear's eyes peered open. They glistened in the darkness and followed me suspiciously as I tiptoed to the door.

I'm going to see Björn, ok? Stay here with Snow. Call to me if he wakes up, I asked, although I was unsure whether our telepathic connection maintained its durability when he was in this form.

Bear let out a low rumble and the glisten of his watchful eyes disappeared.

I walked through the black tunnel towards Björn with every other sense but vision guiding the way, which conveniently paced my steps as I approached. My experiment would only work if Björn remained in deep sleep.

When I reached his cell, it was clear he was.

I lowered gently down onto the stone floor in front of the bars. Time was not an enemy that night. If anything, it was a friend. It did not press me to be anywhere else by duty for anyone else by hand of the clock—for the clock, under the influence of the sun and moon had already promised that these hours until dawn were free.

My eyes had adjusted to the dark and Björn's silhouette was visible on the ground. He clearly didn't allow himself the pleasure of sleeping on the mattress, which revealed how deeply his inclination for self-punishment polluted his actions and thoughts.

I closed my eyes and began by tuning my attention entirely into the glow of light in my chest.

With each breath, I let it fill me and then expand into the space around me until I could lock it into place, establishing a protective sphere that would allow me to work with whatever Shadows were present, while avoiding attack. That was my intention anyway. Whether it would work, I couldn't be sure.

It emanated a mild, transparent Air-blue glow. And when I felt safe and centred inside it, I turned my attention onto Björn, scanning his current state of being.

I could feel what the old Shaman had described: a sense of openness and malleability within his energy field that had only recently been concealed behind a wall of armour. The Shadows that had settled comfortably into his system were no longer so concretely settled.

As I held my attention on the Shadows, I realised they weren't as bountiful as they had been originally, which meant my work prior to that night had been successful. He was clearing, emptying.

In fact, he had emptied so much that what possessed Björn now was not a mass of Shadows at all. All that was left was a singular entity: one Shadow.

But it was still no cause for celebration.

It was denser than any other I had felt lift from his being, like a tree with roots and branches that spread throughout his entire system, creating the illusion of fragmentation. The essence at its core was the same. All the pain within him was traceable to one singular trunk.

I felt confronted by the scope of impact one Shadow alone could have over a being, while at the same time, encouraged. If I could access and emancipate the core frame of the entity—the trunk—perhaps all the roots and branches would unhook and unwind alongside it, and Björn would simply be free.

I followed the surface branches of the Shadow deeper into Björn's being, sifting through the dense fog that was like a black cloud enveloping him. It was only then that I realized the fog was a defence mechanism. A smoke screen that functioned to hide the central spirit of the entity from being seen and recognised by someone like me.

When I found its central frame, it felt solid, an etheric iron bar, secured through the centre of Björn's body.

I remained still and activated my heart like a magnet, drawing the spirit through the fog. The celestial magnetism was more efficient than I expected. After some resistance, I felt it loosening, shifting, rising out of its previously locked position.

I opened my eyes and the Shadow was no longer cloaked behind the veil by which it was invisible. I could see now what I had only sensed.

A mass of black L·ight Mȧttẹr lingered around Björn's silhouette, an external expression of the lifting fog that had, only moments earlier, been trapped inside him, permeating through his energetic system.

And through it, the entity became visible in its manifest expression too, rising to the surface.

What I saw was, in fact, a being, but it was semi-transparent. It was the spirit of a Sky person as it would have appeared in form centuries ago, before their planet perished.

It was both human-like in appearance and foreign. Tall and metallic, its silver skin was smooth and shiny, even without the reflection of light. It stood separate from Björn, appearing in the aether just above his sleeping body, not merged with it as I had seen in glimpses previously.

I felt compelled by its dynamic and unfamiliar presence, but I kept my distance. Its metallic face was menacing, not male or female, cheekbones high and jawline sharp as edges. I got the sense it was irritated by my presence. And I was irritated by the intense well of emotion that radiated outwards from it. The same emotion that had been tormenting Björn.

It was shame. Pure shame. The Shadow was shame itself. And it was intense. It felt horrible. Debilitating. Immobilising. But as long as I remained separate, I wouldn't be debilitated by it.

It was exposed now, at least to my eyes, and acute shards of anger struck my chest, shooting out from where it stood, penetrating straight through my protective sphere. While the arrows were of an etheric nature, the pain was cutting and felt no less real. It could have overwhelmed me, but I didn't let it.

I *knew* pain. We had become allies. My tolerance to suffer extreme volumes of uncomfortable sensation was high. But I realised in that moment, I did not have to stand there and merely endure it.

I lifted my forearm in front of me, calling on more concentrated Air Magic to cast an additional celestial shield of armour that protected my heart from further attack.

The shards ceased reaching me.

I remained centred, not breaking focus, as the pain dissipated. I had arrived at a critical moment and was not prepared to lose sight or sense of this ancient entity who was determined to return to its new residence inside the man I loved.

With the Sky Spirit somewhat separated from Björn's body, the glow of his true spirit became visible in contrast below. But a plethora of black roots extended down from the Sky Person, who was still very much hooked in. An entanglement of Black L·ight Måttęr was intertwined with the streams of white light that made up Björn's aetheric body.

The magnetic field that I'd used earlier amplified inside my chest.

I felt a moment of uncertainty. I had not planned for what to do with the entity once it was exposed. Nor did I know how to break the magnetism between us now that it had been established.

Under the influence of my attention, the magnetic draw grew richer, and the being, with its dark eyes dead set on mine, surged towards me.

But its eyes were no longer malicious.

They, like mine, were afraid.

Now that it was there, visible in front of me, it seemed too giant to truly confront, the violent might of its presence too immense. I couldn't possibly match it if it continued forth, but I didn't know how to stop it. It had an intelligence, a consciousness of its own, that I could not dictate and did not understand well enough to manage.

But I was also aware that my sudden angst was of no service, not to me, so I softened my gaze and the heat inside my chest softened with it.

My racing heartbeat slowed.

I tried to cut the cord that connected us but realised it couldn't be cut, for it wasn't a cord. It was just as it felt: two magnets drawn together by a gravitational pull. I would have to destroy the celestial magnet I'd carelessly created and secured over my heart.

But it was all happening too fast. I couldn't focus. I hadn't prepared for this. I hadn't considered what might happen if my metaphysical experimentation actually progressed.

That was when I remembered I wasn't alone. There were unseen forces present with me, supreme and divine, that were as passionate about assisting Björn's transition back to freedom as I was. Air Magic, and the purest of White L·ight Måttęr, were in full cooperation with my cause.

As I examined the Sky Entity more boldly, I realised that although it was moving towards me, it wasn't attracted to my energy field.

It seemed that, unlike the case with Björn and other human beings, it didn't *want* to live inside the vessel of my body as much as I didn't want it there. Maybe because it knew better than I did at that moment that it couldn't survive there.

But still, it drew closer, through the wooden bars that had no impact on its movement, for they were solid and it was not.

The more I tried to pull the magnets apart, the faster it flew towards me, until abruptly it came to a halt.

It smacked against my protective light shield.

I was frozen for a moment.

The Sky being was frozen too. Right there, right in front of me. So close.

Now that I could see it more clearly, its eyes were not just glimmering with fear; they were full of fear. Only fear.

I didn't have to *do* anything to provoke it. It seemed my very presence—the expanse of light that was held within the vicinity of my presence—terrified it.

The field of fear that extended outwards hit me with such intensity I could have been swallowed by it, but I didn't allow it to stir up any fear of my own, and so it remained separate. The energy travelled at rapid and incomprehensible speeds into me, but it did not stick. It disappeared straight through me. Through the epic light inside my chest.

The being began to shake and shiver until, as abruptly as it had hit the wall of light around me, it burst.

Like a silent explosion it dissolved into black mist, into Black L·ight Mátter, Black Magic. And before I could do or think anything, all that remained of it swept into me.

It breached my protective shield and I was enveloped by the same black fog Björn had been. Like the fear, I felt it pour into my chest in a channel of dense black mist.

I thought it was transferring into me. Perhaps in that moment, I *should* have been afraid. But I felt a sense of okayness, for at least it was no longer trapped in Björn.

And as it reached my heart, a beam of bright white light shone out from my chest, as radiant as the sun.

Before that moment, I had felt its exquisite power dwelling within me, but I had not seen it. It was stunning, brilliant, blinding.

The black mist didn't spread through and infect my body. Instead, it dissolved into the light that was my body. No density could survive the supreme expanse of power that poured from my heart. Infinite.

I fell back.

My entire body vibrated as if struck by an electric voltage more immense than anything I'd experienced before.

I couldn't think.

The racing sensations were all-encompassing. I felt electrified, like I too could burst and shatter into all the tiny particles that reverberated inside me. That's the only way I could explain it, and doubted I'd ever try to. It was too strange. Too profound. Too unexplainable.

No one was there to witness it. The experience was mine alone. And there was a sense of sacredness in that. The only eyes that could have seen it were Björn's. And he was still, somehow, asleep.

I was tempted to wake him up, curious as to whether he would feel any immediate difference.

But my body was struck by the weight of a heavy, overdue exhaustion. I could have dropped to the ground right there, but I did not want my presence to trigger Björn in any negative way when he woke. I dragged myself away from his cell and meandered back towards my room.

The tunnels were still pitch black. There were no lights to guide me, but I slid along the wall, using its support as both an escort and brace to alleviate the weight of my fatigued body.

I barely noticed the human standing in the corridor as I slid deliriously along the cold stone wall. My concentration was fixated on my feet alone, and the propulsion of each step forwards.

A faint orange flame caught my eye, and I was surprised to lift my head to find Bŏdhi blocking my path, lantern in hand, its glow illuminating his face. I fell into his broad chest without a thought.

Before I could summon the energy to even wonder what he was doing up at that hour, he answered.

"I went to see you earlier. To talk to you. I couldn't sleep. I waited outside your room, but you were gone for a long time. I just wanted to know you were ok."

"I'm ok," I mumbled.

I felt so safe in his arms. So held. So content. I lost all control over my body and began drifting, falling, heavily into sleep right there in the dark tunnel.

A light laugh rumbled through his chest. "You can't sleep here, Maya," he said, amused.

"Just a few minutes," I said, but fell swiftly from that world, and into a deep and dreamless sleep.

CHAPTER FORTY

W HEN MY EYES OPENED again, I was in my bed, but I couldn't recall how I got there. I remembered my interaction with Bŏdhi before I crashed. He must have carried me.

I rolled over to see Snow, surprised he hadn't woken me up as he usually did, but Bear was the only other being within my eyesight. He was awake but lying lazily on the same patch of stone upon which he slept, chin resting on the ground while his eyes watched me regain consciousness.

Bear, where's Snow?

I was still testing whether this form of celestial communication was available between us when he wasn't in dragon form.

Your mate has him.

My mate?

He slept here last night, on the floor beside you. When Snow woke up, he took him so you could keep sleeping.

It took me a moment to adjust to hearing his voice in my head while his brown eyes and bear face simply stared up at me.

He's not my mate.

I read the energy world, the indirect exchange between people. I will discount your words if they do not match what is spoken by the language of your body, Bear said simply.

Your complicated minds deceive you. You humans lie and are often unaware you're lying.

I may have liked you more when you didn't use words, I said, although I appreciated his directness.

His chest rumbled, and I realised the sound was his expression of a laugh.

It is not my preferred language either. But no judgement from me, he said of the apparent non-verbal implications between me and Bõdhi.

Yeah, well, that would be hypocritical, wouldn't it? I said in reference to his multiple lovers, or mates or...casual seed spreading—whatever it was labelled in the animal world.

You should not judge yourself either. Love is a frequency that cannot be controlled or suppressed. It lives free. And you have permission to live free also.

We're talking about love now?

Love is everywhere, in many expressions. Maybe it doesn't always mean what you think it means, he said.

I don't know your Björn, but this man Bõdhi cares for you deeply. That is what I do know.

The sound and resonance of Bear's voice was deep and mature, and the slow, articulate pace in which he spoke emphasised the wisdom in his words.

Is this weird? To be talking like this? I asked, perhaps as a subtle attempt to avoid the topic. A subtle, or not so subtle, way to 'lie'.

A little, he agreed, and rose to his feet, pushing open the door with his nose.

It was simpler when he was just a bear. But I also appreciated the clarity through which he saw the world. He didn't have the same hooks and fears and biases and ideas of right and wrong that jaded the way we humans interpreted things.

He looked back at me before he left and let out a familiar whining noise that I knew as goodbye, returning to Bear language.

I laughed and shook my head.

Better? he asked.

I honestly don't know.

I was wary not to leave Snow for too long after the previous day's events, so sought where Bõdhi had taken him before considering doing anything else, like checking on Björn.

I checked all the most obvious places, including his room, and then his kids'. They were all empty.

I had slept later than usual, and the working day had begun for most of the community; people moved about all through the cave.

I finally found Phŏenix with Moānā and Tasmai on either side, hands interconnected. She was walking them to the section of the cave dedicated to schooling—although it was a very different kind of education to what we had in the City. It could barely fall under the same label.

"Have you seen Bõdhi and Snow?"

"We saw them earlier this morning, but not since, sorry," Phŏenix said.

Once upon a time, there were things called mobile phones, through which you could send a text out into the aether and receive one in return from the person you wanted to reach within minutes. A phone would have been convenient at that moment.

But there was still one place I hadn't checked, and it was there that I found them.

In the glow worm cave.

Snow was laughing while Bõdhi waded his little white body through the dark, glimmering water, teaching him to kick. I stood back, watching them for a minute or so. They were alone, and my heart shone brighter at the sight of their bonding.

A myriad of tiny, fluorescent blue lights lit the cave and delicate, almost transparent strings of a silk-like substance hung from the ceiling, so fine they swayed lightly, even though the air was still. The same sense of enchantment settled over me as it had the previous times I'd visited.

And the same spark flared up inside me the longer my eyes lingered on the exotic, dark-skinned man who held my son through the water, as it had every time I was in his presence recently.

The spark of magic in the presence of magic. I assured myself.

 Or maybe it was love. But a different kind of love, like bear had suggested; *Love is everywhere, in many expressions. Maybe it doesn't always mean what you think it means.*

Maybe magic was a form of love, just as love was a form of magic.

"Mumma!" Snow sensed my presence before I stepped out of the shadows.

My gaze was soft, relaxed. I couldn't tell if it was the glow of the room reflecting off him, but his auric field was more vivid than usual. It was white. Pure white. I walked closer, to the edge of the water, and the light that surrounded Snow didn't dissipate. It was not an illusion. He was enveloped by Pristine White L·ight Måttẹr.

My eyes shifted to Bõdhi, whose aura was also visible. It wasn't unusual. Auras often drifted in and out of my sight. I didn't usually take much notice of them. But today, there was something significant about the L·ight Måttẹr that drifted in and around the boys.

The colour that encapsulated Bõdhi was harder to see; a deep and electric blue. The colour of the ocean. It blended into the dim, blue-tinted hue of the room.

Snow reached out his hand and Bõdhi carried him out of the water to meet me, wrapping him in an over-sized towel. Bõdhi didn't mind the water on his skin. He remained shirtless and shiny.

I held Snow tightly in my arms, kissing his cold cheeks.

I'd seen all the colours before, but never pure white—apart from around Nirmala and her Axscendant Chaiṭãnya, who I gathered were the embodiments of the spirit element.

My heart beat hotly as something dawned on me that I wasn't sure I wanted to let dawn.

So, I didn't let it. Not yet.

"Are you alright?" Bõdhi touched my arm.

The electricity was too much. I flinched away.

"Sorry, just…" I didn't want to tell him, because exploring it with him out loud would make it real.

But whatever I was seeing was burning to be acknowledged.

Literally.

Physically.

Snow let out a cry of agony and clasped his hands together, holding them urgently to his chest. I thought for a second it was his heart, but he was too young for a heart attack.

He screamed, and I was glad we were a decent distance from the central caverns, for it was piercing.

I was lost for what to do. I was lost for the source of the problem, so I just held and rocked him.

"Shhh," I stroked his silky hair, which was whiter than it was blonde. "What is it?" I whispered quietly, although inside, my panic was loud.

But he just cried again in pain and held his tight fists up to show me. They were glowing even brighter than his aura, brighter than the glow worms that surrounded us. The light was radiant, his fists like miniature suns, beaming but white. Pure white.

I looked to Bõdhi, whose expression was as helpless as I felt. But his eyes were wide; he could see it too.

Snow's fists sprung open and striking light burst outwards, upwards, in channels that reached for the sky. White Magic.

When the outpour of light faded, what was left within the centre of both of his little palms were two bright red gashes, engraved deep into his supple, blood-smudged skin.

But they weren't anything like normal gashes, primarily because they were not caused by any external blade. They were self-inflicted, drawn by some kind of mysterious metaphysical blade that none of us could see.

Snow cried again as the celestial blade continued to cut along his skin with a slow kind of precision that led me to believe it had intelligence.

What if it was a Sky being, like the one I'd seen last night, punishing my son for what I did to it?

Impossible.

But it was beginning to appear that nothing was impossible.

Bŏdhi was quick to take action while I tried to peer into the realm of the unseen, but it was hard to truly arrive there when my heart beat so fast, thudding in my brain, disrupting my concentration.

Bŏdhi swept his own palms out to face the waterbody and drew up two channels of water that he contained, then touched his cold hands over Snow's palms, releasing the water to wash them clean.

Snow's body relaxed. His pain eased. He lifted his tense face from my chest, cheeks streaked with tears. His panicked breath slowed as he calmed.

Bŏdhi lifted his hands from Snow's.

The red gashes were healing at a supernatural pace, and now that the blood had been washed away, we could clearly see two identical carvings in the centre of each palm.

I watched the skin around the cuts mend itself before my eyes, but not completely. Two perfect scars were left that began to glow the same pristine white glow that had shone from them in brilliant beams moments earlier, bright as lasers.

I recognised the drawings immediately.

Bŏdhi leaned closer.

"Is that… is that one of the symbols from..." He looked up at me, eyes filled with the same mix of emotions mine were.

I nodded before he finished his sentence.

"Spirit. Aether," I told him.

"The space between the air, earth, fire, water. All of it. The element that is the fabric upon which all other elements are painted."

"Pure as pure," Bõdhi said, eyes brushing over Snow's smooth, pure white skin.

His ice-like, light blue eyes.

His abnormally calm, soulful expression, that had returned only moments after expressing such acute pain.

"He's one of…" He could barely say it. He barely needed to.

"The cluster," I finished. Although I didn't want to.

"But he's so young. Surely he can't be asked to…do whatever it is we're being asked to do."

I felt a sense of comfort in knowing Bõdhi felt equally as conflicted by this newly uncovered knowledge as I did.

"But he is," I said out loud, only as a way to get a little closer to accepting it myself.

Snow was staring between us and his hands. Pure curiosity.

His expression did not carry the concern that ours did. Perhaps he'd already been aware of what he was.

He reached both hands up and over to touch each of our cheeks. The power of his touch was gentle and loving but powerful all the same. The gracious power of Yin, of Spirit, of Aether. So tender one could only truly receive it in the stillest of stillness.

His arms weren't long, and I could feel the closeness of Bõdhi's face next to mine, my heart sparking against his.

"Mumma, your hands," Snow said.

His voice carried the same serenity as his touch. I didn't get to hear it often, for he didn't often choose to use it. Where was the need for excessive words when one's experience of the world rested in a space that was so much richer, deeper, and more refined? A space of no words, that no word could express.

I sat down on the bright green moss at our feet, and Snow sat directly in front of me. I held out my palms as requested. He held out his and placed them over mine.

He stared down with great concentration. The relationship between us in that moment felt unusual, for it did not feel like mother and child. At that moment, he was my teacher, not I his.

The magic within his chest shone brighter, brighter, dripping down his arms and into his palms. I could feel it as potently as I could see it, moving, flowing in brilliant white rivers.

Acute pain shot through the centre of both my palms, like razor-sharp blades slicing my skin. But the severity quickly mellowed, watered down by the divine tenderness of Snow's touch. It became simply a sensation. Manageable. And because pain did not steal all of my attention, I was able to acquiesce and perceive what was unfolding more clearly.

White L·ight Måttęr shone down from Snow's palms, as if the magic he carried was both creating and soothing the cutting sensations at once.

My hands began to glow too, in a brilliant silver blue. The colour of the Air element. I could feel its presence all around me, enveloping me, seeping into my cells. Magic.

When he lifted his palms, there were gashes in the centre of mine. Precisely carved and perfectly reflective of the Air symbol from the drawing. And just like his had, they healed at a supernatural speed by which I could watch in real time as the skin sewed itself back together, leaving plump scars in the place of the initially raw, red wounds.

Snow's slight body swayed, tired, but he gathered himself. His eyes sharpened with renewed purpose as they landed on Bŏdhi, who had been silently watching, wary not to interfere. We both knew what Snow's eyes were requesting.

I leant down and kissed his forehead before shuffling aside to let Bŏdhi take my place.

Snow repeated the same process he had with me. As expected, when he lifted his palms from Bŏdhi's, painted upon them were two identical Symbols for water.

All eyes watched once more as the skin healed around the Symbols, leaving scars that emitted a glow of vivid, electric blue L·ight Måtter. The colour of a deep sea. The colour of the water element. Water Magic.

The stillness in the room was so rich, so effervescent, and the power that flourished between us, as the monumental presence of each element rose to the surface of our beings, was a kind of boundless force I'd never experienced before.

A low rumbling noise echoed through the cave, followed by a tremor that shook the ground, startling each of us from the sacredness of the moment. I doubted that it was caused by what was occurring between us, but I couldn't be sure.

It didn't last long, but while it lasted we were frozen in place, unsure of what to do if it escalated.

I supposed we should run to the entrance. Being trapped inside a monstrous hollow rock was the most dangerous possible place to be if what we were experiencing was the inception of an earthquake.

Bŏdhi took my hand impulsively and gripped it tight.

Light on his feet, I could feel his sense of readiness to take action if the situation called for it. The electricity of our palms in direct contact pulsed up my arm and through my body. I knew he felt it too.

But the tremors ceased, and the low rumble faded. We waited, listening, but it didn't return.

Snow crawled to me and fell into my lap, exhausted, but I knew not to worry, for I'd been in a similar state that previous night. I knew the energetic demand of elemental experimentation.

I held him, allowing him to rest, while simultaneously allowing myself to process all that had just unfolded.

Silence prevailed once more.

I began to wonder if exhaustion would always be the price of metaphysical work, or if there was a way to contain a certain amount of internal stamina while working with the magic of our elements.

It was probably an important skill to explore and practice. If we were forced to use our powers in the face of an unrelenting force such as the Sky People—which I assumed we would be—we couldn't afford to drop limp halfway through when the energy of our physical form had been spent.

Surely there was a way to merge with the source of our elements so completely that we could work *from* it, *as* it, instead of just *with* it...

I remembered how depleted I'd felt the previous night, the way I'd fallen limp in Bõdhi's arms like Snow presently was in mine. I'd forgotten our short, unexpected interaction, but remembering it struck my curiosity.

"What was it you wanted to talk about last night?" I asked.

He remained quiet, but I knew he heard me and was contemplating his answer. His eyes darted down to Snow who had fallen swiftly into sleep in my arms. I placed him down on a towel beside me, giving Bõdhi my full attention.

"This probably isn't the right time," he drifted off.

"I want to know," I said, his hesitation amplifying my curiosity. "It must have been somewhat important if it was keeping you up enough to come wake me up in the middle of the night..."

"That's exactly it," he said. "I can't sleep. And it's making me do things I shouldn't, things that don't make sense, like going out in the middle of the night with the intention to disrupt *your* sleep just to relieve myself from this thing I've been carrying around on my chest. Unsure of how to express it, or if it should be expressed at all..."

He was speaking around corners, and I was chasing the back of his words for their meaning.

But some part of me was already aware of where his trail was leading. I quietly wished I hadn't encouraged him to speak, while quietly pleased I had.

"I can't think straight, is the problem," he continued. "I can't focus on anything. The fields, the kids. It's the strangest thing, food is uninteresting and sleep is…" He shook his head, and finally took a direct approach.

"Love has hit me like a tidal wave, and I don't know what to do with it. I've never felt it before like this, and I have become the most useless, dysfunctional human because of it."

I wanted to interrupt him but I let him express what he needed to express.

"I know you love Björn and I know when he gets better you will be together like you were before, but I can't suppress this feeling."

I couldn't hold his gaze. My face was burning. So was my heart, even though I knew he was just confused.

"I'm sorry. I also know that this is the last thing you want to hear. Because I've been watching you, probably too closely. Every time there is a moment of intimacy between us you deflect it. But I also watch the way your body responds to mine, before the mind interferes, and robs us of what might happen if..." He drifted off, his green eyes locked onto mine now, so vivid against his dark skin.

I finally allowed the intensity of the feelings he spoke of, the feelings I'd been suppressing, to wash through my body.

"…If we both let go of these ideas of right and wrong. These rules. Barriers. And allow…" I drifted off.

Without thinking, my body leant forward just enough to encourage his to edge forward too, our chests drawing closer like magnets. I shifted onto my knees and crawled, absentmindedly, to bridge what was left of the gap between us, then stopped. Caught by my own sense.

"But it's not love," I said, only inches away from his face.

His expression turned confused. I sat back.

"It's magic," I told him, sure now that the magnetic chemistry between us was a product of the magic we shared, and magic alone alone.

His brows furrowed. He shook his head as if to argue, but was interrupted by the earth that shook too. It was just a tremor, but it rumbled louder than before.

Snow woke abruptly and looked at me with started eyes. I picked him up and stood.

Bǒdhi was already up standing beside me. We didn't need to vocalize the fact that now wasn't the time to finish our conversation.

"I going to find my kids," he said. "And see if anyone knows what's going on."

The earth had stopped shaking but still, we ran through the tunnels toward the community centre. I stopped when we passed the tunnel that led down to Björn.

"I'm really sorry to ask this, but can you take Snow? And keep him safe with you?"

Bǒdhi hesitated, eyes darting between the tunnel and me. All was still in the cave again, but we could not completely rule out potential oncoming danger.

He let me go.

"Of course." He took Snow into his arms and we both continued running, but in opposite directions.

CHAPTER FORTY-ONE

*A*IR. *Water. And now Aether.* I thought as I ran. Three of the elements had now been found.

Breathless, I slowed, beginning to dismiss the rumbling we felt as some kind of loud work happening above us, or maybe even the power of the magic that was being united between us.

Fire?

It didn't take me long to recognize that Bear, in his almighty dragon form, may well have been our cluster's fire representative.

We were proving ourselves to be a more eccentric bunch than I initially imagined, and I felt more uncertain than ever as to who might possibly reveal themselves as our earth element. But then again, like the others, whoever it was may already be in plain sight.

I hadn't told Bõdhi yet of the bear/shapeshifter/fire-breathing dragon situation. It was not something that could simply be told.

And I hadn't consoled Bear with my inclination that he might be part of our cluster. Perhaps he already knew. But if that were true, why would he hide it?

I didn't lock in my assumption, but I left it in the back of my mind to explore when Bear returned from his day's adventure.

There was still work to be done with Björn.

I was eager to see him after what happened with the Sky entity. I couldn't be sure that it was the only entity that had attached itself to him. Even if it was, I couldn't be sure that it meant he would now be free. I knew from experience that time played a significant role in letting go of patterns of the body and mind, even once the original source of them has been eliminated.

But when I reached the dark cavern of his prison, he wasn't there.

The wooden branches that had contained him were splintered and broken. He had clearly escaped. *Which could mean something equally perfect or terrible.*

I was surprised by his strength. He had no weapon with him in the cavern, yet it looked like there had been an explosion.

I didn't give myself the option to fret yet over how or why or who may have voluntarily let him out.

For the second time that day, I found myself racing around the underground maze to find one of the men that had a home in my heart.

Continued in Book Three - The final book in the series.

AFTERWORD

If you liked this novel, your reviews and ratings are highly valuable to help other readers find it!

To stay updated on Book Three, you can subscribe to Sita's newsletter at;

www.sitabennettauthor.com.au

ABOUT AUTHOR

Sita Bennett is a West-Australian Author, Actress, and Filmmaker from the small coastal town of Margaret River.

She writes fantasy adventure novels inspired by eastern mysticism and ancient wisdom from multiple cultures, that follow smart, sensitive, resilient & determined young women on quests for truth and freedom in chaotic worlds.

She also co-creates independent films with her brother, Frank Bennett, that explore the mysteries of consciousness. Together, they co-founded Lightdance Productions.

All of Sita's work follow stories of self-discovery, transformation & love as characters find their unique personal power within.

www.sitabennettauthor.com.au

She Who Rose From Ashes

Exerpt

A Prequel Novel to Maya of The In-Between that follows different characters, but is set in the same universe decades earlier.

I DON'T HAVE AN INTRODUCTION

I don't have an Introduction.

I cannot start by sharing with you my recent past; it would be too confronting.

Nor can I accurately reveal any hint of what lies in my future; it is more mystical and obscure than I am yet to grasp.

But I can invite you in to my present.

My now.

Here, but not *here.*

A present experience of a past trauma, where the linearity of time is more fluid than it ordinarily seems, and I embody someone I once was.

These experiences are not unusual for me. They don't often last long either, but they are all-encompassing when they re-surface from where they hide in my subconscious. They reveal more of where I'm going by developing my understanding of where I came from . . .

Red.

Flames.

A shrill scream. Pain.

Burning.

Suddenly, I'm burning.

Skin blistering, sweltering. Sweat dripping, pouring. Scorching steam envelops me, and putrid black smoke stings my throat. My lungs shrink.

The flames devour my feet, ankles, legs. I'm chained to a stake; there is no escape. I'm forced to simply breathe and burn.

But as I breathe and burn from the safety of my bed in a relatively bare apartment in Taiwan, a small slither of my sleeping consciousness is aware that this is not *real*, a dream, or a premonition. Modern punishments for the mastery of Magic have become far more sophisticated — that I know from personal experience. What I'm experiencing now is a memory.

But that small slither of sleeping consciousness that is aware, is overpowered by the intensity of my body's desperation to survive. The trauma of the past trapped in the now, warning me to run.

Run again.

For it's not just one lifetime's memory of burning that my body carries. As more memories return, I'm starting to see that death by flame has been a re-occurring pattern over the multiple lives I've lived on earth.

Besalú, Catalonia, Spain, 1841

Rain lands lightly outside my window, and a hazy white frost creeps along its edges. I lie half-naked on top of my winter sheets, and while the night air feels like ice on my bare skin, the sensation of burning overwhelms me—my body traumatised by past events that seem fixed on repeating. I have been here before, but not here.

A dark shadow lurks over my bed—the shadow of fear. It's infiltrating the air I breathe. A mass blacker than the night, its presence is like death. I'm paralysed. Fear cripples me.

My body quivers as I force myself to slide from the illusionary safety of my bed and tiptoe across the worn floorboards to hatch down every window and lock of my quaint strawbale cottage. They are not here yet, but every sense in my body is switched on, hyper-aware of their approach. It was ignorant to think we had more time. We should have acted sooner, faster.

The fog-drenched forest that extends for miles in each direction is dead silent, all of nature sleeping, as I should be.

Echoing waves of a turbulent sea roll and rumble in the far distance.

An insect cries out.

The first flame flickers in the darkness, bright red against pitch black, and I duck, heart racing rapidly while simultaneously missing a beat. I tuck myself against the low corner cupboards of the kitchen and squeeze my eyes shut; trying to keep my attention on pacing the air, I suck desperately into choked lungs.

Hiding. Always hiding.

But I am not alone in my hiding. For there are others like me. Just four.

We act. We disguise ourselves as regular townsfolk. We blend in and pretend we're one of them. But we are not. We're a different breed, an alternate race of humans entirely, while still just human enough to move through the world unnoticed.

In this era, they call us Witches; in a past life, we were Toltecs. Whatever the label, we are defined by the magic we embody—the unrivalled well of power at the core of our being. Everything that we are threatens the mundane republic that the Dynasty has fought to build, control, and maintain since its inception centuries ago.

We must hide. Or die.

A brick of fear presses down my caving chest. I could almost let it kill me, surrender, and allow my heart to simply stop, but the body's intelligence transcends that of the mind. It won't allow for an apathetic departure. It's adamant to survive this. I'm adamant to survive this. If not for me, then for them. My cluster.

A frantic shuffling of leaves.

An escalating thump of boots.

A man's voice in the distance… followed by another.

A startling bang on the door, then the window. The flickers of torchlight paint shadows onto the pale wall in front of me that look not like men but demons.

I feel sicker than sick.

There was a time when I looked death directly in the eye and decided I would be unafraid when it came to take me, for the exquisite sense that it wasn't death, but a return to Source drowned out my previous misconceptions.

But that was before. Before I found him. Them.

This work is too important. The Mystic circle calls on five to be completed. And not just any five. If I die –

The sound of shattering glass stings my ears, and I flinch as the penetrating stone smacks a hole in the fragile wall opposite. Shards scatter over my body, and as they prick my skin, I know they'll be the very least of the damage this body will endure tonight.

My eyes flash open to the same wall, or at least it appears so from this angle, but the shadows have vanished, and the shards of glass are no longer scattered around me.

Sleepwalking.

The night is silent and cool, but my body still burns from within, still paralysed by the same fear of flesh-eating flames. It has followed me here.

Pressed into corner cupboards beneath the wide window of a similarly designed kitchen, my body is immobile, and I remain unmoving for a timeless time, focusing on the rise and fall of my chest. My eyes are glued wide open just in case the town's watchmen have followed me here too. It's impossible, but I'm beginning to wonder once again where the lines truly lie between the conscious and subconscious realms as they continue to blur.

A light bluish glow illuminates the bare wall as the first glimpse of pre-dawn washes in, and sweeping sounds roll in the distance, this time coming from car wheels instead of waves.

I jump as a horn honks, the lump of fear trapped in my chest reacting to the subtlest sounds, slow to meet my mind that understands it as an encouraging sign. It means I'm now far, far away from the world in my dreamscape—the dreamscape of my past. A horse's neigh would have been the closest resemblance to a car horn back then.

I watch the gradual migration of light across the wall before me, wide awake and highly alert as the rising sun shines through in rays and dust drifts gently in the stagnant dusk air. As daylight prevails, the fear fades, creeping back into the shadows where it'll hide until the dark of night allows its full expression once more.

Once more... The number of times I've hoped that's all it will be.

But I've learnt better than to hope now. Hope, in this area, is a seemingly sweet disillusionment that only becomes the catalyst for intensified pain when the shadows return.

If I *expect* their return, I can prepare. Prepare to stand up taller, allow the light within me to expand wider, so wide there's no space left for darkness to survive.

But like the moon shades the sun's light each cycle of night, so does this particular fear possess the power to overshadow me.

Even in my earliest childhood memories, darkness was terrifying. And while my night terrors were dismissed as 'normal' by my parents, their magnitude was beyond any childish fear of ghosts and monsters. It was a fear of flames, hunters, men, torture, shadows, death.

It *was* and still *is*.

Because I still don't understand it. Not fully. It makes no linear sense. Every time I think I've healed the fear, a new layer of it rises to the surface. A new memory of a different life, all of which ending not just in premature death, but murder. It's as if the memories are stacked on top of each other, waiting to be uncovered, intensifying the deeper I penetrate.

So, I continue to practice deeper surrender and develop a warrior heart that might become robust enough not to weaken under any traumatic sensation, no matter how ancient and intense.

I release the pressure of my back against the hard kitchen cupboards and exhale a full breath. My muscles loosen, and my body regains mobility.

The sweet sounds of birds in their early morning song lighten my heart, and I finally stand, only now realising how long I've just been sitting here, *feeling*, processing the relevance of this new memory against the maze of memories that continue to return in dreams and visions. They are all linked, and they all lead me closer.

Closer to *them*.

Closer to the freedom I will need to embody to stand strong against the forces of resistance that exist today, the forces of Black, who are equally as determined to see us fall as they have been in every lifetime past; in which we have in fact fallen.

I can see that each of these pockets of fear stored within my system weaken me and compress the true expanse of power that is my being. If we are to complete our purpose, I will need to be clean, clear, free of the weight of my past. It's obvious that it was intense fear that crippled me in the memory I received last night. Depleting, debilitating. It was essentially fear that killed me, for I lost the strength to fight back.

I run the kitchen tap and watch as the glass I hold fills with pristine water, imagining what it might feel like to be so clear, so pure, so weightless.

It's a kitchenette in a small, condensed apartment. Simply furnished with the bare necessities of survival. I'm not here to indulge in comforts and make a home. I'm moving, travelling, searching for the only ones that can help me execute what's been calling me since birth:—the ones who are the only constant thread throughout all my memories. In every life I've lived and remembered, they have been there, moving with the momentum of the same purpose.

Well, them, and magic.

They are what weave each mysterious vision into something coherent, and I'm sure that if I have returned to live another cycle of life in yet another body, they have too. They are here, somewhere on this earth.

They have to be.

At first, as a child, the call of magic was a whisper that was only ever mine, for I sensible enough to understand that expressing it aloud would be dangerous. The people of this modern time are still as frightened of and threatened by Magic as they were centuries ago when I was burned under the label 'Witch'.

It just expresses itself a little differently now.

The fear is less obvious, more of an undercurrent, governing everyone and everything. Anyone who exists and behaves outside of the ordinary is attacked by those who are too dependent on the structures of ordinary life to see beyond it.

Ordinary is comfortable, change is scary, and unconventionality is inconvenient—a disturbance to the system. This was obvious to me from a young age, so I played the game and kept the Magic that lies within me a secret.

Well, I tried to.

I attempted ignoring it in the years I attended school, suppressing the whispers in a misled desperation to be normal, but was quickly forced to surrender to the truth that 'normalness' has never been in the cards for me.

The whispers became an irrepressible yell, a pressing momentum, a flame in my heart that might have burned me alive if I didn't start to listen. So I dropped all my attempts of avoidance and listened.

And here I am, in a cheap apartment on the outskirts of a developing township in Taiwan, still listening.

I turn to gaze out through the window into the day.

Vivid green splashes of plant life, distant mountain ranges, and ancient stone temples appear even more enchanting amongst the plethora of shiny iron buildings. Both nature and capital, the old and the new stand upon almost equal ground in their rivalry for the space to breathe and be.

Pastel shades of pink and orange blend into the light blue sky, visible through the smog between where I stand and where the sun rises over the silver city. The contrast never fails to jar my eyes. Scattered cranes and stagnant machinery raise their stiff necks from multiple construction sites where they anticipate the moment they're aroused into motion. It's obvious that if the infrastructure continues, the capital will soon win dominance.

There are no lengths of flat land left still free of buildings. Most of the natural world exists on the mountain ranges and holy places that are protected by the monasteries and Buddhist organisations determined to conserve their history and sacredness where they can.

Thanks to their gentle activism, Taiwan is still somewhat protected, unlike the majority of other overdeveloped, overpopulated, and overmined countries I've travelled through. The land. Nature. The temples, culture, *history*. It's *supposed* to be protected. There *are* laws.

But already, it would appear those laws are being steadily discounted by the 'people's demand' for *more*.

Even so, the holiness of this land beams through. Through all that is manmade, the divinity of this country remains; *touched* but indestructible.

According to forgotten history, Taiwan was a sanctuary for people like me long ago when Mystics, Sëers, Light Bearers, and Enlightened ones were forced to retreat from China under Chairman Mao's Communist regime. That's what drew me here initially: the promise of ancient wisdom and gentle-natured beings. And the expanse of light that is still held by the country is undeniable, ever-present, even if only dim.

I turn the blue knob of the shower and slip under an icy stream. It shocks my naked skin, invigorating every cell to awaken with the day, and washes off the residual fear.

Clear mind. Clean thoughts. Clean energy.

I roll up my sleeping mat to create more space in the small square area that triples as my bedroom, living room, and dressing room and wind the stiff window wide open. The soft white curtains sway and dance on a mild wave of wind, and all the sounds of the busying street below wash in with the fresh morning air.

A motorbike dashes along the thin, wearing road, weaving around cars and the subtle smell of spicy omelette buns and dumplings drift up from the quaint family-run restaurant below where they serve traditional Taiwanese breakfasts.

I live on one of the older, poorer streets in town, but I prefer it here. The people are somehow simpler despite the general air of chaos.

Geographically, there are no large gaps between the rich and the poor. This city was once an aged but revered Buddhist village and the developments have not yet been fully integrated. Around the bend of a slum or street of worn and weathered humble homes can be rows of shiny skyscrapers, electronic billboards and slick new roads, creating vast contrast between one block to the next.

With hand resting over heart, I tune my attention inwards.

Inhale, exhale.

The rhythm of my breath slows and elongates. My eyes shut as I drop deeper into the vastness that lies within and around me, the source of life itself.

I turn on my travel speakers, letting my body merge with the sounds that begin to vibrate into the air. Erratic bursts of energy govern un-rhythmic, semi-chaotic movements until I lose all sense of self to something greater, something eternal.

As the tempo mellows, I sway, returning to rhythm, to breath, to the gentle waves of motion in the air itself. Immense presence, peace, and beauty overwhelm me.

I lower and cross my legs on the floor. Eyes closed, I feel myself dropping deeper into the sea of stillness that rests at the heart of my being. There is no fear here, only curiosity - although I have abandoned my quest for direct and obvious answers. The voice of the divine speaks in mysterious languages, speaks through nature, people, and life itself. Life seems to reveal just enough to work with each day—just enough to become a fuller version of what I am becoming.

What I know to be true in this moment is that I know very little, and the more I seek, the less I know. But what I do know is not known by many, for what I seek is sought by very few. And what I am, it seems, is so rare that I have not seen nor heard of the existence of another, although I know there are at least four out there somewhere, most likely hiding, like I have been.

You may be wondering at this point then, who and what, exactly, it is that I am. But my answer might not please you, for it is the nature of the human mind to demand that all things be comprehendible within the labels we are given by the English language to process them.

In this moment of this lifetime, I haven't come across a label that encapsulates all of what I am and what I carry.

A label that defines *who* I am is perhaps harder to refine. How can one claim an identity when she has been visited by memories and experiences of multiple identities she's been before? Even just within the span of this life, it has not been solid enough to wrap into something singular.

My legal name is Iris, but it hasn't always been, nor is it the name I use in day-to-day life. I was named Ember at birth for the unusual shade of my eyes that look like the dusty white grey floor of a fireplace. But that is no longer the name on my passport, nor is my nationality Australian, although it was originally.

I am human, not yet an adult nor still a child. But I have abilities that other humans do not have. Magic that I have not found traces of in books or historical texts. Magic that has been buried with all the past bodies I have worn by ones who are determined for its existence not to be acknowledged.

I am neither good nor bad. I have done exceptionally bad things with exceptionally good intentions, and if I were to be found by the wrong people I would be imprisoned. Again.

What I know with certainty is that there is a pressing purpose within my being that has been carried through each of my lifetimes, demanding of my unbending attention. It cannot be ignored while I serve a prolonged prison sentence for something I did that was arguably out of my control, and arguably necessary.

And while I do not yet understand myself in detail what it is that's so important I feel justified in my defiance of the law and moral decency, I invite you in on my journey of discovery, and ask in return only for your open mind and heart.

For what I find is profound. Although I haven't found it yet.

. . . Find the full novel at www.sitabennettauthor.com.au!

Acknowledgments

A final acknowledgment of all who have supported the creation of this series.

Firstly, to my dearest loved ones - my tribe - Your encouragement and undying, unconditional love and support is what pushes me to keep writing through the waves of self-doubt and most of all, through the hardships that life spins. With special mentions to;

Mum & Dad. (Gary & Lara Bennett)

My Brother & Sister Frank & Shanti Bennett.

My lifelong friend & Sister of the heart - Shyama.

The closest thing I have to a Shaman - Rohan Heaton - And his support of my novels through The Inner Peace Foundation of W.A.

The first readers of my books - Shakti, Nadja, Amy & my nan, Judy Bennett - Thank you!

Now, to those who were part of practically bringing the novel into form;

My amazing, intuitive cover designer Thea Magerand.

My editor Meredith Anderson.

And Regional Arts W.A - who helped fund my time in developing the story.

And finally, I acknowledge you, the reader, for sharing with me your time, heart and attention.